THE
BUCKSKIN
LINE

Forge Books by Elmer Kelton

Elmer Kelton

THE
BUCKSKIN
LINE

FORGE®

A TOM DOHERTY ASSOCIATES BOOK
NEW YORK

THE BUCKSKIN LINE

A Forge Book
Published by Tom Doherty Associates, LLC
175 Fifth Avenue
New York, NY 10010

www.tor-forge.com

Forge® is a registered trademark of Tom Doherty Associates, LLC.

ISBN-13: 978-0-7653-6056-4
ISBN-10: 0-7653-6056-X

First Edition: August 1999
First Mass Market Edition: July 2000
Second Mass Market Edition: March 2008

Printed in the United States of America

0 9 8 7 6 5 4 3 2

THE
BUCKSKIN
LINE

• Prologue •

The Texas Rangers had their beginnings in 1823, when land impresario Stephen F. Austin raised a volunteer company of ten men to act in defense of his colony in Mexican Texas. Rangers served during the decade of the Texas Republic and rode alongside the United States Army in the war against Mexico. Later in the years before and during the Civil War, volunteers manned a ragged picket line along the western frontier, guarding against Indian incursions. They had no official title but were commonly called rangers or ranging companies, minutemen, or spies.

During Reconstruction they were disbanded and replaced by a state police force, which did some good work but was badly stained by internal corruption and unwarranted cruelties. When the Confederate Texans finally regained the right to vote they dissolved the hated state police.

The reorganized state legislature created two battalions of Texas Rangers in 1874, giving them for the first time their official name and the famous star-in-a-circle badge, which was to become the stuff of legend.

This is a story of the early days, when small companies of poorly paid, poorly fed volunteers in homespun cloth and buckskin rode an unmarked frontier line for a primitive Texas that had only a toenail hold on survival. They had no uniform, no badge, not even an official name. But they had a job to do, and against all odds they managed to do it.

The story begins with one of the most unlikely events in early Texas history, the great Comanche raid that led to the sacking of Linnville town on the shores of the Gulf of Mexico.

PART
I.

· 1 ·

He was Comanche, and he was known among the People as
Buffalo Caller. Once in a time of hunger, when he was a
fledgling on one of his first hunts, the older and more experienced men had ridden their horses to exhaustion without
scaring up so much as one lone, lame bull. But Buffalo
Caller, riding alone, had heard a faint and distant bellow. He
had responded in the voice of a buffalo, and the buffalo had
answered him. The calls led him to a small herd in a hidden
canyon.

It was not buffalo he hunted now. He scouted as a wolf
for the largest assembly of raiders the Penateka band had
ever put together, moving to strike the land-greedy, hair-
faced American settlers of Texas. Beside him against the
Texans rode Swift as the Antelope, so named for his fleetness
of foot.

Buffalo Caller tingled with excitement over the sights he
was about to behold. He had never seen an ocean or even a
boat, so it strained his imagination to visualize what old men
had described around their campfires. If the veterans had not

let fanciful dreams overcome the realities of memory, those wonders lay no more than half a day's horseback journey ahead of him. It was claimed that the great water stretched so far one could not see all the way across. None of the People had ever ventured out upon it to determine how far it extended, for they were of the land, not of the sea. It was said that white men's boats might travel for many days without touching shore and that fish larger than horses lived in the dark and frightening depths.

Buffalo Caller doubted much of what he had heard. It sounded typical of the white *teibos*' lies. He had forded many rivers, and he had visited lakes wider than the rivers, but none were so wide that he could not see the opposite side.

Where he rode now was far to the south and east of the short-grass prairie and the limestone hill hunting grounds he was accustomed to roaming. A journey of many days had brought the massive Comanche war column into a gently rolling land of sandy soil and tall, summer-cured grass much different from the higher, drier land the Penatekas claimed as home. The hot, humid wind carried a smell foreign to his experience and left a faint suggestion of salt upon his lips. Summer heat sent sweat rolling down from beneath his buffalo-horn headdress and into his paint-streaked face, burning his eyes.

The foreignness of this land made him uneasy despite the persistent gnawing of curiosity. Though he wanted to see the great water for himself, he would be relieved when they finished what they came to do so they could return to country more suited to his experience.

What they were about was vengeance, blood for blood. In the early spring many tribal leaders and warriors had met with white chiefs in San Antonio de Béjar's council house to discuss an earlier agreement by the Comanches to free all their captives. Some had reconsidered the promise and balked, holding out for stronger terms. Talk had led to quarrel, and quarrel to the loosing of arrows and an explosion of gunfire. When the smoke drifted away, more than thirty Indians lay dead and dying in the council house and in the foul dirt of San Antonio's narrow streets.

In retaliation the People had killed most of the remaining white captives, but those had not bled enough to wash away the stain of the San Antonio disaster. The indignant Penatekas had undertaken this huge punitive expedition, carrying them far beyond their normal range, all the way eastward to the Gulf of Mexico. He did not know how many of the People were on this grand adventure. He had attempted to count them on his fingers and thumbs, but the task overwhelmed him. They were so many that they defied his understanding of numbers. Their horses left the grass beaten down and the ground scarred in their wake like the slow passage of a large buffalo herd. Though the object was war, many women and children had come along to watch and cheer as their warriors carried calamity to the white enemy.

Mexican allies guided them, for they knew the route. They knew how to pick their way through the sparsely settled region and avoid detection until time for the great force to loose its thunder and lightning. Buffalo Caller understood that the Americans had won this land from the Mexicans in a fierce war. Mexico wanted to take it back and had sent emissaries to the tribes, promising many good things in return for their aid. Buffalo Caller cared nothing for Mexico, for the first raid in which he had ridden had been against Mexicans. He had fought them often and had killed many. But he welcomed any chance to strike the Texans. A temporary alliance with a former adversary was justifiable if it promised victory over an enemy hated even more.

Antelope pulled up on his rawhide reins. "The wind brings the smell of smoke." He raised his head, sniffing, testing.

Antelope was notoriously subject to quick judgments and quick action without considering where they might lead. Buffalo Caller smelled only dust, for the ground was so dry it had cracked open in places. The soil would all be up and moving on the wind were it not bound by a heavy stand of brittle grass, the result of last spring's rains. He drew the skin taut at the edge of his right eye, trying to sharpen his vision. He decided Antelope was right, this time. "I think I see a house. It is beyond the timber, there."

His companion thumped the heels of his moccasins against

his mount's ribs, putting him into a trot. "If they have horses, we shall take them."

Buffalo Caller feared that Antelope's zeal would make him forget their real mission. "Taking horses is not what you and I have been sent to do."

The principal concern so far had been to avoid premature detection as the army of warriors moved along. The wolves were to overtake and kill any whites who might observe their passage before the trap was sprung. That precaution seemed less important now because scouts had reported that the town of Victoria lay only a short distance ahead. The Americans would soon know of the column's coming. One Mexican guide had lived in Victoria until the Texans drove him out, and he itched for retribution. Victoria had been chosen as the first target.

Buffalo Caller recognized Antelope's determination. He relented, knowing Antelope would do whatever he wanted, regardless of advice to the contrary. "If we find horses, there is no reason they should not be ours." He set his dun horse into a trot that matched Antelope's pace.

Antelope grunted. "If we find any teibos, we will take their scalps as well as their horses." His taste for vengeance was strong. A brother's blood had soaked into the floor of the San Antonio council house.

"So long as we do not leave our own."

Emerging from a small patch of timber, they saw a man afoot in a cornfield, wielding a curved knife to cut heads from the stalks, tossing them into the bed of a wagon drawn by two horses. His back turned, he did not see the warriors' approach.

Antelope said, "You take the horses. I will take the man."

Not until he heard the hooves did the farmer turn. He wasted a long moment frozen in startled disbelief as the two Comanches rushed down upon him; then he ran for the rail fence. Antelope's arrow struck him in the middle of his back. He fell forward onto his face. The warrior leaped from his horse, vaulted over the low fence and knelt beside the dying man, slicing a patch of scalp with his knife. Buffalo Caller saw no need for undue haste. He climbed over the fence and cut the two horses loose from the wagon. They were docile. What human beings did to one another concerned them little.

Antelope raised the bloody trophy for Buffalo Caller to observe, then looked toward the log cabin. "There may be others."

Whoever was at the house might have a rifle or shotgun. Buffalo Caller saw none here. This was far from normal Comanche range, and the once-formidable Karankawas native to this region had been reduced to a pitiable scattered few. The farmer probably had seen no reason to burden himself with a weapon in the field. "We have the horses. That is what we came for."

Antelope insisted, "If you leave one wasp, it will rebuild the nest."

"But if they fire upon us, we must leave. We can do no good for anyone if we are dead." It was not that he feared death. A warrior who died in battle was promised a happy afterlife. But the life he was living here gave him pleasure, for he was yet young, and so were his two wives. He would enjoy this life as long as he could. The next would endure forever, so he was in no hurry to begin it.

They approached by way of the barn, larger than the cabin and built of rough boards instead of logs. His gaze was focused on the house, for if there was to be trouble it would come from there. Antelope touched his arm and pointed in silence. Beneath a roof that extended beyond the barn, a woman sat on a stool, milking a cow. Like the man, she faced away from the Indians and was unaware of them.

The two warriors slipped down from their horses and moved toward a log fence that separated them from the barn. Buffalo Caller climbed to the top and swung his legs over. A log cracked beneath his weight. Startled, the woman looked around, saw him, and jumped to her feet, spilling the bucket of milk. With a cry of fear, she ran to the barn door and turned, a pitchfork in her hands.

Buffalo Caller had never seen a pitchfork and did not know what use it was meant for, but he recognized that the sharp steel tines could pierce like a lance. She made a threatening gesture, thrusting the fork toward him. She shouted,

but her words meant nothing. White people's talk was like
the grunting of their stinking pigs.

He entertained the thought of taking her along, for his
wives would welcome a slave woman to lift some of labor's
weight from their shoulders. Too, he had never taken a teibo
woman into his blankets, and he wondered how different one
might be. But she came at him with the pitchfork, and he
had no choice. He fitted an arrow to the bowstring and drove
it into her heart. She died quickly, with little sound and little
struggle.

He had noticed from the first that her hair was reddish,
like the hair of a buffalo calf. He knelt over her and lifted a
strand of it, wondering if she might have colored it somehow.
But none of the color came off on his fingers, so he decided
it was natural. It would be a great curiosity when he showed
it to his friends. He made a wide circle with the keen blade
of his knife, wanting to keep as much of the hair as he could.
He placed his foot on her back and pulled on the scalp. It
tore free with a sucking sound.

He heard a movement in the barn and turned quickly,
bringing another arrow out of the quiver. He stopped, for in
the doorway stood a small boy with hair redder than his
mother's. Buffalo Caller could only stare.

Antelope spoke from behind him. "Are you frightened of
a baby? I will kill him for you if you are afraid."

"I am not afraid, but I have never seen hair of such a color,
not on a human being." He recognized that the Americans
were humans, though of a lesser order. The Comanches were
the real people, the True Human Beings.

Antelope said, "The Texans have hair of all colors." He
brought out his knife and moved toward the child.

Buffalo Caller blocked his path. "My wives have given
me only girl babies so far. I will take this boy for a son."

"And carry him into the fight? He will be a burden."

"But I can teach him to be a good hunter. He could keep
us from hunger when we are old."

"A white-skinned Penateka with hair like fire? Who ever
saw such a thing?"

"The buffalo will not care about the color of his hair."

The People had often taken Mexican children and raised them as their own. Captives helped offset the death rate caused by war and by accidents during the hunt. Since Americans had begun moving into Penateka lands, a sprinkling of lighter-skinned children had also appeared in the lodges. Most who survived the trauma of the first weeks would assimilate into the tribe. In time a majority would forget their past lives and become as Comanche-born.

Antelope argued, "We should kill him. The color of his hair is like blood. It could sour our medicine."

"What has hair to do with medicine?"

The boy looked in bewilderment at his mother's body. He whimpered as Buffalo Caller picked him up and tucked him under his right arm.

Antelope said, "I cannot tolerate a squalling child." He touched the handle of his bloodstained knife. "If he cries, I will cut his throat."

Buffalo Caller shifted the boy to his left arm and drew his own knife. "You will have to cut mine first." It was unthinkable that one of the People might kill another, but he would inflict grievous pain with the blade if Antelope made it necessary.

His companion backed off. "Then do not let him cry."

"This one is too brave to cry. Now let us go. We do not want to miss the big fight."

"First I will burn the house." Antelope's eyes pinched in warning. "If you are wise, you will kill that red-haired boy."

Buffalo Caller tightened his hold on the youngster. "Go on. Set your fire."

Buffalo Caller had seen white-man towns before. He had visited San Antonio in his early youth, riding boldly up and down its streets, challenging any and all to come out and fight him. It was a way of demonstrating his bravery to other young men in the event any might have doubted it. No townsman had accepted the challenge face-to-face, but Buffalo Caller proudly bore the scar of a bullet wound inflicted by some coward who hid inside a doorway to shoot him. When he painted himself for ceremony or battle he always made a black circle around the scar so everyone would see and know that bullets did not easily kill him. For a fighter, scars were marks of honor.

The column crossed a creek north of Victoria and paused while warriors took time to paint themselves and their mounts for battle. The paint carried strong medicine and helped ward off bullets. Buffalo Caller had turned his small captive over to the care of his younger wife, Whippoorwill. While women and children waited, the warriors split to make a circle around the town. Buffalo Caller saw no sign that the raiders' approach had aroused alarm. That surprised him. He could only surmise that the column had been mistaken for something other than what it was. It was known that members of the Lipan tribe sometimes visited the town for friendly barter, and Mexican horse traders came occasionally with large *caballadas* to barter or sell.

A shout from one of the chiefs traveled quickly around the circle, picked up and relayed by other voices. The charge began with high-pitched yelling and a thunder of hoofbeats as warriors urged their horses into a run. Not until then did the town's citizens begin to realize they were under attack. The first resistance was a scattering of gunfire from buildings on the outskirts. That resistance soon mushroomed into desperate firing from the more central part of town. Warriors and horses began to falter and fall. Despite the Texans' slowness to recognize their danger, they put up a strong and costly defense.

Buffalo Caller brought his horse to a quick stop after a bullet passed his ear, singing like a locust, then whining off the stone wall of a house. He saw his companions beginning to pull back. It seemed prudent to follow. Only someone who had yet to prove his valor or who valued glory above life would willingly plunge into a hailstorm of bullets fired by determined men hidden behind walls that arrows could not penetrate.

He did not have to prove his courage anew. This was not

a day he would choose to die. There was yet much he had not seen.

Someone shouted that horses had been found just outside of town. Buffalo Caller withdrew from the siege. Though he had come for blood vengeance on the Americans, he would also be pleased to take their horses.

He was amazed at the number. Mexicans had been loose-herding several hundred on the prairie before recognizing their danger and fleeing into the protection of the town. Buffalo Caller guessed they had brought the horses to trade or sell. He would not have expected this welcome bonanza. With enthusiasm he pitched into the rounding up of these horses and many others from nearby farms. By the time the gathering was done, the horse and mule herd had grown to tremendous proportions. Moving, it raised a towering cloud of dust, like an early-spring windstorm out of the west. Even if the invaders were to turn back now, this had been a most profitable venture.

Others in the band had killed several men unfortunate enough to fall into their path and had stolen a white woman and her baby. After camping along a creek that night, they continued on their way, driving the great band of captured horses and mules. They came upon two men in a wagon, killing one but somehow losing the other despite a diligent search.

The white woman's baby began to cry. The impatient Antelope wrested it from its mother's arms and impaled it on a spear. The baby quivered and died while the woman screamed.

Buffalo Caller thought that a regrettable waste. The child might have grown up to be useful. He did not feel pity for mother or child, however. Both were Texan, and pity on an enemy was a dangerous indulgence for a warrior. An enemy spared was an enemy who might have to be faced again another day.

Linnville was a small but prosperous seaport, its several warehouses holding goods brought in by ship for wagon and cart transport to such inland towns as San Antonio and Nacogdoches.

As had been the case at Victoria, the townspeople took little notice of the approaching warriors. Buffalo Caller guessed the huge horse and mule herd had misled them into assuming the visitors were traders like the Mexicans at Victoria, bringing animals to barter or sell.

Citizens of the town began to shout and scream as they belatedly recognized the disaster thundering down upon them. They were too late to mount a defense the way those in Victoria had done. By dozens they scrambled toward the shore. Men, women, and children ran in desperation. They piled into small boats tied to the wooden pier and frantically rowed away into the sea.

Farther out, Buffalo Caller saw what appeared to be a large house floating, a curl of black smoke rising from its tall chimney. Beyond the steamship, he could see nothing but water and more water, endless to the horizon, reflecting the sunlight and burning his eyes. He stared in wonder. People had told him of such strange things, wooden houses that sat atop the water, but he had never quite believed them.

He saw warriors kill a white man and drag two struggling women out of a boat, one white and one whose skin was black. They also captured a child.

Antelope shouted, "Too many are getting away." He forced his horse out into the surf, trying to catch one of the boats and its shrieking passengers. Buffalo Caller followed so far that the water rose up and soaked his moccasins, chilling his feet. He loosed a couple of arrows, but the boats bobbed like fallen leaves on the waves, and the stone-tipped shafts fell harmlessly into the gulf. He chose to waste no more, though Antelope kept trying. Buffalo Caller turned back, for the town lay open and defenseless, awaiting the raiders' pleasure. Several townspeople lay dead in the streets, caught and killed before they could reach the boats.

Buffalo Caller moved toward a large building a short distance from the docks. The Mexican guides had promised that the warehouses would be full of goods wondrous beyond imagination. The People could take whatever they wanted and be welcome to it. There was no shame in stealing from Texans, the biggest thieves of all.

Some of the boats went all the way out to the ship that lay offshore. Others stopped and simply floated along out of range, their passengers watching helplessly while the town fell to the invaders like wild plums dropping from a tree.

Warriors who had followed them into the surf turned back to begin a joyous plundering of homes and warehouses. Buffalo Caller entered a store and marveled at the variety of treasures it offered. He had tasted apples in San Antonio, and he found a barrelful here. He bit eagerly into one while he searched the store for other delights. On the shelves he found rolls of cloth, some plain, others in bright colors. Antelope joined him, shouting in glee as he yanked down a bolt of red material and began to unfold it, wrapping it around his shoulders and waist. He picked up a stovepipe hat and jammed it onto his head, bending the feather he wore tied into his braided black hair.

Buffalo Caller thought Antelope looked ridiculous. He would not trade his buffalo headdress for all the hats in the store. But he carried out an armload of cloth he was sure would please his wives. A long string of red ribbon stretched behind him.

He began smelling smoke. Other warriors were setting fire to houses as they finished their looting.

The Comanches celebrated high carnival, sacking and burning while frustrated townspeople witnessed the destruction from sanctuary far out on the water. Late in the afternoon, wearying warriors began to draw away. They had packed many of the captured horses and mules with goods taken from Linnville homes, stores, and warehouses. Buffalo Caller laughed at the sight of a mule with ribbons tied in its tail, kicking at a bolt of blue cloth that dragged in the dust behind. Many of the men wore white-man clothes and hats of various descriptions. The wind tugged at several open umbrellas. Antelope had placed a hat on his horse's head after cutting slits so it would fit over the ears. It was proper that the horse wear a Texan hat, he said, for it had been taken from a Texan corral west of San Antonio.

Hardly a building remained intact. Most not already burned to the ground were ablaze now as the raiders retreated. A heavy pall of dark smoke hung over the town. Linnville would be little but ashes and ruin when its citizens mustered courage to row back from the sea. Then they would know the true price of Texan treachery.

It mattered not that the people here probably had nothing to do with what happened in the San Antonio council house. They were white. In the eyes of the People, vengeance against one enemy was vengeance against all. They had no patience with individual responsibility, separating the guilty from the innocent. All their enemies were guilty.

Buffalo Caller noted that the head of the column was moving in a northwesterly direction. That pleased him. In a few days he would be back in the familiar and pleasant surroundings of his own country. He had gazed upon the big water once, had felt its wetness and tasted its salt. His own eyes had witnessed a great house that floated upon the sea. He had not seen the fish as large as horses, but he had seen enough. His curiosity was satisfied.

He thought of the boy he had taken and the pleasure a son would bring to his lodge, even one whose hair was red. It was time now to go home, to enjoy the fruits of conquest. It was time for dancing and celebration, for the proud telling of great and daring deeds.

· 2 ·

Warren Webb enjoyed riding alongside Michael Shannon on the wagon road to Linnville. The jovial farmer was pleasant company, never short of stories to tell. It mattered not whether they were totally true or were partly a construction of an imagination enriched by Shannon's thirty years or so of drifting from Tennessee across Arkansas and Louisiana and finally down the Texas coast. He had entered into every conflict he could reach, however far it might have been out of his way. Mike Shannon had never seen a fight he did not want to mix into, bringing all the gusto other men put into games and horse races.

Though summer heat made each mile seem like two, conversation helped relieve the weight of fatigue. And if Shannon's speech easily lapsed into the profane, that too afforded its guilty pleasures. For Webb to use such language would be unseemly if not actually forbidden by the Scriptures. He was a circuit-riding minister whose small farm was sadly neglected because of the travel requirements of his higher calling. Coming from someone else, a little profanity offered a tantalizing hint of wickedness, a minor and harmless rebellion he found refreshing. Shannon seemed little inhibited

by the fact that his riding companion was a man of the cloth
who carried the Word far past the forks of the creek where
settlers could not afford a live-there preacher.

He said, " 'Y God, Preacher Webb, this country is gettin'
so choked up with people, they'll pretty soon be stumblin'
all over one another. I'm studyin' on movin' west, out on
the Colorado River. There's land to be had there, not half so
dear as this on the coast."

Shannon did not own the tract he plowed. He simply
squatted on unclaimed land, using it until he tired of it or a
rightful owner came along to take possession from him and
his wife. In such a way had generations of poor farmers
progressed slowly westward from the Alleghenies to the
Ohio Valley and across the Mississippi into Texas, amassing
little of the world's goods but incurring little in the way of
debt and obligation. They could plant and harvest a crop,
then leave when the spirit moved them or a real owner came
along with the deed. Shannon had already done that more
than once, though he was little if any older than Webb, and
Webb would be thirty come October.

For many, squatting was a means of survival in a country
where cash was a stranger to most men's pockets. Now and
then a farmer might roll up his sleeves and fight when someone came to move him, but most accepted their lot and
looked to the west, confident that they would soon find a
better place. It was a melancholy fact of life that trailblazers
rarely profited like those who followed in their tracks. One
sowed. Another reaped.

Webb would miss having Shannon around. "Surely you'd
not depart our midst before you've harvested your crop."

"And leave the fruits of my labor for somebody who never
broke a sweat? Old Mother Shannon never raised no halfwit
sons, 'y God. I figure we'll leave in the fall and locate us a
place. I'll break the land this winter and have her ready to
seed in the spring."

Webb understood the pioneer wanderlust, for he harbored
a liberal case of it himself. It had caused him to leave his
boyhood home in Alabama and had brought him by fits and
starts to the Republic of Texas after the revolution against

Mexico. "I'd not mind followin' after you, Mike. I've an itch to be seein' new country."

"Come with us, then. There's fever in this low ground, and I've noted that you've got an unhealthy cough. There's others movin' out yonder. Where there's people there's a need for somebody to teach the ways of the Lord, lest they go heathen."

Shannon was right. Webb's lungs sometimes ached, and often he felt himself short of strength. He was tall of frame but so thin he sometimes wondered how he managed to cast a decent shadow. He attributed his condition to the humidity and smothering heat of this region near the Gulf of Mexico. A higher elevation should be better for his health.

Shannon said, "It ain't good to stay in one place too long—dulls a man. You wear out one farm, you move on to another. That's what the Lord put the land here for."

"I don't know that He meant for us to wear it out."

"He must've, 'y God, because He gave us so much. There ain't no end to it." Shannon made a broad sweep with his arm toward a horizon flat and endless.

For a while Webb had been aware of a tan cloud hovering low in the northeast. He had first thought it might be a dust storm, because the weather had turned dry of late, but it occurred to him that the wind did not seem strong enough to raise that much dust. Besides, the cloud appeared localized, moving slowly westward.

Shannon thought along similar lines. "Kind of odd doin's yonder, don't you think?"

Webb had seen large horse herds stir dust like that, but this seemed an out-of-the-way place for traders to be taking a remuda, away from the major settlements. "Might be a group of immigrants, strayed off of the main trail to look for grass."

"If so, maybe they're in the mood to hear the Word, and might be me and you could get us a woman-cooked meal."

"You had a woman-cooked breakfast this mornin'. Your Dora is as good a cook as ever I ate after."

"But I can't remember the last time I had a cup of real

coffee that wasn't stretched out with parched grain. Maybe them folks have got some."

Webb had intended to be at the Linnville settlement by dark, but he supposed tomorrow would be soon enough. If these people were in need of preaching, it was his obligation to offer it. "Let's go see about that coffee."

First sight of the horses aroused a strange sense of foreboding, a queasy feeling of finding himself in the wrong place. "Did you ever see so many in one bunch, Mike?"

Shannon hauled up on the leather reins. Ordinarily given to shrugging off life's everyday aggravations with an easy "Aw, what the hell?" he appeared suddenly alarmed. "Somethin' queer-lookin' about this. They ain't no traders, and they ain't no movers. What they are is Indians, 'y God!"

Webb could not believe this at first. The only Indians he had seen this near the coast had been small gatherings of Tonkawas, the poorest, raggedest people he had ever encountered, come to barter or beg. Folks said they could be ferocious as hungry wolves against their enemies the Comanches, and that they even had cannibalistic tendencies. To him they had appeared harmless except for a little sticky-fingered thievery.

These were not Tonkawas.

Shannon said, "I hope you have favor in the eyes of your Maker. He'd better not let them see us before we get into that timber yonder."

Webb thought it prudent to be running while he consulted the Lord. He applied his spurs and drew his rifle from its long scabbard beneath his leg.

It seemed impossible that they were not discovered, but the passing Indians gave no sign they had noticed.

Shannon said, "They think we're part of their bunch."

"Our clothes and hats ought to tell them different."

Shannon turned for another squint-eyed look. "A lot of them are wearin' hats, too. The store-bought kind, and I'd bet you a U.S. dollar they didn't buy them."

A few wore coats as well, despite the summer heat. A couple had them on backward, buttons in the rear. Many horses and mules were laden with blankets and bolts of cloth.

Trophies of war, proudly displayed.

Shannon tried to make a rough count but gave it up. "Looks to me like there's a couple thousand horses and mules, and maybe a thousand Indians. Odd thing is, they've got squaws and children with them."

"But who are they? Where'd they come from?"

"Comanches, and I'd guess they're fresh from lootin' the hell out of some place. Headin' back to their own country now, most likely."

"God pity any poor souls they happen upon along their way."

Shannon frowned, mulling on that thought. "There's some farms out yonder, the direction they're travelin'. They'll gobble up them folks like wolves gobble a rabbit."

"We could circle around ahead of them and give warnin'. How's your faith?"

"Strong enough, long as I'm ridin' with a preacher. The Lord ain't goin' to let nothin' happen to you."

The column inched along, the animals traveling in a walk. Webb could see women and children. Were it not for the evidence of loot being carried away, he might take this for a tribe peacefully moving from one hunting ground to another. He saw no outriders, though it stood to reason there must be some somewhere. "They don't seem to be in a hurry or worried about anybody jumpin' them."

Shannon said, "I'd feel safe too if I was them. It'd take an army to jump a bunch the size of that."

Riding at an angle away from the Indian column, the two remained within the cover of the timber to its southern edge. Webb looked back. "We ought to be far enough now." He set his horse into a long trot, paralleling the Comanches.

Shannon spurred alongside him, glancing warily in one direction, then the other. "They didn't pick all them doodads and all them horses and mules off of the trees. I'd wager they've left a string of dead folks behind them."

"First we need to look after the ones still alive. I'll pray for the others when I have the time."

At the first farm they found a man and his wife working in a garden just south of a log cabin. The farmer listened to their report with suspicion. "A bunch of Indians that size don't seem likely. You sure you didn't just see them in a bottle?"

The farmer's wife seemed to believe right off. She brought her hands to her mouth to stifle a cry.

Shannon was not inclined toward patience when calamity bore down. "I been known to sip a little whiskey now and again, but Brøther Webb don't drink, nor is he given to lyin'. Take a look at that dust comin' yonder. It ain't no sea breeze, 'y God."

The urgency in Shannon's voice began to temper the farmer's skepticism. "But Comanches, this close to the coast? Must be a bunch of Tonks, or maybe Karankawas."

"There ain't that many Karankawas in the whole nation. Wouldn't make no difference anyway. One'll kill you as dead as the other. You've got to get out of here."

The farmer at last believed, and with belief he reached a state bordering on panic. "Martha! Get the young'uns ready. I'll hitch up the team."

The woman rushed screaming into the cabin. Webb and Shannon helped the farmer harness his mules and saddle his horse. Webb boosted the woman up onto the seat while Shannon lifted three frightened children into the bed of the wagon.

The farmer pointed. "You'll find the Johnson family over thataway where you see that stand of trees. Old Man Blessing and his boys are a mile or so further on. They're the last ones I know of in that direction." He put his horse into a run, trying to catch up to the fast-moving wagon. The woman was applying the whip, and the children clung desperately to the wagon's sideboards to keep from being bounced out.

The Johnsons required no persuasion. Webb had known the young family at camp meeting, and they accepted his word. Their only question was which direction they should run. They wasted little time gathering up a few possessions and quitting their place.

Shannon watched them with regret. "Ain't apt to be much left here when they come back."

"There'll be the land."

Abner Blessing was a towering, rawboned farmer whose broad shoulders appeared to sag under their own weight. Webb had once heard him declare that he had "fit Injuns all over hell and half of Georgia" before coming to Texas. He was ready to take these on. The Blessings had built their cabin of stone, befitting a family of great strength. He pointed to his three grown sons, all rough-cut out of raw oak, in his image. "Me and my boys ain't givin' up our place. We'll take our stand behind them stone walls."

Webb argued, "You'd just as well try to wipe out a hornet's nest with a sharp stick. I don't doubt your fightin' spirit, Mr. Blessing, but you know what happened at the Alamo."

"Them fellers killed a heap of Mexicans."

"But they lost the battle."

"Me and the boys, we've worked hard to build what we've got here." Reluctantly Blessing turned to his sons. "Tom, Bert, Jim . . . go gather the horses and mules. Them varmints may burn the house, but be damned if they'll add our stock to their string." The young men hastened to comply. Shannon moved to help them. Blessing said, "I hate to leave here without a fight. Where you reckon them red devils've been?"

Webb could only shrug. "They were comin' from the direction of Linnville when we saw them."

"Linnville." The farmer clenched his fists, his knuckles bulging like pine knots. "I've got a sister there, and her family. You don't reckon . . ."

"I don't know."

Misery came into the man's blue eyes, followed by a building anger. "Everybody can't just up and run. There's bound to be somebody with the guts to stand and fight."

"Maybe, if the Comanches didn't leave everybody dead behind them."

"Maybe me and the boys can put some fightin' men together. There's four of us to start."

"Six. Mike and me, we'll go with you." Webb looked to Shannon for silent confirmation.

They struck southward, driving the family's extra horses and mules several miles before they came upon a brush-lined creek. Blessing told his sons, "Scatter the stock down in there. I doubt the redskins'll come this far off of their line of march."

That done, he said, "Let's be headin' for Linnville." He led off without waiting for argument. Webb offered none, and Shannon seemed as eager as Blessing for a fight.

They pushed their horses into a lope for short distances, then slowed to a trot to conserve the mounts' strength. Webb could see the cloud of dust to the north, marking the location of the Comanche column.

The oldest of the Blessing boys, Tom, drew up on the reins. "Listen. I think I hear shootin'."

Webb first thought the Indians might have caught one of the families he and Shannon had warned. But he decided that was not the case; the sound indicated many guns.

The elder Blessing said, "Somebody's done lit into them. Come on, boys, or we're liable to miss the fight." He spurred off toward the dust. His sons struggled to catch up.

Webb gave Shannon a questioning glance. Shannon said, "Hell, Preacher, who wants to live to get old and decrepit?"

They never managed to close the distance between themselves and the Blessings, but presently through the dust they could see a back-and-forth surging of men and horses. Rifles and pistols snapped in a desultory manner. Webb reined up, for he wanted to grasp the full situation before riding into the middle of it. He saw a large company of white men dismounted, shooting at horseback Indians who circled them. Farther ahead, the main column of Comanches hurried away with their women and children, their horse and mule herd, while this detached set of warriors fought a delaying action.

Blessing and his sons had halted, watching the fight from two hundred yards. Uncertainty held the big farmer back, though he chafed to ride headlong into the scrap. "We'd probably all get killed if we was to try to break through. Maybe we can do them fellers more good from out here."

Shannon said, "At least, 'y God, we can give them devils somethin' else to be worryin' about."

The men dismounted. Webb tied a knot in the end of his split leather reins and slipped them over his arm so the horse could not easily jerk away. He dropped to one knee and aimed his rifle as he heard shots fired on either side of him. After the flash, a white cloud of smoke blossomed around the barrel. He could not see if he had hit anything.

Some of the Indians immediately split off and charged toward the six men. Anticipating this, two of the Blessing boys had held their fire. While four reloaded, the pair took their time in firing. A horse went down, and the charge broke up. The Indians zigzagged in a rough circle, reconsidering. By the time they decided to rush again, the reloaded guns blazed a second volley. One of the Indians fell from his horse. The others halted, two grabbing him up between them, carrying him back toward the main group.

Soon the larger column had moved well beyond the skirmish. The nearby Indians broke their circle and began to travel slowly in a westerly direction. Those who had firearms kept shooting back in the direction of their adversaries. The company of white men continued firing toward them. The range became too great for accuracy by either side.

Shannon said, "Looks like they've had enough entertainment for a while. Let's go see how the boys yonder made out."

A rough count told Webb that the company was made up of more than a hundred men. Most had managed to hang on to their horses through the fight, though a few animals were wounded and at least a couple lay dead.

A horseman rode out to meet the six incoming riders. "Welcome, men. You almost missed the skirmish."

Webb thought he knew the face. "Seems to me I've seen you at camp meetin'."

The man nodded. "You're a preacher, as I recollect. We're volunteers out of Victoria. We've followed this bunch all the way from Linnville."

Blessing pressed, "Linnville? What happened there?"

"They took the town by surprise. Killed several folks, burned down just about everything. Ain't much left but ashes."

Blessing swore, mostly under his breath. "I have a sister in Linnville."

"Most of the people got away in boats. Like as not she

did, too. The dead were mostly menfolks, I think. They tarried too long, fightin' a losin' battle."

Blessing swallowed and looked at his sons, then back to the man from Victoria. "You-all ain't givin' up the fight, are you?"

"We haven't even started yet. We'll nip at their rear 'til more outfits catch up to us."

Webb said, "There's more on the way?"

"The alarm's been sent out in all directions. There'll be some rangin' companies along, I expect."

Several Victoria men stood in a circle, heads bowed, staring down at a man on the ground. It was evident that he was dead.

Shannon said, "Since we've got a preacher with us, I expect you-all would like some words spoke."

One of the bystanders said, "We'd appreciate it mightily."

Webb removed his hat, and the others followed suit. He said a brief prayer for the stranger who lay before him. One of the Victoria men said, "Pray that before we get through, we send most of them bloody-handed Comanches after him."

Webb doubted the propriety of such a prayer, but at the moment, standing in the presence of death, he could think of no reply. Most of the Victoria men took solace in the fact that they appeared to have killed or wounded several Indians. It crossed Webb's mind that he might pray for those too, but he dismissed the thought. The devil had sent them; the devil could have them.

The captain of the volunteers came forward. "I'd be pleased to have you men join us if you have no company of your own."

Blessing was torn. "I ought to be seein' about my sister."

His son Tom placed a large hand on his father's shoulder. "You go find Aunt Bess. Me and Bert and Jim'll do the family's share of the fightin'."

The two brothers signaled agreement. Blessing cleared his throat and shook hands with his sons, each in turn. "I've always been proud of you boys. A man couldn't't've asked for better." Shortly he rode away, toward whatever was left of Linnville.

Tom Blessing told the captain of the volunteers, "We got cousins in Gonzales. They'd be mighty put out if they was to miss the main fight. Reckon we've got time to go and fetch them?"

"You might run into Indians along the way."

"It'll be their own fault if they mess with us Blessings."

The captain glanced toward the dust left by the departing Comanches. " 'Til the ranger companies show up, there aren't enough of us here to do more than pester their rear guard a little. If you can gather up some more help, go with my blessings."

Shannon said, "Me and the preacher'll go with you, Tom. Just in case you do run into some Indians." He glanced at Webb. "All right, Preacher?"

"You said it yourself: who wants to get old and decrepit?"

· 3 ·

Riding at the rear of the long column, Buffalo Caller looked back toward the white men who trailed behind like wolves following a buffalo herd. Their pursuit had become something of a game—parry and thrust, feint and retreat—in an effort to draw warriors into a trap. After a couple of these episodes resulted in a few casualties, the Comanches had become slow about rising to the bait.

Buffalo Caller saw no reason such a superior force should play the white man's game. The People had all the advantage. It appeared to him that the whites were trying to delay the Indian retreat by pecking at its edges. They probably hoped for reinforcements. He doubted that they could muster enough fighting men to mount any serious challenge against a force this strong. Should they try, it would only mean more scalps dangling from war lances, more celebration when the People were back on their home ground. Buffalo Caller would welcome a stiff fight. Linnville had been so easy he almost felt cheated.

Swift as the Antelope kept looking back, sweat running from beneath the band of the white-man stovepipe hat he had worn since they had sacked the coastal town. Because of the heat he no longer wore red cloth wrapped around his body, but he had not abandoned it. He had it loosely rolled and tied behind his rawhide-covered saddle. It was for his wife, he claimed.

Antelope was impatient, as usual. "We should strike them like the lightning. We could kill them all before they have time to catch a breath."

They had tried that already, though with only a small portion of their fighting force, expecting the Texans to flee in terror. Instead, the hair-faces had surprised them with a stiff resistance. Several warriors had had to be carried away after the skirmish.

"There is time enough," Buffalo Caller said. "Let them become tired and hungry. Sooner or later they will begin to straggle. Then we can cut them to pieces."

"But they are growing stronger. More teibos keep joining them."

"All the more of them to die."

He had noticed small groups joining the pursuers periodically, but the Texans remained relatively small in number. Buffalo Caller was confident that they were much too weak to make any meaningful dent in the Comanche column, strung out so far now that he could not see the head of it. If the enemy should have the poor judgment to try, their blood and bones would enrich this prairie ground, and the grass would grow stronger for years.

Antelope opened his hands, showing all his fingers. "With this many men I could run them all the way back to the water."

He had always been prone to overstate his accomplishments and sometimes took personal credit for deeds performed by others as long as he did not expect to be challenged by someone who had been there.

"Go, then. I will marry your widow and give her many sons."

"You have two wives already, and your seed produces only girls. You have no son except that Texan boy."

Buffalo Caller saw danger in Antelope's eyes. Antelope had repeatedly made veiled threats against the child since they had taken him from his dead mother's side.

"The boy is not your concern."

"I tell you again, that hair is an ill omen. It looks like blood. I had a dream last night. The boy will bring evil. If you do not have the stomach to do what must be done, let me." He clasped the deer-horn handle of his knife.

Buffalo Caller stiffened. "You will not touch him!"

Antelope roughly pulled his horse away and joined other warriors, but a dark scowl said the question was not settled. Buffalo Caller knew their friendship, though of long standing, would not be enough to protect the boy. Antelope believed strongly in medicine and omens. He had a remarkable ability to sense the presence of dark spirits when no one else was aware of them.

Buffalo Caller believed in medicine as strongly as anyone, but his guardian spirits often disagreed with Antelope's. Antelope claimed to carry the power of the badger, and certainly he possessed that animal's belligerent temperament. Still, Buffalo Caller sometimes wondered if Antelope was not misled by Coyote, the trickster. Coyote was always up to mischief. He liked to play with men's minds and lead them into folly.

Antelope's implied threat began to play upon the mind of Buffalo Caller. To reassure himself that the boy was all right he put his mount into a long trot, passing the rear guard and going around the massive herd of stolen horses and mules. The women and children rode near the head of the column, where they were considered safest from attack by the trailing Texans. He sought out Whippoorwill, the younger and prettier of his two wives, the one he had chosen to accompany him on this long journey. She carried the boy in front of her on a high-stepping sorrel mare taken from the Mexican traders at Victoria.

"Is he all right?" he asked, though he could see no evidence to the contrary. The boy still wore his homespun clothes, now dirty and beginning to ravel from the stresses of traveling. He did not look Comanche, but the shirt and trousers would have to last until the band made its way back to the homeland. Then he could be put into something more suitable.

"He does not understand anything I tell him," Whippoor-will said. "At times he talks, but they are not words I know."

"He will learn soon enough to speak like a Comanche. Has Antelope said anything to you about him?"

"This morning, as we broke camp. He said the spirits came to him in a dream and told him we should kill the red-hair before he brings death to us."

"Watch out for him. Do not let him get close to the boy."

"What if he is right? What if the red-hair is bad medicine?"

"My spirits have told me no such thing. Antelope makes wind and thinks it is spirits speaking to him."

Satisfied for the time being, he dismounted and let his horse graze the dry grass while he waited for the column to pass. Its movement was slow as a turtle's, he thought. He remembered his doubts when the council first decided to allow women and children to accompany this grand punitive excursion. Ordinarily it would be considered too dangerous, but so many warriors had massed together that the expedition seemed secure enough to allow such luxury. It was argued that the outnumbered whites would fall like dry leaves in an autumn wind. Though resistance had proven strong enough to turn the raiders back from the heart of Victoria, Linnville had been crushed like a beetle beneath a warrior's moccasin. The spoils had been extraordinary. Those who had chosen to remain behind in the homeland would soon be ashamed for their timidity.

The rear guard came along after a time, and Buffalo Caller grasped his horse's mane, pulling himself up. His eyes met those of Antelope for a moment before Antelope looked away. What he saw there convinced him that once they reached home he would have to remove his family from Antelope's reach.

A warrior known as Feared by His Enemies pulled up beside him. "More white men have joined their brothers back there." He pointed his chin toward the horsemen, who trailed at a respectful distance.

The number had increased; that was evident. "There are still far more of us than of them."

Feared by His Enemies held up three fingers. "It has been three days, and they have not given up."

"They will, or we will destroy them when we get back into our own country."

Before camping that night, Buffalo Caller noted where Antelope located himself and found a place far away for Whippoorwill and the red-haired boy.

The next morning was the fourth since they had chased the boats into the big water. The column had been traveling on gradually rising ground. The air was drier and less oppressive than at the coast, though the summer sun began spreading its heat soon after its rising. He could not yet see them, but Buffalo Caller could visualize the limestone hills not far ahead. Soon the People would be back in their own environment. The raid had been more than satisfactory, especially in terms of the wealth they had taken, but it would be good to breathe the familiar air of home.

The unexpected approach of four Texan horsemen seemed more an affront than a threat. Surely they would turn back when they saw the full strength of the Comanche force. But they did not. Antelope gave a shout and led several rearguard warriors in a charge. One of the Texans fired, and a warrior fell. The charge broke up in the face of unexpectedly fierce gunfire. The warriors turned back, rejoining the rest of the rear guard.

The Texans kept coming.

From a flank, a second group of Texans broke out of a fringe of live-oak timber and quickly halted, seeming surprised by the number of Indians they faced. They turned back into the trees. This time Buffalo Caller joined other warriors in pursuit. Yelling for blood, they charged into the timber. The Texans retreated, though one somehow lost his horse and ran after his companions afoot. In their haste to get away they appeared unaware of his predicament.

He turned with terror in his eyes to meet death as the warriors rode him down. They celebrated over his scalp, but the celebration was short-lived. Gunfire erupted farther ahead. A larger Texan force plunged into the exposed flank of the main column. Buffalo Caller heard shooting, loud shouting, cries of dismay.

The herd panicked, breaking into wild stampede. Thousands of hooves drummed against the prairie sod. Some of the pack animals lost their loads, the contents bouncing as they struck the ground. Long bolts of colored cloth came unfolded, dragging along behind them in the dust and the grass.

Unbelievable! There could not possibly be that many Texans. Buffalo Caller looked around with wide eyes, confusion giving way to fear. His wife and the red-haired boy were up there where the Texans were on the attack.

It was his place to stand his ground and fight, but he could not. He had to see to Whippoorwill's safety, and the boy's. He put his horse into a hard run, passing the rear-guard warriors, flinging an arrow at a Texan who popped up ahead of him. He missed and had no time for a second try.

Though the whites had trailed for four days, their sudden bold attack had taken the column by surprise. Some warriors were trying without success to stop the stampede of the loose horses and mules. Very quickly they had to give up that attempt and fight for their own survival against the yelling, fighting teibos who seemed now to be everywhere.

Just ahead, the women and children were fleeing, surrounded by a thin guard of warriors. Some were already falling behind and being swallowed up by the rapidly advancing Texans.

The Comanches' supreme confidence seemed to have evaporated. They were caught up now in a wild rout, no longer an organized force but a thousand individuals running for their lives.

Antelope appeared like a vengeful specter out of the choking dust. His stovepipe hat was gone, his face twisted in fury. "I told you!" he shouted. "That red-hair has brought this calamity down on us."

His intention was clear. "No!" Buffalo Caller protested. He fitted an arrow to the bowstring. He could not kill An-

telope. For one Comanche to kill another was unthinkable.
But he could kill Antelope's horse.

He heard the thud of a bullet. His own horse faltered,
missed a stride, then went down. Buffalo Caller rolled away
from him in the dry grass. He pushed to his feet, the dust
burning his eyes, choking him. He felt around desperately
for the fallen bow and found it. He looked up but saw Antelope nowhere. The warrior had disappeared in the brown
cloud raised by all those pounding hooves.

He tried to catch a riderless horse but was bumped hard
and flung aside, falling to his knees. Another loose horse
leaped over him, a sharp hoof striking his head. Buffalo
Caller fell on his face, stunned, spitting out dirt and dry
grass. He tried to push to his feet but could not. His scalp
burned like fire.

He heard a shout and saw a Texan bearing down upon
him, a pistol extended at arm's length. Buffalo Caller tried
to roll out of the way. He saw the flash and felt the hard
shock as a bullet drove into his ribs.

A blanket of darkness descended over him, but not before
he gave way to despair. He was powerless to save the red-
haired boy from Antelope's vengeance.

Warren Webb could only guess at the number of volunteers
and ranging companies who had gathered to challenge the
Comanche invaders, but he feared they were not enough. The
new Republic of Texas had little in its national treasury except hope, and it could ill afford to pay the number of rangers
it needed to patrol its broad frontier. Webb and Michael
Shannon had once answered a call to enlist in a minuteman
company during an Indian scare but had never received the
promised wage. Even those officially enlisted as full-time
members of ranging companies were sometimes obliged to
pay their own way. They had little advantage over civilian
volunteers except their official-sounding titles.

Webb had never been this far inland, so the country was
new to him. The word had been spread that all available

Texas forces—organized ranging companies as well as volunteers—would gather at Plum Creek, which lay ahead. There, win or lose, they would stage the confrontation before the Indians could reach their hill-country sanctuaries.

Shortly after dawn, scouts had come into camp to report the Indians were just a few miles away. Webb and Shannon had attached themselves to a group of volunteers headed by Captain Mathew Caldwell, known as "Old Paint" for the white splotches in his beard. Caldwell gathered his company around him and made a rousing speech. They knew him as a battle-seasoned veteran of the revolution against Mexico, a man always cocked and primed for a fight.

"Boys," he declared, "there are a thousand Indians. They have our women and children captives. But we are eighty-seven strong, and I believe we can whip hell out of them!"

An approving murmur arose from the men.

Caldwell shouted, "What shall we do, boys? Shall we fight?"

Loud cheers gave him the answer.

A biblical phrase came to Webb's mind: *the faith of the mustard seed.* He thought it more likely that the Texans would be the ones who got hell whipped out of them, but the infectious enthusiasm among the settler congregation convinced him that to voice a contrary opinion would be to cry out in the wilderness, a voice lost in the wind.

Mike Shannon said, "Better cinch your saddle up tight, Preacher. We're fixin' to have ourselves a run, 'y God."

But in which direction? Webb wondered. He took some comfort in the knowledge that Caldwell's eighty-seven were only part of the force converging for the fight. It had been reported that Colonel Ed Burleson was on his way up from the Colorado with a large company including Chief Placido and several Tonkawa Indians, blood enemies of the Comanche. But even so, the invaders would still be greatly superior in number.

Though most of the men favored Caldwell, Old Paint acceded command to Felix Huston, a major general of the Texas army. Under Huston's orders the Texans moved into concealment to await Burleson's arrival. The Indians appeared first, a long, thin column stretching for several miles across the prairie, people and animals moving in and out of the dust like spectral figures, seen a moment, then disappearing.

Shannon said, "They have to know we're somewhere about because they've been trailed the whole way. Talk about arrogant . . . they must figure they can swat us away like so many horseflies."

Maybe they can, Webb thought. But he began to take hope. It occurred to him that the Comanches did not seem to know much about large-scale military tactics. They should realize their strung-out column was vulnerable to being flanked, cut and diced into sections. They must regard themselves as invulnerable because of their number.

Pride goeth before a fall.

He tried to make a rough count of the horses and mules but found it impossible. There might have been two thousand, even three. A considerable number carried plunder the Comanches had acquired in Victoria and Linnville.

Burleson arrived with his men. What caught Webb's attention most was the contingent of Tonkawas, all afoot and stripped to no more than breechclout and moccasins, their bodies painted for war. They wore white cloths tied on their arms so the Texans would not mistake them for Comanches in the excitement of battle. Most did not know one Indian from another.

Distant firing indicated that the fight had opened, though Webb could not see the action and had no idea which way the contest might be going. A contingent of Comanches charged upon Webb's group, yelling, firing what rifles they had, loosing arrows that made a peculiar singing sound as they flew. Their initial strategy was clear: to pin down the Texans while the main body escaped with the women and children, the booty-laden horses and mules.

Webb had never seen a more splendid spectacle, savage though it was. One Indian cast aside an umbrella he had carried to shade himself from the sun. He came in a run, waving a war club. On his head was a beaver hat with red ribbon tied around the crown. A ribbon of the same color streamed from his horse's tail. Webb found himself so fascinated, watching, that he did not take aim. The Indian was within twenty yards when someone's rifle brought him down. The beaver hat rolled on the ground. The Indian reached for it, but the wind carried it away. His fingers clawed the ground, and he died.

Shannon shouted, "If you ain't goin' to use that rifle, give it to me."

"I'll tote my load." Webb bore down on a warrior who wore antelope-horn headdress. Hit, the Indian twisted and laid forward on his horse's neck but managed to hold on as the horse galloped away from the fight.

Webb lost sight of the overall battle, for he was concentrating upon his own small part of it. He could hear firing all around him, the exuberant yelling of the Texans sensing victory, the war cries of the Comanches. The Tonkawas, though on foot, charged into the fray with a fury like hell unleashed, slashing, clubbing, scalping their enemies while they still breathed. It was enough to turn Webb's stomach had he not been too busy to let the horror of it soak in.

Soon the confrontation was less a battle than a runaway. Unaccountably, the Comanches seemed to have been caught off balance and unprepared. Any semblance of unity was lost. The big caballada of horses and mules was scattering to the winds, many losing their packs, littering the open prairie with all manner of white-man store goods.

Comanches, dead and dying, lay along the trail. Webb had to spur to keep up with the race.

Ahead of him he saw an Indian woman on a sorrel mare, holding a small boy in front of her. A Comanche warrior rushed to overtake her. A husband bound on protecting wife and child, Webb thought. He brought his rifle up, though it was next to useless from the back of a running horse. He felt a pang of conscience for having even considered leaving woman and child without a husband and father.

He realized suddenly that the man was swinging a war club, and the woman was trying to avoid him. She leaned over the boy, holding her arm out to deflect the blow. He heard her scream.

Webb could not believe what he saw. The man was trying to kill the youngster.

The mare stumbled, pitching woman and child out into the grass. The warrior's speed carried him past them. He wheeled his horse about and started back. She screamed again, trying to shield the boy with her body. She brought up a knife, brandishing it at the man.

Webb had no time to consider options. He drove his horse forward to intercept the warrior, who seemed so intent on the boy that he did not see the larger enemy until it was too late. The Comanche's eyes met Webb's, and he raised the club.

Momentum slammed the two horses together. Webb felt himself catapulted out of the saddle. He rolled in the dry grass and grabbed frantically at the rifle. He brought it up and pulled the trigger, but impact had spilled powder from the pan.

The Indian had managed to stay on his horse. He reined it around and came back, holding the club high. Webb instinctively raised the rifle, trying to let it take the blow. The club came down hard against his left arm. A sharp stab of pain told him the bone was broken.

Mike Shannon appeared suddenly, coming up behind the Comanche. Wild-eyed and shouting, he jammed the muzzle of his rifle against the painted body and fired. Blood spurted from the Indian's stomach as the bullet tore through him and exited. He tumbled from his horse and writhed on the ground, pressing his hands against a huge hole that gushed red. He struggled, then lapsed into a quiet quivering as life drained away.

Broken arm throbbing, Webb turned quickly to look for the woman. He saw her on hands and knees, gasping for breath lost in the fall. The knife lay on the ground beside her right hand. The boy stood beside her, bewildered.

Only then did Webb notice that the child's hair was red, his frightened eyes blue. He wore the homespun clothing typical in poor farm families. A white captive, Webb realized, probably taken in Victoria or Linnville. He looked as if he might be two years old, perhaps three.

"Come to me, lad," Webb said.

The boy hesitated. The Indian woman cried something and reached toward him. Webb knew Comanches often killed their captives when they were under pressure, so he kicked the knife away. He placed himself between the child and the woman, lifted the boy with his right arm and turned to catch his horse. The youngster clung tightly to his neck.

Shannon rode in close, drawing a pistol because he had not had time to reload the rifle. He gave the woman a hard look. Webb feared for a moment that he might shoot her.

"Spare her," Webb said.

"Less'n she makes a move toward you." He frowned. "Got your arm busted, looks like. Better let me carry the boy. White, ain't he?" He leaned down and drew the lad up in front of him in the saddle.

The woman pleaded in words Webb did not comprehend, though her expression told him she did not want to give up the child. Knowing she would not understand, he felt compelled nevertheless to try to explain. "The lad has people somewhere. He needs to be back with his own kind."

The mare had risen to her feet and was walking shakily. Webb motioned toward the woman, then toward the mare. "You'd best be slippin' away while you can."

She understood his motions if not his words. She hopped upon the mare's back. Crying, she made one last plea, holding out her arms. Shannon turned the boy away from her. She gave up and moved westward in the direction of the general runaway, though she kept looking back at the boy in Shannon's arms.

A volunteer rode up, eyes ablaze with excitement, sweat running down his face into a stubble of beard. His hands were bloody, but the blood did not appear to be his own. He pointed toward the fleeing woman. "Ain't you goin' to shoot her?"

Shannon said, "I never shoot women without I have to."

"Indian women make babies, and babies grow up to do murder. If you ain't goin' to shoot her, I will."

Shannon set the boy down upon the ground and eased the

muzzle of his rifle in the horseman's direction. "Do and you'll answer to me."

The man's face went scarlet. "You wouldn't shoot me over a Comanche squaw."

Shannon's voice was crisp. "I might. And then again, 'y God, I might just whip the hell out of you."

The man lowered his weapon. "One day her sons'll come to take your scalp, and you'll wish you'd killed her before she bore them."

"They've got plenty of fightin' men left up yonder if you're bound on more killin'. Go get *them*."

The fight, what was still left of it, had swept on past. "I figure to." The volunteer looked down at the boy on the ground. "You takin' Indian boys to raise, are you?"

"Look closer. He ain't an Indian."

The rider's eyes reflected surprise. "Good thing he ain't, because I'd be of a mind to kill him before he has a chance to grow up and kill me and mine." He rode on.

Shannon watched until the man was swallowed up in the dust. He turned back to Webb. "Yonder's a bunch of men gathered. Maybe there's a doctor amongst them. Your arm needs lookin' after."

Webb carried a medical book in his saddlebags with his Bible and administered limited physical aid along his circuit because real doctors were scarce in settlements beyond the main towns like San Antonio and Houston. But he doubted he had the fortitude to set his own broken bone. He mounted, careful not to use the left arm.

Shannon rode up to the small group of Texans. "Anybody recognize this young'un?"

No one did.

"What's your name, lad?" Webb asked.

The boy did not reply. Webb repeated the question. "What do your folks call you, your daddy and mama?"

The boy murmured, "Davy. Me Davy."

"What do they call your mama? And your daddy?"

"Mama. Daddy."

He saw that further questions would yield nothing. The boy was too young to know his family name.

Shannon inquired about a doctor but found there was none, at least not in this group. A young man with an upturned moustache and a German accent said, "Is best we bind that arm anyway, so it will not stay always crooked."

Webb came near fainting as the German pulled the arm straight, then tore a long strip of blue cloth off a bolt that had fallen from a pack animal. He bound it around a temporary splint, a rough piece of live-oak limb. Webb broke out in a cold sweat, his body trembling. But he managed to keep his head as the young man hurried the task.

"August Burmeister is not doctor, but the arm will not crooked be."

Shannon was impressed. "Where'd you learn to do up a broken arm like that?"

"In the old country, in Westphalia. I was a soldier in the army."

"How come you to be in Texas?"

"I did not like to be a soldier in the army. In the old country they tell of Texas. When they do not watch, I walk out to the *niederland* and the sea. On a boat I come to Galveston, to look for myself."

"Hell of a sight you're seein' here." The sounds of battle trailed away to distant spotty firing. Shannon said, "We gave them a royal whippin', 'y God. There'll be a trail of Comanche bones all the way to the mountains. They'll study long before they ever come this far again."

Evening fell. The arm throbbed, and Webb knew he was running a fever. He and Shannon shared a camp with the Blessing brothers and a small gathering of volunteer rangers in the service of the republic. Nearby, another group sang and shouted. The Tonkawa scouts who had accompanied the white men on their punitive strike were celebrating victory. Webb wondered how one tribe could be induced to aid the Texans in their fight against other Indians. The only answer he could see was that they did not consider themselves to be of the same people despite the fact that white men regarded them that way. The Tonkawas, a small and vulnerable tribe, saw the Texans as allies in their long struggle against domination by the stronger and far more numerous Comanches.

Shannon went over to watch but did not remain long. He came back, looking a little pale. "They're roastin' meat over yonder."

Webb was aware of that, for it smelled good. He assumed the Tonkawas had cut up one of the horses or mules killed in the fight.

Shannon asked, "Did you notice that some of them dead Comanches had their limbs chopped off?"

Webb had not. His broken arm had taken precedence over other considerations.

Shannon said, "Right now them Tonks are feastin' on the haunch off of a Comanche. They've got a couple of hands and a foot roastin' on the coals."

Webb thought at first that Shannon was joshing him, but his friend's expression was serious. Shannon said, "They invited me to join them. I said I was already full."

The Tonkawas had a reputation as cannibals, eating flesh from their enemies in ceremonial rites. This trait they shared with another coastal tribe, the Karankawas, who had been implacably hostile to the first settlers and by now had been hunted almost to extinction. It was said other tribes held Tonkawas and Karankawas in contempt for their consumption of human flesh and gladly killed them on sight.

Webb shuddered. He wished he had not smelled the roast on the Tonkawa fire. "Praise God they're our friends and not our enemies."

"Me and you wouldn't suit them much as enemies. We'd be too tough and stringy to eat." Shannon turned his attention to the rescued boy with the reddish hair. "What we goin' to do with him, Preacher?"

"Nothin' we *can* do except ride back over the trail the Indians left and ask if anybody knows him."

"Chances are that the Comanches killed his folks when they stole him."

Webb felt his throat pinch with pity. He had considered that probability. "If we can't turn up his family we'll have to find somebody who'll give him a good home."

Shannon seated himself on the fallen trunk of a lightning-struck live oak and lifted the youngster up into his lap.

"Davy, is it? Nice name. He'll be a good-lookin' young'un when he gets his face washed. That rusty-colored hair means he'll be a fighter someday. Reckon he's Irish?"

Webb was pleased that Shannon was warming to the boy. "All I know is that he's not Comanche."

"He'll be needin' a woman's care. My Dora'd be right pleased to keep him 'til we find his own folks."

"And if we don't find them?"

A fly buzzed around the boy's face. Shannon brushed it away. "Dora always wanted a big family, but as you know, she ain't been able to bear. She'd take this young'un as her own and be glad for the chance."

"I'd keep him myself, only I've got no wife to see after him. I couldn't take him on the circuit with me, and I couldn't leave him."

"Then it's settled. This boy'll be good company for Dora. We'll treat him like he was born to us and give him a good Christian raisin'. That's a promise, 'y God."

Exhausted, the red-haired youngster drifted off to sleep in Shannon's arms. The Irishman smiled.

Webb tried to smile too, but his arm hurt too much.

PART
II.

• 4 •

Rusty Shannon realized the morning was off to a bad beginning when he stepped out onto the open dog run of the double log cabin and saw that the mule team was not in the corral. He had personally penned them last night so he could get a daylight start in the field. They had included a big gray mule named Old Zach, one of a pair Daddy Mike Shannon had brought home from the Mexican war. The mule was smart as paint, but it had never learned to untie a knot in a rawhide string or push open a heavy gate that always dragged the ground and strained a man's muscles to lift and move it.

Rusty trotted out to the pen and saw the gate slumped half open, dead weight against its leather hinges. Leaning down to pick up the rawhide strip, he saw that it had been cut. He became aware of moccasin tracks, and his heartbeat quickened. Instinct made him look up, his gaze sweeping the open ground between the cabin and the river. His stomach, warm and full from a breakfast of coffee and cornbread, honey and venison, seemed to do a quick turnover.

"Daddy! Daddy Mike!"

He had taken to calling his foster father *Dad*; it sounded more mature. But in a moment of excitement he reverted to the name he had used since boyhood.

He started back toward the cabin in a hard run. Mike Shannon limped out of the kitchen onto the open dog run, one arthritis-knotted hand raised to shield his eyes from the rising sun. His graying whiskers had not felt a razor in a week or more. His thick gray hair was disheveled, for he had not taken time to use a comb. He combed his hair only for company, and he had no reason to expect any.

"What's all the noise, young'un? Fox been amongst the chickens again?"

Rusty was too old to be called *young'un*, but he supposed Mike would hold to the habit as long as he lived. No one knew Rusty's age, exactly. The best guess was that he should be a year or so on the far side of twenty.

"Indians, Dad. Indians got the mules."

Mike Shannon snorted. "Ain't seen an Indian here since . . ." He did not finish the sentence. He had seen a lot of Indians in his time, most of them over the sights of a rifle. He had been in so many skirmishes that they tended to run together. When he began telling about them, one incident often became mixed with another. He contended that the fine details did not matter so much as the innate truth and spirit of the story. Even a village idiot could cite dry facts.

Michael Shannon hobbled out to meet Rusty and accompany him back to the corral. He had come home from the Mexican war a dozen years ago with two mules and a sense of duty fulfilled. But he had gone off on an Indian campaign a year or so ago and came home with a wounded leg that still pained him every day. He had had to lean heavily upon Rusty to work this farm that the state of Texas had awarded him for service. Texas had little cash to pay its volunteers, so they often went unpaid despite the best intentions of governor and legislature. But it had land aplenty. It sometimes settled its debts with real estate.

Mother Dora came out onto the dog run, arms folded as if they were cold, thin shoulders slumped. She had been ill of late for no specific reason that met the eye. Preacher Webb was the nearest thing to a doctor within a day's ride, when he was not off to some distant point carrying the Scriptures to the farthermost settlers. Webb knew a lot about poultices and potions, but he could not fathom what was wrong with her. Country women tended to age rapidly on the frontier. An old saying declared that Texas was heaven for men and horses but hell for women and dogs. She had simply worn herself out, for a woman's work began before daylight and did not end until she crawled into bed, exhausted.

Rusty asked no foolish questions. He preferred to figure things out for himself or leave them alone. He handed Mike the cut string. "Look at the moccasin tracks."

Mike said, "Them thievin' rascals." A hint of admiration crept into his voice. "Snuck up here in the night, 'y God, and got off with them mules without us hearin' a thing." He squinted at Rusty. "You *didn't* hear anything, did you?"

"No, sir. I'd've raised a holler." For a fleeting moment Rusty wondered if Mike might think he heard but was scared to do anything about it. Mike should know him better than that. Rusty never went looking for a fight but did not run from one if it came looking for him. He had learned from Mike that skinned knuckles heal, but wounded pride just festers.

It struck Rusty that the family's brown dog should have raised a ruckus. It never let so much as a raccoon approach the place at night without sounding an alarm. Sometimes, lacking anything else to bark at, it just barked at the moon. He found the dog lying in the grass, an arrow driven deeply into its body. It might have barked a little before it was struck, but no one in the cabin would have paid attention if the racket stopped quickly.

Mike tugged at the arrow. It was too deeply embedded to be pulled out easily. He examined the shaft. "Comanche."

Comanche was a word that sent a chill up a man's back. It traveled up Rusty's and down again.

Mike grumbled, "A fool dog he was, but good company." He wasted but a moment in regret. "We're not rich enough that we can afford to furnish work stock to the Comanche

nation. Ain't but one thing to do, and that's go after them,
'y God."

"Afoot?" Rusty asked.

"I saw our horses grazin' down by the river just at sundown. Maybe them redskin thieves missed them in the dark.
You go see."

Rusty had trotted a hundred yards before it dawned on
him that he was not armed. But it was unlikely the Indians
still lingered. On a horse-stealing raid they tended to strike
hard and get away fast.

He thought the chance of getting the mules back was about
the same as finding a pot of gold down by the river. But he
would not tell Mike so. He was as conservative with words
as he was with the little bit of money that ever came into
his hands. Visitors had spent the night at the Shannon farm
and left the next day believing Rusty was deaf and dumb.

People not well acquainted with the family often assumed
that Rusty had been born to it. Many did not know that Mike
Shannon and Preacher Webb had taken him from the Comanches on the battlefield at Plum Creek. The minister had
ridden many long miles and made a lot of inquiries before
abandoning hope of identifying the boy. Mike and Mother
Dora had regarded him as their own and gave him their family name, for he had none of his own.

The only thing markedly different about Rusty was his
reddish hair, which had gained him his nickname. Mike always said red hair went with a name like Shannon anyway;
it was the Irish coming out.

Hardly anyone except Mother Dora ever called him by the
only name he had brought with him: David. She clung stub-
bornly to it, though everyone else had long since called him
Rusty.

At times, when he lay half asleep at night, Rusty could
almost remember his true mother—not so much what she
looked like, for he could never quite conjure up her face, but
something vague about the way she felt cradling him in her
arms and the sound of her voice talking and singing to him.
He remembered the warm and comforting feeling of love. It
was not much, but it was enough to make him wonder, to

give him a sense of loss, of something missed that he would never recover. It saddened him at times, even as he remained grateful for the Shannons. Had he been able to choose his parents, he would have wanted them in the Shannon image.

Still, he often wondered who he really was.

Though he made no claim to being a tracker, the broad trail led him to guess that the Comanches must have been riding or driving seventy-five to a hundred horses and mules. A lot of people besides the Shannons had been set afoot. But he found the two Shannon horses grazing calmly a hundred yards from the river. As Mike had said, the Indians had probably overlooked them in the dark.

Rusty walked up to the gentler of the pair, a black much favored by Mike. "Easy, Alamo, easy." He spoke softly until he could rub the animal's shoulder; then he grabbed a handful of glossy mane and swung up bareback. He guided the horse with his knees and gentle pats on the neck. "Come on, Alamo. You too, Goliad."

Mike Shannon was pleased as Rusty brought the two horses to the cabin and put them in the pen from which the mules had been stolen. "I was afraid we'd have to go afoot."

That would have been futile sure enough, Rusty thought, though he did not say so. The federal army's foot soldiers had never been able to catch up to any Indians, though they had worn out a lot of shoe leather trying.

Mother Dora left the dog run and came out, her steps careful and slow as if she were unsure of her footing. She did not often criticize her husband, however much she might deplore his fighting nature. But this time she said, "You're goin' off on a fool's errand, Michael. Even if you catch up to them, what'll you do? Get yourself killed, more than likely, and David with you."

Mike Shannon had never admitted defeat in his life, even if it faced him nose to nose. When his time came to die, he meant to go down fighting. "We'll come up with somethin'."

She asked, "How far do you think you can ride? What about that bad leg?"

"It's a long way from the heart. Saddle up, Rusty, then let's go get our guns."

In the cabin, Rusty fetched down from its pegs a flintlock rifle Mike had brought home from the war with Mexico. It was the only one the family owned. He handed it to Mike.

From a corner he took an old shotgun Mike had carried to Texas in 1836 in hope of using it on Mexican general Santa Anna, or *Santy Anna,* as Mike called him. He was just in time to be on hand when Sam Houston took that fancy gentleman's measure on the battleground at San Jacinto. Mike had felt cheated, getting to participate in only a single engagement, so one-sided that it was over almost before it began. He had to wait ten years for another full-blown war to break out. Mother Dora had reluctantly given her blessings and sent him off with a company of ranger volunteers to fight Mexico as his forebears had fought the British in two earlier wars.

Scouting for the United States Army, Mike and other Texans under command of Colonel Jack Hays had harried the enemy all the way to Veracruz and Mexico City. Rusty had heard him tell many a rousing tale, most of them more or less true, allowing for a little enthusiastic stretching of minor parts that otherwise would not have been so interesting. A faded and battle-worn U.S. flag hung in a place of honor on the kitchen wall.

A muzzle-loading horse pistol usually rested on a set of pegs beneath the rifle, but it was missing. A greasy-whiskered neighbor named Fowler Gaskin had borrowed it weeks ago. Gaskin was notorious for borrowing first one thing and then another, sometimes asking, sometimes just coming and getting. He was also notorious for not bringing anything back. If the owner wanted it, he had to go and get it . . . if Gaskin hadn't misplaced it somewhere or sold it to somebody. A couple of weeks ago he had borrowed Mike Shannon's best mule, Chapultepec. He hadn't asked but had chosen a time when the menfolk were elsewhere. He led the animal out of the corral and told Mother Dora, "I need the borry of your mule," then had shouted "Thankee!" back over his shoulder as he rode away bareback. The bridle had been Mike's, too.

It might just be that the Indians had missed the Gaskin

place, Rusty thought. If so, the Shannons still had one plow mule after all. They could team him with Alamo if they had to, though it would hurt Mike's conscience to hitch the black to a wagon or plow. Especially alongside a mule.

Indian raids were no longer commonplace along this section of the Colorado, though they still occurred with regularity farther west. Texas had been a state in the union for more than ten years now. Federal troops guarded the frontier, but most were infantry, restricted to guard and garrison duty and ill equipped for pursuit of the Comanches' light cavalry. Several times Mike had enlisted in the state's volunteer ranging companies for limited periods. Horseback, they moved faster than the federals, were burdened with less equipage, and did not have to answer to every pip-squeak bureaucrat misled into an overappraisal of his own importance.

Rusty had no clear recollection of ever having seen a Comanche close up, though faint and confusing fragments of memory sometimes came to him unbidden, so elusive he could never grab hold of them. He knew Indians had carried him away from his original home, and he was aware that he had stayed with them a short while. Mostly he remembered being bewildered and frightened, not able to understand.

Mike checked the rifle and the shot pouch that went with it. "Mother, we'll drag that dog off before we leave. He'll be stinkin' before long."

The dark circles beneath her eyes seemed heavier this morning, and her hair had never looked quite so gray. "I wish you wouldn't go. You're not as young as you think you are. How far do you think you can travel?"

"I rode many a mile and crossed many a river durin' the war."

"That was ten years ago, before a Comanche bullet ruined your leg. There are lots of things you used to do that you can't anymore."

Fearing the two were about to plunge into a full-blown argument, Rusty stepped out onto the dog run to avoid being a witness. He saw riders approaching and shouted, "Company comin'."

Mike hobbled out with the rifle cradled in his arms, ready

for use. "Hard to believe they'd come back for more. They already took more than enough."

"It's white men," Rusty said. "Looks like Tom Blessing in the lead."

Mike squinted, uncertain. His eyesight was not as keen as it used to be.

Blessing had often served as a captain when the state treasury got a few dollars ahead and the governor called ranger companies into service. Several times Rusty had watched Mike ride away with Blessing and others in search of Indians or bandits or to put down one of the foolish but bloody feuds that seemed always brewing in the older settlements of Texas. A year ago Mike had gone off under command of Captain John S. "Rip" Ford on an expedition against hostiles. The rangers and federal troops had been aided by friendly Indians to whom the Comanches were longtime enemies. They had devastated a large village, but Mike had come home with a wounded leg that would have been amputated had he not resisted with his shotgun and threatened to shoot anyone who touched him.

Rusty was aware, from stories he had heard, that Blessing had been present when he was recovered from the Comanches at Plum Creek. He had always felt that he owned his life to Tom Blessing, Mike Shannon, and Preacher Webb. He was pleased to see Preacher Webb riding just behind Blessing. Every man was armed. It was plain that they were trailing the Indians.

Blessing's pale blue eyes were a major contrast to his fierce black beard speckled with gray. He had a deep, booming voice that bespoke authority. "Mike, I judge by the tracks that you-all had visitors last night."

"We sure enough did. Tried to clean us out of horse and mule flesh, 'y God. Me and Rusty was fixin' to take up their trail."

Blessing seemed more amused than surprised. "Just the two of you?"

"Didn't figure on Dora goin'."

"Mind if we join you?"

"Me and Rusty'd be tickled for the company, long as you don't get in our way."

Rusty's heart leaped with excitement at the thought of riding with the volunteer rangers. He had long wanted to, but Mike had always said he was too young. Mike easily forgot how young *he* had been when he set out for Texas on his own.

Preacher Webb moved forward, looking relieved. "Thank the Lord that the Indians were after stock more than scalps."

Blessing said, "They took some scalps to the east of here, though. Killed most of a family, stole a woman and a boy."

"A boy?" Mike Shannon said. He glanced at Rusty. Rusty guessed he was remembering Plum Creek.

Blessing said, "Last time I saw you, Mike, that leg was still in bad shape. You sure you're ready for a long ride?"

" 'Y God I'm always ready. You never seen me lag behind like some people." He directed his gaze to Fowler Gaskin, sitting on Mike's mule Chapultepec.

Gaskin held a hand behind his right ear, trying to hear better. He was thin as a slab of bacon, his face ruddy with tiny red veins threaded across it, his ragged old vest spotted with tobacco juice and remnants of past meals. He took more sustenance from a jug than from a plate.

Rusty said, "Dad, there's Chapultepec. They didn't get him."

Gaskin growled, "I wish they had. He's the roughest-trottin' mule I ever rode. Looks like you-all could keep a better one around for your neighbors to borry."

Ordinarily Rusty was careful to speak respectfully to his elders, but he had no respect for Fowler Gaskin. Neither did anyone else around here that he knew of. "You didn't ask, you just came and took him. We could've told you he's a plow mule, not a ridin' mule."

He figured Gaskin would have no stomach for a close view of the Indians. At the first sign of a feather he would probably find out just how fast Chapultepec could run, in the opposite direction.

Blessing seemed to figure that way too, for he gave Gaskin a chance to turn back. He managed deference, but it was clearly a strain. "It's apt to be a hard ride, Fowler. At your age I'm sure you'd rather be at home watchin' over your family."

Gaskin did not watch over his family very well under the best of circumstances. He and his wife and daughter Florey barely tolerated one another, and Gaskin did not even like his two sons much. Neither did Rusty. Eph and Luke Gaskin used to lie in ambush, waiting to chunk rocks at him when he came into range. Usually they scampered as soon as Rusty began hurling the same rocks back at them. His aim was better. The Gaskin boys were too lazy to practice, but Rusty was not. Lately the brothers had outgrown rock-throwing but still baited him and threw insults.

The whole family was a lean and hungry lot, looking to reap where others had sown.

Gaskin seemed torn. Rusty suspected he had come this far only because someone had shamed him into it.

A tall, angry-looking man named Isaac York pushed his horse against the mule Gaskin rode. "Go back, Fowler, and leave the fightin' to people who know how to kill Indians! You'd just be in the way."

Though Gaskin was a man of little pride, and for good reason, that little made him stubborn enough to refuse. "I've come this far. I'll go the whole hog." He spat on the ground and gave York a look of defiance. Rusty was surprised that he could rouse up that much gumption.

Mother Dora said, "I wish you wouldn't take David. He's just a boy."

Blessing gave Rusty a quick study. "Maybe you haven't looked at him close, Miz Shannon. Rusty's a man."

Rusty warmed at Blessing's acceptance. He had waited a long time for it.

Blessing said, "We're goin' on, Mike. When you're ready, you can lope up and catch us."

Pulse racing, Rusty watched the men ride away, Gaskin trailing behind on the mule. The faces were known to him, and most of the names. They were neighbors, friends of Mike's, farmers and tradesmen from the settlement five miles downriver. Each had his own life and his own interests, but in times of challenge the community pulled together. In that way it had survived the poverty of the early years, the pressure from Indians and from Mexico.

Though that country had relinquished formal claim on Texas after the Mexican war, many people on both sides of the border had never acknowledged the treaty. They regarded Texas as Mexican territory and sometimes raided north of the Rio Grande to bolster their point. This, in turn, invited retaliation by Texans, who felt no compunctions about raiding into Mexico, often less from patriotism as from expectation of personal gain. Even up here on the Colorado River, far north of the Rio Grande, settlers could not feel secure against the border troubles. Only a few years ago a Mexican army had invaded all the way to San Antonio, capturing the district court in session and taking Texan prisoners back to Mexico. There had been hell to pay over that incident and the retaliations that followed. Always ready for a scrap, Mike Shannon had ridden off on a punitive expedition. Wisely, he had stopped at the Rio Grande. Some who crossed the river had paid with their lives.

Preacher Webb said, "I'll wait and ride with you-all." He dismounted and stepped up to Mother Dora. His voice was full of concern. "How do you feel, Dora? Any improvement?"

She attempted a faint smile that never quite came to life. "I know better than to lie to a preacher."

Webb turned to Mike. "I wish you'd stay and watch over Dora. It's time you left the fightin' to younger men."

"I ain't any older than you are."

"I've got no sick wife at home."

Dora said, "He's set his mind to go, Preacher Webb, so let him be. I can take care of myself. Always have." She turned toward the cabin's kitchen door. "I'll sack up some vittles. And you-all had best take blankets. The nights can get chilly out in the open."

Mike nodded. "Go fetch them, Rusty."

Rusty was so excited at riding with the volunteers, at calling himself a ranger if only for a few days, that a small thing like blankets would not have crossed his mind. But he rolled up a blanket apiece for himself and his foster father.

Dora Shannon came out of the kitchen and handed Rusty a bulging cloth sack. "There's coffee and some bacon and salt. And the biscuits from breakfast. You be real careful, son." She hugged him, and he felt the wetness of her tears when their cheeks came together. Many a time she had bid Mike good-bye this way.

Mike said, "The young'un'll do his duty."

"Duty." She spoke the word with irony. "Duty'll be the death of you someday." She put her thin arms around her husband. "Don't take any chances tryin' to get our stock back. We can buy more somehow. Just bring yourself back in one piece, and make sure nothin' happens to David. He's the only son we'll ever have."

Mike tried to dismiss her concerns. "We probably won't catch up to them anyway." He turned. "We'd best be movin', Preacher."

Webb gave Dora Shannon one more worried look. "God bless this house, and all who live in it." He swung into the saddle and spurred his brown horse into a trot.

Rusty waved his floppy old felt hat and shouted back over his shoulder to his foster mother, "Don't you worry. We'll be comin' back."

If she answered, he could not hear her for the wind.

"We *will* be comin' back," he repeated, softer now, and more to himself than to Mike or Preacher Webb.

For years he had worked the farm without anything exciting happening to him. Following the plow and the mules day after day, year after year, he had dreamed of joining a minuteman ranging company as Mike had so often done. He had seen himself riding boldly into action, making Mike and Mother Dora proud of the raising they had given him. Now his backside prickled with anticipation.

The three did not press their animals to catch up quickly. Mike said they had plenty of time because they were unlikely to overtake the Indians before tomorrow or next day at the earliest. They moved along in a stiff trot, gradually closing the distance between them and the other volunteers without breaking into a run that would tire their horses. The hooves of the stolen animals had beaten down the grass and left a wide band of tracks that anyone could have followed.

Most members of Blessing's little band had fought Indians, and several had seen action in the Mexican war and border skirmishes.

It felt natural to Rusty that he ride alongside Preacher Webb. Several times he had accompanied Webb on his preaching circuit when he had no pressing responsibilities at home. The minister had always been pleasant company and a good teacher without blatantly appearing to try. He was widely read and could talk at length on subjects totally foreign but fascinating to Rusty. Moreover, he withheld his sermons for the pulpit. His best preaching was done by example, living the kind of life he urged upon others. If the man had any vices beyond a little affinity for horse races and a bachelor's way of staring wistfully at good-looking ladies, Rusty had not seen it.

He had long marveled at the man's stamina. The minister would sometimes ride until fatigue dulled his eyes and he could barely stay in the saddle. Yet once Webb reached his destination and found a crowd waiting to hear him, his shoulders straightened and his weak voice took on the power of the Word.

"The Lord never gives us a job to do without He gives us the strength to carry it out," Webb often said.

His left arm was crooked, having healed that way after being broken by an Indian club at Plum Creek, so Rusty had been told. The arm was always subject to the miseries when weather changed, but the minister never let it handicap him if work needed to be done.

He and Mike and Rusty caught up when Blessing's men stopped for a noon rest. The trail was still plain. Rusty thought, though he did not say so, that it was a mistake to pause while the Indians rode on. But the pursuers' mounts could only be pushed so far and so fast. The Indians could switch to fresh horses from among those they had taken.

Blessing's men had to make do with what they had. If a
mount gave out or went lame, its rider was out of the chase.

The ranger captain walked out to meet the three incoming
horsemen. "Better get down and let your mounts blow a little." He waited for Rusty to dismount. "Your daddy has been
sworn in so many times there don't seem any point to it. But
I'll swear you in if you want me to. You'll not likely see a
dime of state money, but at least you can put in a claim . . .
for whatever that's worth."

Rusty had not even considered that he might be paid. Mike
had always told him that a man owed it to his neighbors and
to his country to serve when duty called, and he should never
ask about reward. "You just ask what they want you to do.
It's your way to pay for the privilege of livin' in Texas and
the United States of America."

Rusty had been no more than seven or eight years old at
the time, but he remembered how joyfully his foster father
had celebrated when Texas gave up its status as a free republic and became a state in the union. Mike had declared,
"If it hadn't been for my daddy comin' over from the old
country when he did, we'd still be in Ireland today, workin'
a shriveled-up potato patch and starvin' to death, 'y God."

Indeed, the Shannons had come near starving a time or
two when they first broke out their present farm. But determination and helpful neighbors had allowed them to survive.

Rusty told Blessing, "I don't worry about pay, but I'd take
it kindly if you made me a ranger, even for a few days. So
would Daddy Mike, I think." His foster father had always
been proud of the times—some short, some long—he had
served in a ranging company.

Blessing administered a brief oath that officially made
Rusty a member of his company for whatever time his service might be deemed necessary. He stated that Rusty was
obliged to furnish his own firearm and horse and was to be
paid a daily allowance from the state treasury should such
monies be available. "The state insists on the first part,"
Blessing said. "It's a lot more flexible as to the last. I'm
sorry I can't give you a badge to wear, but I don't have one

myself. Badges wouldn't impress a Comanche much anyhow."

From Mike's stories, Rusty knew the rangers did not stand on ceremony. They had no official uniform, no official badge, not even an official title. They were most often called simply rangers or ranging companies, minutemen, and sometimes spies. Their rules were mostly made up as they went along, based on common sense and the realities of the moment. The main requirement was that they do the job or bust themselves trying. Sometimes they did indeed bust themselves, but more often they did whatever they thought it took to get the job done. If they happened to maim or kill a few more people than was really necessary . . . well, that was just too damned bad. It was ranger logic that such casualties resulted from folks being in the wrong place at the wrong time, and they were probably guilty of something anyway.

Blessing did not call a halt until dusk faded into darkness. He stopped where the steep banks of a near-dry creek bed would hide their meager campfire from view should the Indians send scouts to survey their back trail.

The men needed rest, especially Mike and Preacher Webb. Mike rubbed his bad leg and winced with pain when he thought nobody was looking. The minister seemed wrung out like a freshly washed shirt. He gripped his crooked arm as if the miseries had set in deep.

Blessing offered, "Oscar Petrie had the foresight to bring a bottle of whiskey if that would help you, Mike."

Mike accepted with gratitude. "Oscar Petrie is the smartest man I know."

Blessing turned to Webb. "How about you, Preacher?"

"After I have made whiskey the subject of a hundred sermons?"

"It has medicinal properties."

Rusty remembered that Mother Dora had put coffee in the sack of grub she had given him. "I'll boil you some coffee, Preacher. I never heard you sermonize against that."

"And you never will. When the Christians drove the Turks from the gates of Vienna, the Turks left their stores of coffee

behind. I feel sure that was the Lord's notion of a proper gift
to His faithful."

Rusty had no idea where Vienna was. Probably not in
Texas, or he would have heard about it.

He noticed that Isaac York kept pacing back and forth atop
the creek bank, staring toward the north. Blessing called,
"Isaac, you'd better get some rest while you can."

York's voice was harsh. "I doubt that woman and boy they
stole are gettin' any rest."

"You can't do them any good if you're too worn out to
keep up."

"Moon's risin'. Plain as the tracks are, we ought to be able
to follow them pretty soon."

"We'll never catch up on dead horses. Come on down."
Blessing poured a tin cup almost to the brim with steaming
coffee and held it high as enticement. York descended from
the bank. A black man who always accompanied him took
the coffee Blessing offered and handed it to him as if it were
his place, and his only, to serve York.

York said, "Go get you some sleep, Shanty." He squatted
near the fire, a towering man with a slight hunch to his broad
shoulders. Rusty studied the brooding face, made bloodred
and fearsome by the flickering reflection of the coals. He
knew the man mostly by reputation. He was said to be a
ferocious fighter in any scrap with Indians. Mike had fought
side by side with him in the Mexican war. He said York
seemed to take that conflict as a personal crusade and killing
as many enemies as possible a personal obligation. Back
home, York was known as a heavy drinker and dramshop
brawler always looking for a new war to fight.

Though Mike Shannon was a good scrapper himself, he
gave York room except when duty called them together.

Rusty was intrigued by the man's intensity. He eased himself down at Preacher Webb's side and asked, "What do you
think of Isaac York?"

Webb considered the question gravely. "He's been to the
edge of the pit and looked down into the fires of hell. He's
a good man to have at your side in a fight, but some dark

day the fire will draw him in. You'd not want to be at his side then."

Rusty stared at the troubled face and shivered.

It seemed he had barely gone to sleep when Mike shook his shoulder. "Time to saddle up and go, young'un. Tom Blessing's given the word."

Rusty's body resisted at first. He was painfully stiff from lying on the ground, and his stomach was uneasy because of the need for more sleep. But he felt a renewal of yesterday's excitement at riding with these men. Moreover, he was ashamed to lag when he saw that the minister, much older than he, was up and moving. So was Mike, limping heavily as he saddled his horse. Looking to the east, Rusty saw no sign of sunrise.

Webb seemed to read his thoughts. "Moon's still up. The Lord has given us light enough that we should be able to follow the trail, plain as it is."

The sun was three hours high when they came upon the place where the Comanches had spent the night. Buzzards had already found what remained of a horse they had slaughtered and roasted. They led the pursuers to something else as well.

Rusty took one look at the naked, bloody corpse of the woman and quickly turned away. The exhilarating sense of adventure vanished. He almost lost his quick breakfast of coffee and cold biscuits. He leaned far out of the saddle in case it all came up.

Isaac York went into a frenzy, spurring toward the buzzards, firing his pistol at them, cursing them and all the Indians that ever lived. The birds rose sluggishly into the air. One of York's bullets struck home, and black feathers exploded. The buzzard fell to the ground and flapped one wing, futilely trying to rise again.

Fowler Gaskin stared at the body with bold curiosity as if he had never seen a woman naked before.

Preacher Webb's voice had a sting. "Have you no decency

in you, Fowler?" He dismounted and untied the blanket from behind the cantle of his saddle. He shook it out and covered the woman with it, removed his hat and began a quiet prayer. The other men bared and bowed their heads. Rusty sensed a quiet fury rising among the group, though no one spoke while Webb prayed. Even York managed to contain himself, but barely.

The prayer finished, York faced Blessing and took an accusatory stance. "They probably done this to her while we was takin' our rest last night."

Blessing seemed stunned by the sight of the dead woman. That surprised Rusty, because he had always regarded Blessing as a man who could not be shaken. Blessing said, "We couldn't have gotten here in time to stop it if we had ridden straight through." He turned to the other men. "Look around. The boy may be here somewhere, too."

No trace was found. The boy evidently was still with the Indians.

"Damn them!" York's eyes were wild. "The only way to stop them is to kill them all—every last redskinned heathen for a thousand miles!"

"You know we can't."

"Why not? Who'd stop us?"

"The United States Army. They'd stop us at the reserve."

Rusty was aware that a reservation had been set up on the Brazos River in North Central Texas for those Indians who would come to council and formally agree to peace. He knew from what he had heard around the settlement that even some southern Comanche bands were there. Other Comanches remained unfettered, ranging at will across their accustomed hunting grounds and beyond, occasionally raiding southward all the way into Mexico. Most Texas residents would not have minded—might even have cheered—if the attacks had been confined to Mexico, but of course they were not.

The settlers were distrustful, even hostile to the concept of reserve Indians. It was common belief that raiding parties ventured out from the reservation, then fled back to the army's protection once they had committed their depredations. This was accepted as fact, though some of the warriors now on the reserve had sided with the whites as scouts and fighting allies in two recent major campaigns against hostile Comanches.

Comanches preyed upon other Indians as well as upon the white settlements. They saw everyone around them as either friend or enemy. They had few friends.

York cried, "The federals! They don't do a damned thing to protect white people, but they'd shoot us all to save their Indian pets."

Blessing did not argue. Rusty had a strong feeling that he agreed even if he did not say so. The captain said, "Preacher, we never thought to bring a shovel, but there's a plenty of rocks here. Reckon you and Rusty can cover her decent and then try to catch up to us? We'll move on as fast as we can without killin' the horses."

"We'll do our best by her."

Blessing sought out Gaskin. "Fowler, why don't you stay and help?"

Gaskin was quick to dismount. "If you say so, Tom, but you know I'm ready and rarin' to go on."

York looked down a last time at the blanket-covered body. "We ought to kill them all and send them back to hell where they came from!"

The black man called Shanty rode beside him, talking quietly, trying to calm him. "You liable to bust a blood vessel, Mr. Isaac. You know what happened to you the last time."

Rusty had heard that York got into a violent argument at the settlement and went into some kind of fit. Witnesses had feared for a few minutes that he might die.

As the men rode away, Rusty asked, "Was this lady maybe some kin of York's?"

Webb shook his head. "I doubt he even knew her. But out here we're so few that in one sense we're all kin."

"I just thought from the way he acted . . ."

"A few years ago, down on the Brazos, he and Shanty went to help a neighbor raise a cabin. When they got back he found his own cabin burned and his wife dead. The Comanches did to her what they did to this poor woman, and killed his two little girls besides. Such a thing has driven stronger men than Isaac York out of their minds."

Rusty and Webb wrapped the blanket around the body and began picking up rocks. Fowler Gaskin made a halfhearted effort but contributed only a few stones to the mound. He kept mumbling about the likelihood that the rangers would run into an ambush. "Tom Blessing don't know what he may be gettin' into."

"He knows what he's doin'," Webb said. "He always does."

When the minister decided the body was covered with enough stones to discourage wolves and coyotes, Gaskin declared, "This sorry mule is about give out."

Webb suggested, "Then the best thing for you to do is go on home. You wouldn't be of much use on a worn-out mule."

Gaskin tried to look disappointed, but the relief in his eyes made him a liar. "You tell Tom Blessing how bad I hate to have to drop out."

Webb was much kinder than Rusty thought the situation warranted. "He'll understand. We all do."

Gaskin rode away, putting the mule into a stiff trot. The animal was not too tired for that.

Rusty wasted little time brooding about Gaskin's desertion. He stared regretfully at the grave. "It don't seem right— no fitten grave, not even a marker, no kinfolks to say goodbye."

"What's here is just the clay, not the soul. The Lord's takin' care of her now."

Bitterness crept into Rusty's voice. "Where was He last night when she really *needed* takin' care of? He could've struck them butchers down."

"It's not given to us to know His reasons. He tests the strength of our faith."

"I'm not real sure about mine right now. I don't think He's even lookin' in our direction."

"Lad, this is no time to yield to blasphemy."

"You think He's liable to strike *me* down?"

"You're young. You have but little notion how cruel man

can be to man. You'll learn, though, and you'll need a strong faith to get you through it."

"I'd have a stronger faith if I could see a dozen Comanches layin' here dead."

"You might not like it once you saw it. Be careful what you pray for, lest it be given unto you."

· 5 ·

Buffalo Caller, stripped down to breechclout and moccasins and a few streaks of paint, allowed the horses and mules to be driven past him in a generally northward direction. He held tightly to the rawhide rein of the bay horse he rode and looked southward along the trail they had just made. He saw no one, but he sensed that the Texans were back there somewhere. He had seen them in a dream last night. He could feel them in his bones. A blind man could follow these tracks, and the Texans were hardly blind.

Ordinarily this would trouble him. On most horse raids he took every precaution to make the trail difficult or impossible to follow. But this time was different. This time he had a purpose.

A young brave drew up beside him and studied the tracks. "If we divide the horses it will be much harder for the Texans to follow."

Buffalo Caller felt the prickling of impatience. He was the leader of this raid. The young men's fighting ability was as yet unproven. It was not for them to question his judgment. But he put down the flare of resentment, for this was Black Horse, son of an old friend who had died at Texan hands long ago, after the big raid on Linnville. Buffalo Caller avoided ever saying Antelope's name, though it crossed his mind from time to time. It was not good to speak the names of the dead lest one summon their ghosts. Ghosts were often known to be unfriendly, though in life they had been family and friends. Antelope might feel he had ample cause to be unfriendly because Buffalo Caller had drawn a knife on him to defend the Texan boy of the red hair.

Buffalo Caller thought occasionally of the boy, wondering if he yet lived. Whippoorwill had said he was alive when the Texans took him from her, but only because a Texan bullet had struck down Antelope as he tried to kill the youngster. Buffalo Caller knew that dark spirits could summon all manner of ill fortune to fall upon child and adult alike. Diseases once unknown to the Comanche had spread among them with a vengeance after the white man's coming. The spotted sickness was the worst, snuffing out the lives not only of children but of their elders as well, leaving many lodges in mourning.

The white man had much to answer for.

He had often thought upon Antelope's warning that the boy's red hair was bad medicine and could bring misfortune upon them all. True, the big fight had been a disaster for the Comanches. Buffalo Caller had almost died of a bullet wound and later had had to make his way afoot all the way from the battlefield to the encampment on the plains. Many a long and sleepless night, he had pondered Antelope's warning and wondered if it might have been correct.

In the fight, Buffalo Caller had lost the scalp of the red-haired woman who had been the boy's mother. He wished he could have burned it, for at times he felt its evil had followed him. He had encountered a few white people with red hair in the years since. He had drawn away from them as if they carried the spotted sickness. He had not considered killing them, for he feared the possibility that evil spirits dwelling within them might transfer themselves to him at the moment of their deaths. Shamans had said this could come to pass. A wise man did not risk the displeasure of malevolent spirits.

Blinking against the bite of dust, he looked toward the herd of horses and mules. He could not see the white boy they had taken. He had feared all along that one of the young warriors might take it in his head to kill the youngster as Antelope had tried to kill the other one long ago. That would be contrary to Buffalo Caller's order, but the young men were not bound to obey if they chose otherwise. A war leader could not compel; he could only use his powers of persuasion and hope they were strong enough. He had given his approval for the young men to violate and then butcher the white woman in hope that spilling her blood would cool the fire in their own. She had been a burden anyway, weeping all the time. How could white men expect to raise strong sons if the mothers were weak?

It had long been a Comanche observation that captive children should be separated from their mothers as soon as possible if they were to make a successful conversion to the ways of the People. Texan and Mexican mothers tended to exert an adverse influence. This boy, who appeared to be three or four summers old, had the chance to become a good warrior once his mettle had been tested. The young men had been quirting him at intervals and jabbing the points of their arrows into his skin to determine if he was of strong spirit. So far he seemed to be. He had cried a bit at first, then had grown sullen. This morning he had lashed out at a couple of his tormenters. Buffalo Caller took that as a good omen.

He put the bay into a lope to catch up and pass the herd. He noted with satisfaction that the captive boy appeared sound enough, riding in front of a young warrior who had suggested that he might take the lad as his brother. Buffalo Caller said, "He has borne up well. Do not let them torment him anymore."

He rode beyond the herd to where Wolf That Limps was scouting out in front. He said, "We have entered the reserve. We must be watchful and not fall into the hands of the soldiers."

It was well known that horseback troops of the White Father in Washington patrolled the perimeter of the Indian reserve, as much to protect their wards inside from hostile whites as to prevent those wards from slipping away and committing depredations. Buffalo Caller had only contempt for Indians who gave up their freedom and allowed themselves to be penned like cattle, accepting whatever paltry gifts the White Father deigned to give them. A real man would choose to range free, hunting buffalo, raiding his enemies, and living from the land, or he would die fighting, as wild horses sometimes died rather than submit to the rope. Moreover, Buffalo Caller was resentful because some of the reserve Indians had aided soldiers and rangers against those Comanches who still chose to remain outside, living in the old ways. Many a weeping widow had mutilated herself in mourning for husbands who died at the hands of these pet dogs from the reservation.

Most Texans could not distinguish between tribes. Reserve Indians who rode with them against the Comanches had to tie white cloths to their arms so the whites would not kill them by mistake. Buffalo Caller knew that most settlers believed the reserve Indians were taking advantage of their protected status to commit theft and murder in the settlements, then flee back to safety under the soldiers' guardianship. The Texans were chafing at a chance for vengeance.

So was Buffalo Caller. He thought it a delicious irony that the whites themselves might give him that revenge.

Wolf That Limps said, "Would it not be much safer to go around the reserve? The soldiers do not range far. They would never see us."

"If we are careful they will not see us anyway. But the Texans will follow the tracks. They will believe those who live on the reservation have made this raid. Sooner or later they will fall upon them with gun and knife. The ones who helped them against us will pay for what they did."

"Are the whites so easily fooled?"

"They are bad-hearted people who do not know Comanche from Waco or Caddo or Kiowa. They will kill our enemies for us and believe they have done a great thing."

The sun had not traveled much farther overhead when a warrior approached from the south in an easy lope. Buffalo Caller had sent him to watch the back trail.

"The Texans are coming," Black Wing said, turning and pointing. "They follow the trail just as you wanted."

"Onto the reserve?"

"Yes. But the horse soldiers will stop them soon. They also are coming."

Buffalo Caller had not counted on the soldiers, but after a moment's consideration he decided benevolent spirits were indeed riding with him today. It might be even better than he had planned if the soldiers and the Texans confronted one another. Perhaps some would be killed. Even if not, this would only anger the Texans more against the traitorous people who lived on the reserve. One day soon the Texans would rise in fury, and the Comanches would have vengeance upon those who had brought the rangers and the soldiers against them.

He caught up to the others and signaled for them to stop the herd. "Now," he said, "the trap is sprung. It is time we divide and disappear like smoke."

The horses and mules were split into small groups whose tracks would be difficult to follow. If the Texans managed to get past the soldiers and penetrate this far, they would be confounded by loss of the trail. It would seem obvious to them that the reserve Indians were the authors of their trouble.

Black Wing said, "You are clever, elder brother."

"I have studied the Trickster. Coyote is a good teacher."

Isaac York was livid. "See there, Tom, what I been tellin' you? These tracks have led us straight onto the reserve."

Blessing appeared torn, believing even as he wished he did not. "Don't you think I can see for myself?"

"You didn't want to, but there's the evidence right before your eyes. How much longer we got to put up with this before we do what we ought to've done before they ever moved them red heathens in here?"

"The agents've said all along that they're keepin' the reserve Indians under control. I can't say I trusted them all, but I trusted Robert Neighbors." Neighbors was the chief agent, approved by both the federal government and the governor of Texas.

"That dead woman back yonder tells you he lied. She tells you they all lied. We'd just as well have a rattlesnake den in our backyard as to have this reserve here."

"I don't know what we can do about it."

"We're fixin' to get a chance. Yonder come the yellow-legged soldiers."

Rusty turned to look in the direction York pointed. A small federal patrol—he counted seven men—moved rapidly up from their right flank. The officer in the lead waved his hand as a signal for the Texans to halt.

York said, "There's twice as many of us as there is of them. We ain't stoppin' for them, are we?"

Blessing raised his hand. "Let's see what they say about these horse tracks."

Mike drew his horse up beside Rusty. "If any trouble starts, young'un, you get out of the way. Your mother would never forgive me if I let you get shot. Especially by a United States soldier."

So far as Rusty knew, Mike had never retreated in his life. "If you don't run, I don't run."

The officer reined up and glanced first at York, then at Blessing, trying to decide which was the leader. Both had a formidable look, as if they were ready for the war to start. Blessing did not leave him wondering long. "Do you have business with us, sir? If not, we have business of our own."

The officer took on an imperious tone. "Are you aware that you are trespassing? You crossed over the reserve boundary some miles back."

"With good reason. Some of your wards butchered a woman back yonder, and they kidnapped a boy. Besides that, they've stolen a big bunch of horses and mules. We intend to get them back."

"None of our Indians are out. We have been making certain of that."

"Look at the tracks. They speak for themselves."

The officer gave the trail only a moment's attention. "If

any of our Indians have a captive, we shall see that he is freed. If livestock has been stolen from you, it is the responsibility of federal troops to recover them. Now, gentlemen, you will turn around and leave!"

York leaned forward in the saddle and pointed a finger straight at the officer's nose. "We've come to free that boy and get our property back. And we intend to make some of your red pets pay. If you think you can stop us, you'd best count your soldiers and then count us."

The officer's face reddened, but he yielded no ground. "This is a federal reserve. You have no right to be here."

Blessing said, "It may be a federal reserve, but it's in Texas, and we are officers of the state of Texas, duly sworn. If your reserve Indians are not guilty, who is?"

"That must be determined. By us, not by you."

"You'll have to shoot us to stop us. It'll look bad in Washington, federal troops shootin' citizens who only want to get back what's rightfully theirs."

The officer did not answer. Rusty could see doubt in his eyes.

Blessing took silence as a positive sign. "All right, boys, let's go ahead." He turned his back on the officer and touched his heels to his horse. The rest of the volunteers followed. Rusty's mouth went dry as he saw the soldiers draw rifles. Blessing saw, but if he had misgivings he did not betray them. He kept riding, his back straight and stiff. After a few tense moments the officer shouted an order and the soldiers put the rifles back into their scabbards. He signaled for his troopers to follow the ranger volunteers. He spurred forward, pulling up abreast of Blessing.

"You are all under arrest, you know."

"The hell you say." Rusty knew both Blessing and the officer had been bluffing, and Blessing had made his bluff stick, at least for the moment. He could see how ludicrous the situation was, seven troopers trying to arrest a group of armed and determined Texans more than double their number. But he could not laugh.

Neither could Mike or Preacher Webb. Mike kept his voice low. "Stay close to me, young'un. Right now it wouldn't take but one fool on either side to spark a small war."

"What'll we do?"

"One thing we *won't* do is fire on federal soldiers. I fought beside them in Mexico. I won't fight against them."

Webb said, "Wise words, well put."

The passing of miles gradually drained away the tension. Rusty decided that neither Texans nor soldiers wanted a fight, except perhaps Isaac York. The officer calmed enough to begin a conversation with Tom Blessing, who explained to him the settlers' fears and frustrations.

The officer said, "I assure you we are not uncaring. We are doing our best to keep the reservation Indians contained. But at the same time we have a responsibility to protect them against harm from outside."

"You've already shown that you can't protect *us*. All we're after now is justice, and to get back that boy and our stock. We'd rather have you with us than against us, but we'll do what we have to no matter which way you go."

Blessing stopped his horse and looked at the ground. He rode a little farther and stopped again. "They've split off into several bunches. We can't follow them all."

Mike frowned at Rusty and Preacher Webb. "Ain't no way to tell what bunch took the boy."

Webb nodded. "It won't matter. Whichever trail we follow, it will soon disappear. I'm surprised they've let us track them this far."

The officer overheard. "They did it because they wanted you to follow. It's a Comanche trick to make you believe our reservation Indians were responsible."

Isaac York argued, "Ignorant savages, they're not smart enough to figure out a scheme such as that."

"You've not seen them from my vantage point. Just because they cannot read books does not mean they lack native intelligence. They are as smart as any of us."

"You sayin' it don't make it so," York retorted. "Ain't no two of them got the brains of a white man."

Exasperated, the officer went silent.

Blessing chose a trail that seemed the largest. "We'll follow this one and see where it takes us."

It did not take them far. It led to a stream that the officer said was a tributary to the Clear Fork of the Brazos. There it vanished. Tracks were visible to the edge of the water, but none appeared on the other side. Blessing divided the detail, sending half upstream and half down. The soldiers also split, half following one group of Texans, half the other. The officer remained with Blessing.

The search was futile. The point of exit could not be found.

Isaac York fumed. "Crafty bastards. Let's go back and follow one of the other trails."

Blessing shook his head. "Wouldn't be of no use. It'd end up just like this one. When they want to, Indians can disappear like dust after a whirlwind."

"We can't just up and quit. Let's search every village on the reservation 'til we find them."

"We're out of grub, and we've just about rode our horses down. Besides, do you think seven soldiers are all there is? The lieutenant can go and fetch however many he needs to stop us. And he will."

The officer's eyes were fierce. "You can count on it."

For a moment Rusty feared he was about to see York go into a fit like the one they talked about at the settlement. York said, "I'll go by myself if I have to. Just me and Shanty."

The little black man pulled in beside him as if to give weight to the threat.

The officer said grittily, "I'd have you in irons before the sun is down."

Blessing turned to look grimly over his men. "That won't be necessary. We're goin' home . . . unless you've still got a foolish notion that we're under arrest."

"I bow to reality. But I warn you once more: this reserve is protected ground. Trespass again and you will face the full might of the United States Army."

Blessing looked up the stream in the direction the trail had led. "Damned little might you've ever shown against hostile Indians."

The officer promised, "We'll search the reserve for the boy and for your stock. But I believe they are beyond the reserve now, bound for Comanche country."

Blessing's voice was bitter. "Believe what you want to, but you'd better find that boy. Otherwise we'll be back, and you and your army can go to hell!"

Rusty expected the soldiers to accompany the Texans across the reserve boundary, but they did not. The officer said, "I'll get reinforcements and some Indian trackers. We'll follow up on the trails." He led his troopers away.

York watched them. His voice was sour. "Ain't nothin'll come of it. Them soldiers couldn't find an elephant in a hog pen."

Rusty had a gut feeling that the captive boy would never be found. "What'll they do to him?"

Mike Shannon stared to the north, where the Indians had probably gone. "They'll make a Comanche out of him or they'll kill him."

"That's what they'd've done to me, isn't it? But you and Preacher Webb got in their way."

Mike's face showed despair. "I'm afraid there ain't nobody goin' to get in their way this time."

The volunteers had ridden north like a military unit, heads high, driven by a stern determination. Retreating southward now, they straggled without order, shoulders hunched in an attitude of failure. The mood was contagious. Rusty felt an emptiness that went beyond hunger. He had eaten nothing since yesterday noon.

"We didn't accomplish a thing," he lamented to Mike.

Mike only grunted. "It ends up this way more often than not. Many a time I've ridden a hundred miles after Indians and never seen a feather. But we've got to try or we'd just as well pack up our wagon and go back to wherever we came from."

Preacher Webb added, "There's no shame in losin', provided you made an honest effort. There's shame only when you give up before you start."

Rusty heard Isaac York raise his voice. "Yonder's a pair of tepees."

They stood three hundred yards away, within easy water-carrying distance of the stream.

Blessing said, "Probably just a family or two out huntin' for meat. The ones we're after wouldn't camp where they're so easy found."

"They're Indians, ain't they?" York put spurs to his horse and set him into a run. Behind him the black man Shanty tried vainly to catch up. He had no spurs. He did not even have shoes.

Blessing called in vain for York to stop.

Mike said, "We'd better go after him. Ain't no tellin' what he's crazy enough to do." He put his black horse Alamo into a lope. Rusty and Blessing and the others followed.

Rusty saw two women scraping flesh from the hide of a deer. Three children played nearby until they heard the horses and saw the oncoming riders. They fled into scrub timber alongside the stream. The two women screamed. An elderly man stooped to come out through the open flap of a tepee. He motioned for the women to run, then pushed him-self as erect as his age would allow and waited for the horsemen.

York shot him.

One of the women turned back and hurried to the fallen man. She knelt at his side, then pushed to her feet and rushed at York, screaming at him and shaking her fists.

He shot her, too.

By then the rest of the Texans arrived. Blessing shouted in a rage, "Goddamn you, Isaac York, put up that pistol!"

York said, "I ain't through yet. There's still more of them."

Mike Shannon drew the old pistol he had brought home from the Mexican war. "Put it away, or 'y God I'll shoot you!"

York gave Mike a look of pure hatred. "They're gettin' away. I saw a boy amongst them young'uns."

Blessing said, "I saw him, too. He was an Indian boy. Put up the gun, Isaac."

York resisted. He looked down at the dead man. "There's one good Comanche. He'll never kill another white woman or steal a white boy."

Mike said, "These're not Comanches. Take another look."

York shrugged, unmoved. "Makes no difference. They're Indians. One or another, they're all alike." He started to ride after the others.

To Rusty's surprise, Mike Shannon spurred up beside York and pulled him from his horse. The two men landed together in the grass and began to fight. Blessing stepped in to separate them. "That's enough. Both of you, back away."

Shanty placed himself protectively in front of York. York was shaking and shouting incoherently. Rusty quickly dismounted and gripped Mike's arms. "No more, Dad. It's over with."

Preacher Webb stood between the dead man and the wounded woman. He removed his hat and began a prayer in a voice almost too low for Rusty to hear. "Lord God, forgive us all."

Blessing's face was scarlet. Rusty thought he looked as if *he* were about to go into a spasm. "Isaac, there's no tellin' how much trouble you may have got us into. Bad enough killin' the old man, but shootin' a woman, too?"

York trembled in the aftermath of rage. "They killed a white woman. I hope this one dies. She won't be birthin' no more babies to grow up and kill white folks."

Blessing saw the futility of argument with York. "If the troops heard the shots they'll be comin' to see what happened. We'd better put the reservation behind us as quick as we can." He waved his hand and set off southward in the lead, putting his horse into a long trot.

When the Texans departed, the other woman and the children emerged from the timber and set in to wailing. Rusty felt a chill.

Darkness lingered in his foster father's face. Mike Shannon said, "Young'un, we did accomplish somethin' after all. We killed a defenseless old man and maybe a woman. Ain't that somethin' for a ranger to be proud of?"

As Mike and Rusty turned off toward the farm, leaving

the rest of the volunteers, Tom Blessing said, "You-all consider yourselves still sworn in. If things go the way they're pointed right now, I'll be needin' you."

Mike did not wait for Rusty to react. "Just holler any time. But next time leave Isaac York to home."

Rusty was not sure he would want to go again, not if the next mission turned out as this one had.

Preacher Webb brought the call. He rode up to the cabin one morning, his grim expression indicating he carried a message of importance. He delayed its delivery until he had inquired about Mother Dora's health.

Mike's worried eyes reflected the burden he had carried lately. "I'm afraid the medicine ain't helpin' her. Most days it's all she can do to get out of bed. Me and Rusty been doin' the cookin' and all."

Webb entered the cabin. He returned in a few minutes with a deep frown. "I wish we had a sure-enough doctor to see after her. Isn't much I can do that I haven't already done."

"You've done your best, Preacher." Mike grimaced. "The rest is up to the Almighty."

Rusty feared the Almighty was looking somewhere else. But he would not say so where the minister could hear.

Webb said, "These are dark days. I suppose you've heard the talk that Texas may pull out of the union?"

Mike grunted. "I have, and it's damned foolishness."

"A lot of people are dead serious about it. And there's been more trouble up on the reserve. A bunch of white men rode in there and started a fight. When it was over there were dead on both sides. So the army has been ordered to move all tribes off of the reserve . . . take them north of the Red River into Indian Territory."

Mike scowled. "Even the ones that helped us fight the Comanches?"

"That's what we're told. I'm afraid most Texans don't put much faith in Indian loyalties."

"Damned poor piece of business. What ever became of gratitude?"

"Tom wants to take some of us up there and help see that the move stays peaceful."

Mike observed, "Then he'd best not take Isaac York."

"Isaac's not goin'. And neither are you, Mike. You'd best stay here and watch over Dora."

Rusty expected Mike to roar in angry protest because he had always welcomed any opportunity for adventure. Instead, he seemed almost relieved at not going. His easy acceptance brought home to Rusty—though he needed no reminding—that his foster mother was failing.

Mike gripped Rusty's shoulder. His legs might be weak now, but his hands were strong as steel. "You'll have to serve for both of us, young'un. It won't be a happy sight to watch. Gather up what stuff you need. I'll go saddle my black horse for you."

Rusty remembered the bitter ending of the last trip and did not want to go. But Mike had drilled the notion of duty into him too deeply for him to voice his reluctance. He rolled a blanket, collected a little grub and the rifle, and went in to say a hasty good-bye to Mother Dora. She clutched his hand as if she feared she would not see him again. She whispered, "Hurry back as soon as you can."

"Just a week or ten days, Preacher Webb says. It won't be forever."

"Not for you, but maybe for me."

Rusty blinked back the threat of tears and tried to make light of the turbulence he felt. "I'll be back before you know I'm gone."

Mike led the saddled horse out of the corral and watched Rusty tie the blanket behind the cantle. "Tom Blessing is a good man, so listen to what he says. But don't put all your faith in other people, because sometimes they can be wrong. Do your own thinkin'. In the long run every man has got to answer to himself, and *for* himself." He looked up at Webb, in the saddle and waiting. "Keep an eye on him, won't you, Preacher?"

"Don't you worry about Rusty. You take care of Dora."

Rusty and Webb cut across the river and put their horses into a trot. They intercepted Blessing and six others after a couple of hours. Webb explained about Mike's remaining behind. Blessing took the news with regret. "I always felt that everything would turn out all right when I could see Mike Shannon at my side. You've got a big pair of boots to fill, Rusty."

Rusty did not know how to reply. Webb smiled. "He'll fill them. He's still gettin' his growth."

Rusty glanced quickly over the men and was pleased to see that Isaac York was not among them. He had lain awake many nights, his mind's eye seeing York shoot the old man and the Indian woman over and over again. The memory usually brought him to a cold sweat. He would seek a balance by remembering the white woman so cruelly butchered, but that made him feel no easier about York. The man had a streak of madness in him, Rusty thought. Given provocation, there was no telling what he might do.

It took the rangers two days to reach the boundary of the reserve. There they met a couple of similar volunteer companies gathered to keep the peace. Looking at their determined faces, Rusty suspected that a few might welcome any excuse to break the peace instead, to kill a few more Indians before they were moved out of the state and, in theory at least, out of reach. Besides the rangers, a number of civilians came straggling along, well-armed and talking loudly. It was apparent that they were not burdened with the weight of good intentions.

Rusty was relieved to see a large contingent of U.S. Army troops on hand to accompany the march out of Texas. Without their protection, he suspected, many of the Indians would not live to see the Red River.

Major Robert Neighbors, the Indian agent, accompanied the final group of refugees that started the long northward trek. Rusty heard him mutter something about Philistines and the exodus from Egypt.

Rusty saw grown men weeping. He saw an Indian woman throw her arms around a tree and refuse to move until two soldiers forcibly pulled her away. He saw a travois with a woman lying on it, her shoulder heavily bandaged. He could not be sure, but he thought she was probably the one York had shot. If so, she had survived the wound. He hoped she would survive the long trip, the travois bumping along on rough ground and jarring her mercilessly.

The rangers followed at a respectable distance. It was plain to Rusty that the Indians were bitterly opposed to the move, forced upon them so suddenly that they had not had time to gather most of their livestock. He could imagine what would happen to the animals. As soon as the troops were out of sight, opportunists would drive off all the horses and cattle they could find. Even if the government permitted a delegation of Indians to come back for a roundup, they would find that most of their property was gone.

Finally watching the long, sad column cross the river into the territory, Tom Blessing said, "We'll all breathe easier with them gone."

Preacher Webb replied, "No matter how we may want to justify it, this is a damned poor reward for the help they gave us against the Comanches."

Rusty had never heard the minister use the word *damned*, at least not in that manner. It showed the depth of his feelings.

Blessing said, "You've got too busy a conscience, Preacher. There's times a man has to lock it away and do what needs to be done. The white man and the Indian are too different to live side by side. We tried it, and it didn't work. Somebody has to give way. There's a lot more of us than there is of them."

Rusty listened in a quandary, swinging at first to Blessing's view, then back to Preacher Webb's, and finally hanging uncertainly somewhere in the middle. Daddy Mike had talked a great deal about the recent campaign against the Comanches who shunned the reservation. He claimed that had it not been for help from the reserve Indians, the expedition would have had no chance. Still, correctly or not, most people believed the reserve Indians were responsible for much of the raiding.

It was hard to know what was right. Watching the last of the Indians trail off into the distance, he was glad the decision had not been his to make.

*   *   *

North of the Red River, a satisfied Buffalo Caller sat on his horse at the edge of a stand of timber and watched the straggling column making its way toward a new homeland the federal government had staked out. This was what he had hoped for, why he had made false trails into the reserve. He felt no pity for the distress he saw among the evacuees. They had aided the teibos against the Comanches. They deserved whatever misfortune the dark spirits might visit upon them.

Now perhaps they would understand what the Comanches had known all along, that the whites were a treacherous and grasping lot, stealing everything they saw. Given their way, they would drive the Indian to the edge of the Mother Earth and push him over into the great emptiness.

Up to now the reserve tribes had regarded the Comanches as their enemy. Perhaps this would show them who their true enemy was.

· 6 ·

Rusty watched with misgivings as Mike Shannon threw his saddle up over his horse's back and buckled the girth. "Don't you think I ought to go with you?"

Mike adjusted his coat, for the wind carried a chill. "Ain't no need. I'm just goin' to the settlement to have a drink or two and visit what friends I've still got left."

Lately there had been much less talk about Indians than about a proposed Texas referendum on secession from the union. Most people along the river seemed to favor joining the new Confederacy. Mike vigorously opposed it, so long-time friends had been falling away from him.

Rusty said, "At least, don't be talkin' politics. It'll just get you into another fight."

"Why shouldn't a man say what he thinks when he knows he's right? Them boys've got no idea what they're talkin' about. Wantin' to take Texas out of the union . . . they've forgot how hard we fought to get *in*."

"It won't make a particle of difference what you or anybody else says in a little cotton-gin settlement most people never heard of. It'll be decided in places like Austin and San Antonio. That's where the big votes are."

"Just the same, if a man don't exercise his right to say what he thinks, pretty soon they won't let him say anything."

"Even Tom Blessing has given up on the union, and he used to be as strong for it as anybody. He says a little bunch of Yankees up north are tryin' to boss everybody. Says it's time to rise up and tell them to go to hell before we lose all our rights."

Face reddening, Mike shook his finger at Rusty. "Don't you ever let me hear talk like that comin' out of your mouth. I was born American. I've fought under the United States flag. I'll not stand idle while anybody talks against it . . . not you, not anybody." He swung up onto the horse. "Not anybody, 'y God!"

Watching Mike ride off eastward on the wagon road, Rusty felt chastened by the harshness of his foster father's voice. He should be getting used to it, he thought. Always one to speak his mind and opinions with his fists, Mike had been increasingly argumentative since the secession talk became serious. Moreover, he had taken to drinking considerably more since they had buried Mother Dora at the edge of the oak grove west of the cabin. Nobody had ever quite decided what her ailment was. She had simply faded before their eyes, becoming grayer and thinner, losing strength until one day Mike and Rusty had come home from the field and found her dying.

In a voice so low he could barely hear it, she had asked Rusty to look after his father. He had promised he would, but he feared he had done poorly at living up to the promise. Mike Shannon was too old to take orders from Rusty and too headstrong to accept advice. He had come home from the settlement more than once with his face bruised, his knuckles skinned and swollen.

Some of it was patriotism, Rusty reasoned, but some was simply a result of grief and restlessness, a combination too much for Mike to bear with grace.

Rusty was wrestling with his own feelings about the secession question. On one hand, he could see his father's side of it. The fiercely partisan Mike had drummed patriotism and duty into him from the time Rusty was old enough to understand the words. On the other, he could understand why Tom Blessing had joined so many in disillusionment with the federal government. It had long promised to protect settlers but had not delivered. The troops it sent to the frontier were limited in number and too often foot soldiers, incapable of anything more than holding a defensive position. Cavalrymen were so few that they were unable to keep Indians from stealing army horses out of the military's own corrals.

Yet the same Washington officials responsible for such unwise decisions felt obliged to exert increasing control over the daily lives of the faraway folk they served so poorly.

Some people were saying the whole problem was over slavery, but Rusty did not accept that. Tom Blessing owned no slaves, yet he staunchly defended secession on the grounds that the federals were becoming dictatorial. The only slave Rusty knew in these parts was Isaac York's man Shanty. Whatever York's faults, and he had many, he treated Shanty more like a friend and partner than a piece of property.

Maybe the whole notion would run its course and blow over like a whirlwind that raises a lot of dust, then falls away. Rusty did not relish the prospect of having to make a choice.

He harnessed old Chapultepec. The mule had recently caused a fistfight between Rusty and the Gaskin brothers. Twice Mike had asked Fowler Gaskin to return the animal he had borrowed without a by-your-leave. Gaskin always had an excuse for keeping it a little longer. Seeing Mike's growing impatience and afraid he was on the verge of getting into a serious quarrel with Gaskin, Rusty rode to the neighboring farm alone, determined to fetch the mule home whether the Gaskins liked it or not.

They had not liked it. Fowler Gaskin had a way of looking pathetic as a beggar on a village square when he wanted something, and he usually wanted something. "Boy, you don't know how it is to be poor folks. We can't afford to buy a good strong mule for ourselves. We'd be obliged if you-all'd let us keep the use of this'un just a few more days."

Rusty acted as if he hadn't heard. "Where's he at?"

"He ain't real handy right now. Tell you what, I'll have one of the boys take him home the first of next week."

Suspiciously Rusty demanded again, "Where you got him?"

Gaskin backed away, half a step at a time. "Truth of the matter is, he ain't here. He's over at the Joneses."

By this time the two Gaskin brothers had come up to stand on either side of their father. Rusty could see fight in their eyes.

Anger rising, Rusty was in a mood to accommodate them. He balled his fists. "How come he's at the Joneses? Thought you borrowed him for your own use."

"Old Man Jones offered me fifty cents a day to hire him, and me and the family sure do need the money."

Rusty could feel heat rising in his face. He prepared to remount. "I'll go over to the Jones place and fetch him."

Gaskin took hold of Rusty's bridle reins. "You can't do that. Old Man Jones paid me for ten days, and he ain't used them up yet."

Rusty trembled with anger. "Then I reckon you'll have to give him his money back."

"But it's done spent, and I don't know how I'll go about gettin' any more."

"You might try sendin' your boys out to work."

"You act awful high and mighty, Rusty Shannon, because you-all have got a bigger farm and a lot more money."

"You've got just as much land, but you're all too lazy to work it proper. As for money, I can't remember the last time we had twenty dollars cash."

He lifted his foot toward the stirrup, but Eph Gaskin grabbed the back of his coat. "You ain't goin' noplace."

Rusty whirled and swung a knot-hard fist at him. Gaskin's head snapped back under the impact. The other brother rushed in, and Rusty found himself entertaining two at the same time. The scrap lasted only a minute or so. When it was over, both younger Gaskins were sitting on the ground with bruises and contusions, showing no inclination to get up.

Fowler Gaskin shook his fist but dropped it quickly when Rusty took a step toward him. "I'm a crippled-up old man. The law wouldn't like it, you hittin' a crippled-up old man."

Eph Gaskin did not arise, but he growled, "We'll get you, Rusty Shannon. You just wait, we'll pay you back."

Rusty said grittily, "You'd better worry about how you're goin' to pay back Old Man Jones for the loss of the mule."

Riding away, he could hear Fowler Gaskin railing at his sons for letting "that redheaded son of a bitch" whip both of them. Rusty rubbed his skinned knuckles in satisfaction. It had been the best day's work he had done all winter.

It had been three days since the fight. Now Rusty hitched Chapultepec alongside a young mule Mike had traded for. The young one had a double portion of stubbornness and only a small portion of the older mule's intelligence. It was constantly testing the limits of Rusty's patience, but at least it helped keep his mind occupied so he did not dwell on grief over Mother Dora or brood too much on the troubles brewing between North and South. These seemed far away except when Mike went to the settlement. Then they came close to home.

Rusty had the wagon half full of deadfall timber when he stopped to drink from a jug he had brought beneath the seat. His attention was caught by movement on the road from the east. Preacher Webb approached on a bay horse. The minister altered his course when he spotted Rusty down by the river. Rusty held the jug high so he would see it. "Water, Preacher? It ain't coffee, but it's wet."

"Much obliged." Webb dismounted and tipped up the jug for a long drink. "I never could understand why so many people insist on whiskey. Water is better by far." He wiped his mouth on the frayed sleeve of his coat and glanced toward the cabin. "Is Mike anywhere around?"

"He's gone to the settlement."

Webb's face looked pinched. "I must have missed him somewhere on the way. Wish I'd gotten here in time to head him off. Things are commencin' to get ugly."

"How ugly?"

"Ugly enough. There's been a lot of agitation stirred up

against those who oppose secession. I'm afraid it's gettin'
dangerous."

Rusty suspected Webb had heard about the fights Mike
had had over the question. "He's always taken care of himself."

"He's never seen old friends turn into enemies before. It's
been bitter enough to cause a few killin's."

The minister's apprehension was infectious. Rusty began
to feel it, too. "It might do some good if you'd talk to him.
He doesn't listen to me much. Still figures I'm just a kid."

"I'll go back to the settlement and look for him."

Rusty watched Webb ride off. His stomach had been uneasy since Mike had left, and it was worse now. Politics had
brought on this trouble. This could be a happier world if it
weren't for politics and politicians, he thought. He wondered
if Indians had them, too. He decided they probably did. They
fought among themselves just like white folks, sometimes
with even deadlier results.

If he ever found himself in a position to rule the country,
he would pass a law against politics.

Rusty waited supper until almost dark, hoping Mike would
come home. The work and the cold had made him hungry,
however, so he finally fried up some smokehouse ham and
made cornbread. He had almost finished eating when he
heard voices outside. Stepping onto the dog run without taking time to put on a coat, he saw Preacher Webb and Mike
dismounting from their horses. Mike had to hold to the saddle a minute to steady himself. His face was dark with
bruises, his shirt torn and bloody.

Rusty hurried out to help. Mike waved him and Webb
away. He said curtly, "I can get into the house by myself."
Rusty guessed that he and the minister had argued. It was
evident that Mike had been drinking, for no other way would
he have said a cross word to his old friend. Rusty stepped
aside and let him alone.

Mike stumbled getting up on the dog run but caught himself on a post. "Come on in where it's warm, Preacher. Me
and Rusty'll fix you some supper." He weaved his way into

the kitchen side of the double cabin and bumped into a chair. He promptly slumped in it.

Rusty remained outside, shivering from the night's chill. "Who did he fight with this time?"

"Isaac York. Isaac's strong for secession. Shanty managed to get hold of him after a few blows were struck. I took Mike out of there."

"I'll bet he wasn't happy about leavin'."

"He wanted to finish the fight, but I was afraid I might have to bring him home dead. Isaac was mad enough to kill him."

Rusty looked toward the door. "I'm obliged. Come on in, Preacher. Dad ought to be in a better humor after he gets some supper in his belly to soak up that whiskey."

Mike's eyes defied Rusty to offer criticism. Rusty held silent as he fried more ham. Preacher Webb tried to smooth Mike's ruffled feathers by talking of other matters such as the promise of ground moisture for next spring's crops, a new baby he had christened for the Mather family, the rumors about building a railroad into Texas.

None of them distracted Mike. "I ain't finished my discussion with Isaac."

Webb argued, "You know he has a crazy streak in him. He's dangerous."

"I'm an American, born free and raised to stay that way. Nobody can tell me what to say or think."

"A man doesn't have to go around *tellin'* everybody what he thinks. He can keep it to himself and stay out of fights that might get him killed."

"Isaac York ain't seen the day he could kill me, not in a fair fight."

Rusty thought of the old Indian and the woman. "What promise have you got that it'd be fair?"

Mike soon began to yawn. Rusty saw him to bed, then returned to the kitchen and the minister. "I wish we could get him away from here for a while. Ain't there Indian trouble someplace, or maybe somethin' stirrin' down on the border?"

"Not anything serious that I know about. I'll talk to Tom

Blessing. He might cook up an excuse to get Mike away."

"Tom's strong for secession, too."

"But he's too decent a man to put politics ahead of an old friendship."

Tom Blessing showed up one frosty morning as Rusty prepared breakfast. Mike, still stiff and sore from his fight with York, was having difficulty getting out of bed. Rusty had not been eager to push him, for Mike's mood was not forgiving. He had been pulled away from a fight before it was finished, and it rankled.

"Come on in this house," Rusty called to Blessing. "Coffee's ready, and the rest will be in a few minutes."

Blessing paused at the kitchen door, then glanced back toward the room where Mike grumbled to himself, trying to get his clothes on. "Is he all right?"

"He's movin' kind of slow. I guess Preacher Webb talked to you?"

"He did. I'd already heard about Mike's set-to with Isaac. Preacher's right. Tempers bein' the way they are, it'd be smart to get Mike away from here 'til the secession election's over with and things quiet down."

"I'm afraid he doesn't realize how serious things have got. Preacher says there's been killin'."

"Other places. Not here . . . yet."

"Even Sam Houston talks against secession. Why shouldn't Mike?"

"Nobody's goin' to kill Sam Houston. He's a Texas hero. But he's old now, and not many people listen to him anymore."

Mike struggled through the door about the time Blessing finished his first cup of coffee. His shirt was buttoned wrong. The left side of his face was swollen and colored a patchwork of blue and red. He groped for a chair to steady himself and winced in pain as Blessing shook his hand. "You're out mighty early. Sun ain't made it all the way up yet."

"I've come lookin' for a good man. Got a little job of work for him."

"I don't feel like much of a man this mornin'. Almost everything hurts, and what don't hurt ain't workin'."

"You'll be all right soon as I get you on horseback and you work the kinks out of your system."

"Where we goin'?"

"Not we, just you. I've had word from a volunteer company up close to the Red River. They've got some green boys ridin' patrol to keep raiders from sneakin' down out of the territory. They need guidance from an experienced old-timer who won't turn tail and run from the first Indian he sees."

"I reckon I'm your man. What about Rusty?"

Blessing frowned. "I figured you'd want him to stay here and take care of the farm."

Rusty handed Mike a cup of coffee. Mike seated himself and poured the coffee into a saucer. He blew across it and poured it back into the cup but set it down without drinking. His eyes clouded with suspicion. "You sure they asked you to send them a man? Or is this just somethin' you cooked up to get me away from here?"

Blessing hesitated. "They need all the help they can get."

Anger roughened Mike's voice. "So you're fixin' to move old Mike Shannon out of sight because you're afraid Isaac York is liable to hurt him."

"Those boys up there really need you."

"No they don't. As for Isaac, I'd made a good start toward whippin' him when I was dragged off against my will. I'm stayin' here to be at his service if he wants some more of the same."

Blessing set his cup down half full of coffee. "We've all got your best interests at heart."

"You can serve my best interests by leavin' me the hell alone. Mike Shannon ain't ever run from a fight."

Rusty could think of several strong arguments, but he knew they would be futile. When Mike's eyes took on that defiant look, a four-up team of mules couldn't pull him loose.

Blessing said, "I thank you for the coffee." He pushed his chair back from the table.

Mike's voice softened a little. "You've come a long ways. You'd just as well have breakfast with us."

"Somehow I don't seem to have any appetite." Blessing shook Rusty's hand, then paused at the door to look back at Mike. "I'd give you some advice if I thought you'd take it."

"I won't seek Isaac out, if that's what worries you. But if he comes lookin' for me, I won't be hard to find."

Discouraged, Rusty followed Blessing out onto the dog run. "I thank you for tryin'."

"Isaac's as stubborn as Mike is, but I'll go talk to him. And you keep an eye on your daddy. Tie him up if you have to."

Rusty walked back into the kitchen. Mike looked up from his breakfast. "I think I can see Preacher Webb's fine hand in this. And yours too, like as not."

"None of us want to see you get hurt."

"What hurts the worst is knowin' you don't think I can take care of myself anymore. You figure I'm too old?"

"No, but this is a new situation. Preacher Webb says a lot of people are talkin' war."

"I've been to war before. I'm still here."

Rusty gave in to frustration. "Maybe *I* ought to go up to the Red River and quit worryin' about you."

"Maybe you ought to."

Rusty knew he would keep worrying if he went halfway around the world. "What am I goin' to do with you, Dad?"

"Nothin'. Just admit that I'm a grown man and let me do things my own way."

You always did, Rusty thought, but he held his tongue.

Walking out to the barn, he began to wonder about his real father. If he were living today, would he react to the current situation the same way as Daddy Mike? Would he be for secession or for the union, and would he be willing to fight for whichever he believed in?

I wish I'd known you, Rusty thought. *Maybe if I knew which way you'd have gone, I'd know which way to go myself.*

A young heifer heavy with calf had not been seen in a couple of days, then showed up with her udder swollen and her sides flatter than they had been. Rusty could tell that she had calved. She probably had hidden the baby somewhere in the timber along the river, where it would be fair game should a wolf or a coyote come prowling about. He saddled Mike's black horse, Alamo, and followed the heifer at a distance, hoping to find the calf and bring it into the pens, where it would be safe until it was stronger and better able to survive.

As he expected, the heifer led him to her new offspring. The calf lay in some heavy undergrowth where she had left it. The heifer tossed her head belligerently as Rusty dismounted and led the horse toward the hiding spot. Warily, for a new mother could be dangerous if anything threatened her baby, he eased close to the calf. It eyed him without fear until the heifer snorted and began to paw. It arose on shaky legs. Rusty caught and lifted it up, stretching it belly-down across the saddle. Its umbilical cord was dried but not yet lost.

He tried to soothe the heifer's anxiety with a calm voice. "Sook now. Sook." Holding the wriggling calf, he swung up behind the saddle and put the horse into a slow walk. The heifer slung her head, offering fight, then began to follow, bawling.

He was halfway back to the cabin when he heard a shot. In the crisp air the echo reverberated through timber along the river. He thought at first that Mike had fired at a varmint, but the report had not sounded like Mike's rifle.

He shivered with a sudden cold fear and put the black horse into a long trot, then into a lope. He came near losing the calf as it struggled and kicked. The heifer fell behind but kept coming. At the pens, Rusty slid to the ground and lifted the calf down, then looked fearfully toward the woodpile, where he had last seen Mike chopping fuel for the cabin.

"Dad! Dad, where are you?"

He heard no answer. He trotted toward the tall stack of dead timber and called again.

Hearing a muffled voice, he checked his stride, trying to determine from where the sound had come. He heard it again, a rasping "Rusty!"

Mike lay on his stomach near the chopping log. He tried to arise, but he could do no more than push up on one elbow, then slump back. Rusty saw blood spreading across the back of Mike's old shirt and staining the wood chips upon which he lay. The ax was beside him where he had dropped it as he fell.

Rusty fought to keep from crying. "I'll get you to the house." Mike cried out in pain as Rusty tried to lift him. Rusty eased him onto his back, placing Mike's hat beneath his head.

"Don't move me no more. Don't move me."

"You'll bleed to death if I don't get this blood stopped."

"Won't do no good. Son of a bitch, he's a better shot than I thought." Mike coughed up blood.

"It was Isaac York, wasn't it?"

"Didn't see." Mike's voice dropped to a whisper. "If he'd only made it a fair fight . . ." He reached out. Rusty took his hand. Mike gasped, trying to speak.

Whatever he wanted to say, it died with him.

Eyes afire, Rusty bent over his foster father and cried as he had when Mother Dora died.

A cold realization gradually crept over him while he knelt, gripping Mike's lifeless hand. It staggered him as he absorbed its full import. So far as he knew, he had no blood kin, not anywhere. He did not even know who he really was, and it was improbable that he ever would. Now the couple who had given him a name and a home and the security of their love had been taken from him.

For the second time in his life, he was alone.

Rusty was disappointed at the small number of neighbors who came to pay their final respects to Mike. He had not fully realized the deep feelings many people held about secession, or how much they had resented Mike's firm stance against it. For some, his record as a ranger and the many times he had volunteered his strong arms for service to the community were not enough to erase the stain of his political leanings.

Rusty told Preacher Webb, "Now I can see who his true friends were."

"Don't blame them too much. We may be lookin' at a war, and war takes a hard toll on friendships. If this one comes to pass, it may even break up families. The Mike we knew couldn't deny his true convictions. You wouldn't have wanted him to."

"I would if it could've saved his life."

"You'd have lost respect for him, and he'd have lost respect for himself."

"Nothin' is worth somebody murderin' him." Rusty cast a dark look toward the sheriff, who stood at the edge of the small gathering, gesturing broadly as he expressed his opinion that Texas should cut loose as soon as possible. "*He* don't seem any too concerned over catchin' Isaac York and bringin' him in."

"There isn't any proof that Isaac did it."

"Who else would've? You were there. You helped break up the fight between him and Dad. And he's not here for the funeral. He's afraid to come because he knows I know he's guilty. So do lots of folks, whether they'll admit it or not."

"Several other neighbors aren't here either, but that doesn't mean they murdered Mike."

The sheriff caught enough of the conversation to arouse his interest. He walked up to Rusty, his face burdened by a deep frown. "Son, you've got a right to be upset, but you've got no right to accuse anybody without you can show proof. You got that proof?"

"I didn't see him, but I know. I think you know, too."

"If I'd always really known half as much as I thought I did, I'd be the smartest man in Texas. We're here to bury your daddy, not to set off another killin'. And that's what it'll lead to if you keep makin' accusations. It'll come down to you or him, and I'd have to lay my bet on him."

Rusty knew his resentment showed, and he didn't care. Mike wouldn't have, either. But he said no more, and the sheriff turned away to resume his lecture on politics. He had a receptive audience. Just about everybody here was ready to cut ties with the union.

Despite their political feelings, a few friends like Tom Blessing from around the settlement had come to be with Rusty when word spread about Mike's death. Blessing and a couple of others had dug the grave while Rusty and Preacher Webb fashioned a coffin out of rough-cut pine torn from the side of the cow barn. There had been no extra lumber lying around. It cost too much to waste.

Rusty stood numb at the graveside, unable to absorb all of Webb's eulogy, the recounting of Mike's brave deeds and exploits, of his and Dora's devotion to one another, of their unselfishness in taking an orphaned boy to raise as their own. Rusty's mind ranged back to the earliest events he could remember with any clarity. Always, it seemed, Daddy Mike and Mother Dora had been there to pick him up when he fell, to encourage him when he faltered, to cheer him when he did something well. Blood kin could have done no more.

Carried back in time by his memories, he did not hear the minister call for a closing prayer. He did not bow his head until he blinked his eyes clear of tears and saw that the others were all looking downward.

A strong arm fell upon his shoulder. Tom Blessing stood beside him, sorrow in his light blue eyes. "Son, it'd do you good to get away from this place for a while. I've got a job for you."

Rusty coughed his throat clear. Blessing had tried to send Daddy Mike away to keep him from harm until the secession fever subsided. Now he had the same idea, except this time it was to put distance between Rusty and Isaac York. "What'd become of this place?"

"It does a field good to lie fallow a year or two and rest, same as it helps a man to pause in his labor now and again to give thanks for the Lord's bounty. The place won't go anywhere. It'll still be here when you come back."

"I've got a thing or two that needs doin' first."

"You're thinkin' of Isaac York. I can tell by the look in your eyes. Forget that. Come to my house, and come prepared to travel."

While the grave was being filled in, the visitors began to drift away. Preacher Webb waited. He talked quietly to first one and then another but did not take his eyes from Rusty for long.

Fowler Gaskin had surprised Rusty by coming to the funeral, though without his two sons. He hung back until almost the last, then approached Rusty, his voice tentative. "Boy, I hate to be askin' you at a time such as this, but I know Mike's clothes won't fit you. I was wonderin' if you was of a mind to give some of them away? I sure could use a good winter coat."

The audacity of the man caught Rusty standing on his left foot. "The dirt hasn't even settled over his grave and you've already come scavengin'. Get the hell out of my sight, Fowler!"

Gaskin backed off. "Just felt like I ought to ask before somebody else comes along and carries everything away. After all, me and your daddy been neighbors a long time."

"A lot too long."

Gaskin gave Rusty a hard look while he mounted his slab-sided old mule. He kicked the mule vigorously and rode off, mumbling.

Rusty noticed Webb watching closely. The minister said, "First time the Gaskins catch you gone, they'll help themselves to whatever they want of Mike's stuff."

Rusty had not thought of that. "We'll head them off. You probably know some poor folks who could use Dad's clothes."

"They'll be grateful to you." Webb's expression darkened. "I heard you tell Tom Blessing you have somethin' to do before you leave. I don't like the sound of that."

"Would you have me turn my back on what happened to Dad?"

"Better than to do somethin' you might be sorry for the rest of your life."

"I won't be sorry."

The Isaac York place lay north and a bit west of the cotton gin and general store that were the nucleus of the settlement.

Rusty had been there just once, when Mike was trying to trade mules. York had been half drunk, and the black man Shanty had done most of the dickering for him. It had struck Rusty odd, seeing a man supposed to be a slave assuming that kind of responsibility for his owner. Mike had not been one to take advantage of a drunk, but even if he had, Shanty had been too sharp a trader to let him get away with it.

Rusty had hardly slept last night, trying to decide what his course should be. By rights he should shoot York down like a dog, but he would not shoot him in the back. He would prefer that York be looking at him, knowing what was coming and why.

As he rode he kept turning over the options in his mind. Maybe he would not shoot York at all but instead force him to confess, then stand back and let the law hang him. Hanging was a more fitting death under the circumstances. A bullet ended things too quickly. Still, there was always the chance that the law would not mete out the punishment York deserved. After all, Mike had been a union sympathizer, and the community was strongly pro-Confederacy.

The longer Rusty pondered, the less sure he was about what he would do. But he felt that when he got there he would know. Mike had always said that when the time came to act, most men knew instinctively what to do.

"Trust me," he had advised, "and if I ain't there, trust yourself. You'll know what's right."

Rusty went suddenly short of breath as he rounded the winter-bared cotton field and saw the cabin ahead. Trembling, he reined up and drew Mike's old pistol from its scabbard to recheck the load. He had never fired the pistol much and did not fully trust it. He liked a rifle, for he could hit anything he saw over its sights. A pistol, extended at arm's length, seemed unwieldy and felt heavier than a rifle, though it was not.

He started for the cabin but changed course when he saw York seated on a wooden stool beside the door of a log shed, soaking up the meager winter sunshine. York raised a jug on the crook of his arm and drank.

Drunk, like as not, Rusty thought, disappointed. He had

hoped to find York sober and able to understand fully what was happening. On the other hand, if he was drunk he might not have his guard up. It might be easier to draw a confession out of him.

Rusty dismounted twenty feet from York and drew the pistol. York blinked, trying to clear his eyes. "Who are you?"

"You know me. I'm Rusty Shannon."

"I can't quite make you out." York kept blinking. He was too drunk to see straight.

Rusty seethed. "You were seein' all right when you shot Mike Shannon. I'm here to make you pay for it."

The slave Shanty stepped out of the shed, staring with wide eyes at the pistol. "Please, boy, put that thing away."

York pushed to his feet but swayed and braced one hand against the shed wall. "You sayin' I shot Mike? How could I? I been drunk for three, four days."

"Not too drunk to shoot him in the back. And you'll admit it, or I'll shoot you where you stand."

A firm voice said, "No you won't."

Rusty turned quickly. Preacher Webb and Tom Blessing stood behind him. Webb reached out. "Give me the pistol. You're too young to get yourself in this kind of trouble."

Rusty was too surprised to move. Webb quickly gripped the pistol and pushed the muzzle down, then gave it a twist that wrested the weapon from Rusty's hand. "I was afraid you'd take a notion to do this."

Rusty choked from frustration. "He's got it comin'."

Blessing said, "You have no proof. He says he's been too drunk to leave the place. Shanty yonder backs him up."

The black man nodded, relieved that the pistol had not been fired.

"What else could Shanty say? Isaac owns him."

Blessing said, "I'll admit that from the looks of things you could be right. Isaac and Mike both left mad after their fight broke up. But these are bitter times, and there's other people around who didn't like Mike's politics. You can't kill a man on suspicion."

"That's more than he killed Mike for." Shaking with anger, Rusty reached for the pistol. Webb turned, keeping it from him.

Blessing said, "Settle down, son. I promise you we'll look into Mike's killin'. If we find proof that Isaac did it, he'll pay. But that's not for you to do, it's for the law."

"I talked to the law yesterday. The sheriff won't do a damned thing. He as much as told me so."

Webb said, "Have faith, lad. The Lord finds His own way to punish the evildoer. If it was Isaac, he'll settle accounts with the Almighty. If it wasn't . . . you wouldn't want an innocent man to burden your conscience as long as you live."

"I've got no faith in the law, and not a hell of a lot in the Almighty. How come He wasn't watchin' over Daddy Mike?"

"It's not for us to understand His ways."

"*I* sure don't. If He really punishes the evildoers, how do we know He didn't send me here to strike Isaac down?"

"He wouldn't have let us stop you."

Blessing laid his heavy arm on Rusty's shoulder, as he had yesterday. "I told you before, you need to get away for a while. Let things here take their own course. That job I tried to give Mike . . . it's still waitin'."

"Job?" Mike was too upset to remember. "What job?"

"South of the Red, in a minuteman company scoutin' for Indian sign. Turnin' them back if they cross into Texas. The boys are shorthanded up there."

Rusty glared at Isaac. "What about *him*?"

"He won't be goin' anywhere. If it's proved that he killed Mike, he'll still be here when you come back. Or hung."

It wasn't enough. Rusty wanted him to pay now. But he could see that it was not to be. Even if York went on trial, chances were strong that a secessionist jury would acquit him. "You're tryin' to protect him. That's why you want me gone."

"We're tryin' to protect you from yourself, and maybe from some others. There was hard feelin' against Mike. Some of that feelin' is bound to be laid over onto you. It's best for you and everybody else if you're not seen around here 'til this secession business quiets down."

Rusty could not take his gaze away from York. Shanty stepped protectively in front of his owner.

Reluctantly Rusty shrugged. "All right, I'll go. Do I get my pistol back?"

A flicker of a smile crossed Webb's face. "I'll ride along part of the way with you and give your pistol back when I feel like it's safe."

"Isaac York won't be safe 'til he's dead."

· 7 ·

Paper was scarce, so Tom Blessing sketched a map on the back of an old order he had received from the governor's office in Austin during one of his limited terms in volunteer ranger ranks. "You'll remember the Fort Belknap country from when we went up north to attend the Indian removal. You oughtn't to have much trouble findin' the company camp. When Texas secedes, there won't be anybody but our own volunteers watchin' the frontier. Just a buckskin line, and a thin one. That's why they need you up there."

Rusty studied the map. "There's several rivers to cross between here and there."

"You'll cross a lot more if you stay with the rangers. You just mind what goes on around you and be careful. Some Indian would be tickled to hang your red hair on his lance."

Preacher Webb handed Rusty a book. "Put this in your saddlebag. It'll be good readin' for you of a night."

Rusty saw what the book was. "I'll be carryin' Dad's old pistol in there. You think it and the Bible fit together?"

"Samson prayed, then slew his enemies with the jawbone of an ass. Lord knows it sometimes takes violence to bring peace."

Blessing said, "I've known many a man who carried a Bible in his pocket and a pistol on his belt. I'd rather ride with that kind than them who just carry the gun."

Rusty reasoned that it could do him no harm to make room for the book. Whether he read much from it or not was another matter. Though Mother Dora had read from hers every day, it had not saved her from the wasting illness that carried her away. Mike Shannon had been a strong believer, after his fashion, yet a bullet had found his back.

He wanted Preacher Webb to feel contented. With the Shannons gone, the minister was the only real link Rusty had to his past. "Thanks for the book, Preacher. Don't you reckon it's time we got started?"

Webb said, "I'm ready."

Rusty stepped past the sagging door of Blessing's cabin and turned to where he had tied Mike's favorite horse, Alamo. The mule Chapultepec stood patiently waiting, a pack on his back. Rusty told Blessing, "I'd appreciate it if you'd keep an eye on Fowler Gaskin. Soon as he knows I'm gone, he's liable to carry off everything that's not rooted down." He had already let Webb give Mike's and Mother Dora's clothes to families who needed them.

Blessing shook Rusty's hand. "You're doin' the right thing, goin' away for a while."

"I'm not forgettin' Isaac York."

Blessing said, "But forget about takin' your own vengeance. Leave it to the law." He looked at Webb. "And to the Lord."

"For now." Rusty turned his eyes toward the Colorado River. Beyond it lay the Llano and San Saba, the Brazos . . . and how many more?

He said to the horse and mule, "I hope you-all can swim."

Following a faint wagon road that led in a northwesterly direction, Rusty and Webb made a dry camp the first night. They ate a meager meal of cold cornbread and pork Tom Blessing's wife had sacked for them. In his lingering grief,

Rusty had not felt like eating much since Mike's death, so he took his supper mostly in boiled coffee stretched with parched grain.

Webb studied him a long time in the faint light of a modest campfire that barely held back the night's chill. "I don't like the look in your face. I'm afraid you still have murder in your heart."

"Won't matter how far we go. Whatever's inside, I'll carry along with me."

"You'll have other things to think about besides revenge. Distance will give time a chance to cool the passion."

"I don't want it to cool. If the law doesn't settle with Isaac, I will. Won't make any difference how long it takes . . . a month, a year, ten years."

Webb's eyes held pity. "That book I gave you . . . I could cite you some passages. It might help you to read them."

"I don't see you readin' out of yours."

"I don't have to. I know it by heart."

Toward noon the third day Webb turned off the wagon road and bore northeastward.

Rusty looked back to be sure the pack mule was following. "Aren't we goin' out of our way?"

"Some people I know have a farm off yonder. They'll make us welcome, and the womenfolks are fine cooks."

Though Rusty still had little appetite, he perceived that Webb was eager to make the stop. The minister enjoyed being among friends, and given any chance, he made friends of almost everyone he met. "I don't reckon there's any big hurry about me gettin' to Belknap. The main thing was to get me away from home."

"These people's name is Monahan. Lon Monahan is a good farmer and a good man. You'll like him. You'll like the whole family."

Rusty was not keen on making new acquaintances right now. They would try their best to make him feel good, and he didn't really want to feel good. Mike's death hung over him like a dark cloud. He was not yet ready for the sunshine.

Webb added, "They've got a daughter about sixteen or seventeen. Her name is Geneva. Pretty as a china doll."

That's an old bachelor for you, Rusty thought. *Go miles out of his way to keep from missing a pretty woman.* He suspected Webb's definition of pretty was undemanding.

Rusty found the Monahan farm larger and neater in appearance than the Shannon place. It bespoke prosperity, at least by the modest standards of a Texas still in its settling-down stage. The main house was built of sawmill lumber rather than logs, though an older double log cabin still appeared to be in use. He suspected it had been the Monahans's first home and had been set aside for older family members or the boys of the family, a fairly common usage in such cases. Like the main house, the newest, largest barn was of lumber, the smaller barn and sheds older and of logs. A low rock fence surrounded a large garden. Out past the big barn, two men were building a new corral, stacking trimmed oak branches between double oak posts to form a fence. It was typical wintertime work for a farmer who had nothing to do in the fields.

Webb said, "There's Lon Monahan, out yonder with one of his sons. We'll stop and say howdy before we go up to the house."

Monahan's sun-bronzed features, droopy-brimmed felt hat, and brogan shoes would mark him anywhere as a farmer no matter how far he might stray from the plow. He wiped a huge hand on the bib of his faded overalls before reaching out to shake with Webb. "I swear to God, Preacher, it's damned good to see you."

Webb said, "You remember Mike Shannon? This is his boy Rusty."

Monahan's grip was strong enough to crush bones. His broad, easy smile added to the creases of middle age but made Rusty feel at ease with the farmer. He did not always meet strangers well. "Pleased to make your acquaintance, Mr. Monahan. Preacher has told me a right smart about you." He hadn't, really, except to warn that Monahan's language tended to be salty.

"I knew your daddy in the Mexican war. Hell of a good feller. I hope he's well."

Rusty looked at the ground. "No, sir, he's dead."

"I'm sorry. How . . ." Monahan broke off as Webb gave him a quick negative signal. "We'll say a prayer for him tonight at meetin'. You *are* goin' to stay and conduct meetin' for us, ain't you, Preacher? I'll send the boys out with word to the neighbors."

Rusty suspected Webb had anticipated Monahan's request. In any case he appeared pleased by it. Webb said, "Sure enough. I've always got time to share the Word."

Wherever he went, people expected him to conduct prayer meetings. Many who lived far from sizable settlements rarely had an opportunity to attend church. For them, circuit-riding ministers met a deeply felt spiritual need.

The other fence builder finished wedging a branch tightly into place and joined his father in greeting the visitors. He was a strapping youth near Rusty's own age. Monahan introduced him as his oldest son, James. "You-all tie your horses and go on up to the house. Clemmie'll have dinner ready directly. Been a while since we've had a real soul-cleansin' around here, so she'll be damned tickled to see you, Preacher."

Rusty sensed that the welcome was genuine, not put on for appearance's sake. He found it easy to like Monahan. The sunburned James seemed cut from the same cloth. Rough hands and muscular shoulders bore the stamp of hard work.

James asked Rusty, "You like to hunt?"

"When I've got time."

"Maybe after supper we'll go up the river a ways and see what we can find."

Lon Monahan said, "Not tonight. We're goin' to have meetin'. Maybe Rusty can stay around a few days."

"Can't. I'm supposed to report to the ranger camp up north of here."

James shrugged. "Rangers don't range all the time. Maybe when you get a little time off."

Walking toward the house, Webb said to Rusty, "I baptized all the Monahan children. I baptized you too, remember?"

"I remember. I thought you were fixin' to drown me."

"Just tried to wash away all your sins."

"I was maybe six years old. How many sins could I have had?"

"The Lord and me looked to the future. I think we headed the sins off pretty well, up to now."

"And now?"

"You're a grown man. From here on it's up to you."

Rusty doubted that Clemmie Monahan weighed ninety pounds. When she first stepped out onto the porch he took her for a half-grown girl. Closer, he saw her lined face, her graying hair, her work-hardened hands. Building this farm had left the marks of wear and worry on both her and her husband. Her face lighted up as she recognized Webb.

"Preacher!" she shouted. "Come on in this house."

Quietly, so only Rusty could hear, Webb said, "Now, lad, there is a handsome woman."

"Handsome? Maybe she was once."

"She still is. Beauty is not what you see on the outside but the spirit you know is within."

Webb bowed to the woman in a courtly manner so ingrained that Rusty doubted he realized he was doing it. Rusty self-consciously tried to emulate him but knew his was a poor imitation. Webb introduced him. Mrs. Monahan's expression turned sad for a moment when the minister told her Rusty's father was dead. He did not state the cause, and she had the good manners not to ask.

"He'll be missed, your father," she said. "Well, you-all come on in and rest a spell." She called to a boy working at the barn. "Billy, take care of the horses. And watch that mule. He's liable to kick."

The boy, about fifteen years old, shouted back, "Yes, ma'am." He led the two horses and Chapultepec into a corral.

Clemmie Monahan said, "I expect you'll want to wash off some of the road dust. There's a wash pan on the back gallery. Geneva, see that there's water in the bucket out there."

A girl appeared in the doorway. She was almost a duplicate of her mother except for being a generation younger. To call her slender would have been charitable, Rusty thought. Skinny was more like it. But she had a pleasant face, eyes filling with curiosity as she looked at him. In the room's poor light, he could not tell what color they were.

He blushed as he realized he was staring and that she was staring back.

She said, "I already did, Mama, soon as I saw Preacher Webb comin'. Brought in fresh drinkin' water from the cistern too. Figured he'd be thirsty."

Webb accepted the hospitality with easy grace. "Such a fine welcome from such handsome young ladies reminds an old bachelor what he has missed in his life." He glanced back at Rusty. "And should be a lesson to a young one."

The girl smiled. Rusty felt his cheeks warm. He wanted to say something to cover his discomfort, but he conjured up no words that seemed appropriate. He was conscious that his clothes were dusty and trail-worn. He touched a hand to his face and felt several days' growth of stubble. Mother Dora would have pointed to Mike's razor and suggested that he use it.

The girl Geneva kept looking at him. "Does he ever talk?"

Webb grinned. "I've seen him go for days without sayin' a word except 'Please pass the cornbread.' "

Defensively Rusty said, "I don't talk just to hear myself." Feeling slightly wicked and trusting that Webb would take it with good humor, he added, "I'm not a preacher."

Clemmie Monahan said, "Leave the gentlemen be, Geneva, so they can wash for dinner. We've both got work enough to do in the kitchen."

Webb was first at the washbasin. Drying himself on a square of homespun cotton cloth, he smiled. "You've not been away from home enough, lad. You need to work on the social graces."

"You have them, but they never got you married."

Webb's smile faded. "The ladies I fancied always seemed to fancy someone else."

Rusty had long suspected Mother Dora was one. It could be that Clemmie Monahan was another.

Webb emptied the wash pan so Rusty could pour fresh water into it. "Besides, I've been on the journey too much to have any normal life at home. My circuit, and the times

I've ridden away with the volunteers . . . I could not ask a good woman to sit in a lonely cabin and wait for me."

"I'll bet there's some would've been willin'."

"Perhaps, but it would've been unfair to ask it of them."

"Haven't you wanted to?"

"Once or twice. I always managed to think better of it. I hope you never have to look at yourself in a mirror and face a decision between your needs and your duty."

"I don't expect I'll ever be a preacher."

"There are other duties that demand all one has to give. If you should ever hear the call, you'll understand."

The family was large and the table long, with benches on either side, chairs at each end for Lon Monahan and his wife. Clemmie was on her feet much of the time, bringing food to the table, pouring coffee. Geneva sat opposite Rusty, where he could steal glances at her. Two younger sisters and the youngest brother, Billy, sat beside her. On the bench with Rusty and Webb were the oldest brother, James, and Clemmie Monahan's father, a small, thin man named Vince Purdy. He squinted as if he had a hard time seeing. Rusty suspected his sight was slowly failing. His knuckles were knotted with arthritis.

Lon Monahan asked, "Been much talk down you-all's way about this secession foolishness?"

More than just talk, Rusty thought darkly, but he let Preacher Webb answer.

"There has. There are bitter feelin's on both sides."

"Same here, I'm sorry to say. Serious enough that I'm afraid it could lead to bloodlettin'."

Clemmie protested, "Lon, don't be scarin' the children."

"It's the truth. I ain't seen folks get so worked up since the war against Mexico. This may be worse, because it has neighbor buttin' heads with neighbor. Damndest notion I ever heard of, wantin' to pull out of the union! Don't you agree, Preacher?"

Webb looked about the table before he answered. "Every argument sounds good while you listen to it. Then you hear an answer from the other side, and it sounds good, too. As a minister I think I'd best stay out of it."

"The way it looks, everybody's goin' to have to choose a side, like it or not."

"I'm on God's side, and God wants us to live in peace."

Monahan's eyes were fierce. "There won't be peace if Texas pulls out. We'll find ourselves in the damnedest war this country ever saw."

Clemmie broke in. "This is no fit subject for the dinner table. James, pass your daddy the gravy."

In deference to her, the conversation turned to subjects that sparked no controversy, such as speculation that a railroad might be built to haul farm produce from the interior to a gulf port, and the need for a soaking rain.

Rusty only half listened to most of it. He did not know enough about railroads to voice an opinion, and all the talk in the world would not bring rain so long as the wind was out of the west. He kept his chin down as if he were concentrating on eating, but he lifted his gaze to Geneva, across the table. Somehow she didn't seem quite so skinny as he had first thought. The longer he looked at her, the more he wanted to look. He did not have a lot to judge her by. Girls of her age were scarce down on his section of the Colorado River. He had gone to school with Fowler Gaskin's daughter, Florey, but she looked too much like her brothers to arouse any interest. The only person he knew uglier than the Gaskin brothers was their father.

After dinner James saddled a horse and set out eastward to notify neighbors that Preacher Webb would conduct services that evening at the Monahans'. Billy Monahan rode north and west.

Lon Monahan shouted after James, "You tell them to be sure and come! Ain't a one of them but what can stand a damned good dose of salvation!"

Rusty thought it might not have been necessary for the boys to ride out. Monahan could have stood on the porch and hollered loudly enough to reach everyone within four or five miles.

Clemmie admonished, "Lon, is it necessary to use that kind of language in front of the preacher?"

"Hell, he's heard it all before. A little honest swearin'

wipeth away anger and bringeth peace to the soul." He winked at Rusty.

Rusty was reminded that Mike Shannon had looked at it that way too, and the thought brought sadness. Mike had had much in common with Lon Monahan besides their political leanings.

Clemmie noticed Rusty's expression. She said, "You're lookin' kind of down, son. Not feelin' good?"

Rusty did not want to get into a discussion about what had happened to Mike. He replied, "Just thinkin' over what Mr. Monahan said about war."

Clemmie turned on her husband. "See what you done, talkin' so free? Some things you'd ought to keep to yourself."

Monahan said, "Ain't no dodgin' what's true." Once the boys were gone, he suggested, "We'd just as well forget about fence buildin' today. Preacher, I'd like to show you my horses. Traded for a nice little set of mares and a sorrel stud since you were here last."

"As I recall, the Comanches cleaned you out last year."

"I'm hopin' the volunteers can keep them crafty devils from comin' south." He looked at Rusty as if for verification.

Rusty found Geneva looking at him too and felt compelled to make some kind of answer, even if it meant nothing. "I'll just be followin' orders, but I expect we'll do the best we can."

Monahan said, "The country you've got to cover is big, and there won't be many of you. Seein' how poor Texas is now, I can't understand how anybody thinks it'd be better off by quittin' the union. Everything the union's been doin' for us, we'll have to do for ourselves."

Rusty could see the other side of the argument. "A lot of folks don't think it *has* done much for us."

"A lot of folks are wrong. I'm afraid they're fixin' to find that out."

Rusty was not overly interested in seeing Monahan's mares. He would rather have stayed and gotten acquainted with Monahan's daughter, but he felt it his obligation as a guest to act pleased and accept in good grace whatever courtesy the host extended. He rode out with Monahan and Webb.

Monahan said, "If it hadn't taken us so long to borrow horses to ride, we'd've caught up to them Indians and got our own back. As it was, we trailed them all the way to the Red River, me and James and Billy."

Webb was incredulous. "The three of you? What would you have done if you'd caught up to the Indians?"

"Like I said, we'd've took back our horses. By the tracks there wasn't but six or seven hostiles. Me and the boys could've whipped up on them easy."

The stallion made a threatening rush at the three horsemen, but Monahan put him to flight by waving his hat and shouting at the top of his voice. Rusty thought he might have flushed birds out of the trees half a mile away.

By the time they returned to the house, the first neighbors had begun arriving a-horseback, in wagons and buggies. Most brought food in baskets or sacks to help the Monahans feed the expected crowd. Rusty was introduced to so many that he had no chance of remembering the names. It had always been that way when he had accompanied Preacher Webb on his circuit. Prayer meeting was more than a religious event. It provided a rare excuse for a social gathering where the men could swap yarns, horses, and dogs. Women could exchange news about weddings and births and discuss whatever they had been able to learn about fashion in faraway places like St. Louis and New Orleans.

This gathering also provided a forum for extended discussions on secession. Rusty noted that the preponderance of opinion favored pulling out. Monahan's was definitely a minority view. In another setting the debate might have sparked violent quarreling, but here the visitors respected the host's views even as most disagreed with them.

Clemmie Monahan walked out onto the porch, drying wet hands on an apron. She told her husband, "Appears to me that just about everybody's here and lookin' hungry."

Her father said, "I sure am."

Lon Monahan asked Webb, "You want to eat first or do it after the preachin'?"

"Minister first to the body, then the soul will be ready for the Word."

Old Vince Purdy said, "Amen."

Preacher Webb broke up the scattered conversations by calling for the visitors to bow their heads. He beseeched the Lord to heal divisions and restore peace to troubled hearts.

He had barely reached the "Amen" when a large man of commanding presence rode up on a big white horse, trailed by three riders whose subservient manner indicated they were in his pay or in his debt. The man wore a long black coat, open so that no one could miss seeing the pistol he carried in his broad waistband.

Lon Monahan was obviously displeased about the late-arriving guests, but he showed himself a good host by walking out to meet them. "You're late, Colonel, but we're just fixin' to eat supper. There's plenty for all of you. And Preacher Webb ain't delivered his sermon yet."

Rusty heard Vince Purdy mutter, "Colonel Caleb Dawkins. I'd rather be bit by a hydrophoby dog."

Dawkins did not dismount. He seemed seven feet tall in the saddle, a huge man with shoulders that looked wide enough to bump a doorway on both sides and hands big enough to choke a mule. "We have not come to eat or listen to platitudes." His voice was deep and resonant, like Monahan's, and chillingly calm. "We have come to see how many choose to align themselves with traitors."

Stung, Monahan struggled to recover his composure. "You'll find no traitors here, Colonel Dawkins. There is scarcely a man in this crowd who has not answered the call against Mexico or against the savage."

"We've a different enemy this time. You and your family have openly allied yourself with the northern union. I must assume that those who break bread with you support you in your sedition."

The accusation aroused angry shouts from among the visitors. Half a dozen men surged forward in protest. The three with Dawkins dropped their hands to their weapons, and the threat cooled. Dawkins remained unmoved, showing no emotion. He seemed to be above anger or fear.

Monahan's face colored. "Damn you, Colonel, you've just abused the hell out of my hospitality." He moved toward the man, but Preacher Webb stepped in front of him.

Webb said, "You are wrong, Colonel Dawkins. A vote here tonight would probably be ninety percent for secession. These people have come for a prayer meeting, not a political fight. I would invite you to join us in fellowship and worship."

Dawkins looked at Webb as if he were a beggar on the street. "You call yourself a man of God, yet you sup with one flagrantly disloyal to his state. The devil rules here tonight, not God." His chilling gaze swept over the crowd. "I warn all of you, judgment day is coming. When the vote is taken and Texas secedes, a swift and just punishment will be visited upon all who are not on God's side." He leaned forward, piercing eyes fixed on Lon Monahan. "Be warned. You will be the first."

Rusty was reminded of Isaac York. This man could have been York's close kin except that York was highly excitable, where Dawkins was stolid and cold. Rusty could not help shivering.

James Monahan, trembling with anger, reached down to pick up a rock. "Git off of this place, Dawkins, before I chunk you off."

Lon Monahan caught his oldest son's throwing arm and held it. "This is for your daddy to take care of." He looked up at Dawkins. "James said it as good as I could: Git! Else I'll be forced to stomp hell out of you in front of the Lord and everybody."

Old Vince Purdy joined his son-in-law. "And damned if me and James don't whip the other three."

Caleb Dawkins could have been leaving church for all the emotion he showed in departing. The men with him followed without speaking, though they kept looking back over their shoulders as if expecting trouble to run and catch up.

James hurled the rock, missing Dawkins by only a couple of feet. "We could've beaten him, Pa. Him and that hired trash with him."

"He ain't worth skinnin' our knuckles over. He talks

strong because it's the only way he can get anybody to listen to him."

Webb said, "*I* listened to him, and he scared me."

"God save us from zealots." Monahan turned his back on the retreating Dawkins. "He'll keep. Right now we've got company."

They did not have it for long. Caleb Dawkins's appearance sapped all the pleasure from the gathering. Conversation was subdued as the people ate. Preacher Webb sensed the crowd's distraction and trimmed his sermon short. Guests thanked the Monahans for their hospitality and Webb for his message, of which most had probably heard little. They saddled horses and climbed into wagons and buggies, then headed off in several directions.

"I'm sorry, Preacher," Monahan apologized. "Everything kind of went to hell after the colonel got here."

"It wasn't your fault."

"He's been itchin' for a killin' ever since he came into this country. Everybody knows he's a little crazy."

"That makes him all the more dangerous."

Rusty asked, "Who is he, and how come you-all call him colonel?"

Monahan said, "He was one once, in the war against Mexico. Hung a couple of men for cowardice because they retreated without orders when the Mexicans was fixin' to overrun them. Got cashiered out of the army. He never could see where he'd done anything wrong. He's hated the federal government ever since."

Rusty saw worry in Geneva Monahan's eyes, and for the first time he was certain of their color: blue, like his own. He felt an urge to put a protective arm around her, but he did not know just what he could protect her from or how he would do it.

Clemmie jerked her head to beckon her daughters. "Come on, Geneva, you and the other girls. We've got some cleanin' up to do."

Lon Monahan looked glumly toward the last departing guests, three hundred yards down the wagon road. He said to his sons, "We'd best be gettin' the stock fed. The horses probably think we've forgotten them."

James grumbled, "I still say we could've whipped them. I was cocked and primed to do it."

Lon replied, "You're too eager to fight, son. Time you've been in as many scraps as me and your granddaddy and the preacher, you won't be so anxious for another one."

Rusty and Webb trailed behind, prepared to help. Rusty said, "If I was Lon Monahan, I'd never be more than a step away from a gun. Dawkins sounds a lot like Isaac York, and everybody knows what Isaac did to Daddy Mike."

"We don't know that for sure."

"I'm as certain as if I'd been there and seen it. And one of these days he'll pay."

"Vengeance is best left to the Lord."

"When the day comes, I'll give the Lord some help."

The next morning Rusty went out before breakfast to saddle Alamo and pack Chapultepec for an early start. Preacher Webb walked with him but remained outside of the corral. Rusty said, "I thought we were leavin' today."

"*You* are, but I'm not goin' the rest of the way with you. Looks like I'm needed here."

Rusty suspected the quarrel between Monahan and Dawkins weighed heavily on the minister's mind. "Maybe I'd better stay with you."

"You're obliged to obey orders and go on. I feel my obligation is to try to pour oil on troubled waters. I smell blood in the air."

Rusty paused, his hand on the rope that tied the mule's pack. "You don't reckon Dawkins would do somethin' to the family . . . to the womenfolks and all?"

"I doubt he's crazy enough to hurt the women. People around here would turn against him in a minute." Webb seemed to see through Rusty's eyes and into his mind. "You're worried about the girl."

"Her and all of them. They're good folks."

Webb nodded. "Good people, caught up in bad times. I'm afraid that's been the way of the world since the first days. We won't see the end of it in our short span upon the earth."

The family filed into place at the table. Rusty waited until everyone else was seated, then took the position he had been given at the end of a bench across from Geneva and the younger girls. Lon Monahan's eyes were tired, his shoulders sagging. After Webb said grace, Monahan gulped half a cup of coffee. He tore a biscuit in half, started to eat it, then laid it on his plate. His face was grim.

"I didn't sleep none last night," he said. "Caleb Dawkins kept runnin' through my mind. Ain't there somethin' in the Scriptures, Preacher, about handwritin' on the wall?"

"It foretells things to come."

"The handwritin' is on the wall here. Texas is about to pull out of the union. When it does, all hell is liable to bust loose. Fanatics like Dawkins will run wild and free, for a while at least. They'll be comin' after folks who've talked against Texas pullin' out."

Clemmie protested, "Everybody around here is your friend, Lon, even if they don't agree with you. They wouldn't let him—"

"He won't ask them. He'll just go ahead and do it, or try to."

James's voice was confident. "You've always been able to take care of yourself, Pa. And we'll be with you, all of us."

"I couldn't ask for a better family. But anything that puts me in danger puts you-all in danger, too. The way I see it, we've got two choices. We can stay and tough it out, or we can leave here before the trouble starts."

Geneva cried, "Leave? But where would we go?"

"I hear that a few folks've already gone south to Mexico. Or we could move west out to Arizona or California. Maybe even to Oregon, where there ain't no north nor south, where there won't be no war."

Clemmie demanded, "What about the farm? We've worked so long and so hard—"

"The Vanderfords've been after me a long time to let them

buy it. We could be halfway to Arizona before Dawkins and his crowd even know we're gone."

James stood up, fists clenched. "Turn tail and run? That ain't like you, Pa. It ain't like *us*."

"You're way too young to remember the runaway scrape, when Santy Anna marched across Texas, bent on wipin' us all out. A lot of brave folks packed up and ran because they didn't see any other way to survive." He looked at Webb. "You know what I'm talkin' about, Preacher?"

Webb nodded sadly. "I'm afraid I read the handwritin' on the wall the same way you do."

Rusty saw anguish in Geneva's eyes and wished he could do something to ease it. He said, "There ought to be somebody who could do somethin'. The rangers, maybe. There's more to the rangers than fightin' Indians. Aren't we supposed to keep the peace?"

Webb said, "When Texas secedes there won't be any peace to keep. Not likely to be much of a government, not for a while. May not even be any rangers."

James declared, "To hell with Caleb Dawkins. We'll fight him. We'll kill him if we have to."

Webb cautioned, "You shouldn't speak of killin'. Don't even think of it."

Rusty imagined he could hear Clemmie's teeth grinding. She declared, "This place is ours. We built it from nothin'. We're not goin' to Mexico or Oregon or anywhere else. We're stayin' right here."

Lon Monahan's gaze moved to the other members of the family—Billy, Geneva and her sisters, Clemmie's father. "You-all say the same? Even knowin' the risk, you're bound to stay?"

Geneva looked at Webb. "There'd be risk on the trail too, wouldn't there, Preacher Webb?"

Webb's eyes were sad. "Indians. Sickness. Outlaws. No tellin' what-all."

Geneva said, "Then we'd just be tradin' one risk for another. Maybe a bunch of them."

Clemmie folded her arms, her eyes stern. "Here at least we know what the danger is. It's got a face, and that face looks like old Caleb Dawkins. There never was a time, on the sickest day of your life, that you couldn't beat the whey out of that son of a bitch. Pardon me, Preacher."

Monahan's eyes brightened. "I just wanted everybody to know what we're up against and to let you have your say." He turned back to Webb. "I've told you before, and I'll say it again. I've got the best damned family of anybody I know."

Webb still looked sad. "I envy you your family, but I do not envy the position you're in."

Monahan shrugged as if his worries had largely evaporated. "Long as we stick together, ain't nothin' can whip us." He turned to his breakfast.

Webb ate little. Monahan's renewed cheer had not transferred itself to him. Rusty finished his eggs and biscuits and pushed to his feet. "I wish I could stay longer, but I've still got a ways to travel." He shook hands with Monahan and with each member of the family, including the smallest of the girls.

Geneva said, "You'll be comin' back this way sometime, won't you?"

"That is my intention." He lingered a moment, held by the sparkle in her eyes.

Webb said, "I'll walk out to the barn with you."

They strode in silence to where the horse and the mule were tied. Rusty asked, "You sure you can do anything here?"

"There is no certainty in this life. I'll do what I can to keep the peace. The rest is up to a greater power than ourselves." He grasped Rusty's hand. "Be careful. The Indians have been given a bad bargain, and they're mad. You had nothing to do with it, but you're white. That makes you fair game."

"I'll watch out."

"I'm proud of you, Rusty. You were a good boy, and you've grown up to be a good man. Now go and be a good ranger."

Riding away, Rusty looked back. He already missed the comforting presence of Preacher Webb. Except for the farm itself, Webb was the only remaining strong tie to his life with Mike and Dora Shannon. He saw the Monahans scattering, each to his or her own chores, and regret was a wrenching pain. For a while he had warmed himself in the glow of this closely knit family. Now he mourned anew the loss of his own, for he was alone again, rootless and adrift.

· 8 ·

It was not a lot farther to Fort Belknap, and Rusty did not push hard. He did not want to wear down his animals. Tom Blessing had not indicated there was any particular hurry. His main concern had been to put distance between Rusty and Isaac York until feelings cooled down. Rusty stopped occasionally to allow the horse and mule to graze and to give himself an opportunity to study the land. He had counted the rivers and streams he had crossed and knew there were more than Blessing's rough map had indicated. But good water made for a good country.

From time to time he came upon scattered small gatherings of buffalo, their winter hair rough and matted. He was tempted to shoot one just for the hell of it, but Daddy Mike had taught him long ago to kill only for meat, not for pleasure. If he shot one of these shaggy animals he would have to leave most of the carcass to spoil. Mike would say that was wasteful of Nature's gifts, and not pleasing in the sight of the Lord.

Despite his edgy feeling of aloneness and vulnerability, he found pleasure in traversing the rolling plains after breaking out of the cross timbers and its scrub-oak country. They were different in many ways, both in terrain and in vegetation, from the Colorado River region of his upbringing. It was not entirely new to him. He had seen the area before, going and coming back from following the Brazos reserve Indians on their reluctant march to new and less desirable country north of the Red.

It required no stretch of his imagination to understand why they so hated leaving after having set down roots near the Clear Fork of the Brazos on land pledged to be theirs forever. Forever had proven to be painfully short. Though most had no cultural inclination toward being farmers, many had put forth an honest effort to learn, to break out fields and plant crops the way the white agents showed them. Then they had been hurried away under military escort, obliged to leave most of their livestock for the whites who moved in behind them.

Yet Rusty understood the other side of the argument. Warfare was an integral part of Indian life—at least for the horseback Indians who roamed the plains. Warrior status was coveted by every ambitious young male. Only through war and the hunt could he prove himself worthy of being regarded a man. A life without war would be idle and pointless, too dreary to contemplate. Sometimes war was fought against nearby tribes. More often the targets were American settlers and Mexicans, whoever came handy.

To these people of European extraction and vastly different culture, it was intolerable to live in constant fear of potentially hostile neighbors. Most could recall violent deaths of kin and acquaintances at Indian hands. In many a home, chilling family stories were told and retold about depredations against forebears in the Alleghenies, the Mohawk and Ohio Valleys, the Southeast, or down in Mexico. A rumor of Indians could panic a community or arouse it to arms.

Coming into the region that had been the reservation before removal, Rusty saw a few new cabins. Some structures built by or for the Indians were occupied. Settlers had not wasted time moving into the vacuum after the former residents were dispossessed. He knew there had been political string-pulling well ahead of the removal and that hunger for land had been at least as potent a motive as fear in breaking up the Brazos reserve.

His opinion about these new settlers was immaterial, whether favorable or otherwise. As a ranger, paid or not, he would have to defend them against re-invasion by the displaced Indians. Since removal, any Indian found inside the borders of Texas was assumed to be hostile and subject to being shot on sight unless accompanied by federal or state officials. Even then he would be regarded with suspicion and kept under watch lest he try to take back by force that which he regarded as having been his.

Rusty came to a creek he thought too narrow to be the Clear Fork. He was sure it was not on Blessing's crude map. Nearby stood a new picket cabin built of upright oak logs and covered by a sod roof that he doubted would keep all the rain out. The sod was thick enough and heavy enough to pose a hazard if it became saturated with water. Its weight could collapse the cabin into a heap of ruin and bury anyone unlucky enough to have sought shelter inside. But perhaps its owner was better at farming than at carpentry.

A man was stacking stones, building a rock fence around a garden plot. He was so intent on his work or whatever else was on his mind that he remained unaware until Rusty was almost close enough to reach across the fence and touch him.

"Howdy," Rusty said.

The man jumped backward, bringing a large rock up defensively as if to brain Rusty with it. A trickle of brown down his chin showed he had been chewing tobacco. He swallowed most of it. "My God!" he exclaimed after a moment's startled silence. "You could've been an Indian. Why don't you make a little noise before you slip up on a feller?" He dropped the stone and spat out what remained of the tobacco, coughing in an effort to bring up some that had lodged in his throat.

Rusty said, "This old mule sloshes like a water barrel on a wagon. You must've been studyin' hard not to've heard us."

It took the farmer a minute to get rid of the tobacco and calm down. "Maybe I was. I need to pay more attention if

I'm to keep livin' in this country. Just because they've moved the Indians out don't mean they might not come back."

"Could you blame them? They were given this land, and then it was taken away from them."

"It wasn't me that gave them the reservation, and it wasn't me that told them they had to leave. Damned government never did ask my opinion about anything. If I hadn't took up this place, somebody else would've. Can't blame me for that, can you?"

Rusty shook his head. "Seems like it doesn't do much good to blame anybody. It's a mess, and we have to live with it the best we can. Mind if I water my stock at your creek?"

"The creek ain't mine, just the land that runs up to it. If you and your animals drink it all up, them fellers downstream will just have to take care of theirselves." The farmer had recovered from his momentary fright, though Rusty suspected it would take longer to get over the tobacco he had swallowed.

"I'm on my way up to Fort Belknap. I've been through here before, but I'm a little hazy about the distance."

The farmer studied the horse and mule, satisfying himself of their soundness. "You'll make it in another day easy enough. Less if you lope up a little. What kind of business draws you to Belknap?"

"I'm reportin' for duty there."

The farmer's eyebrows went up. "You look kind of young to be one of them minuteman rangers."

"Captain Blessing thinks I'm old enough."

"You're liable to age in a hurry. Some hard old boys hang around in the brush outside of Fort Belknap. They don't take kindly to the law messin' with their business."

"What kind of business?"

"Some peddle whiskey up north of the Red River, on the Indian reservation. Others go up there and steal Indian horses. When the Indians get mad enough or drunk enough to start raisin' hell, it's always somebody innocent that gets hurt. They don't try to find the ones that's actually caused their trouble. Anybody white will do."

Rusty decided the farmer was not going to invite him to break bread with him or to spend the night. It was early in the afternoon anyway. He could make several more miles before time to camp.

The farmer said, "I don't ordinarily give advice where it ain't been asked for, but you look like some mother's nice young son. If I was you I wouldn't advertise too high about bein' a ranger. Some of them rough boys might decide to leave you layin' out on the prairie and pretend like the Indians done it."

"Once I join the company I'm assigned to, there won't be any secret about who I am."

"Rangers up in this country generally travel in packs, or at least in pairs so one can watch the front while the other watches the rear. Indians ain't the only danger around here, not by a long ways. You heard about agent Neighbors gettin' murdered in Belknap? Just because he tried to help the reserve Indians."

Rusty had heard. He had also heard that the ranger company caught the murderer and made short work of him. "I suppose some of those rough boys pass this way from time to time?"

"I try to see very little and tell even less. If I was to peach to a ranger, somebody might come by here some dark night and blow my light out. If any of them was to ride up here now and see me talkin' to you, and they found out you're a ranger, they might get the same idea. So I'd take it kindly if you'd water your stock and move on."

Rusty pulled the mule's lead rope. "I'm obliged to you for the water and the words of wisdom."

"They never cost me nothin'. Watch out for yourself. I'd hate for your mother to have to grieve for you."

Rusty saw no point in saying that he had no mother, no father, no kin that he knew of. The farmer had his own problems.

*   *   *

He tried to be watchful, for he knew this could be dangerous country, but he missed seeing the band of horses until they came boiling over a hill and swept down toward him. A rider galloped along in front, pointing the way. Several others rode alongside and behind, keeping the animals moving at a fast clip. Rusty felt a wild jolt of apprehension, thinking the horsemen were Comanches. His fear eased as he saw they were white. He realized that Comanches were in the habit of taking horses north, not south.

He pulled to the left to be out of the way. The driven horses began spilling past him, though the man who rode point reined around and came directly toward Rusty. He was followed quickly by two men who had been riding swing alongside the remuda.

The point rider gave Rusty a close scrutiny without speaking. His hard gaze brought back Rusty's uneasiness.

Rusty offered a tentative "Howdy."

"I don't know you. Who are you?" The man was young enough that his several days' growth of whiskers looked soft and uneven.

Not much older than me, Rusty thought. But he saw hardness in the eyes and the set of the jaw. "My name's Rusty Shannon. What's yours?" He extended his hand.

The rider did not answer the question or accept Rusty's hand. "Where you headed?"

"Up the country a ways." Rusty remembered the farmer's admonition about not revealing his mission.

"What for?"

"Lookin' for kin." That was not quite a lie. He always harbored a faint hope that he might run into kin somewhere, though he would have no way of recognizing them if he did. It was frustrating not to know what his real name had been.

The suspicious gray eyes had a piercing quality that compounded Rusty's discomfort. The other two horsemen had pulled up on either side of the point rider. Rusty sensed threat in all three. Whatever they were up to, it was not good.

The point rider asked, "You sure your kin ain't in the federal army? Or maybe the ranger spy company up there?"

"I don't know anybody in the army, or in any spy company either." It was true that Rusty didn't know anyone in the ranger company *yet*.

He strongly suspected these were Indian horses, stolen off the reservation. The threat of war had raised the price of horses enough to tempt even an honest man, much less one already inclined to be a thief. Rusty's life might not be worth a brass peso if these men knew his true business. He made an effort to keep his hand still, not to let it move down toward the stock of his rifle. He doubted he would live to bring the weapon clear of leather. "I don't mean to hold you fellers up. You look like you're in a hurry."

The three men glanced at one another, indecisive. The last of the loose horses trotted past, two riders following. Another rider spurred up from far behind, his face flushed with excitement. "What the hell have you stopped for? They're right behind us!" He pointed in the direction from which he had come.

That threw the others into a similar state of excitement. The point rider drew a pistol from his hip. He brought it up as if to aim it at Rusty, then changed his mind.

The man who had come up last shouted, "Shoot him, damn it, and let's get out of here!"

The point rider hesitated. The other drew his pistol to do the chore for him. The point rider pushed between him and Rusty. He said, "They *might* hang us for horse stealin', Pete. They'd sure as hell hang us for a killin'." He stared hard at Rusty. "Reckon you can forget what we look like?"

The muzzle of the pistol was leveled on Rusty's stomach. "I've already forgotten."

He had not, however. The images of the man with the pistol and the one named Pete had burned themselves indelibly into his memory.

Pete looked back, his voice desperate. "We'd better let the horses go. We can't save them and our scalps too."

Reluctantly the point man said, "All right, there'll be more horses another time." He turned back to Rusty. "I wouldn't stay here if I was you. You're fixin' to meet up with a bunch of real mad Indians."

Rusty's anxiety over the horsemen was replaced by anxiety over what was coming next. He saw a thicket a couple of hundred yards away. "Don't let me hold you back."

The horsemen put spurs to their mounts and quartered southeastward in a hard run. They motioned for two men who still rode on the near side of the remuda to quit the bunch and join them. The stolen horses at the rear realized they were no longer being pushed and slowed down. A few stopped and nickered for their running mates. Rusty touched his heels to Alamo's sides and put him into a long trot. Chapultepec lagged so that Rusty had to turn loose of the lead rope to prevent being pulled from the saddle. He circled back to recover the animal.

"Damned mule, you're liable to get me killed."

The delay prevented him from reaching the thicket in time. More than a dozen riders appeared on the hill where he had first seen the stolen horses. As they galloped down the slope, several split off and came after Rusty while the others continued pursuit of the remuda. There was no doubt this time. These were Indians. Rusty saw that he had no chance to reach the thicket. He pulled hard on the reins and slipped the rifle from its scabbard, then stepped quickly to the ground.

Even as he did so, he knew he had no chance. He might shoot one, but the others would cut him down before he could reload. He held his breath until his lungs ached, then sucked in enough air to fill them and stood with the rifle at arm's length in a posture of surrender.

Daddy Mike had always said the worst thing a man could do was to give himself up to Indians, but the only other option he saw was to go down fighting. It seemed futile to kill just one when he could see half a dozen coming at him. He waited, his heart pounding and his mouth dry as old leather.

He wished Preacher Webb were with him. Preacher could charm his way into or out of almost any situation. Rusty whispered, "Lord, if You're really up there and payin' any attention, You'd better do somethin' quick."

The first Indian to reach him shouted furiously and pointed toward the horses still moving southward. Rusty did not understand the words, but the tone was unmistakable. The rest surrounded him in a hostile manner. He knew they assumed he was one of the thieves.

He pointed in the direction the real thieves had taken. They were still in sight but fading rapidly into the distance. "Yonder go the ones that stole your horses. It wasn't me."

He realized they probably did not understand what he was saying. He hoped they understood his gestures. He pointed again. "Yonder they go."

A voice came from behind him. "How come you didn't go with them, bub?"

He had not noticed that one of the men was white. *Lord,* he thought, *maybe You were paying attention after all.* "Because I wasn't with them in the first place."

Being white did not mean the man was friendly. He had a hangman's look about him, darkly suspicious eyes peering from beneath the drooping brim of a weather-beaten felt hat, his mouth a flat line barely visible through heavy brown whiskers. "You tryin' to make us believe you just happened into them?"

"Yes, sir, or they just happened into me. I was headed the other direction, to Fort Belknap."

Several sets of dark and glittering eyes stared accusingly at him. He suspected some of the Indians understood enough English to get the gist of what he had said. They argued among themselves. One pointed to the mule. Rusty feared he was claiming the animal, which would mean they had made up their minds he was a thief. He shivered, wondering how it felt to take an arrow in the chest or to have a war club smash his skull.

The white man listened intently to the Indians' conversation, which he seemed to understand. Rusty assumed he was some kind of scout or interpreter. When the talk dwindled away, the man told Rusty, "Walkin' Eagle says there wasn't no mules among the bunch that was stolen."

Rusty began to hope. "Not this one, for sure. I brought Chapultepec with me all the way up from the Colorado River. Alamo too." He pointed to the black horse's brand. "That's the Shannon brand, an S with a bar under it. I'm Rusty Shannon."

The name meant nothing. The man pointed to the brand and said something to the Indians, part in spoken words and part in sign. They argued, but when the argument quieted down, Rusty was fairly sure none of them was claiming the brand. He breathed easier.

The white man demanded, "What's your business at Belknap?"

Rusty pondered his answer. Given what had been done to them in recent times, it was unlikely these Indians had any good feeling toward the rangers. He repeated the evasion he had offered to the horse thief. "I'm lookin' for some kin."

"Who are they? Maybe I know them."

"Our family's the Shannons." That was not a lie.

"I don't recall any Shannons up that way. You sure they're there?"

"I'm not sure of anything. But I thought I'd look."

Rusty could see that several Indians who had followed the thieves had abandoned that chase and were helping run down the loose horses. He saw a couple of army uniforms as well.

The interpreter said, "I don't like to call anybody a liar 'til I know for sure, but let's just say I ain't done wonderin'. Soon's the Tonkawas finish roundin' up their horses, we'll all head back toward Fort Belknap together. We'll see if we can find any Shannons."

Rusty was mildly surprised. "Tonkawas? I figured these were Comanches."

The man seemed short of patience. "That's one big trouble with you people in Texas. You never could tell one Indian from another. It's caused you no end of grief, and them, too. The Comanches are as wild as deer."

"These looked pretty wild too, comin' at me like they did."

"If they was the killin' kind of Indian, you'd already be halfway to hell and smellin' the smoke. The Tonkawas don't mean harm to anybody, except Comanches. They used to give you Texans a lot of help against the wild Indians. The reward you gave them was to kick them across the river."

Rusty remembered the sad exodus, but under present circumstances he had no intention of letting them know he had been there.

The Indians had turned back the leaders of the stolen horse herd and were pushing the bunch in Rusty's direction. The two army men rode ahead, reining up as they reached Rusty and the interpreter. One of the pair bore himself with exaggerated dignity, which led Rusty to assume he was an officer of some kind. *Probably a lieutenant,* he thought. Daddy Mike had always said lieutenants tended to have an inflated view of their importance. By the time they made captain, most had had their egos punctured often enough to let the excess air out of them.

The officer gave Rusty a study of the most negative sort. "I see you captured one of them, Harrison."

The interpreter had not introduced himself. Now, at least, Rusty knew his name.

Harrison replied, "We're inclined to believe he's not one of them. He says he was on his way north and just happened to run into the thieves. None of the Tonks claim his horse or mule."

The officer continued his hard scrutiny. "Perhaps. Not all have seen them yet." To Rusty he said, "If you are what you claim to be, I must say that I find fault with your choice of company."

"They weren't any company of mine. It looked for a minute like they were fixin' to shoot me." He considered showing the note Tom Blessing had written for the captain of rangers but decided it might be well to wait until they reached Belknap. He did not know the army's opinion of the rangers. If it was like the rangers' opinion of the army, he had better keep his mouth shut.

The officer said, "What matters most is that the Indians recovered their horses. To be on the safe side, we'll turn you over to the authorities as we pass Belknap. If they find no fault with you, they'll free you quickly enough." He scowled. "They do not seem to find much fault with people who steal from the Indians."

Rusty decided against continuing to proclaim his innocence. He had already said more than usual, and the lieutenant would keep doubting him anyway.

The officer asked, "Should the occasion arise, do you think you could identify the thieves?"

"One or two, maybe. Most of them were too far away." Under duress Rusty had implied a promise of silence to the thieves' point rider, though he did not feel honor bound to respect it. With luck he might never be called upon to face that moral decision.

Though technically not a prisoner, Rusty felt like one. Should he try to escape his mixed escort he suspected he would be run down or shot. He decided to make the best of the present situation inasmuch as he was being taken where he had intended to go in the first place.

The lieutenant rode on one side of him, Harrison on the other. The lieutenant had little to say. Rusty suspected he did not like talking to inferiors more than necessary, and it was clear enough that he saw Rusty as an inferior.

Harrison interested Rusty the most. "Where'd you learn how to talk to Indians?"

"Tonkawas, mainly. The only talkin' I ever done with the Comanches was with the business end of a gun. I ain't no Texan, but I lived there awhile, near the Tonks. They're good people if you overlook their eatin' habits."

"Like what?"

"Ain't nothin' pleases them more than a little barbecued Comanche. Eatin' their enemy gives them some of his strength, the way they figure it. Of course that makes other Indians hate them. Now you Texans have moved them up into the territory and put them smack-dab in the middle of their enemies. It'll be a wonder if the other tribes don't kill them all."

The lieutenant said, "They have the army's protection."

Rusty blurted, "Like the army's always protected Texas?"

The lieutenant's pained expression showed that the barb had bitten into the flesh. "I suppose you are one of those who plans to vote for secession?"

"I doubt I'll get a chance to vote one way or the other. If I did, I'm not sure which way I'd choose."

"Perhaps you have not heard. The vote is to be taken this coming Saturday. There are a few counties in the northern section still strongly pro-federal, and the German colonies near San Antonio. The rest of Texas seems bound and determined to charge up Fool's Hill."

Rusty had not realized the voting day was imminent. The news shook him a little. Daddy Mike had predicted bad trouble once the vote was taken. So had Lon Monahan. "What happens to the federal army if Texas pulls out?" he asked.

Harrison said, "The soldiers may find theirselves fightin' Texans instead of Comanches."

The lieutenant frowned. "No, more than likely the army will simply be ordered to withdraw all troops from the state."

Rusty knew many Texans would welcome that result, but he feared they had not thought the implications through. Despite the army's many shortcomings, it had provided the frontier at least a little protection. If it withdrew, Texas would have to fall back entirely upon its own resources: the local militia and rangers or minutemen. During the ten years it had been a republic Texas had never put together enough money to wad a shotgun. It had fared but little better as a state. He saw no reason to expect its position to improve once it was no longer part of the United States.

He remarked, "Looks to me like we're fixin' to cook our own goose."

The officer suggested, "You could vote against secession."

"That wouldn't change anything. I'd about as well try to dam up the Brazos River with a pitchfork."

Rusty kept watching in fascination the Indians who pushed the recovered horses along. Most had changed to fresh mounts, having worn down their original ones in the pursuit. The stolen animals had been driven hard but had not carried the burden of men on their backs. The Tonkawas' winter clothing was a mixture of long breechclouts, tanned leathers, and white-man castoffs. For protection against the cold, some covered their shoulders and torsos with buffalo robes, others with woolen blankets. Some wore earrings and necklaces of animal teeth or shells.

Harrison told him, "You'd best take a good look at them. The Tonkawas are dyin' out."

"These look pretty strong to me."

"As Indians go, there ain't many left. White man's diseases . . . hostile tribes . . . Pretty soon they'll all be gone."

"I expect a lot of people would be glad to dance at the last one's funeral."

"Just you Texans who can't tell Indians apart. If you ever got to know them, you'd see that there's a world of difference between Tonkawas and Comanches."

"The Comanches stole me once when I was little. I can't remember much except bein' scared."

"It's lucky your folks got you back."

"They evidently killed my folks. Other people took and raised me."

"You Texans think because some Indians are bad, they all are. I guess your experience made you hate all Indians."

"I don't hate anybody." Rusty reconsidered. "Except maybe one man, and he's white."

"Indians have got ways of their own. That don't make them good or bad, it just makes them different. These Tonkawas were ready to've killed the horse thieves if they'd caught them, and you'd've heard weepin' and wailin' about an Indian massacre. But do you think white men would've been different? If it was their horses they'd've been hell-bent to hang everybody they caught."

"Texans aren't all alike, either. Because some are bad, you think they all are."

Harrison almost smiled. "There may be an exception here and there."

They were a few miles short of Fort Belknap when a dozen horsemen suddenly appeared three hundred yards in front of them, fanned out as if to offer battle. One prematurely fired a shot, which took no effect that Rusty could see. A soldier who had been riding point ahead of the remuda spurred toward them, his right arm raised, so the riders could see that the Indians had a military escort. One of the newcomers, evidently their leader, waved his hat and signaled for those on the flanks to rejoin the main group. As they pulled together, he motioned for them to hold their position while he rode forward. He swung out to one side and slowed to let the driven horses pass. He gave the Indians a critical study before proceeding to meet the lieutenant. He wore no uniform but carried himself in a military manner. He brought his hand up in a sharp salute, touching the brim of a well-worn felt hat. His back was arrow-straight, his black-and-gray moustache smartly trimmed and turned up at the ends.

In a stiffly formal manner he said, "We were sent a report of Indians passing through the country. It was our fear that they were Comanche or Kiowa."

The words were clipped. Rusty detected a trace of accent similar to that of Germans he knew on the Colorado.

The lieutenant's tone was condescending. "As even a Texan can see, they are Tonkawas."

"Often I have ridden with the Tonkawas. But even they are forbidden now south of the Red River. From where obtained they so many horses?"

The lieutenant plainly was not used to being questioned by civilians who did not show proper deference to their betters. "These horses belong to them. They were stolen off the reservation. And who are you to be asking questions of a military officer?"

"I am August Burmeister, a captain of the state rangers."

The lieutenant was not impressed. "If you Texans were as diligent in going after white thieves as red ones, these Indians might not have found it necessary to come south of the river. But as you can see, they are under federal military escort."

"Ah yes, the federals." Burmeister was not impressed either. He pointed his chin northward. "You are on your way to Belknap, I assume?"

"No. Do you think I would give the trigger-happy citizens of that ill-begotten community an excuse for killing more peaceful Indians? However, we have a man here to turn over to the proper persons." He jerked a thumb in Rusty's direction.

Burmeister tugged at one end of his moustache while giving Rusty an intense scrutiny. "And what is it this man has done?"

"We found him with the horse thieves. He claims he was travelling north and encountered them by chance. We'll leave it to you to determine the truth of the matter. I trust if he is guilty of stealing Indian horses, you will deal with him in an appropriate manner?"

The question was offered in an ironic voice that said the officer had no such expectation.

Rusty saw no harm in revealing his mission now. He took from his coat pocket the map and a note Tom Blessing had written. "I was on my way to Fort Belknap to report to you," he told the ranger.

As the captain read the note, his expression lost its severity. A smile lifted the moustache. "Tom Blessing. A good man he is. I was with him when we battled Comanches at Plum Creek."

"I was there, too," Rusty said.

"How could that be? Twenty years ago, it was."

"Do you remember a little boy there, rescued from the Indians?"

"I do. He was red-haired." The captain gave Rusty a closer study. "It would seem he is still red-haired."

"The name's Rusty Shannon. In the letter, Tom Blessing calls me *David*."

The captain shook his hand. "Shannon. The name seems *bekannt*. Was there not someone called Shannon at Plum Creek?"

"Mike Shannon, my father. Foster father, anyway. They never found out who my real folks were, so he took me to raise, him and Mother Dora."

"A man of the cloth rode with him, I believe. His arm was broken in the fight."

"That'd be Preacher Webb. Him and Daddy Mike were always close."

"They are both well, I hope."

"Preacher Webb still carries the Word to the forks of the creek." Rusty's throat tightened. "Daddy Mike is dead."

"That I regret. They fought a good fight. We all fought a good fight." Burmeister looked back to the lieutenant. "This young man need concern you no longer, Captain."

"Lieutenant."

"Lieutenant. Yes, I should have known." Burmeister's look showed his opinion of lieutenants.

The officer rebuked Rusty with his eyes. "You should have told us you belonged to this company."

"I was afraid you might have less use for Texas rangers than you do for Texas horse thieves."

"I find them similar in many respects. Come along, Harrison. The Tonkawas are getting ahead of us."

The scout Harrison gave Rusty a wink and put his horse into a long trot to catch up with the departing officer.

Burmeister watched the two ride away. "I agree not with this talk of breaking away from the union. But such officers could do much to change my mind."

With a nod he bade Rusty to follow him to where the rest of his ranger contingent waited. One of the men, rangy and hungry-looking, leaned forward, bracing his hands on the horn of his saddle. He wore a tattered buckskin jacket, crudely patched. His face was heavily freckled, and his eyes laughed. "Couldn't you talk us into a fight with them Yankee boys and their Indians, Dutch? We need the practice."

"I have ridden with the Tonkawas as allies. You would not want them for an enemy." Burmeister's moustache lifted at both ends. "Besides, Tanner, you are too skinny to interest them. Not even good soup would you make."

The man named Tanner turned his attention to Rusty. "Looks like they rejected this one, too. He ain't got much more meat on him than I have."

Burmeister introduced Rusty to the group. "David Shannon. Tom Blessing has sent him to join our little company."

Tanner shook Rusty's hand. "Welcome, David."

"Call me Rusty."

"Hope you brought money enough to run us awhile, Rusty, because pay don't come often around here and don't amount to much when it does."

Rusty had only four dollars but saw no reason to admit to poverty. Many in this group had a ragged appearance, which indicated they could not show even that much.

Tanner pointed at Chapultepec. "Worst come to worst, we can always eat the mule."

Somebody shouted, "Ain't that cannibalism, Tanner, eatin' your own kind?"

Rusty decided he was going to like this bunch.

• 9 •

Before they reached the tent camp, two men passed them, racing horses at breakneck speed across the open prairie and shouting in glee. It looked like fun to Rusty, but Burmeister frowned. "They have not enough to do when they do not ride the line. They will break a horse's leg one day, or a man's neck. But I cannot forbid them. Two months' pay they are owed."

The camp crowded against a clump of timber a short distance from Fort Belknap. The military post that had lent the small settlement its name had been vacated by the army a few years earlier. Rusty suspected the rangers had been placed away from the town so they would be less exposed to urban temptations. However, lack of spending money accomplished that purpose. The state required each man to furnish his own horse and firearms, and it was to supply the other necessities. The spartan nature of the camp indicated to Rusty that the state's definition of *necessities* was poor and lean. Texas was rich only in ambition and spirit. Its leaders had nothing in their pockets except their hands, but they gave voice to extravagant dreams. Texas was a great *someday* land.

Burmeister watched Rusty remove the pack from Chapultepec. "I wish I could say the state will pay you for use of the mule. Promises I can give you. Money I cannot."

"Wasn't money that I came for."

"For what *did* you come?"

The primary reason was that Tom Blessing had told him to, but he doubted that was what Burmeister would want to hear. "Duty. Daddy Mike always preached that we owe it to our neighbors to serve wherever we can."

"A wise man, your father. I hope he taught you well in other things."

"He taught me to plow a straight furrow. He taught me to hit what I aim at."

"Did he teach you to know what you should aim at and what you should not?"

Rusty frowned. "I'm not sure what you mean."

"Never mind. When it is important, I think you will know."

Burmeister queried Rusty at length about the horse thieves he had encountered and jotted a few notes in a small book. Rusty doubted that he had told enough to be useful.

Burmeister frowned. "If you see some of them again, it would surprise me none. There are in this vicinity those who have little regard for property other than their own."

As the captain moved away, the lanky Tanner edged closer, observing Rusty's saddle and other accoutrements. Rusty thought about counting the freckles on the ranger's face but decided that would take until dark, even if Tanner held still.

Tanner said, "You ain't long off of the farm."

"How can you tell?"

"Your hands are set in the shape of a plow handle, and ain't nobody but a dry-dirt farmer would be ridin' a saddle as old as that."

Rusty felt defensive. "It keeps me on the horse."

"What you want to do is catch you a lawbreaker that's got a good saddle. Shoot him and confiscate the saddle as contraband. If a man is a sure-enough shot, he can put a good outfit together in almost no time atall."

Rusty was momentarily taken aback until a twinkle in Tanner's eyes told him the ranger was trying to run a sandy on a newcomer.

Tanner said, "That's how I got my saddle. Only it turned out he was innocent. The joke was on me."

"I'll bet you both got a laugh out of it."

Tanner grinned. "You've got to kill a high class of criminal to get ahead. Poor folks never carry anything worth confiscatin'." He pointed to a nearby tent, the canvas old and badly stained. Rusty suspected it leaked like fishing net, should rain ever chance to fall.

Tanner offered, "I'll help you carry your stuff."

There was not much of it, but Rusty accepted the offer, grateful for the welcoming manner. "What all does the company do?"

"Mainly just patrol, watchin' for sign of Indians comin' into the country. Most of the time it's dull and tiresome. Now and then we get a little excitement, like today when we thought we was about to do battle with a bunch of Comanche horse thieves. That one flickered out like a candle in the wind. Most of them do."

"What about Captain Burmeister? You get along with him all right?"

"Dutch? Sure. Don't let his way of talkin' fool you. He can't help it if he don't talk good like me and you. He came from someplace over in Europe . . . Westphalia, he calls it. I don't know just where that is; I ain't been further than San Antonio myself. I just know that he was a soldier over there a long time ago, and he took French leave—snuck off and left them."

"I don't suppose he's ever snuck off and left this outfit."

"Never. A man smart as he is could be set real pretty by now if he'd put his mind to it. He's spent too much of his life volunteerin' and not enough takin' care of his own interests. Acts and thinks a little too much like a Yankee for some people's tastes, but he'd charge hell with a bucket of water. And most every man in this outfit would follow him into the fire."

Inside the tent Rusty saw several bedrolls spread on the

ground. Tanner pointed to an open spot. "There's your bed."

"My bed?"

"You wasn't lookin' for a cot, was you? This ain't exactly the Menger Hotel. The rangers get bed and board from the state. It gives them ground to roll out their bed, and it lets them eat all the game they can shoot for theirselves."

"Mighty generous."

"Ain't as bad as it sounds. We get a payday now and again when the politicians in Austin don't spend it all first. Ain't much to waste it on anyway . . . bad whiskey, slow horses, loose women ugly as mud."

"But you're makin' it a better country to live in."

"Ask your Tonkawa friends about that. The way we've treated them, they might not agree."

Two rangers came riding in from patrol, one carrying a deer carcass tied behind his saddle. Tanner hailed them. "Looks like fresh venison again tonight. I'd give a month's pay for a bait of good salt pork."

Rusty had left some hanging in the smokehouse back home. The Gaskin family had probably sneaked over and stolen it all by now.

Tanner introduced him to Jim and Johnny Morris, brothers who had brought in the deer. They had the same ragged appearance as Tanner, though Jim wore a new buckskin shirt that seemed out of place with his frayed and patched woolen trousers. Tanner raked charred bits of wood from a shallow pit and coaxed a few sparks into blazing life amid a small pile of shavings.

He hung a coffeepot from a steel bar over the fire and melted deer fat in a skillet, preparatory to frying the meat. "I'm no more than a fair to middlin' shot, but I'm a pretty decent cook when I've got somethin' to work with."

Jim Morris commented, "He fixes a pretty fair possum."

Not all the rangers Rusty had seen around camp were as lank as Tanner, but none ran much to fat. He could easily see why.

As they finished the fried venison, Captain Burmeister walked over from his tent. He carried a notebook and pencil.

"I must have information for Austin so you will be paid. Perhaps."

He ran his finger down a short list of questions, beginning with name and birth date. Rusty explained that he did not know his birth date or even his birth name, reminding Burmeister that he had been picked up on the battlefield at Plum Creek.

Burmeister said, "It makes no difference. A few men in this company know their true name but use another. I am at peace with it. Now I must ask—"

Tanner interrupted. "Pardon, Dutch, but look what's comin'."

Rusty turned as he heard horses approaching camp. Burmeister squinted, then uttered a few words of German that by their tone suggested profanity. Rusty quick-counted ten horsemen. He knew the man at the center and thought he recognized a couple of others.

"Caleb Dawkins," he said.

Burmeister gave Rusty a surprised look. "You know the colonel?"

"Met him. He spoiled a good supper a few nights ago."

"For me he has spoiled several. But he is a citizen. We must show respect." Burmeister walked out to receive Dawkins. His voice was edged with irony. "To what, Colonel, owe we this pleasure?"

"It's no pleasure for me, Burmeister. I have with me my son and several other men who just lost a large number of horses to raiding Indians. They barely escaped with their lives."

Rusty was certain now. At least one of the riders had been with Dawkins when he had threatened Lon Monahan. He turned his attention to two more who moved up almost even with the colonel. They had been among the thieves who had stolen horses from the Tonkawas. One was the young man called Pete, who had urged the point rider to kill Rusty and move on. The other was the point rider himself, who could have shot Rusty but chose not to. The point rider's eyes met Rusty's and locked on them. Recognition was immediate, and so was sudden fear. The young thief surreptitiously shook his head, silently pleading that Rusty not give him away.

Burmeister said, "We saw but one band. They were Tonkawas with federal escort. They had just recovered horses stolen by white renegades."

Rusty studied Dawkins, wondering if the colonel knew the truth or if the thieves had duped him. Nothing in the man's expression gave a solid indication either way.

Dawkins said, "Did you have anything more than their word that the horses they took had been stolen?"

"The word of a federal officer."

"Federal officer!" Dawkins spoke the words like a curse. "I had rather trust a gypsy horse trader." He turned to the young man beside him, the one called Pete. "That wouldn't be the same Indians you told me about, would it, son?"

The reply was so quick it overlapped the question. "No sir, Papa, the ones that chased us was sure as hell Comanches. And the horses they took was mine, bought and paid for over east. We wouldn't lie to you."

The young point rider looked again at Rusty, silently begging. The one called Pete carefully avoided Rusty's gaze. That he had recognized Rusty was almost certain.

Dawkins said firmly, "I assume you intend to pursue the matter, Burmeister?"

"Patrols are out. They will find the trail if one there is, and we will pursue. Tell me where it happened."

Pete proceeded to offer an ambitious lie. He placed the raid well to the east of the point where Rusty had encountered first the outlaws, then the Tonkawas. He was vague and uncertain when Burmeister asked him to describe the horses, their number and their brands. His excuse was that he had just recently bought them from a number of farmers and had not yet had time to become familiar with the individual animals.

The ranger had to maintain appearances, though the sarcasm in his questions made it clear that he saw through the hoax. He said, "Whoever took the horses, they are by now across the river. There it is forbidden for my men to go. Your friends can go to the federal officers and make a complaint."

Rusty knew that was a polite way of closing the matter, for going to federal authorities was the last thing either Dawkins or the horse thieves would want to do.

Dawkins seemed vindicated by the rejection. "I told my son you would give him no satisfaction. You so-called lawmen helped the federals protect Washington's pets while they were on the Brazos reserve, and you have no stomach for facing them now."

Burmeister's ire began to rise. "Always the rangers are in the middle. The settlers said it was the Indians we protected. The federals said we were with the settlers against the Indians. You are free to complain to Austin or to the federal authorities. I stand not in your way."

"I will not talk to any federals, and I can see I'm wasting my time talking to you. You're a foreigner anyhow."

"How long is it you have been in Texas, Colonel Dawkins?"

"Twelve years. I'm proud to say I came from Mississippi."

"More than twenty years I have been here. So who is the foreigner?"

"At least I can speak proper English. There'll be changes after the election. When Texas is free of the Yankee yoke, you and your whole damned command will have questions to answer. I suspect it is infested with unionists."

Burmeister took an angry step toward Dawkins, then stopped, his feet planted apart in a challenging stance. "We have no more to say, Colonel. You are free to go."

"Hell yes, I'm free, and I intend to stay that way. I don't have to ask your permission to come or to go. But you'll wish you'd never seen me."

"That is my wish already."

Dawkins made a point of being slow to turn away, as if allowing the full weight of his disdain to settle upon Burmeister and the men around him. Pete remained beside him, and the young point rider was quick to follow, as if afraid Rusty might be about to turn the rangers loose on him.

Rusty wondered why he hadn't. It would have been easy to have pointed a finger. His hunch was that Dawkins did not know what his son had been up to. It would have shut him up in a hurry if Rusty had told. But Rusty had been dissuaded by the desperation in the young point rider's eyes. He remembered that the thief could easily have killed him but had not.

We're even now, he thought. *Next time I catch you in the wrong, I don't owe you a thing.*

Tanner stood slouched and looking like a scarecrow with hands in his pockets, his ragged buckskin jacket open and flapping in the wind. He said, "That Dawkins is a peculiar son of a bitch, ain't he?"

When the riders had pulled away, Burmeister faced Rusty. "I believe among those men were the very thieves the Tonkawas chased. Did you not recognize them?"

Rusty did not want to lie, but neither did he want to betray the point rider. "I never saw most of them very close. I didn't care to accuse somebody and turn out to be wrong."

"Next time, accuse. If a man is innocent, we can turn him loose. If he is guilty . . ." He left it at that.

If Rusty had hoped distance would lessen the pain of Mike Shannon's death, his first night in the ranger camp proved the hope to be futile. Long before dawn he awakened out of a violent dream in which he saw Daddy Mike lying dead beside the woodpile. Standing over him was a drunken, laughing Isaac York, a smoking rifle in his hand. Though in his dream Rusty held a pistol, he was unable to raise it. His arm hung stiff and useless at his side. Crying in frustration, he struggled but was unable to move. Isaac York drifted away like a wisp of smoke stolen by the wind. The opportunity to kill him was gone.

The rest of the night Rusty lay with his eyes open, listening to the snoring of fellow rangers. Moonlight filtered through the thin canvas so that he could see the forms of the others sleeping on the ground. He turned onto his right side, then his left, his stomach and his back, trying in vain to be comfortable. The ground was hard and unyielding. After a long time he began hearing a rooster crow somewhere in the distance. He turned back his blanket and found his hat, then his trousers. He had slept in his shirt because his shoulders were cold. He pulled on his boots after shaking them to be certain no unwelcome tiny visitor had crawled into them during the night.

Tanner sat up and stretched, yawning and blinking his eyes. "I ain't heard the call yet."

"Me neither, except for a rooster. Go back to sleep."

"Too late now. You've done woke me up." Tanner had stripped down to long underwear. He hobbled to the front of the tent and peered through the flap. His thin legs reminded Rusty of a spider. "It'll be daylight directly anyhow. You want to start the coffee?"

"Just as well. I've got nothin' better to do."

"We'll be headin' out to ride the line this mornin'. I hope you've rested enough to make a long sashay."

"I wasn't sent here to rest."

"What *was* you sent here for? You kill somebody or somethin'?"

"I was sent here so I *wouldn't*."

Tanner's jaw dropped. "You want to tell me?"

"It's not somethin' I like to talk about." He thought about it, though, whenever his mind was not occupied with the urgencies of the moment.

Tanner sat on his bedroll and tugged at his bootstraps until his feet found bottom. "You'll not likely kill anybody up here unless it's Indians, and probably not even them. I'll bet I've been up and down that line a hundred times, and damned few trips did I see as much as a feather."

"That's all right with me. I've got no grudge against any of them except maybe the Comanches."

"I heard what you told Captain Burmeister about them stealin' you when you was little. You'd be a Comanche yourself today if somebody hadn't rescued you. A redheaded Comanche. Now wouldn't that be a sight to behold?"

Burmeister's long-ago service as a soldier made him try to maintain some semblance of military order in the ranger company, though Rusty quickly saw that the men did not consider themselves soldiers. They submitted to morning formation and roll call, but their notion of standing at attention was decidedly informal. Some chewed and spat tobacco. A couple smoked black and odorous cigars. Company sergeant Whitfield, chunkily built but muscular as a blacksmith, impatiently read the roll as if he considered it a waste of time better spent on more fruitful activity. Some of the men talked among themselves or looked at the sky as if appraising the chance for rain or snow. The roll call was indeed unnecessary except as a faint stab at military routine because the sergeant and the captain both knew who was here and who was out on the line.

The sergeant said, "All present and accounted for except one, Dutch." He frowned as if he had bitten into a sour apple. "Private Haskins is absent without leave again. But I already told you that." Whitfield's tobacco-stained moustache, heavy and unkempt, lifted and fell with each word he spoke. It was in sharp contrast to the captain's moustache, neatly trimmed, its ends upturned.

Burmeister shrugged. "How long must it be before he learns he cannot dry up Fort Belknap? Always, freight wagons bring fresh whiskey. And where does he get the money to buy?"

"There's people in town who buy it for him. I think they get him drunk so he'll tell them what we're doin' out here and what we're fixin' to do. There's many that don't want rangers interferin' in their business."

"Detail someone to bring him. Handcuff him to a tree until the whiskey has gone from him."

"Was it left to me, I'd give him a lick or two with a quirt and send him packin'."

"Sober, he is a good man."

"Drunk, he's useless to himself and to this company. But you're the captain, Dutch. If you want to keep him on the payroll, that's your business."

"On the payroll? I think you make the joke. How long is it since we have been paid?"

"Money is one thing I don't joke about. I've never had enough that it ever got funny."

Burmeister's gaze sought out Rusty. "Haskins was to be

on patrol today. David Shannon, you will take his place."

Rusty was not certain of the proper response, so he made an effort at a salute. He said, "You bet."

Burmeister winced.

Rusty whispered to Tanner, "Did I do somethin' wrong?"

"I think you're supposed to say, 'You bet, *sir.*' "

The patrol moved northward toward the Red River. At first Alamo looked back, wanting to travel southward toward home. But after a half mile or so he reconciled with reality and plodded along, keeping good pace with the other horses. Rusty studied the riders around him. They had little of a military look about them. Their clothing was a rainbow of colors and a random mix of homespun cotton, wool, and buckskin, most of it showing the effects of rough use.

He remembered what Tom Blessing had called the volunteer patrols along the frontier: the buckskin line.

Tanner asked Rusty, "You any good at followin' tracks?"

"I've trailed deer. Followed a wolf one time for two miles 'til I found its den."

"This ought not to be too tough, then. We'll be watchin' for horse tracks that don't belong."

"How do you know which ones don't belong?"

"When the hair raises up on the back of your neck."

Sergeant Whitfield was in charge of the patrol. He seemed a man not given to smiling easily, for Rusty had seen no sign of levity about him. Nor did he have much to say beyond the orders necessary to get the patrol under way. Despite his considerable size, Whitfield seemed to sit easy in the saddle. He set the pace, an easy trot the horses could maintain for long stretches of time.

Rusty soon saw that the sergeant had a way of watching the ground without missing anything that happened around him. Once, seeing distant dark objects that aroused his suspicion, he detailed Rusty and Tanner to ride out and investigate. "Don't get too close 'til you're sure it's not Indians. I don't want to explain to the captain why I let a couple of chuckleheaded boys get themselves killed."

Tanner assured him, "I've already laid out my plans for the day, and gettin' killed ain't on the list." He made a half-hearted attempt to laugh but dropped it when he received no response from Whitfield. The sergeant was all business.

Rusty noted that though Tanner seemed on the surface to shrug off the notion of danger, he was cautious in his approach to the dark specks Whitfield had seen in the tall grass. Tanner carried his rifle across the pommel of his saddle, his right hand nervously rubbing the wooden stock.

Two buffalo bulls jumped up, snorted, and loped away in an awkward rocking gait, grumbling at the disturbance. Relieved, Tanner expelled a long breath. Rusty realized he had been holding it.

Tanner said, "At least it'll give the sergeant somethin' to write in his report. 'Jumped two buffalo. Found no Indians.' "

"The day's a long way from done. How do you know we won't find any Indians?"

"If there'd been any around, they'd've already killed them two bulls for meat."

Tanner's professed confidence did not lessen Rusty's watchfulness. He found himself looking to the horizon more than to the ground where any horse tracks might be. But he reasoned that sergeant Whitfield was watchful enough for both of them.

They camped on the south bank of the Red River. Whitfield detailed Tanner to make bread and Rusty to brew the coffee. Rusty dipped the pot into the river to fill it. Somehow the water looked a bit less muddy in the pot than it did out in the channel, though it still retained some of the red clay color.

Tanner saw Rusty's uncertainty. "A little mud makes for stronger coffee. They say our bodies are made of clay anyhow. But if it bothers you, grow yourself a moustache like the sergeant's. Then you can strain your coffee."

Whitfield had started a fire. Rusty hung the pot on a short steel bar and looked at Tanner. "Did you ever have a serious thought in your life?"

"Sure. I've tried cryin' and I've tried laughin'. I like laughin' better."

Sergeant Whitfield looked reproachfully at Tanner. "I want to hear you laugh someday when the Comanches swarm down on us like a bunch of hornets."

Tanner turned to kneading dough, which had a faint reddish tinge from the river water he mixed with the flour. "You'll be way too busy to listen to me."

The meager supper of bread and salt pork and coffee left Rusty wondering how much Red River mud he had ingested and whether it might leave any lasting damage to his digestive system. He had been too hungry to notice if it had any distinctive flavor.

Sergeant Whitfield beckoned him a little distance away from the rest of the men. Whitfield seemed reluctant to broach his subject. "Ordinarily, I don't ask a man about his politics. Who he votes for is his own business. But you know the people of Texas are votin' right now as to whether or not they want to stay in the union."

"So I've been told."

"We won't get a chance to vote out here, but just the same, we'll be in the stew when the pot comes to a boil. You heard Colonel Dawkins. He's just one of a great many that's ready to breathe fire and brimstone after the vote is counted. It's goin' to be almighty important where every man stands."

"My daddy was strong for stayin' in the union. A lot of good friends are for pullin' out. If I could vote, I don't know which way I'd swing."

"I don't know if you'll be able to sit on the fence. They're apt to tear it down, and you'll be forced to take a stand."

"Then I'll stand with Texas. Not the union, not the confederacy, but Texas."

Whitfield's mouth was grim. "That suits me, but there's lots of people it won't. You may be in for hell."

Rusty thought back to the pursuit of the Comanches, to the finding of the butchered woman. He thought back to the murder of Daddy Mike. He said, "I've already had a taste of hell."

*   *   *

Good news travels afoot. Bad news rides a fast horse. The election results were quick to reach the frontier, and they held no surprises. By a strong majority, Texas voters had supported secession. The report brought cheers in Fort Belknap but found a mixed reception in the ranger camp. Though a rumor had spread quickly among the men, Captain Burmeister called them into formation to make the announcement official.

His face was solemn, his voice so subdued that Rusty could barely hear it. "Men, the news is come. The vote was as we have thought, for secession. Very soon the Texas legislature will meet. No longer will we stand under the flag of the United States."

The men waited in silence, contemplating their individual futures, until Tanner asked, "If we ain't Americans anymore, what are we?"

Burmeister stared at the ground. Rusty thought he saw tears in the captain's eyes. "That, you must each decide. Almost thirty years now, I have been an American. An American I will remain."

He turned and walked back to his tent without dismissing the formation. Sergeant Whitfield gravely watched him go. "All right," he said finally, "dismissed."

The following morning Burmeister called the company into formation and turned the command over to Whitfield. "Until they send someone, you will be in charge. Perhaps they will send no one. Then the company is yours if you want it."

Uncertainty creased Whitfield's face. His heavy moustache seemed to droop. "The whole country's fixin' to turn upside down. They may not want any rangers at all. Where'll you go, Dutch?"

"Across the river. I will offer myself to the federal army. If they do not want me . . . perhaps to Colorado. Texas under a different flag cannot be my home."

"It won't be the same without you."

"With or without me, it will not be the same again." Burmeister shook Whitfield's hand, then turned to the men who stood in loose formation. "May God be with us all."

Rusty felt a catch in his throat. He had not been here long enough to know the captain beyond a modest surface acquaintance, yet in a strange way he felt he had known him always. He lent his voice to those of the men, who all shouted their individual good-byes.

As Burmeister rode away, leading a pack mule, Rusty heard a man behind him say, "The captain was a foreigner when he came here, and he was still a foreigner when he left. He never was a real Texan."

Angrily Whitfield turned on him. "He's a hell of a good man, and as good a Texan as you'll ever see. I'll not have you or anybody else speak ill of him."

The man's voice indicated no backing down. "What about you, Whitfield? You for the union or the Confederacy?"

Whitfield looked at Rusty before he answered. "I stand with Texas."

PART
III.

· 10 ·

Buffalo Caller had left his horse and the rest of his raiding party in the cover of timber while he walked to the edge of the muddy river for a careful look at the other side. To his right, the sun had descended almost to the horizon and was reflected in brilliant colors against a few flat clouds barren of rain. It had been a dry summer and fall. The horses had not fattened as he would have liked for the journey, but a full moon was near. If the enterprise was to be undertaken at all, it must be done now. Shorter days promised that winter's bitter breath would soon blow across the land. No Comanche liked to travel when snow lay heavy on the ground and ice crusted the edges of every stream. That was a time to hover near the lodge center's fire and recount the glory deeds of olden days.

Buffalo Caller paused at the edge of the brush that lined the upper bank. His gaze searched the far side. He had no reason to fear the bluecoat soldiers, for most had gone away to fight a white man's war somewhere to the east. He knew that on the Texas side of the river, the bluecoats were regarded as an enemy just as the Comanches themselves were.

He did not understand why white men had gone to war against one another, but the reasons were of no importance. What mattered was that the teibos were distracted by their own fight. Many white men had left the Texas settlements to join the war, leaving the countryside thinly defended. It had become easier for raiding parties to reenter their old hunting grounds and escape with whatever spoils they were able to garner along the way. Many settler families had abandoned homes on the leading edge of the frontier, retreating eastward to the relative safety of the older settlements. Others had gathered into makeshift forts for mutual protection, venturing out only in numbers sufficient for a meaningful defense.

Buffalo Caller hoped the white men's war would go on forever. Perhaps the People might regain the lost portions of Comanchería. It was theirs by the sacred right of conquest. They had won it the honorable way, in war, wresting it from the hated Apaches and other claimants. They had not stolen it piecemeal like the white man, but boldly and swiftly at a high cost in blood. They had held it with lance, arrow, and club until the Americans had come swarming in, numerous as the ants and greedy as the fat hogs they brought with them.

He watched until the sun disappeared beyond the source of the broad, shallow river, for they would wait until darkness before crossing. Not once did he see any sign of white men. Lacking the bluecoat soldiers anymore, the Texans had only scattered roving groups belonging to a warrior society known as rangers. They could be ferocious when encountered, but with help from benevolent guardian spirits a raiding party could usually go around them. Buffalo Caller had always been careful to observe the requirements of his spirits and avoid their displeasure. Rarely had his medicine proven weak.

When darkness had swallowed the shadows and before the moon rose to magnify its brilliance in the water, he decided it was time to cross over. He felt no need to voice orders, for the People's way was fully democratic. It was each warrior's right either to follow the leader or to head off in his own direction. Buffalo Caller had never lacked for warriors eager to accompany him, however. Seldom did one of his raids fail to reward them with horses, and more often than not, their victories yielded a few scalps as well. It was always good to make the white men bleed for their perfidy.

He grasped his pony's mane and pulled himself up onto its back. Of late he had become aware that his knees no longer had the spring he remembered from his youth. Exertion that never used to bother him would set his heart to pounding. But though the body had slowed and gray was invading his once-black hair, the mind had gained in wisdom. Among the People, age was accorded respect. Lessons taught by experience offset the weight of years. He paused at the riverbank to take a final look, then put the pony into the water. He did not have to look back to know that his warriors followed. He could hear their horses splashing.

They were good men—young, of course, except for his friend Broken Leg, who was perhaps becoming too old for the kind of fast travel that would be expected of him the next few days and nights. Buffalo Caller had been hesitant about allowing him to come along, but Broken Leg had pointed out that they were the same age, born the same winter in a tribal encampment sheltered by high walls of the caprock. Buffalo Caller had reluctantly accepted him, though he feared his friend might handicap the party in an emergency. He hoped some young warrior would not die because of the old one.

Especially his own son Jackrabbit, still unseasoned but eager to learn. Whippoorwill had finally presented him with a son after he had given up on his wives having anything but daughters. This was to be Jackrabbit's first major raid.

They traveled rapidly once they had put the river behind them. At one point they saw a distant campfire, and some of the young men wanted to investigate. Buffalo Caller dissuaded them. The fire might belong to a few hunters, and a hunter camp was unlikely to yield as many horses as could be expected deeper in the white men's country. Or it might belong to the Texan warrior society, in which case an attack would only stir up an unnecessary fight and gain few, if any, horses. The rangers seldom took with them more than one mount per man, and they did not easily give them up.

He knew the way well, for he had hunted buffalo all over this region south of the Clay-Colored River in the time before the white men had come to dominance. He took precautions to travel as much as possible on hard ground where tracks would not be obvious, though there was no way to avoid them altogether. When the riders came to a narrow stream that flowed in the general direction he wanted to travel, he had them put their horses into it and avoid the muddy banks, which would preserve sign of their passage. They rode until sunrise, then pulled out onto a gravel bed and took shelter in a heavy stand of scrub oak.

Buffalo Caller was well aware of the minutemen patrols that watched for raiding parties' tracks. He wished for rain that would wash away all sign, but for a long time now, the skies had yielded no moisture. The winds were dry. Given time enough, wind could destroy tracks, too. If he could not have rain, then he hoped the spirits would give him wind. It might blow dust into the eyes of the rangers so they would not see what lay at their horses' feet.

He looked critically at Broken Leg, asking how his friend was enduring the ride though he knew Broken Leg would not admit it if he were dying of pain. "Ask the young men how *they* are doing," Broken Leg replied. "I have been on many long rides before."

Too many, Buffalo Caller thought. "If you become too tired, turn back. There is no need for you to hurt yourself."

He gave men and horses a few hours to rest, then mounted and reentered the stream that would swallow their tracks. He and the others were stripped for war, traveling light so they could move swiftly when the time came. They counted on their ability to endure hunger and live off the land. They could feast when they returned home with the prizes of war.

Buffalo Caller rode far out in the lead, where he could detect any hazards before the others were exposed. He knew the risk of traveling by day, but the party could not spare the time to move only at night. They needed the visibility of a full moon for the horse-stealing phase of the trip, and it would be gone if they tarried too long on the way.

They held up once and dismounted to make themselves less conspicuous when Buffalo Caller spotted two wagons moving in a northerly direction, directly in their path. The young warriors coveted the horses that pulled the wagons, but he pointed out again that larger rewards awaited them if they would be patient and not reveal their presence too early. Once they struck, the countryside would be alerted and their only recourse would be a fast retreat with whatever booty they had managed to take.

Their third night brought them to a valley where Buffalo Caller remembered that white farmers had plowed up much of the grass to grow corn and cotton and feed for their many horses. "This is the place," he said. "We will go to the end, then come back up the valley and gather all the horses and mules we can find."

Broken Leg had lagged much of the day, catching up only at nightfall when the others slowed their pace. He slumped on his horse, plainly tired but admitting nothing. "I remember this valley. Here we killed many buffalo."

"A long time ago," Buffalo Caller said. "Now there are no buffalo, only spotted cattle." Perhaps if the white men's war continued long enough, the teibos would kill off one another and the buffalo would return. He had eaten flesh of cattle but found it not so strong or so rich with flavor as that of the buffalo. To his taste, even mule meat was better.

He looked up. The moon was in its brightest phase. They would need all of its light to see by as they swept the farms clean of their riding and draft stock.

Past the last farm, where the valley flattened out into a long and gentle downward slope toward a distant river, he halted and reined his pony around. "Let us gather horses." The warriors spread out in an irregular line and started back in the direction they had come. In a short time they were pushing ahead of them more horses and mules than he could count on his fingers four times over, and much of the valley still lay ahead.

This, he thought, was going to be one of the greatest raids of his life. He put aside the pain which had invaded his joints. Exhilaration overwhelmed any feeling of fatigue. He looked for his son and was pleased to see Jackrabbit riding ahead of the other young men. His gaze sought out Broken Leg, who appeared as invigorated as Buffalo Caller felt. Perhaps it was right after all that he had brought his friend.

They came to a farm where half a dozen horses and mules stood inside a closed pen. When one of the young men tried to open the gate, a rifle blasted, and for a second or two the burning of gunpowder lighted an open area between two sections of a cabin. Yelping like coyotes, two of the young men rushed the rifleman and struck him down before he had time to reload. They burst through a door. Buffalo Caller heard a woman scream in fear, then cry out again in agony. The cry was cut short.

Buffalo Caller rushed to the cabin and pushed through the door in time to see Jackrabbit dragging live coals out of a fireplace and spreading them across the rough wood floor. Buffalo Caller quickly raked the coals back onto the hearth. "White men farther up the valley might see the fire. They would know we are coming."

"I did not consider such a thing, Father," the young warrior said ruefully.

"You must learn to think, or you will not live to be an elder."

On the dog run, the other warrior was taking the fallen rifleman's scalp. He held it up for Buffalo Caller to see, along with the longer hair of the woman.

"She was with child," the warrior said. "So we have killed three."

Buffalo Caller was more interested in the fact that the echo of the rifle shot might have carried a long way up the valley. "You will have time later to show off your scalps. We are losing too much of the night."

Looking back, he almost wished he had let his son burn the cabin. He would like to burn all the cabins and leave no trace that white men had ever come. They were, to him, a curse upon a land once pure and fruitful, now despoiled by plows and cattle and hogs.

By daylight the warriors passed over a hill that marked

the upper end of the valley. In front of them, strung out over a considerable distance, trotted a large band of horses and mules. Buffalo Caller tried to count them by fours but gave up after two attempts brought him two different answers. They were enough. Now the challenge would be to get them out of the country without being stopped by the white men's warriors.

He asked Broken Leg, "Are you all right?"

Broken Leg beamed with delight. "I am a young man again."

"Good, for we have two long days' ride ahead of us before we reach the river. Even the young men will be feeling old."

He was aware of pursuit, though it was tentative and did not press hard. He saw two horsemen trailing a comfortable distance behind. It would be folly for two men to attack the raiders, but they could hang back and keep the horse herd in sight, hoping for reinforcement somewhere ahead. He tried to ignore them, but after half a day they irritated him like an itch he could not scratch away.

He picked two of the young men he judged to be the most seasoned and told Broken Leg, "Keep the horses moving. We will catch up when we have swatted the gnats behind us."

He led his two warriors out into a thicket and motioned for them to dismount. They squatted on their moccasined heels to wait. Patience was drilled into potential hunters and warriors from the time they were boys. It was as much a part of their training as learning accuracy with the bow, for often they were forced to lie in wait for hours until game approached close enough to kill.

The two white riders passed the thicket. They were too intent upon the heavily marked trail to see the three men, even had the warriors not been so well hidden. One of the young men arose, and Buffalo Caller motioned for him to crouch again. "We will wait until they are well past, then we will come up behind them."

The surprise was swift and complete. The white men were unaware of danger until the three Comanches were within easy arrow range. By then it was too late even to bring a

rifle into play. They fell, and the two younger men had a
scalp apiece to show off when they returned in triumph to
the larger group.

Buffalo Caller gave the two bodies but a quick glance, for
white men were of little interest to him once they were dead.
The young warriors tied the fresh scalps to their horses'
manes and took the reins of the two mounts they had just
acquired. They led them into a trot, then into a lope as Buffalo Caller set the pace. They were a long while in catching
up to the rest. He slipped the bridles from the horses' heads
so the animals would not trip on the reins. He tied the bridles
to the saddles, which he left in place. He did not like white-
man saddles himself, but probably he could trade them to
someone who did.

They were within half a day of the river when a group of
horsemen appeared without warning over a low hill and
fanned out in challenge. Buffalo Caller had begun to hope
he and his party would escape unscathed, but he saw that it
was not to be. He stopped and counted the horsemen, who
were as yet far beyond arrow range. They might simply be
aroused citizens, who sometimes fought bravely but usually
not well. On the other hand they might be rangers, better
organized and savage in a fight, tenacious as hungry wolves.

Several of the young warriors gathered around him, eager
for combat. Buffalo Caller counted the white men a second
time and knew they fell well short of the Comanches in number. He pointed to several of the warriors, including his son,
and told them to put the horse herd into a run. "The rest of
us will stay behind and hold back the Texans."

The young men protested. They all wanted to participate
in the battle. Buffalo Caller reasoned, "We have traveled far
and endured much for these horses. Do you want to lose
them now?"

The young men quarreled over who should stay with the
horses and who should seek the glory of killing more Texans.
Buffalo Caller saw that his arguments were useless. There
would always be more horses. One sought battle honors
wherever the opportunity presented itself. He took a long
look at the herd, which was becoming more strung out and

more scattered as it pulled away from the quarreling warriors.

He could understand the young men's wish for glory. He had known it himself when he was their age. Now he had gained glory enough over the years, and he had a high appreciation for the value of horses.

Reluctantly he said, "Let us make a quick fight of it, then, so we do not lose everything we came for."

The young men yelped and shouted and charged wildly toward the Texans. Buffalo Caller thought he saw confusion in the ranks of the whites. He hoped they would scatter and run. If they did, the fight would degenerate into a race, and death would come swiftly for those whites who rode slow horses.

To his dismay, the white men stepped down from their saddles, dropped to their knees, and aimed their rifles at the warriors who bore down upon them. A quick rattle of gunfire left two horses riderless and a third horse down. Buffalo Caller saw Jackrabbit still astride and was thankful he was not one of the fallen.

He hoped the warriors could overwhelm the Texans while they paused to reload their rifles, but it quickly became evident that some had held their fire to avoid such a calamity. They spaced their shots so their line would not have all its rifles empty at one time. Buffalo Caller felt sure then that these were rangers.

The Comanche charge broke up, the warriors reeling back uncertainly. The rangers immediately remounted their horses and made a charge of their own.

A ranger spurred straight toward him, rifle in his hands. Buffalo Caller strung an arrow in his bow. The ranger's hat blew off, and Buffalo Caller was startled to see that his hair was red. Old dreams, long pushed aside but never forgotten, flashed in his mind like a flare of gunpowder. Even as he released the string and let the arrow fly, he knew it would miss.

The ranger fired the rifle, but the motion of his horse spoiled his aim. Buffalo Caller heard and felt the impact of the bullet striking his pony in the chest. Before he could jump free, he was slammed against the ground. The crushing weight of the pony rolled over him, pressing him hard into the dirt. He tried to crawl free, but his leg was pinned.

He grasped desperately for the bow that had fallen in front of him. He clawed at the ground but could not quite reach the bow. He strained to pull himself forward. His heart pounded hard as he tried again to reach the bow and failed though he stretched every muscle in the effort. He felt that his medicine had soured. Helpless, he steeled himself to receive the bullet that would kill him.

The ranger's black horse was wild-eyed, nostrils flaring in excitement. In the saddle, the ranger seemed to tower above Buffalo Caller like the high walls of the People's winter encampment. Numb, suddenly cold, Buffalo Caller saw that the man was young, like the warriors in the raiding party. The black horse danced nervously, threatening to run away. The ranger drew a pistol from its holster and tried to bring the horse under control.

Buffalo Caller spoke to his spirits, asking them to be ready to receive him, for the ranger was too close. He could not miss.

He heard a shout. Broken Leg galloped up, bow in his hand, an arrow fitted against the string. The ranger whirled and hastily fired his pistol. Broken Leg's arrow drove into the young Texan's leg. With a cry of pain, the ranger dropped his rifle and bent over in the saddle, losing his hold on the reins. His horse broke into a run, away from the fight.

Instantly Broken Leg was on the ground. He tugged at the pony's rein but received no response. The horse was dead. He pushed against the body until Buffalo Caller was able to pull his leg free.

"Quickly!" Broken Leg said. "Up behind me before more Texans come."

Buffalo Caller hopped, for the leg felt numb and threatened to crumple beneath him. He retrieved his bow and shield from the ground as well as the rifle the ranger had dropped. Broken Leg jumped onto his horse's back, then leaned down, arm extended, helping Buffalo Caller up behind him. Looking back over his shoulder, Buffalo Caller could see that the rangers and the warriors had become scattered over a broad area. Firing was sporadic. The fight was winding down to a draw, neither side a clear winner.

It was just as well. The stolen horses were badly scattered too, but as the warriors regrouped they could probably recover a substantial number. The young men had had the taste of battle they had wanted, so they would be content despite losing some of their horses.

Buffalo Caller was relieved to see no sign of pursuit. Several warriors had broken away from the engagement and were coming up behind. Jackrabbit was among them. The rest would probably be on their way shortly as they extricated themselves.

He asked Broken Leg, "The ranger you wounded . . . did you see his hair?"

"For a moment. I thought I would have his scalp, but I only wounded him. It was more important that I rescue you."

"His hair was red."

"That I saw. I thought it was colored with clay."

"I have had bad dreams about a red-hair. He spoiled my medicine. He would have killed me had you not come."

"Perhaps it was your medicine that brought me."

Buffalo Caller had not considered it in that light. "Perhaps. I am glad you persuaded me to let you come, old friend. But for you, I would be with my grandfathers."

Broken Leg agreed. He would make much of it when they returned to the main camp and the boasting began. Buffalo Caller could not begrudge him the glory.

Broken Leg said, "My medicine was good today."

Buffalo Caller shuddered, the dreams heavy on his mind. "If ever I see a red-hair again, I hope you will be with me. His medicine is stronger than mine."

Rusty Shannon almost despaired of stopping the runaway horse. The heavy firing had frightened Alamo into a blind panic. Each stride brought excruciating pain, seeming to drive the arrow deeper into Rusty's leg. It had glanced off the bone. Blood flowed freely, warm and gummy to his fingers as he awkwardly holstered the pistol and grasped the shaft of the arrow. He struggled in vain, trying to pull it out.

The reins trailed on the ground, dropped along with the rifle when the arrow had struck. Reins could be a hazard. Looped, they could snag on a tree branch while a horse ran. If split, like these, a running horse could step on them, jerk his head down, and take a hard fall.

Through his pain, Rusty recognized that danger. He leaned forward, trying to grab a rein. Light-headed, he could not reach it without tumbling from the saddle. Yet he knew that at any moment Alamo could turn a somersault. Rusty stood a strong chance of being crushed beneath him.

He was aware of another horse closing from the left. He assumed the rider was a Comanche, come to finish him off. He felt helpless to defend himself, though he drew the pistol again. Blood on his hand made it feel sticky as syrup.

Tanner's shout relieved his fear. "Hold on, redhead. I'm comin'." Tanner pushed his horse up against Alamo and reached down, his bony hand grasping the reins. He dallied them around his saddle horn. "Got you." He slowly brought both horses to a stop. Alamo breathed hard, eyes rolling in the aftermath of fright. "Damn it, Rusty, you're bleedin' like a stuck shoat."

Blood had spread down Rusty's leg to the stirrup and the toe of his boot.

Tanner said, "I'll get you back to the rest of the bunch. Wouldn't want some stray Indians to catch us out here by ourselves and pick us off. Say, I'll bet that arrow hurts like hell."

Rusty's head seemed to spin. He was in some danger of falling from the saddle. He attempted three times before he managed to shove his pistol back into the holster. It tried to stick to his hand. "Damn right it hurts."

"We'll get it out soon's we can. Me and Captain Whitfield, we're pretty good at pocketknife surgery."

Pocketknife! The thought did not encourage confidence. But anything to lessen the pain.

Tanner said, "I seen you miss that Indian. You were so close, I don't understand how you kept from hittin' him."

"Alamo was faunchin' around too much." Rusty did not know how anyone could make a good shot from the back of a running horse.

"Maybe you've taken a case of buck fever. You ever shoot at anybody before?"

"Been tempted, but I ain't done it." Rusty hoped the interrogation would stop. He hurt too much to think straight.

"Captain'll want to know. Just tell him about the horse. You don't have to say nothin' about buck fever."

Rusty did not want to feel resentful of his friend, but he could not help it. "Did *you* kill any Indians?"

"Brought down a horse. Set an Indian afoot and it's almost as good as killin' him. Except he'll be back to shoot at you another day. But if it wasn't him it'd be another one. The world don't seem to run short of Indians."

It did not seem to run short of unnecessary conversation, either. Rusty tried to close his mind to Tanner's rambling. He realized Tanner was talking in an effort to bring his own excitement under control. "Yes, sir," Tanner said, "we scattered us some Comanches."

"But they're gettin' away. Looks like they've still got most of their horses." Rusty could see that much through eyes pinched with pain.

"Well, me and you can't be held responsible. We're just followin' orders. I don't hardly know who we're workin' for anyway, the state of Texas or the Confederate States of America. Ain't neither one paid us lately."

Since Texas had joined the Confederacy, its affairs had descended into confusion and controversy. State officials in Austin quarreled with national officials in Richmond over the financial responsibility for protecting the frontier. Most recently they wrangled over a new Confederate conscription law that threatened to strip the outlying settlements of the already deficient manpower needed for their defense. Texas officials resisted the law and as yet were refusing to enforce it in the western counties. Confederate authorities in Richmond saw Indians as a distant problem easily ignored while Yankee soldiers were pounding rifle butts against their doors.

Tanner led Alamo while Rusty gripped his saddle with

both hands. Shock was setting in. He felt himself in danger
of slipping to the ground. Tanner had to catch him and ease
him back into the saddle. The ranger never stopped talking.

"Hang on, pardner. I see some of the boys gatherin' just
ahead yonder. If you fall now you're apt to break that arrow
off, and we won't have enough left to grab ahold of."

Rusty tried to focus on the rangers ahead, but it was like
looking at them through a fog. He did not recognize the one
who rode out to meet him until the man spoke and he knew
the gruff voice to be Captain Whitfield's. The former sergeant had been promoted after August Burmeister's departure.

"Bring him over here under the tree, Tanner. We've got a
couple others to patch up, but at least we didn't get anybody
killed."

Rusty felt himself being lifted from the saddle. Though
the men tried to be gentle, there was no way to move him
without causing the arrow to cut deeper into the flesh. They
laid him on a blanket. With the point of a knife, Whitfield
ripped a long slit in the leg of Rusty's trousers. His hands
carefully explored around the shaft. "It's gone most of the
way through. I can feel the point stickin' out just a little on
the underside. If we try to pull back on it, the head is liable
to break loose and stay in there. Best thing is to shove it on
through."

Tanner's voice was uncertain. "That's liable to hurt a right
smart."

"But it'll be over with before he can holler. You-all hold
on to him."

Rusty cried out in agony as Whitfield's strong hands
pushed the shaft, and the arrow cut the rest of the way
through the leg. He must have fainted for a moment, because
when he became conscious again, he saw Tanner fingering
the blooded arrowhead.

Whitfield said, "Now to pull out the shaft. Hold him
again."

Rusty felt a sharp pain, then the ground dropped away
from under him. He was conscious of something being
poured into the wound and wondering how anything wet

could burn with such ferocity. Then there was a flash of fire, and consciousness left him altogether.

He had no sense of time, but he was aware that the sun was going down when he managed to open his eyes. He heard Tanner's voice. He seemed to have heard it all during the time he had been unconscious, but he supposed that was hallucination. He felt a hard throbbing in his leg and a sense of severe burning.

Tanner was saying, "About time you quit lazin' around and woke up to your responsibilities. You goin' to sleep your life away?"

Rusty looked down at his leg, wrapped with cloth. "What did you-all do, set me afire?"

"We cauterized that wound. Ain't but one way, and that's with hot steel." Tanner drew a bowie knife from a sheath on his belt, opposite the pistol he carried. "Heated this 'til it glowed red. Probably took all the temper out. It won't be much account from now on."

"I'll buy you another, if we ever get paid."

Tanner shrugged. "We're liable to be old and gray by then." He reached into his pocket. "Here's you a keepsake. You may want to use it for a watch fob." He handed Rusty an arrowhead. Rusty knew it was the one that had gone through his leg.

"I don't have a watch."

"Maybe you won't be a poor man all your life."

Captain Whitfield stood over Rusty, hands on his broad hips. "I hope you shot the Indian who put that arrow in you."

"I didn't hardly even see him. I was tryin' to shoot another one, but my horse kept dodgin'."

"I don't know that we killed any of them. We bloodied them a bit and got back a part of the horses they stole. The price was a little high, though. We've got two wounded besides you. Your leg is the worst."

The leg throbbed and burned as if a fire blazed inside it. Rusty felt as if it were about to fall off. He had a bad moment as he mulled over the thought of losing it. "How bad do you reckon it is?"

Whitfield's face creased. "Bad enough. We need to get you

someplace where people can take proper care of you."

Tanner suggested, "The Monahan farm is down yonder a ways. I'll bet they'd put him up."

Rusty asked, "Monahan? Is that Lon Monahan?"

Tanner nodded. "You know him?"

"Met him on my way up to Fort Belknap, is all. Can't say I know him real well."

"They're a hotbed of unionists, him and his family, but otherwise they're good folks."

Whitfield growled. "Look around you, Tanner. This company itself is a hotbed of unionists. Most who don't favor the union have already left to join the Confederate army. You're one of the few who haven't."

Rusty knew Tanner's loyalty was to the Confederacy. He remained confused about his own. He could not in good conscience support last year's secession, yet he understood Texans' frustrations with the union. "I wouldn't want to cause the Monahan family any trouble."

Whitfield said, "You wouldn't add a speck to the trouble they've already got. You might even be a help to them."

"The shape I'm in? I don't see how."

"There's been agitation against the Monahans. Wouldn't take much to stir the hotheads into somethin' real mean. Havin' a ranger stayin' there might calm the waters."

Rusty had heard ugly stories about mob violence against unionists farther east in the state. "If it came to trouble, I don't know how much help I could be. This bad leg . . ."

"You represent the authority of the state of Texas. Most people will respect that. Those that don't . . . well, you might have to shoot one or two of them." His eyes narrowed. "Speakin' of which, are you real sure you were tryin' to kill that Indian? There's some who flinch when it comes to actually pullin' the trigger."

The thought startled Rusty. He had not considered that his own reluctance might have caused him to miss. The Indian had been pinned down, helpless, an easy target.

Too easy, perhaps. That might have been the trouble.

Whitfield said, "It's no disgrace to hate havin' to kill. I've got no use for a man who kills because he likes to do it. I'll fire him out of my company quicker than a jackrabbit can jump."

Rusty considered, then said, "It was my horse. Kept faunchin' around." But now that the question had been raised, he could no longer feel completely sure.

Whitfield started to turn away but stopped. "Maybe your life didn't depend on it just then. But you'd better be sure you can do what you have to when your life *does* depend on it. Otherwise, you're dead."

· 11 ·

Tanner rode south to the Monahan farm. Two days later he returned to the camp at Belknap with Lon Monahan, his son Billy, and a wagon. Monahan climbed down over the right-hand front wheel and tied the lines to the brake. He walked to Rusty's tent and ducked to enter through the open flap. "Looks like you got yourself a little too close to the Indians. Didn't anybody ever tell you that they bite?"

"I guess I wasn't thinkin'."

"Soon's Tanner came and told us, we sent for Preacher Webb. He's near as good at healin' the body as at healin' the soul."

"It'll be good to see him. It's good to see *you*, Mr. Monahan."

Tanner gave Rusty a critical study. "You're lookin' mighty drawed."

Tanner had looked "mighty drawed" to Rusty ever since they had first met. He had barely enough flesh to hold his bones together. "The worst day I ever had, I looked better than you do. But you look pretty good to me right now, you and that wagon."

Monahan nodded at his son. "You hurry and spread a couple of blankets in the wagon. We'll do good to make it to the farm before dark tomorrow."

Billy complied. Rusty gritted his teeth and held his breath while Tanner and Billy lifted him. Movement set the leg to hurting badly again. Tanner threw Rusty's saddle, blanket, and few possibles into the wagon bed, then tied Alamo on behind. He said, "Before you get into another Indian fight, you'd better train this horse to mind."

"It was his first time up so close. Mine, too."

"Probably won't be the last. Now, don't you linger any longer than you have to. The state ain't payin' you to idle around."

"Or for anything else." Rusty reached over the sideboard to shake Tanner's hand. "You watch out some Comanche doesn't slip up on the blind side of you and cut your hair."

Monahan and his son climbed up onto the seat. Monahan cautioned, "It'll be rough in spots, so take a grip. The Comanches never built any roads out here, and neither has the state."

Tanner stood with narrow shoulders slumped and watched the wagon pull away. Rusty felt a tug of regret at the parting. He had been with the company more than a year now, patrolling the line, watching for Indian sign, and seldom finding any. Yesterday's engagement was the closest he had come to being in a real fight where he could see the color of the enemy's eyes. But he had enjoyed the life despite its lack of comforts, despite its sometimes monotonous routine, despite the slowness of pay scanty by any standard and irregular in arrival. He had enjoyed the bond that had grown among members of the company, riding together, camping together day after day, playing cards, occasionally racing horses.

Jim and Johnny Morris had shown him how close brothers could be, though they argued about trivial matters from time to time. Rusty had grown to regard Tanner as a substitute for the brother he never had. But Tanner had family back in the East Texas blacklands and had taken leave a couple of times to visit them. He wrote and received letters at fairly regular intervals. Rusty had received no letters except an occasional brief message from Preacher Webb, nor had he anyone else to write a letter to. When other men talked of their families, he was achingly aware that he had none.

The Monahans did not make a lot of unnecessary talk on the way south to the farm. They knew the rough ground caused Rusty considerable pain, and they did not bother him with useless conversation. The elder Monahan held the reins. He was careful to seek out the most benign terrain he could find, though much of the time he had little choice. One way was as rugged as another. Rusty managed to doze for short periods when the going smoothed out, though he remained always conscious of the throbbing in his leg.

The Monahan women met the wagon in their front yard. Geneva Monahan said nothing but pressed the palm of her hand against her mouth, her stricken eyes telling Rusty what she was thinking.

Clemmie anxiously looked over the sideboard. "My land, he looks more dead than alive. I hope you-all stopped along the way now and again to let him rest."

"Couldn't afford to," Lon replied. "If dark had caught us we'd've had to camp a second night. Wanted to get him here to your tender mercies the fastest we could."

"Let's carry him into the house. Preacher Webb ain't showed up yet. Lord knows how far Papa has to ride to find him."

By that, Rusty assumed that Clemmie's father had gone to search for Webb. He realized he had not seen Geneva's older brother or heard him mentioned. He asked, "Where's James?"

Lon and Clemmie Monahan glanced at each other before Lon answered, "We ain't sure, exactly. It's best that we don't know."

Clemmie said, "The conscript officers came lookin' for him. He had to slip away in the middle of the night. Wasn't nothin' else he could do. He didn't want to go to war against the union."

The conscript law had put many young men on the run, some who had unionist leanings and some who simply did not want to be drafted into the Confederate army. By Richmond law it had become part of the ranger mission to find and bring in conscript dodgers, though Whitfield's company had exerted itself but little in that direction. Many of the rangers might have joined the fugitives had their frontier service so far not exempted them from military service.

Rusty said, "I thought you-all made up your minds to stay here no matter what."

Lon said, "The sons of bitches was fixin' to take James away. He didn't have no choice."

Clemmie fretted, "I'm afraid Billy's next. He's sixteen. Another year or so and he'll be of age."

Rusty knew that some boys as young as fifteen and sixteen were serving, though to his knowledge it was by their own choice. He felt a surge of bitterness. "I don't know who wanted that stupid war in the first place. They sure didn't ask me what I thought."

Lon stared down at a knotty fist. "In a way, I reckon they asked all of us. Texas called a vote on secession. A majority said yes."

"But they didn't ask for war."

"I'm afraid both camps was itchin' for it. I can't fault one side more than the other, but us Monahans have always stood for the union."

"In spite of it drivin' your son away?"

"He'll be back. When this war burns itself out, people'll come to their senses, most of them. As for the rest, the hell with them."

Clemmie said, "Right now we've got a different fight on our hands. Let's quit talkin' and carry Rusty into the house. We'll take off the dirty wrappin' and see what that limb looks like."

Rusty felt a small, warm hand slip into his. Looking up, he saw Geneva's worried eyes. "Don't you fret, Rusty. We'll take care of you."

He felt better already, a little.

Removal of the binding agitated the wound. Geneva had to soak the final pair of wraps because dried blood had stuck the cloth to the skin. Rusty sucked a sharp breath beneath his teeth as the binding was pulled free.

He did not look down. He did not have to, for the grim

reaction of the women told him more than he wanted to know. Clemmie demanded, "What did they burn you with, a brandin' iron?"

"A knife. Said they had to cauterize the wound."

"Roasted it, more like. But maybe they saved you from gangrene."

A dark fear had lurked in the back of Rusty's mind almost from the first. He had not permitted it to rise all the way to the surface. When no one volunteered further comment, he asked the question in a shaky voice. "You reckon I'm fixin' to lose my leg?"

Clemmie managed an answer. "Not without we give it a hard fight. I'll be glad when Preacher Webb gets here."

"I doubt he can doctor it any better than you can."

"But he's got more say with the Almighty."

They lighted a lantern and hung it on the porch in case Webb should arrive in the night. It could as easily guide marauding Indians, but nobody mentioned the risk. Rusty had just dropped off into a fitful sleep when he heard a commotion on the dog run. The door swung open, and Webb entered, removing his flop-brimmed old hat and pitching it against a wall. He did not break his stride until he reached the cot where Rusty lay in the cabin's kitchen.

Clemmie's father, Vince Purdy, followed Webb. He looked small and wizened and tired.

Clemmie explained, "We cleaned the wound the best we could and put on fresh bandagin'."

Webb placed his hand on Rusty's forehead, checking for fever. He turned back the blanket and touched the bandage but withdrew his hand without untying the knot that held it. "We'll leave well enough alone 'til mornin'. Since the Lord hasn't taken you already, maybe He's not got a place fixed for you yet."

Rusty said, "If there *is* a Lord, I was lookin' Him square in the eye. The Comanche who put the arrow in my leg was tryin' to put it in my heart."

"God has saved you for other work."

"I had my front sight leveled against another Indian. You think the Lord saved him, too?"

"The Indians are His creatures, same as we are. Maybe He has other work for that one, too."

Rusty was inclined to believe that his nervous horse was the cause for both misses, but he did not feel like arguing religion with Webb at this time of night. "It's awful good to see you, Preacher."

"And you. I'm glad you've managed to stay out of trouble, at least 'til your scrap with the Indians."

Rusty understood the reference. "I don't suppose Isaac York has drunk himself to death yet?"

"No, but he's tried." Webb frowned. "You've been away more than a year. I'd hoped you'd forgotten about Isaac."

"I can't forget him. Every time I think of Daddy Mike, I see Isaac York too. I will until he dies, or I do."

"Leave him to heaven, Rusty."

"Or to hell."

Rusty forced himself to look at the leg when Webb unwrapped it the next morning. It was swollen, the color running from red to blue, but at least he saw nothing to indicate the onset of gangrene. Crusting had begun along the edges where Tanner's knife had seared the wound. He thought it smelled a bit too, but that could have been something Clemmie had applied to it last night.

Anxiously he asked, "What do you think, Preacher?"

"There are better things to do than burn it, but I suppose there was little choice out in the field. I'm afraid the burn will leave a bigger scar than the arrow would have."

"A scar won't bother me much if I've still got a leg."

"It'll take a while, but I think you'll heal. The main thing to worry us now is blood poisonin'. About the only thing we can do on that is to pray."

Geneva stood beside the minister, hope in her eyes where there had been dark worry last night. "We'll all do that, Preacher."

Webb looked at her as if something about her surprised him. He turned back to Rusty. "That should help as much as any medicine we can give him. I'm not sure Rusty knows how to pray for himself."

Geneva said, "I'll teach him."

Webb smiled.

Rusty spent most of his time lying on the cot the first couple of days, for the pain from the wound reached its peak, and he was too weak to want to move much. After that he became increasingly restless, wanting to be up and doing something. The Monahan family was busy from early morning until dusk, harvesting their feed crop and picking their cotton, which would have to be hauled eastward a long way for ginning. Rusty felt guilt about requiring their attention and eating their food while performing no service in return, especially after Preacher Webb left to attend to his circuit.

Once Rusty was able to sit up for long periods, he insisted that they bring him work to do: harness he could mend, tools he could sharpen. He constructed a crude but workable crutch from a forked branch of oak that Billy brought him. He shaved off the bark and padded the top so it would not rub his arm raw. Though he moved awkwardly, the crutch enabled him to get around the house and the barn. The guilt and the feeling of uselessness left him.

One day Geneva brought him a cup of coffee at the barn, where he was grinding a new edge onto a scythe. "Maybe I can get back to the company before long," he told her.

He heard regret in her voice. "Are you in such a hurry to leave us?"

"No, but I feel like it's my duty to go soon as I'm able to ride. Every day I'm gone, others have got to make up for me. The company's shorthanded."

"What if you'd been killed? They'd've had to find somebody else. Let them find somebody else now."

He said, "There's another consideration besides duty." He had not put the thought into words before, though it had come to him often enough. "Long as I stay in the frontier company, the conscript officers have to leave me alone. But if I quit it, they'll be comin' after me. Then I'll have to go fight the union or I'll have to leave the country like James did. Either way, I couldn't stay here."

"They won't take you 'til that leg heals. Maybe the war'll be over by then."

"Sounds to me like it's barely got started."

Tears welled in her eyes. "First it was James. Now we've got you and Billy to worry about. It's not fair, a bunch of old men startin' a war and makin' the young men go and fight it." She leaned against him and touched his hand. He set down the coffee cup, and she turned into his arms.

It was the first time he had held her. He felt warm and happy and greatly confused. He had never held a girl this way before.

She said, "Don't be in a big hurry about gettin' well."

His crutch slid to the barn's earthen floor. He would have to turn her loose to stoop and pick it up. He let it lie.

Another day, Rusty was leaning on his crutch, brushing Alamo's mane, when Colonel Caleb Dawkins rode up accompanied by half a dozen men. Rusty blinked in momentary disbelief, for he recognized two of them. One was Dawkins's son Pete, who had wanted to kill Rusty the day he had encountered the thieves with the Tonkawa horses. Beside Pete was the point rider who had decided against it.

Dawkins was surprised to find Rusty there. "Don't you belong in the ranger camp up by Belknap?" he demanded, as if it were his right to know and approve or disapprove.

Rusty stiffened at the challenge in the voice. "I do."

"Then why are you here?"

"Recuperatin'. Had a little run-in with some Comanches, and they came out with the best of it."

"You could have chosen a better place for healing. Don't you know this place is a nest of unionists?"

"They're friends of mine. Their politics don't matter to me."

"They should. You are sworn to uphold the laws of the

state of Texas. You should be more careful about the company you keep."

Rusty found a bit of unintended humor in that comment. He studied the young horse thieves, particularly Pete. "That'd be good advice for a lot of people."

Dawkins straightened his shoulders in an attitude of authority. "We are here representing the conscription committee. As a ranger, I expect you to speak the truth."

"I always do, or pretty close to it."

"The committee has declared James Monahan a fugitive. Have you seen him?"

Rusty saw no reason to lie, though he would have had there been a reason. He owed nothing to Dawkins. "I haven't seen him since I came here."

"Do you know where he has gone?"

"Someplace else, is all I know. It's none of my business where he's at."

"As a representative of the law, every lawbreaker should be your business."

Rusty looked at the young men again. Pete appeared suddenly apprehensive. The other could not meet Rusty's eyes. The more Rusty considered it, the more he was convinced that the colonel did not know about the horse stealing.

Rusty said, "I suppose if you had a lawbreaker in your midst, you'd turn him in?"

"Unless it was a Yankee law."

"I don't suppose there's any Texas law against runnin' off Indian horses?"

The puzzlement in Dawkins's eyes indicated that he was indeed ignorant about the thieves in his midst. "Are you saying one of us steals Indian horses?"

Rusty saw nothing to be gained by telling him. "I'm just usin' that as an example. Everybody's got laws they don't like and don't pay any attention to. Even you, I suspect."

"Not I, sir. The law is the law. I abide by it, and I insist that others do the same."

Lon Monahan came in from the field, riding a bareback mule with most of the harness still on him. He rode up close enough to have reached out and punched Dawkins on the nose had he intended to. He looked as if he might be considering it. " 'Y God, Dawkins, I've ordered you off of this place more than once. What do you want this time?"

As before, Monahan's quick anger was in marked contrast to the cold calm in Dawkins's look and manner.

"The same as before. We're looking for your son James. He has been declared a deserter."

"How can he desert somethin' he never joined in the first place?"

"He deserted his duty."

"His duty as *you* see it. He saw it different. You're not welcome here, Dawkins, you nor any of them scalawags with you. I'm tellin' you to leave."

"When we're ready." Dawkins looked across the field, where Billy was dragging a cotton sack. "How old is that boy yonder?"

Monahan's defiance began giving way to uneasiness. "He ain't barely sixteen. Too young for you to be takin' him."

"*You* say he's sixteen. I say he looks older."

"He ain't. We've got his birth date wrote down in our Bible."

"The hand of man can make even a Bible lie." Dawkins began to rein his horse around. "Let's go take a look at him, boys. I say he looks eighteen."

Monahan stepped inside the barn and immediately came out again, carrying a rifle. He aimed it at Dawkins's broad chest. "Touch my boy and I'll kill you!"

For a fleeting moment Dawkins lost his composure. Murder flared in his eyes and made Rusty wish for his own rifle. But the moment passed and Dawkins appeared calm again, at least outwardly. It was just as well, for Lon had the upper hand.

Dawkins drew himself up into a military attitude of full attention. "We are representatives of the conscription committee, duly appointed. You are interfering with the performance of our duties."

"It ain't your duty to take an underage boy against his family's will. Now I'm givin' you a chance to git, and don't be comin' back."

Dawkins lowered his deep voice. "You'll see us again."

"If so, it'll be the same way I see you now, over the barrel of this gun." Monahan's hands were steady, but as soon as Dawkins and the men with him turned away, his hands began to tremble.

The point rider lagged, looking back as if he wanted to say something, but he thought better of it and followed Dawkins.

Rusty had forgotten his pain. It came back to him in a rush, for in his concentration on Monahan and Dawkins he had let some of his weight rest on the wounded leg. He lifted it and rubbed his hand gingerly over the bandage as if that would ease the throbbing. "I thought sure as hell you were fixin' to shoot him."

"I was. The Lord stayed my hand."

"He'll be back."

"I know. And before I'll let him have Billy, I *will* shoot him, 'y God." Monahan's face was grim. "Damn that Dawkins for a hypocrite. He's out roundin' up other men's sons for the army, but he pays the government to keep his own at home."

Rusty appreciated the irony of the situation. While Dawkins lectured gravely about law and order, his own son was stealing Indian horses without the old man knowing it.

Watching Dawkins's retreat, Rusty feared for a minute that the man was going to cut back into the field and make for Billy. Dawkins paused once, as if considering it.

Monahan raised the rifle. "He's still in range, and he knows it."

Dawkins resumed his retreat. Monahan lowered the rifle, relieved. He said, "I'm goin' out and fetch Billy."

He climbed back onto the mule and cut straight across the field, making no effort to spare the unharvested cotton from trampling. Watching, Rusty saw signs of argument between Monahan and his son, though he could not hear the voices. Presently Billy followed his father out of the field, carrying the half-filled sack on his shoulder. He resumed his argument at the barn. "But everybody around here knows I'm only sixteen."

"To Dawkins you're as old as he wants you to be. It ain't you he's really after, but he'll use you to get even with me and James. So you've got to go, son. You've got to go now, because there's no tellin' when he's apt to come back for you." Monahan turned to his father-in-law, who had come up from the house to watch in silence. He carried a shotgun, ready to support his son-in-law if the incident had built to violence. "I'd appreciate it if you'd go tell Clemmie and Geneva to fix up a big sack of grub for Billy. And roll up a couple of blankets. Soon as it's dark, he'll be ridin' out."

Billy's grandfather nodded, his thin face sad. "Just like with James. I don't know what Clemmie's goin' to say."

"Ain't much she can say. It's got to be done or we'll lose the boy sure enough." Monahan turned to Rusty. "As a ranger, maybe you ought not to see none of this. It might go hard with you if the authorities decide you could've stopped it and didn't."

Rusty shrugged. "I'm all crippled up, and my pistol is in my saddlebag where I can't get ahold of it. I couldn't stop it if I wanted to."

Monahan grunted. "You'd better tell them you wanted to, though. Tell them I held a gun on you, if it helps any." He swung the muzzle of the rifle around to point at Rusty a moment, then turned it away. "Now it won't be a lie." Monahan climbed back onto the mule. "I'll go out and see what horses I can find. Billy's got to have a good one."

"Give him Alamo if you want to. He's got a lot of endurance. He just doesn't like guns much."

"I don't think that'll be necessary. But I'll always be grateful that you offered."

The sun seemed reluctant to set, and dusk seemed hours about settling in. Rusty and Clemmie's father stood on the dog run, watching. The old man said, "I wouldn't put it past Dawkins to be hidin' out yonder, spyin' on this place. He's bound to suspect we'll be slippin' Billy away."

Rusty could hear Lon and Clemmie Monahan in the kitchen, giving Billy advice. Clemmie said, "I just wish Preacher Webb was here. He'd know just where James is at, so Billy could find him."

On leaving, James had promised to stay in touch with Webb. Webb could quietly pass James's letters on to the family, whose own mail was almost certainly being watched. The authorities would have no reason to suspect the minister.

When the sky had turned full dark, the family blew out the lamp in the kitchen, throwing the cabin into darkness. Lon Monahan led a saddled horse up from the barn. "You'd best be on your way before the moon rises. You can travel many a mile before sunup."

Billy reluctantly shook hands with Rusty, his father, and his grandfather, and hugged his mother and sisters. Lon Monahan gave him a small leather pouch. "This is good Yankee money we've kept hidden away."

The youngster accepted it tearfully. "Maybe with luck I can bring it all back."

Clemmie said, "Don't trust only to luck. Keep talkin' to the Lord. We'll be prayin' with you."

"I'll be back," Billy said, and he disappeared into the darkness. The women cried.

Lon Monahan laid his heavy hand on Rusty's shoulder. Tightly he said, "Remember, if anybody asks you, you tried to stop him."

"I'm a poor liar."

"Then don't say anything. We'll lie for you."

The women went back into the dark kitchen, shoulders heavily burdened with sadness. Lon Monahan remained outside, stuffing his pipe, puffing harder than normal. Clemmie's father leaned against the corner where the logs joined together at right angles. He kept his grief to himself, though his bony shoulders trembled.

Rusty, not wanting to intrude on their mourning, hobbled out into the packed yard, leaning heavily on the crutch. He looked toward the black horizon, where the moon was just beginning to rise. Soon it would be in full brilliance. The early stars were out. It struck him that moonlight nights were the favorite time for Comanche raids. But Indians were a minor concern at the moment. A much larger and all-consuming war had taken precedence.

He heard a faint commotion somewhere to the west, in the

direction Billy had taken. It lasted but a moment, and afterward he was not certain he had heard anything. He made his way back to the dog run and found Lon Monahan with the pipe in one hand, the other hand behind his ear.

"Did you hear somethin', Rusty?"

"I thought I did, but I'm not sure." He had seen some of the Monahan horses wander down that way to graze just before sundown. A couple of them might have had a brief biting and kicking fight.

Clemmie's father said he had heard nothing. "Half the time anymore, I can't hear it thunder."

Monahan paced the dog run, debating with himself, then said, "I'm goin' to saddle up and ride down that way. Got to be sure nothin' has happened to Billy."

It was Monahan's custom to keep a night horse penned so someone could ride out each morning before breakfast and bring in the work stock. In a few minutes Rusty heard Lon ride by and saw his dark form at some distance in the moonlight. Lon soon faded from view.

Rusty said, "It probably wasn't anything. A couple of horses fightin', or maybe a cow and calf spooked by a coyote."

The old man said, "You're probably right," but his voice carried no conviction. "Can't help worryin' that the boy has run into trouble."

After a time Clemmie came out onto the dog run. "Where's Lon?"

Rusty considered lying to her, for he saw no reason to upset her needlessly. But her father did not give him a chance. "He saddled up and rode off. Thought he heard somethin' out yonder."

Clemmie caught a short breath. "Heard what?"

Rusty said, "We don't know. Probably nothin'. He'll likely come back pretty soon."

But he did not. Rusty guessed that an hour passed, and more. Clemmie came out onto the dog run several times. The last couple of times Geneva was with her. At last she said, "I've got a dreadful feelin' somethin's happened." She

started walking westward. Geneva ran to catch her, clutching
her arm.

"No, Mother. No! What if somethin' is out there? Indians,
maybe."

"I've got to see about Lon and Billy." Clemmie pulled
away from her daughter.

Rusty heard something too far out to see. "Mrs. Monahan,
wait. I think I hear a horse. Lon's comin' back."

"Thank the Lord." She returned to the cabin, Geneva beside her, holding her arm again.

"See, Mother. It wasn't anything."

Rusty began to see the shape of a horse and rider. By the
time they were within fifty yards of the cabin he could tell
that this was not Lon Monahan, nor was it Billy.

The horseman reined up a few feet in front of the family.
He seemed reluctant to dismount. Rusty hobbled up closer
to see his face. He recognized the horse thief who had ridden
point for the Indian remuda. The youth tried twice to speak
before he managed to bring up anything intelligible. "Miz
Monahan, I . . . I don't know how to tell you . . ."

Rusty moved up close enough that he could have reached
out and pulled him down from the horse. "Tell them what?"
When the young man seemed unable to speak, Rusty grabbed
him by the knee and shook hard. "Damn it, man, tell them."

"It wasn't none of my doin'. I didn't want them to do it,
but Colonel Dawkins, he . . . he said it had to be done. And
he done it."

Rusty felt as if he had been showered with ice-cold water.
He shouted, "Did what?"

"He hung Mr. Monahan. And the boy, too. Down yonder
by the river."

Geneva screamed. Clemmie wilted. Her father caught her
as she started to slump to the ground.

• 12 •

Rusty could not speak. He leaned over Clemmie, who lay weeping, and Geneva, who knelt by her mother's side. The old man kept whispering, "God help them. God help them."

A little late for God to intervene now, Rusty thought. He turned to the young horse thief, who had not dismounted and showed no inclination to do so. "Wasn't there anybody who could've stopped it?"

"Nobody stops Colonel Dawkins. When he makes up his mind, there'd better not be anybody standin' in his way."

"So you didn't even try."

"Well, I told him we ought to wait, that we ought to take them to the sheriff. He cussed me for a coward and said if I didn't have the stomach for it, I ought to leave and not ever come back. So I left."

Aching inside, Rusty felt like weeping with the women, but he faced a duty that was more important. "We can't just leave them out there. Would you fetch in the mules and help me hitch them to the wagon?"

The young man bowed his head. "That's the least I can do."

Rusty had to be helped up onto the wagon seat, but once

he was there, the pain subsided. He felt he was able to drive the mules. Clemmie's father sat beside him, his head down. Clemmie cried hysterically, fighting to climb up into the wagon. Her father talked her down, and Geneva held her as the wagon pulled away, leaving the women behind. Rusty rubbed a sleeve across his burning eyes.

The horse thief, who said his name was Smith, rode beside the wagon, pointing the way.

"If we run into Captain Dawkins, I'm leavin'. I'm lightin' a shuck anyway, soon as I help you bring these poor fellers in. I've got no use for a country that goes around hangin' people for not thinkin' the way they're supposed to. Like all them folks over at Gainesville."

Rusty had heard of mass hangings at Gainesville, farther east, where rumors of a unionist uprising had aroused hysteria. "Looks like the world's gone crazy."

"I'm thinkin' it was a short trip." After a long silence Smith said, "I'm beholden to you for not tellin' the captain I had a hand in runnin' off them Indian ponies. He might've hung *me*. He's hell for keepin' the law."

"The law? He just murdered a man and a boy."

"Law and order accordin' to his beliefs. He's got a fire-and-brimstone way of lookin' at things, but he's an honest man, after his own fashion."

"He's a mad dog. Does he know what his son Pete has been up to?

"God no. Fanatic as he is, he might hang Pete, too."

Twice Smith thought he had found the place, only to be mistaken. Rusty was about to despair of finding the Monahans before daylight. Then Smith said, "Light your lantern again. I think this is where they're at."

It was. Rusty had held to a faint hope that somehow Dawkins might have bungled the job, that one or both Monahans might still be alive. He raised the lantern and saw that the hope had been in vain.

The old man wheezed, "God help them."

Rusty wished Preacher Webb were here. He would be a comfort to the women, though it was too late for either him or God to help Lon and Billy Monahan. "I'm afraid God was lookin' somewhere else." He drew the wagon up under the bodies. "Grab ahold," he told Smith, "while I cut them down."

Smith was queasy about the task, taking a moment to summon the stomach for it. Leaning heavily on the crutch so it would not slip from under him, Rusty managed to slice through the ropes. Smith and Vince Purdy gently laid the pair onto the bed of the wagon. Rusty tried not to look at the dead faces, but he was compelled by a force he could not resist. Lon Monahan's eyes were half open. Clemmie's father closed them.

The old man broke down, kneeling beside his grandson, taking one still hand in both of his own. "He wasn't nothin' but a boy. How could any just man do such a thing as this?"

Smith said, "He's got a hard view of justice. It don't allow no extra room. He'd hang Jesus Christ if he thought he was in the wrong."

Rusty repeated something Lon had said once: "God save us from zealots."

Caleb Dawkins was such a man, like Isaac York back home. Worse, perhaps, because York acted in the passion of the moment. Dawkins was cold and calculating.

Purdy spread a blanket over the bodies and blew out the lantern. His voice quavered. "I dread for Clemmie to see this. It'll nigh kill her."

Smith said, "I already been a witness to too much tonight. I'm fixin' to put as much ground under me as I can before the colonel changes his mind. Like as not he'll send after me."

Rusty asked, "Where'll you go?"

"West. There's a heap of rough country out yonder where no ranger or conscript officer is apt to come pokin' around. I'll find me a deep hole and wait for this god-awful war to finish."

"Watch out for Indians. They won't care whether you're from north or south, long as you're white. Especially if they catch you lookin' at their horses."

After Smith left, Purdy said, "First thing come daylight, I'll see if the neighbors can get word to Preacher Webb. At least we can see that Lon and Billy get a decent buryin'."

Rusty said, "I'll go tell the sheriff. He needs to know what's happened here."

Purdy's voice was bitter. "Ain't much the sheriff can do about it. The times favor the likes of Caleb Dawkins, not the Monahans."

Rusty traveled in the wagon, for his leg would not yet permit him to ride a horse. Halfway to town he met the sheriff and his deputy. The lawman's expression was dark and forbidding. "It's rumored this mornin' that somebody killed Lon Monahan."

Rusty's anger quickly rekindled. "Not just somebody. It was Caleb Dawkins. And not just Lon but his boy Billy, too. Taken out and hung like dogs."

The lawman grimaced. "This stupid war . . . how can you be sure it was the colonel? Did you see him?"

"No, but I talked to somebody who was with him." He repeated what Smith had said.

"Smith!" The sheriff spat the word. "The country's fillin' up with men named Smith, and most of them are lookin' back to see who's comin' behind them." Clearly, he had rather be somewhere else. "I'll need to talk to this Smith myself. Is he still at the Monahan place?"

"No, he was afraid of what Dawkins might do if he stayed around. Said he was leavin' and not comin' back."

"I wish they'd all go, somewhere a long ways from here." The sheriff stared at the horizon. "Ain't likely the colonel will admit anything. Not to where it would mean somethin' in court."

"But it was him. Smith told us so."

"You didn't see the hangin' yourself?"

"It was over with before me and Mr. Purdy got there. Everybody was gone except Smith."

"Unless somebody who was there is willin' to bear witness, you're huntin' bear with a switch. You've got no case."

"As a sheriff, you're supposed to do somethin'."

"I'm not a judge. All I can do is make an arrest."

"As a ranger, I could do that, too."

"But whoever you arrested, you'd have to turn him over to the local law, and that's me. Whatever happens after that is up to the court. You know what a court'll say."

Frustration burned like lye in Rusty's stomach. "So there's nothin' to be done?"

"Someday there'll be an accountin'. Caleb Dawkins will stand in judgment like all of us and answer to a higher power than any Confederate court."

"That's liable to be a long time in comin'."

"You're young, and young people are impatient. I'm old enough to know that you've got to have patience. Most things eventually come to pass if the Almighty means them to."

Rusty clenched a fist, wishing he could hit somebody. But he realized the lawman was being realistic, walking a narrow line and looking at reality rather than what should be. Another time, under other circumstances, he might act differently.

Preacher Webb arrived late in the day. Though devastated himself, he consoled the family the best he could.

Rusty grieved much as he had for Daddy Mike and Mother Dora. He told the minister, "I don't understand. There's good people on both sides in this war, and they all say God is with them."

"I'm afraid they haven't asked Him. They wouldn't like His answer."

The subject was painful to Webb, for he quickly changed it. "I see you've put the crutch aside for a cane. Your leg must be better."

"Still itches somethin' awful. Must mean it's healin'."

"Then I suppose you've thought about gettin' back to the ranger company." Webb sounded hopeful.

"Soon as I can get on a horse by myself. But I hate to leave here when the Monahans have got so much to worry about. Nice words seem empty. What's needed is a good killin'."

The minister's face revealed his misgivings. "Vengeance

is mine, sayeth the Lord. You were sent away from home because you talked about killin'. If you talk enough about it, sooner or later you may actually do it."

"I believe I'd be justified."

"All the more reason to rejoin your company as soon as you can."

Rusty counted the neighbors who began showing up for the burying, a-horseback and in wagons and buggies. Aside from family, they numbered only a few more than a dozen. He understood the reasons. Many of the Monahans' friends had fallen away from them once the war began, for most favored the Confederacy. Fear was another factor. The hanging here, like the larger ones at Gainesville, had been a warning to any besides the Monahans who might have unionist leanings or even associate with people who did. Among the few who came, Rusty wondered if Dawkins might have sent a spy or two. He was a big man whose long, dark shadow reached even into the grave.

Webb was taken aback by Rusty's suggestion. He had not considered the possibility that an informer might carry word to Dawkins about those who attended the funeral. "The ones who've come are not easily intimidated. Some have family members in the Confederate service, so Dawkins can hardly charge them with disloyalty."

"Dawkins is a zealot. If he likes whiskey but you like beer, that makes you a traitor in his sight."

"Both sides have their share of blind fanatics. They're the kind who brought on this war."

Rusty said, "I've heard you pray for people to get well. Can't you pray for Dawkins to get sick? A heart seizure maybe, or at least a slobberin' fit."

"That would be a poor use of prayer, and certainly not pleasin' to the Lord."

"It'd please the hell out of me."

Those who came to the funeral avoided mentioning the way Lon and Billy had died. Any death was painful, but deaths from this brand of violence and hatred were especially hard to accept. When Preacher Webb stood over the grave and spoke of madness descending upon the land, Rusty saw several heads nod. He hoped Caleb Dawkins *had* planted a spy here. This would give him something to ponder.

The services over and the grave filled in, the visitors paid their respect to the Monahan women and children and began leaving. The sheriff and his deputy remained to the last, watching for possible trouble. There had been a worry, though slight, that Dawkins might send men to harass and throw fear into the mourners.

The lawman was looking for something else, too. He said, "I thought James Monahan might show up. I've got a warrant for his arrest."

Rusty was not surprised. "Word may not have gotten to him. There's no tellin' where he's at."

"I expect there's folks here who know exactly where he's at." The sheriff glanced toward Preacher Webb. "But I'm glad he didn't come. I'd be duty bound to take him in."

"I know how you feel."

"Do you? You're a ranger. If you see him, you have the same duty to arrest him."

Rusty had not allowed himself to think much about that. The notion was too disturbing.

Relieved that no problem had occurred, the sheriff said, "I didn't think even the colonel would be so eaten up with hate that he'd disrupt a funeral."

Rusty replied, "He hated enough to hang two men."

The younger Monahan girls had strayed off a little way from the burial place, weeping together apart from the adults. They returned in a run, frightened. One shouted, "There's some men hidin' on the river."

The sheriff stiffened. "Where?"

The girl pointed. "Down yonder. One of them is on a big white horse."

Rusty limped out with the lawman. He could not see any men, but he saw the white horse the girl had mentioned, half hidden in underbrush. His first thought was that James had returned to watch from a safe distance as his father and brother were buried.

The sheriff thought otherwise. "Somebody's been spyin' on the funeral crowd. I see Colonel Dawkins's fine hand in this." He gave Rusty a quick look. "Where's your gun?"

"In the house."

"Good. Let it stay there. Been enough men died already." He jerked his head as a signal to his deputy.

Rusty hobbled along on the cane, trailing the two lawmen as rapidly as his sore leg would allow. Realizing they had been discovered, the men on the river emerged into the open. Rusty recognized Dawkins on the white horse, flanked by two riders he had seen before. One was his son Pete.

The sheriff said accusingly, "I thought you had more judgment than to come here, Colonel."

"I came only to observe. I did not intend to be seen."

"Then you ought to've rode a black horse. You've got no business on this place."

"I am a citizen, free to come and go as I choose."

"So were Lon Monahan and his boy."

"Lon Monahan was a traitor, and his son was fleeing conscription."

"You are not the court. You have no authority to hang anybody."

Dawkins gravely considered his answer. "Can you prove I hanged anyone?" When the sheriff did not reply, Dawkins added, "I thought not."

Rusty broke in, "One of your men told us you did it."

Dawkins eyed Rusty with contempt. "As I recall, you are supposed to be a peace officer. If you had been doing your duty, all this need not have happened."

The sheriff told Rusty, "I think you had better step back and let me attend to this."

"Attend to it, then. Arrest him for murder."

The lawman had already explained why that would do no good. He did not repeat himself.

Dawkins challenged Rusty. "You said one of my men told you. Who was he?"

"He said his name was Smith."

"Every scalawag and rascal in the country claims his name is Smith. I have no Smith in my employ."

Clemmie and Preacher Webb came down from the family burying ground, Clemmie's father and Geneva close behind. Rusty could see the two smaller girls huddled together near the new graves. Clemmie spoke in a voice trembling with anger. "Caleb Dawkins, if I'd seen it was you I'd've brought a gun, and that would've been the end of you."

Dawkins pretended he had not heard. He did not look at her.

Sternly the sheriff said, "Colonel, it'll be better for everybody if you turn around and leave here, now."

"That I intend to do. I do not wish to fight with women and children." He looked at Clemmie's father. "Or old men, so long as they sit in their rocking chairs and do not make trouble. But I suggest that it would benefit the community as well as themselves if the Monahan family would load their wagons and depart this country."

Clemmie Monahan moved forward in a cold fury. "This is our home, Caleb Dawkins. We built it from nothin', me and Lon and Papa and the kids. Before we leave it, we'll see you in hell."

Geneva stepped up beside her mother, silently adding emphasis to what Clemmie had said.

Old Vince Purdy joined her on the right. He said, "There ain't a rockin' chair on this place, Caleb, but there's guns. If you come into range after this, we'll shoot you on sight and by God leave you for the hogs."

Rusty felt the hair bristle on his neck. By the tone of the old man's voice, he meant every word.

Dawkins's face masked any feeling he might have had. "Remember what they said, Sheriff. These are dangerous people."

The sheriff said, "You'll do well to remember it yourself."

Dawkins retreated into the dusk. He did not deign to look back, but the two men with him kept turning in the saddle, afraid.

The old man eased up to the sheriff's side. He reached out stealthily, then grabbed the pistol from the lawman's holster.

Before anyone could react, he pointed it at Dawkins's back.

The hammer fell on an empty chamber. The sheriff grunted as he wrested the pistol from Purdy's knotty hand. His angry voice crackled. "That was a fool thing to do."

The old man began to weep. "He killed my grandson."

Clemmie put her arms around her father. The sheriff looked at the pair, anger subsiding, sympathy taking its place. "Dawkins didn't see you do that, and I'll to try to forget it myself. But don't ever pull such a stunt again. It could get you killed."

Purdy's voice was barely audible. "It'd be worth it if I could take Dawkins with me."

Clemmie Monahan said, "Thank you, Sheriff. We appreciate you standin' up for us."

"I'm just tryin' to stay in the middle ground."

Preacher Webb said, "That can be the most dangerous place of all. People shoot at you from both sides."

Clemmie had talked little all day, trying to keep her emotions under tight control. Now she turned to Rusty. "You're a ranger. Can't you do somethin'?"

Geneva protested, "Mother, Rusty's crippled up ... can't even ride yet."

Reluctantly Rusty said, "Your mother's right. Somethin' has got to be done. Trouble is, I don't know what I can do."

In his time with the rangers he had never acted alone. He had always ridden with others and followed the orders of superiors. He wished for that guidance now. "If I arrested Dawkins, I'd have to turn him over to the local authorities. No local court'll convict him, not with times bein' like they are."

The sheriff nodded agreement. "That's the sad facts, Mrs. Monahan. The court would say that all he did was kill a unionist and a young man runnin' away from conscription. Dawkins may be called on to pay at the Pearly Gates, but not in Confederate Texas."

Rusty looked to Webb for advice. The minister had no answers. He supposed there *were* no answers.

The sheriff nodded at his deputy. "We're done here. Let's be goin'."

Webb said, "I'm glad you stood up to Dawkins, Sheriff, but you've probably made an enemy of him."

"He's not liable to forget you either. Even though you're a man of the cloth, he'll figure you've taken sides."

"My side was chosen for me when I saw Lon and Billy in their coffins."

The sheriff faced Clemmie. "After all this, are you sure you want to stay here?"

"More than ever. What's Dawkins goin' to do, hang women and children and an old man?"

"Since he's gotten away with this, I'm afraid he'll think he can get away with anything. Maybe not kill you, but he could shoot your livestock, burn you out . . ."

"He'd better not try. I'd kill him myself."

Geneva put her arm around her mother's shoulder. "This is our home. Caleb Dawkins be damned."

The sheriff regarded them glumly. "I wish I'd stayed in Harris County." He got on his horse and rode off into the dusk, his deputy spurring to catch up.

Preacher Webb did not leave immediately. Rusty assumed he wanted to help the family endure its grief and begin the healing process. Webb periodically stopped whatever he was doing and looked off into the distance as if expecting something. Rusty assumed he was watching for Caleb Dawkins to return.

"Preacher, you don't need to worry. If he comes lookin' for trouble, I'll see that he gets it."

"That's one thing I *am* worried about." Webb looked down at Rusty's leg. "You're bendin' it a lot better. I believe you'll be able to ride soon."

"You're tryin' to get me away from here and back to my company, aren't you?"

"Just as quick as I can."

"All right, we'll see. Would you please catch and saddle Alamo for me?"

The horse had not been ridden since the day of the Indian

fight. He had been enjoying his freedom from work, and he made a little game of eluding Webb until the minister hemmed him in a corral corner. "Now," Webb said softly, "don't you tempt me into language I'll have to beg forgiveness for."

Once caught, Alamo was tractable enough. Rusty held the bridle reins while Webb put the blanket and saddle on. He breathed into the horse's nostrils to remind the animal who he was, in case Alamo was forgetful. He did not have an exaggerated opinion of equine intelligence. He had seen good horses lose all their training after ranging a while with a reprobate, or even in solitude.

Handing Webb the cane, Rusty gingerly raised his left foot to the stirrup and swung the wounded leg over the saddle. A sharp stab of pain told him he was rushing things a little. He managed to put the right foot into the stirrup, but the leg hurt enough to make him wince. He removed the foot from the stirrup. That eased the pain but did not stop it. He felt cold sweat breaking out and shook his head.

"Maybe tomorrow." He dismounted carefully and rubbed the leg in an effort to stop the throbbing that had begun anew.

"I'm sorry. I didn't mean to push you."

In his concentration on trying to ride, Rusty had not noticed that Geneva had walked down to the corral. She watched, troubled. While Webb unsaddled Alamo, Rusty made his way to the fence where she stood. He found himself leaning a bit heavier on the cane.

Anxiously Geneva asked, "You're liable to lame yourself for good, pushin' too fast. Are you so anxious to leave us?"

"No, but Preacher Webb wants me to go as soon as I'm able. He's afraid Colonel Dawkins may cause me trouble."

"Looks to me like you've hurt your leg all over again."

"Irritated it a little, is all. But I've got to keep tryin'. Can't laze around forever, bein' a burden."

"You're no burden. It's been a comfort havin' you here, especially after . . ." She looked away. "Preacher Webb is right, though. Dawkins will hate anybody who helps us. No tellin' what he might do."

"I doubt he'd take action against a ranger. He'd bring the state of Texas down on his head."

"Not if nobody could prove he'd done it, like we can't prove what he did to Pa and Billy."

The second day's effort at riding went better than the first, though it soon set the leg to throbbing again. Rusty had to dismount. He knew he could not make the long ride up to Belknap and the ranger camp on horseback, not yet. He could probably persuade someone to take him in a wagon, but he was not in a hurry about leaving. Maybe in another couple of days.

He made himself as useful as his physical limitations allowed. Preacher Webb joined the Monahan family in the field, picking cotton, cutting feed with a scythe. Rusty kept the tools sharp. Though he felt awkward and out of place, he helped around the kitchen so the women could remain longer at the outdoor chores he could not do.

Often Webb paused in his work and let his gaze search the western horizon. At first Rusty assumed he was worrying about getting back to his circuit. Then he realized the minister was watching for something. Rusty asked him once what he was looking for and received an evasive answer. He did not ask again, but he suspected he knew. Somehow the family had sent word to James.

The thought was troubling, for James's appearance would force Rusty into a painful choice.

"Preacher," he said when he had a chance to speak to Webb alone, "I'm not askin' you to tell me anything you don't want to, but what can I do if James shows up? I'm supposed to arrest him. But the Monahan family took me in, and I don't want to be puttin' James in jail."

Webb pondered. "I didn't figure on your leg bein' so slow to heal. I hoped you'd be able to go back to Belknap sooner."

Rusty took that as affirmation. "So you do expect James to come back?"

"You would, if you were him."

"As fast as I could get here. But I'm not him, I'm me. So I'll keep Alamo in the pen tonight and start for Belknap first thing in the mornin'."

"Your leg still looks angry. Do you think you can ride that far?"

"I'll make a two-day trip of it, and rest along the way."

"I'll pray that James doesn't get here tonight."

The prayer was in vain. Rusty had not been asleep long when he awoke to the sound of voices from the cabin. After the first couple of nights on a cot in the kitchen, he had taken to sleeping in a shed to be out of the way. He laid his blankets aside and reached for his trousers.

A dark figure appeared in the doorway. "Are you awake?" The voice was Webb's. "Stay where you're at. What you don't see, you can't bear witness to."

Rusty knew. "James."

Webb's silence told him enough.

The autumn night air carried a chill. Rusty pulled the blanket around his shoulders. He had an uneasy feeling. "I ain't seen them, but I have a notion Caleb Dawkins or his bunch have been watchin' this place off and on."

"It's the dark of the moon, and James is careful."

"He'd better be gone long before daylight."

"I've already told him that."

Webb left, and Rusty drifted off into a restless half sleep. He was awakened by a quarrel in the cabin. The voices were loud in disagreement, though he could not hear the words. Later he heard a horse moving. He made it a point not to look, but he assumed the horse was James's. He felt relieved that James was leaving and Rusty could truthfully say, in the event he was asked, that he had not seen him. Soon, however, he realized the horse was traveling eastward, not to the west, where James should be going. The thought disturbed him. He threw the blankets aside and reached for his clothes.

As he pulled his boots on, an agitated Preacher Webb appeared in the doorway. "I should have known it would happen," he said.

"What's happened?"

"James has gone to get Caleb Dawkins."

"Dawkins has it comin' to him."

"Violence begets more violence, 'til there's no stoppin' place. I preached that to you when you wanted to kill Isaac York."

"Sometimes I still wish I'd done it. Where does Clemmie stand?"

"She didn't try to talk him out of it. She'd like to spit on Dawkins in his coffin."

"Can't say I'd blame her any."

"But James won't just be a fugitive from conscription. He'll be runnin' from a murder. Sooner or later somebody will kill *him*. Vince and Geneva did their best, and so did I, but James wouldn't listen to us."

Rusty felt an itching along his backside, an urge to be moving. "I should've seen James after all. Worst come to worst, I could've arrested him."

"He wouldn't have let you. You'd have had to shoot him. There wouldn't have been much point."

Rusty looked around the dark shed for his hat. "Maybe I can still find some way to stop him. Would you help me saddle my horse?"

"What'll you do?"

"Try to get to Dawkins before James does."

"But you wouldn't know where to find him."

Vince Purdy shuffled into the shed, shoulders slack, his voice grave. "I know where he'll be at. I'll show you the way."

Any doubts Rusty had about taking the old man along were quickly shunted aside by the fact that he couldn't find the Dawkins place by himself, certainly not in time to help. He picked up his cane, then pitched it atop the cot. If he could ride a horse he should not need a cane. It might just be in his way.

Though only Alamo was in the pen, several other horses stood around outside the gate, waiting for their morning feed. Purdy caught one while Rusty struggled to lift his saddle to Alamo's back. The weight bore heavily on his weak leg. Webb helped him finish saddling, then gave him a boost onto the horse's back. Rusty grunted involuntarily. The leg ached from the exertion.

"The Lord ride with you," Webb said.

"He'd do better to ride with James, and slow him down."

Geneva was there as Rusty rode Alamo out the gate. She reached up to squeeze his hand. Her voice seemed about to break. "James is not the only one at risk in this. You are, too. Be careful, Rusty."

On an impulse too strong to resist, he leaned down and put his arms around her. Urgently he kissed her on the lips, holding the kiss until he felt his lungs would burst.

"I'll be back," he said.

Striking a trot, then a lope, Purdy pointed the way across country rather than follow the winding wagon road.

Purdy worried, "If James gets there before us, I don't know what we can do."

Rusty confessed, "I don't know what we'll do if *we* get there first. But we'll do somethin' even if it's wrong."

Nothing would be without risk. If he arrested James, he would not only alienate the Monahan family but would put James in jeopardy of being dragged out of jail and lynched by the Dawkins faction. At the least, such a move would result in James's being taken by the conscription officers and forced into Confederate service. Rusty could simply warn Dawkins, but that would probably result in getting James waylaid and killed.

Mike Shannon had once told him to have confidence in himself, that he would know the right thing to do when the time came.

He wished Daddy Mike could whisper in his ear now.

The Dawkins farm was quiet. The thin moon shed but little light on it, and the eastern horizon showed no hint of sunup. He saw the dim glow of a lamp in the window of a small log structure, evidently a bunkhouse, and another in the larger house, where he assumed Dawkins lived. A milk-pen calf bawled for its mother. Rusty figured a hired hand was milking, for a lighted lantern was suspended from the rafter of a low shed nearby.

He said, "I wish we could get to Dawkins without stirrin' up everybody on the place." It had been on his mind that he might arrest the man and sneak him away before James arrived. It would be difficult to do without the colonel raising unholy hell and rousing everybody within hearing.

Purdy suggested, "We can circle around his house and slip in through the back door."

A lot of small houses in this part of the country had no back door, but Dawkins's was of a size that would surely have a second way in and out. Rusty hoped it would not be barred. Hardly anyone had locks on doors, though most had provisions for barring the way in event of an Indian raid. A normal lock would pose little difficulty for a determined Comanche.

Rusty's leg burned as if he were standing too close to a fire, but he had no choice except to bear it. He feared it might collapse when he dismounted and stood on it.

He saw a lamp burning in a back room he assumed was the kitchen.

Purdy said, "He's probably havin' his breakfast."

"Maybe I can bring him out without stirrin' up a fuss. You stay here and hold the horses."

"You're liable to need my help."

More likely, Rusty thought, he would get the old man hurt. The Monahan family had suffered enough already. "You just keep the horses ready. We'll put Dawkins up in your saddle, and you can ride behind me."

Rusty eased down from Alamo and tried his weight. The weak leg held, though it trembled a little. He drew his pistol and limped up the two steps to the back door. Just as he started to open it he heard a shout of surprise and an angry voice.

Damn it, James has gotten here ahead of us.

He pushed on the door and found himself in the kitchen. Caleb Dawkins sat at a table, a plate of eggs and ham in front of him, a half-eaten biscuit in his raised right hand. James Monahan stood facing him, holding a rifle. For a man looking death in the eyes, Dawkins seemed amazingly calm.

Not only does he have no heart, he has no fear, Rusty thought. He was at a loss to understand such a man.

He shouted, "James, don't do it!"

James involuntarily swung the rifle toward Rusty, his eyes widening in surprise. Dawkins took the momentary distraction as an opportunity to jump to his feet, knocking the chair backward to clatter against the floor. Instantly James moved the muzzle back to cover him. His eyes seemed afire.

"Don't you move, Colonel."

Rusty saw that Dawkins had no weapon, at least none within reach. He would not have expected trouble at his breakfast table.

For the first time Rusty noticed a gray-haired black woman standing in the doorway to the next room, a cloth draped over one arm, her eyes and mouth wide open. She wheeled and bolted out of sight. A door slammed, and he could hear her excited voice as she went running across the yard.

Rusty said, "Let's get out of here, James. It won't bring your daddy and brother back, killin' Isaac York."

"York?" James puzzled. Rusty realized he had spoken the wrong name. James said, "It won't bring them back, but at least I can make Dawkins pay."

Rusty heard shouting out in the yard. The slave woman had roused the farm help.

Dawkins said, "You hear that, Monahan? My boys'll be here in a minute."

"There's still time for what I came to do."

Anyone else would show mortal fear. Dawkins showed nothing. "If you shoot me, my boys won't let you get away. Pull that trigger and you're a dead man."

James said, "No. *You* are."

He squeezed the trigger, and Caleb Dawkins buckled.

· 13 ·

Dawkins fell forward across the table, tipping it, sliding to the floor, carrying the plate and cup and utensils with him. An agonized groan came from deep inside.

Rusty stiffened in shock. "James, for God's sake . . ."

The shouting from the yard grew louder. James grabbed Rusty's arm. "Come on, we'd better git!"

Rusty had no time to think. He acted by instinct, following James out the back door. His leg threatened to cave beneath him.

He heard a woman's piercing scream from inside the kitchen. He doubted that the slave woman had gotten back so quickly. The scream must have come from Dawkins's wife.

He had given little thought to the possibility that the colonel might have a wife and perhaps other family besides Pete.

Vince Purdy had brought the horses up to the steps. "What happened to the colonel?"

James declared, "He's halfway to hell. I tied my horse out yonder. We'd better ride fast." He sprinted away.

Rusty had trouble getting into the saddle. Purdy reached

down and grabbed his arm, helping lift him. Angry voices arose in the kitchen. The door burst open, and someone fired a shot into the night. Rusty imagined he could hear the bullet whisper by his ear. He fired a quick shot in the direction of the house to discourage pursuit, then spurred Alamo into a hard run. Purdy was close behind him.

The woman's scream seemed to echo in Rusty's ears.

James cut in beside his grandfather. He said, "Let's ride north a while. Lead them away from our place so they won't know it was a Monahan done it."

Rusty began to regain his composure, and with it came anger. "Don't you know you'll be the first one they think of?"

"If you've got any notion that I regret what I done, you're wrong. I've killed snakes and felt sorrier for it."

"You've left a woman a widow back there."

"My mother's a widow."

"What's more, you've outlawed yourself. You'll find every man's hand turned against you."

James's voice had a brutal edge Rusty had not heard in it before. "Anybody tries to stop me, they'll get what I gave Caleb Dawkins."

As the sun appeared, they reached a creek. Rusty looked back. He saw no pursuit, but he sensed that it was coming.

James reined up. "I'm goin' north a ways to lead them astray. You-all ride in the creek to cover your tracks 'til it's safe to go back to the farm." He frowned at Rusty. "Unless you feel like you've got to try and take me in. I'd advise against it."

Rusty swallowed. If he let James go, he would have to lie to the company captain, or at least fail to tell him the whole truth. That went against everything Daddy Mike had drilled into him about duty. "What you did was wrong. I think the world of your mother and your sister"—he glanced at Vince Purdy—"and your granddaddy. But I've got a duty. I'm arrestin' you for shootin' Caleb Dawkins."

James brought the rifle around, pointing it at Rusty.

Rusty said, "You ain't had time to reload. That rifle's empty." He drew his pistol. "But this isn't."

James stared in dismay at Rusty's weapon, then at his own. "You wouldn't kill me, Rusty."

"I wouldn't want to. I'd try to wound you instead, but my leg's hurtin' so bad I can't guarantee my aim."

Vince Purdy's jaw dropped. "Rusty, if I'd ever thought you'd do this . . ."

"I don't like it any better than you do, but I've got no choice. Hand me your pistol, Vince."

Hesitantly Purdy complied. Rusty removed the loads and handed it back to him. Purdy said, "James is a good man at heart. Had a good raisin'. He done what most anybody might do."

"I know. I came awful close to doin' the same thing myself once. But I was lucky. Somebody stopped me." Rusty pointed in the direction of the Monahan farm. "Like James said, you'd better ride in the creek for a ways. Whoever's comin', they'll follow me and James. Tell the womenfolks I'm sorry it had to be this way." He thought regretfully of Geneva. She would take this badly.

"Sooner or later your conscience'll commence to plaguin' you over this."

"It already does, but I've lived with a wounded leg. I can live with a guilty conscience. They're neither one fatal."

James argued, "If you turn me over to the sheriff, I'll be dead before dark. He can't stop Dawkins's people from draggin' me out and puttin' a rope around my neck."

"I'm not takin' you to the sheriff. I'm takin' you to the ranger camp at Belknap. I don't know what the court may do, but at least the rangers won't let a mob get you."

Purdy said, "I'm goin' along with you."

"That's not necessary. I'll see that nobody touches him."

"I'm goin' anyway, and you can't stop me."

The determined look in Purdy's eyes showed where Clemmie's stubborn nature had come from. Arguing with the old man would be like talking to a fence post.

"All right. But I have a job to do, and it's got a bad-enough taste as it is. Don't do anything to make it worse." He looked back. He still saw no sign of pursuit, but his skin prickled. "We'd better be movin'."

This was a poor way to repay the Monahan family, but duty gave him no choice.

James pointed out, "It's a right smart of a ways to Belknap."

"We'll make it."

James looked as if he had a secret he was not sharing. "Mama and Geneva told me about your leg. Reckon it'll hold up to that long a ride?"

"It's held up this far."

In the stress of the shooting and the escape, Rusty had given little thought to his healing wound. Now he became very conscious of its insistent aching. He knew putting this kind of strain on it was a risk, but he saw no option. He had to make it to Belknap. He did not point the pistol directly at James, but he motioned with it. "Let's go."

They pushed the horses as hard as Rusty dared. He could not ride fast enough to outrun the memory of the anguished scream from Dawkins's wife. The rest of her life she would carry the image of Caleb Dawkins sprawled in his own blood, just as Clemmie Monahan would have to live with the sight of her husband and her son lying lifeless in a wagon. War was hell on men, but in its way it was as bad or worse on women, he thought.

The first couple of hours went well enough, though the pain in the leg was increasing. By noon Rusty had to grit his teeth, cold sweat breaking out on his face.

James said, "I'm gettin' hungry. Ain't et nothin' since a midnight supper."

It had been longer than that since Rusty had eaten, but he doubted he could hold anything on his stomach if he had it. He was nauseous, the pain grown almost beyond endurance. "The sooner we get to camp, the sooner you can eat."

Sometime later he realized he was hunched in the saddle. He had difficulty focusing his eyes. Once he tried to throw up, but his stomach held nothing to yield. He had long since holstered the pistol for fear of dropping it.

He felt helpless when James drew up beside him and took the weapon from him. James demanded, "What makes you think you can keep somebody under arrest when you can't hardly even stay in the saddle?"

Rusty heard himself mumbling that James was still his prisoner, but he knew that was no longer true. He was James's prisoner, if James chose to take advantage of the situation.

James's voice stung. "When you needed help, my family took you in like their own. Now look how you paid them back. I ought to shoot you the way I shot Dawkins." He raised the pistol.

Purdy pushed his horse between his grandson and Rusty. He gripped the barrel of James's pistol and forced it downward. "No, James. You've caused grief enough already. Whether you can see it or not, Rusty was right in what he done."

James turned on the older man. "You didn't do me no favors either, leadin' him to Dawkins's place to stop me. My own grandpa."

"Yes, I'm your grandfather, and when you were growin' up I tried to teach you better than what I've seen from you today. I didn't teach you to kill people."

"There wasn't no war then. There is now, and it's all about killin'."

"You're not killin' Rusty."

James lowered the pistol. "No, I ain't. I ought to, but I got a feelin' from my sister that she kind of likes him. Damned if I can see why. So you can go home and tell her I let him live. He can go on to Belknap by himself."

"The shape he's in, he might not make it alone. He's liable to fall off that horse and lay there and die."

"It'd serve him right. I'm strikin' off west, across the country."

"I'll stay with him, at least 'til I can turn him over to somebody who'll see that he gets to Belknap." Purdy pulled his horse in close and embraced his grandson. "You've done wrong, but you're still family. You're still ours."

"Tell Mama . . . well, hell, you'll know what to tell her." James's voice broke. "It won't be safe to write to you, but I'll let Preacher Webb know where I'm at. He can pass the word. Maybe when this damned war is over . . ."

"I may not still be here."

"Sure you'll be here. You'll never die, you'll just turn into an old gray mule and keep on kickin'." James gripped his grandfather's thin shoulders, handed him Rusty's pistol, then turned quickly away.

The old man watched him a long time in silence. Rusty could not see his face, but he could see Purdy's body shake.

Rusty said, "There's a lot of Indians the direction he's goin'."

Purdy wiped a sleeve across his eyes and cleared his throat. "There's worse the other way." He faced around to Rusty. "I'd best be takin' you someplace."

"I'm not as helpless as I may look."

"The hell you're not. You'll never make it to the ranger camp by yourself."

Rusty lacked the strength or the will to put up more of an argument.

They rode without talking for what must have been a couple of hours before Purdy said, "I see a wagon yonder, headin' in the right direction. Hang on tight, because we're fixin' to lope and catch up."

Rusty gripped the saddle horn. He saw the wagon ahead. It appeared to be loaded with freight. Purdy shouted, and the driver sawed on the reins, halting his mules. A black man beside him reached beneath the seat and brought up a rifle, which he held defensively in front of him. Wind lifted his torn, unbuttoned jacket.

Purdy asked, "You-all goin' to Belknap?"

The driver was dressed no better than the black man beside him. He gave the horsemen a long appraisal, slowly satisfying his suspicion. "Yep. Got a load of goods to deliver."

"I've got somethin' else for you to take there. This man belongs to the ranger camp."

The driver was a middle-aged man with a sun-browned face dark as an Indian's where his salt-and-pepper beard did not cover it. He gave Rusty a second close inspection. "Looks like he's got somethin' wrong with him. Ain't no catchin' sickness, I hope."

"He took an arrow in his leg a while back. Keeps agitatin' it to where it ain't healed good."

The freighter regarded Rusty with sympathy. "At least he's still got all his hair on. Mose, spread my blanket roll on top of the load back there so he can lay down."

Purdy supported Rusty as he dismounted, then helped the black man boost him up over the wagon wheel. Rusty settled onto the blankets that covered several wooden crates. Purdy tied Alamo behind the wagon.

The driver said, "It won't be the smoothest ride you ever had, but we'll get you there."

Rusty reached out for Purdy's hand. "I owe you, Mr. Purdy. James would've just left me out there."

"We raised him better than that, in spite of the way he talks. At least now he's goin' someplace that there won't be no conscript officers, no hangin' parties, no fanatics like Caleb Dawkins."

"Don't ever tell me where. I don't want to know."

"You may need to go there yourself someday. The way I've heard you talk, you've got union leanin's of your own."

"I don't noise them about."

Purdy handed the driver Rusty's unloaded pistol and backed his horse away from the wagon. He said, "Give this to him when you get him there. And tell them rangers to take good care of this young feller. He's a right decent sort."

The last Rusty saw of him, Purdy was headed south.

The driver held his questions as long as he could. "He says you belong at the ranger camp. I don't like mixin' into law business. You ain't an escaped prisoner, are you?"

"I'm a ranger, or what's left of one . . . if they haven't fired me for bein' gone too long."

"I'd best take you to the camp before we go into town. There's some folks in Belknap that ain't fond of the law. Feel like it messes in their business too much."

"Some business needs messin' in."

"I heard him say you've got union leanin's."

"My father fought in Mexico for the union flag."

"Well, it don't mean nothin' to me one way or the other. Washington is a long ways off from here, and Richmond ain't much closer. I make a livin'. What happens somewhere else is other folks's business."

Rusty looked at the black man. "They claim the union wants to take away everybody's slaves."

The driver shrugged. "Don't mean nothin' to me. Ol' Mose here, he's a free nigger. Saved up and bought himself, he did. They can't free him if he don't belong to nobody noway. Eh, Mose?"

"God's truth," the black man said.

The wagon hit a rut, and Rusty had to grab a sideboard to keep from being jostled off. "These crates are awful hard. What you got in them?"

The driver thought a minute. "You askin' as a ranger?"

"Not if you don't want me to."

"I oughtn't to tell you, but there's whiskey in them crates, bound for a dram house in Belknap. That's all I know and all I *want* to know. But if I was a suspicionin' man, I'd be inclined to think some of this whiskey is meant to be taken up into the territory and traded to the Indians."

"Knowin' that, you'd still deliver it?"

"If I didn't do it, somebody else would. I've got to make a livin'. Me and Mose, we've sort of got used to eatin' every day whether we need to or not."

The tent camp looked the same as the last time Rusty had seen it. The driver halted the wagon and motioned for Mose to help Rusty to the ground. "This is as far as I dast take you without gettin' me in bad with some of the boys in town."

"I'm much obliged." The leg hurt as Rusty climbed down, using the left front wheel as a ladder of sorts. It almost buckled when he reached the ground. Mose's strong hands steadied him. The black man untied Alamo from the rear of the wagon and handed the reins to Rusty. He also gave him his pistol.

The driver said, "If you see us in town, just act like we're strangers."

They just about were. Rusty never had learned the driver's name, and all he knew about Mose was his name and that he was a free black. He knew also that some of the crates contained whiskey, not illegal in Texas but a violation of union law in Indian Territory. Liquor smuggling was of interest to Texans when it encouraged Indian raids south of the river. Under present conditions of war, neither union nor Confederacy was in a position to make a strong effort against the whiskey trade.

Rusty watched the wagon pull away, then limped toward the corrals, leading Alamo. He wished he had not thrown away the cane. He would whittle a new one to use until the leg was stronger.

Tanner was at the corral, brushing a horse. Surprised at seeing Rusty, he strode out on his long, lanky legs to open the gate. "Looks to me like you rushed things a little. Leg's still botherin' you, ain't it?"

"Got tired of sittin' around doin' nothin'." Rusty unbuckled the girth and slid the saddle to the ground.

Tanner said, "You ain't missed anything here. We've rode a million miles since you been gone, and we ain't seen an Indian, hardly. Things sure been quiet."

"Been dull where I was, too." He did not feel like getting into a long discussion. He would save that for the captain.

"A few of the boys got tired of the routine and joined up with the army. Conscripters've been here too. So far they're leavin' us alone long as we stay on guard with the company. The minute we leave, they'll be lookin' for us to go fight Old Abe."

"I've got no intention of leavin'." However, much depended upon the captain's reaction when Rusty told him about the shooting of Caleb Dawkins and James's escape from his custody. Losing a prisoner was serious business.

"Looks like the folks you stayed with fed you pretty good. Things got so bad on scout a while back that I had to skin and eat a prairie dog."

"How was it?"

"You don't want any."

Rusty saw to it that Alamo had a little grain in a pen by himself where the other horses could not contest him for it. He squared his shoulders. "I'd better go and report in."

"We're shorthanded. The captain'll be tickled to see you."

Maybe not when I tell him everything, Rusty thought.

Captain Whitfield sat at a table, writing. He looked up as Rusty entered the tent. "Shannon. Saw you come in on a wagon. Can't you ride yet?"

"I can, some. Just can't overdo it."

"Then what're you doin' here? You could've stayed longer where you were at."

"Felt like I'd better report to you, sir." Reluctantly Rusty told him everything. He was tempted to leave out the part about taking James prisoner, then losing him, but a deliberate omission would seem the same as an outright lie.

The captain frowned. "So you had him, then lost him."

"I was hurtin' so bad I couldn't see straight. He had my pistol before I knew it."

"Do you know where he went?"

"The last I saw of him, he was headin' west. He couldn't keep up that direction too long, though. He'd be apt to run into Comanches when he got to the plains."

"Probably dropped south once he felt he was in the clear. There's a lot of conscript dodgers hidin' out on the far Colorado and the Brazos and the Conchos. Some of them've been slippin' back into the settlements and stealin' supplies, takin' horses and whatever else comes to hand. As bad as the Indians except they haven't scalped anybody we know of."

"I don't see James Monahan bein' a thief."

"Just a murderer is all?" Sarcasm coarsened the captain's voice.

"He felt like he was justified. Caleb Dawkins hung his daddy and his brother."

"The law would've taken care of Colonel Dawkins the first time it could prove somethin' on him. At least it looks like your James Monahan has saved the state of Texas the cost of that trial, but it'll still be out the cost of his own."

"It'll have to catch him first."

"It will sooner or later. Or kill him." He dismissed the subject with a wave of his hand. "It appears to me that you'd best stay around camp until that leg will let you ride the line. You can find plenty to do on foot."

Rusty was relieved that the captain was not summarily dismissing him. "Yes, sir." He felt that a salute was in order, but he had never been taught the proper way to give one. He made the effort, knowing it fell short of being soldierly.

Whitfield called to him as he was about to leave the tent. "Shannon, are you sure you didn't let your guard down on purpose, out of friendship?"

Rusty thought about it. "I don't think so." Now that the question had been posed, he could not be sure. Perhaps subconsciously he had wanted James to get away and had provided the opportunity without admitting to himself what he was doing. "I couldn't swear to it on the Bible."

"Thanks for an honest answer. Not everybody gives me one." Whitfield waved him away.

Rusty was troubled a little now that the suspicion had been aroused. After all Mike Shannon had preached to him about duty, it was possible he had compromised himself.

Tanner came up from the corrals to meet him. "You look like you're cloudin' up to rain. Catch hell from the captain?"

"No. I'm catchin' a little hell from myself."

He spent the next few days doing chores around camp, raking out the corrals, pitching hay, helping with the cooking. He even shod several horses, a job he would have expected to be particularly hard on the weakened leg. He was gratified to find that the leg was stronger day by day. It was coming back to normal, though the wound was leaving a frightful-looking mark. He had heard that Indians took pride in their scars, sometimes outlining them with paint to make them more noticeable. His was private, to remain forever concealed by the leg of his trousers.

Any damned fool could get himself wounded. The real object in a fight was to win *without* getting wounded, or worse.

Because of the frequent comings and goings of strangers, he paid little attention to a buggy pulling up to the captain's tent, accompanied by several men on horseback. He was currying a horse when an adjutant came into the corral. "Shannon, the captain wants to see you."

Rusty brushed off some of the dirt and horsehair from his clothing and followed the adjutant to the center of camp. He asked no questions. He had found that when the captain wanted the men to know something, he told them.

A broad-shouldered man sat on a chair facing the captain. His back was turned to Rusty.

Whitfield said, "This is Private Shannon."

The big man turned. Rusty's stomach seemed to sink to his feet.

Caleb Dawkins.

Dawkins was pale and seemed to have lost some weight. He pointed his heavy chin at Rusty. "That is the man, captain. Indeed it is. I saw him enter the room just before I was shot."

Rusty was speechless, his tongue stuck to the roof of his dry mouth. His hands shook a little.

The captain said, "Shannon is not the man who shot you."

"No, but he was an accomplice."

Rusty began to find his voice. "I wasn't. I went there to try and stop it."

Whitfield said, "Private Shannon told me he took the culprit prisoner but due to disability was unable to hold him."

Rusty took comfort in the tone of the captain's voice. Evidently Whitfield believed him if Dawkins did not. "I've told the truth, sir."

Dawkins said, "You ran off and left me for dead."

Whitfield said, "Private Shannon was of the opinion that you *were* dead. He left in pursuit of the man who shot you."

"That man was a Monahan, and Shannon has been thick with the Monahans all along. Are you aware, Captain, that they are union sympathizers? I suspect Private Shannon is, as well."

"We do not inquire into our men's politics. Our only interest is in their ability and willingness to face the Indians, and whatever other assignment we give them."

"You have a duty to run down fugitives from conscription."

"When we have time. The Indians are our main concern, and we are spread very thin."

"Then I shall take my case to the governor. We will see what he thinks about officers who shirk their duty and let murderers go free."

The captain's face colored. "You are free to take your case anywhere you wish, Colonel Dawkins. To hell, if that be your choice."

"I see I will get no justice here. Willingham, please help me to my feet." One of Dawkins's men lifted the big man from his chair. Dawkins trembled from the exertion. Clearly, the wound had weakened him considerably. Dawkins raised his hand to his side, his face twisting in pain. Rusty could not see why the bullet had not killed him. He guessed that James had fired in haste, without taking proper aim.

Dawkins said, "I strongly suspect, Whitfield, that your company is harboring men whose loyalties are open to question. I believe Shannon is a unionist, and it stands to reason that some of his fellows are as well. The governor will receive a full report from me, you may rest assured of that."

The captain struggled to control his anger. "Will you be equally eager to report to him that you have taken it upon yourself to hang men you believe are disloyal?"

"You should be careful in making charges you cannot prove."

"And you as well, Colonel."

Rusty stepped aside to allow Dawkins to pass, aided by the man he called Willingham. He felt conflicting emotions, on the one hand relieved that James had not become a murderer after all, and on the other a wish that he had been a better shot. It was unlikely that Dawkins would rest until either he or James was dead. Granted a wish, Dawkins would probably choose to see Rusty and James buried together.

The captain said, "Stay a minute, Shannon." He waited until the sound of horses and squeaking harness told him Dawkins was leaving. "You know, I suppose, that Caleb Dawkins has marked a target on your back. He will be pleased to put a bullet in your chest or a rope around your neck."

"He's a hopeless zealot."

"It's zealots who've brought about this war. Good men can be as dangerous as bad men when they let passion turn them into fanatics. You should be careful not to leave this camp alone. Have other rangers with you wherever you go."

"That's almost the same as runnin' away."

"There's no disgrace in runnin' when the odds are dead set against you. You live, and you fight another day."

"I guess so, but I don't like the feelin'." Another concern came to him. "Am I liable to bring trouble down on you and this company, Captain?"

"Trouble is what we're here for. We can handle it."

"In case the Monahan family doesn't already know, I'd better go warn them that Dawkins is still alive. He might take it in his head to revenge himself on them."

"You stay close. There's nothin' he'd like better than to catch you off by yourself. I'll send Tanner to warn the Monahans."

That brought some comfort, though not enough. "He knows how to find the place."

Soon Rusty was able to participate in routine patrols, short ones at first, then longer as he regained full use of his leg. Now and then the scouting trips turned up sign of Indian incursion, but it seemed more of a probing nature than any effort at full-scale invasion. A couple of times the scouts overtook the Indians and escorted them peacefully if not happily back across the river. More often, the Indians returned on their own before they were caught, usually with horses and mules and occasionally a few scalps. Once they reached the north side of the Red, they were in union territory and out of bounds for any official Texan pursuit. Unofficial civilian pursuit was something else, more often than not bringing retribution upon innocent reservation Indians who had nothing to do with the raids.

Though he deplored the punitive expeditions, the captain understood the fear and anger that prompted them. To most white men an Indian was an Indian, just as most Indians made no distinction between whites. He said, "Whatever it costs and whoever gets hurt, we can't let up our guard. If they ever get the notion they can come across the Red and do whatever they want to without fear of punishment, they'll be here in force."

The Indians were fully aware that the white man's war had crippled the frontier defense and that settlers along the western edge were highly vulnerable. That much was gleaned from conversations with captured Indian invaders given an armed escort back to the line. It was up to the minutemen companies to block hostile incursions to whatever extent they could, lest the dam break and the frontier be inundated by a Comanche flood.

Rusty and Tanner lagged behind Captain Whitfield and two other men in a small patrol scouting far south and east of Belknap. Rusty was half listening to Tanner tell with considerable glee about finding and moving a whiskey runner's stash to see what would happen. The runner accused a rival of theft, and the two men got into a fistfight of monumental proportions in a Fort Belknap dramshop.

"You ever see them Germans make sausage down on the Guadalupe?" Tanner asked. "Them two fought one another all the way across the floor and out into the road. Time they wore theirselves out, their faces looked like a batch of that raw sausage. I laughed 'til I was rollin' on the ground."

"It don't sound like somethin' to laugh about. What if they'd killed one another, and you'd been the cause of it?"

"The world would've been shed of two whiskey runners. All they're good for is to get the Indians liquored up and rarin' for a raid. There's no tellin' how many people have died on account of them, white and Indian both."

"Still, I wouldn't have wanted them on my conscience."

"Maybe your conscience is too sensitive for your own good. You ain't never had to kill anybody, have you? Even an Indian?"

"No, I haven't."

"Time you've done it to two or three that really need it, your conscience won't weigh you down near as much."

A movement to the south caught Rusty's eye. He saw a horseman spurring a sweat-lathered horse toward the patrol. The captain and the two other rangers had already seen and had stopped to wait. The oncoming rider waved his hat. He tried to shout, but he was too hoarse for his voice to carry far.

Tanner said, "I've seen that gent before."

Rusty recognized the man called Willingham, who had been with Caleb Dawkins the day the recuperating farmer visited the camp. The man reined his horse to a rough stop and stirred a small cloud of dust. He coughed, trying to coax his voice into use. "Damn but I'm glad to see you-all. Minutemen, ain't you?"

The captain said, "We're scoutin' from Belknap. You look like you're totin' a load of trouble."

"Trouble enough." Willingham turned in the saddle and pointed in the direction from which he had come. "They raided the Dawkins farm last night. Set fire to a haystack and tried to burn the barn."

"Kill anybody?"

"Not that we know of. Wasn't because they didn't try."

"How many horses did they run off?"

"None that I know of. Ain't had time to take a count."

"Doesn't sound like the Comanches I know. Or the Kiowas either."

"Wasn't Indians atall. White men they was. Colonel says they're some of them conscript dodgers that skulk around in the timber out past the settlements. They was after the colonel personal. Searched the house lookin' for him. Scared Miz Dawkins half to death."

Rusty had a strong hunch. He pushed Alamo forward, facing Willingham. "Recognize anybody?"

"One of the boys said he thought he saw James Monahan among them. Colonel laid low and didn't see nobody, but he's dead certain it was Monahan led the raid."

Rusty had heard reports of petty thievery, blamed on men of the brush who hid out to avoid conscription officers and self-appointed hangmen like Dawkins. He had never seriously considered that James would allow himself to become a thief. But if the raid was aimed specifically at Dawkins, it took on a new and interesting complexion.

The captain told Willingham, "You lead the way. We'll borrow a fresh mount for you at the first farm we come to."

Willingham reined his horse around. "I've heard Colonel say some hard things about you rangers, but he'll be tickled to see you this time."

Rusty had noted that some people who railed at the law's interference in their own affairs were mightily pleased for it to show up when trouble arose.

The patrol spent much of the day in reaching the Dawkins farm. However strong the excitement had been the night before, the place looked calm enough now. Men were working in the fields and around the barn. Rusty saw a scorched area beside the wide barn door, and what had been a stack of hay was just wind-blown gray ashes.

The captain said, "I wonder how come them had to burn the haystack. Seems like a spiteful thing."

Willingham said, "They saw one of the boys run and hide himself in it. They thought he might be Colonel Dawkins, so they burned him out. Singed his whiskers but didn't hurt him."

If Caleb Dawkins was glad to see the scouts he kept his pleasure well concealed. He gave Rusty a moment's attention, then turned on the captain. "It is way past time for you-all to show up, after the trail's gone cold. You ought to've been here last night."

The captain's jaw hardened, but he remained painfully civil. "We can't be everywhere at once. There's a lot of country to cover and only a few of us to do it."

Dawkins repeated the story Willingham had told, with a few extra embellishments and a strong condemnation of James Monahan. "That boy is beating on the doors of hell, and if the law doesn't let him in, I will!"

"Willingham says they made a point of lookin' for you. How come they didn't find you?"

Dawkins glanced away, not meeting the corporal's probing gaze. "They didn't look everywhere."

Willingham had already divulged that Dawkins had taken cover beneath his porch.

The captain said, "At least nobody was killed."

"No thanks to James Monahan. You'd better bring him in. Better yet, kill him where you find him." Dawkins faced Rusty. "Lest somebody turn him loose again."

Pete Dawkins came into the house as the rangers were about to leave. "Papa, looks like we've come up short some horses after all."

Dawkins turned back to the captain. "Well, there you have it. The raid on the headquarters was meant to cover the theft of my horses."

Whitfield promised, "We'll look around and report back to you."

Rusty had no difficulty in finding the trail left by the retreating raiders. Its westward course was plain enough.

Whitfield had been circling in another direction. Finding nothing, he came to Rusty. "What did you find?"

Rusty pointed to the tracks. "No more horses than what they were ridin', the best I can see. If anybody stole the colonel's horses, it was a separate bunch and went off in another direction."

"It could have been like the colonel said. The raid on the headquarters was a diversion."

"Not to James Monahan it wasn't, if he was really here."

"These tracks lead toward the Monahan farm, don't they? I believe he was here."

Rusty could not argue the point. He believed it himself.

Whitfield sent Tanner and the Morris brothers to make a wider circle and look for tracks of stolen horses being driven away. With Rusty beside him, he delivered what information he had back to Dawkins, who waited in front of his house. He said, "We'll go talk to the Monahan family."

Dawkins grunted disapproval. "They won't tell you anything but lies. There won't be peace around here 'til that nest of unionist trash is cleaned out, from the old man down to the women and kids."

Giving in to fury, Rusty dismounted and drew back his fist. Dawkins stumbled backward, trying to avoid the blow he could see coming. The captain grabbed Rusty's arm and broke up the swing before it was completed. "Shannon, he's a wounded man."

"So am I. That makes us even."

Dawkins's cold stare said he was mentally measuring Rusty's neck for a rope.

Rusty declared, "You hurt them women and I'll kill you!"

The captain pulled Rusty away. "Let's go, Shannon. We're doin' no good here."

Rusty resisted leaving a worthy fight unfinished, but Tanner joined the captain in hustling him along to his horse. Tanner said, "Come on, redhead, before you get in trouble."

"The trouble's already here." But he reluctantly gave up the struggle and went along, looking back toward Dawkins.

Riding away, the captain said, "You have to try to put your personal feelin's aside and remember you represent the law."

"Can *you* always do that?"

"I don't go around hittin' people I don't like—unless I think it'll do them some good."

"It would've done *me* a lot of good."

"Maybe I ought to send you back to camp. If we get into a chase after James Monahan, you won't have your heart in it."

"I'll do my duty."

"I'll hold you to that."

Rusty dropped back to the rear. Tanner pulled in beside him. "Looks to me like your conscience is already weakenin' some. Would you really kill him, or are you just talkin'?"

"I hope we don't have to find out."

· 14 ·

Rusty was not surprised that most of the horse tracks veered well to the north of the Monahan farm. James would be too cagy to incriminate his family. But the sharp-eyed captain found a single set of tracks that led toward the Monahans'.

Rusty welcomed the patrol's brief stop for a cold supper. Though the pain in his leg had lessened to a point that he was unaware of it most of the time, fatigue brought back enough that he could not ignore it. While they ate jerked beef and hard bread, the captain asked pointed questions about James. He knew Rusty once had James in custody and lost him. Rusty suspected that most of the rangers believed he had simply let James go. Few blamed him. If Dawkins had any friends in the ranger camp, they kept it a secret.

The captain said, "By the looks of things, Monahan may have thrown in with a bunch of men from the brush."

"I feel like he was just lookin' for revenge against Dawkins."

"We can't stand back and let a bunch of men just run wild. It's our job to catch them or run them plumb out of the country."

"Run them where?"

"A lot of union sympathizers and conscript dodgers have slipped off to Mexico. Others have gone up north to Colorado or out to California. Me, I've got no wish to see James Monahan dead. I'd just like to see him gone. I'd be inclined to look in another direction if I was satisfied he was leavin' the country."

"I'll tell his family that. They'll know a way to get word to him."

They would do it through Preacher Webb, but Rusty would not tell the captain. What he didn't know wouldn't hurt the minister.

Nearing the Monahan farm, Rusty saw Vince Purdy moving out from the house and into the dusk to meet the rangers. His stride was slow and careful. Autumn weather had summoned arthritis into his joints. Purdy's gaze settled on Rusty. "We figured on company," he said. "Didn't know you'd be amongst them."

"I go where they tell me to."

"You're lookin' a right smart better than the last time I seen you."

"I'm able to do a day's work."

"If your work includes catchin' James, he ain't here."

"Didn't figure he would be. But he's been here."

"You're the one sayin' that."

The captain spoke. "The tracks say it. He came by to let you-all know he failed again to kill Caleb Dawkins."

"Is that a fact?" Purdy had the look of an innocent child. He carefully avoided telling a lie; he simply withheld what he knew.

Clemmie Monahan emerged onto the porch. She stood with her arms folded, belligerently silent.

Geneva paused beside her mother, then came down the front steps. Clemmie called for her to come back, but Geneva walked toward Rusty. He stepped down from the saddle to meet her.

She halted a stride short and glanced back toward her mother. Her eyes misted. She reached out as if to touch him, then withdrew her hand. "James isn't here."

"I wasn't goin' to ask you." He looked regretfully at Clemmie, up on the porch. "I don't suppose she understood why I tried to take James to the ranger camp."

"She thought it was poor payment for what we did to help you."

"You feel that way, too?"

"I don't agree with you, but I can see why you felt like you did. You had your duty, and you looked at it the only way you could. Bein' family, we saw it the only way *we* could. I'm grateful you and James didn't come to shootin' one another."

"I couldn't have. I doubt he could either."

"He's still got his mind set on squarin' things with Dawkins."

"I can't blame him, but it's our job to keep him from it."

"What if it means havin' to kill him?"

"I hope it doesn't come to that."

"It might."

Clemmie called from the porch, "Geneva, you come back here." Geneva did not move.

The captain rode up almost to the steps. He took off his hat to Clemmie. "Ma'am, we're lookin' for James Monahan."

"You'll not find him here."

"I don't disbelieve you, but it is our duty to make a search."

"Then do your duty, and be damned." She turned abruptly and disappeared back into the house.

Rusty told the captain, "He'd be a fool to stay here. If we didn't come for him, Dawkins would."

"That's why we need to make a show of searchin'. It's got to look good on our report. Then Dawkins won't have any complaint comin'."

"He'll complain anyway. You heard what he said about gettin' rid of this family. He means it."

Geneva took a sharp breath. "Get rid of us? How?"

"However he has to. Whatever it takes."

She grabbed Rusty's arm. "You-all wouldn't let him do that. Would you?"

The captain said, "Not while we're here, but we're spread too thin to stay."

"We have a sheriff."

"He's got this whole county to worry about. He can't set up permanent camp here. Looks to me like you-all are in a fix." Whitfield looked regretfully at the girl. "I'm afraid with Dawkins it's gone deeper than patriotism and a difference over the war. Your brother has made a personal vendetta out of it."

Rusty protested, "It didn't start with James. It started when Dawkins hung Lon and Billy."

"It doesn't matter where it started. What matters is where it has got to now."

Rusty took Geneva's hands in his own. "I told Dawkins I'd kill him if he hurt any of you. I don't think he believed it. I'm not sure I believe it either."

The captain asked, "Is there any place you folks could go to get away from here for a while?"

"Before Pa died we promised we'd stay here no matter what."

Rusty said, "It's a promise you can't afford to keep. On account of James, you're all in danger if you stay here."

"Mother won't hear of goin'."

Vince Purdy had stood with his hands in his pockets and his head down, listening quietly. Now he interceded. "When everybody made that promise, we didn't know your daddy was fixin' to be killed. Everything is different now."

Geneva gave Rusty an anguished look. "But we've got nowhere to go. We can't live out in the brush like James. There's the young ones to think of."

Purdy took his granddaughter's arm. "We'll try talkin' to your mother. Don't know that it'll do any good." He walked with her up the steps and into the house.

Rusty faced the captain. "I'm not goin' anywhere 'til I know these folks are safe. I'll resign from the company if I have to."

Whitfield frowned. "The conscript officers'll come for you. They'll send you off to Virginia or Tennessee or some-place a long ways from here."

"They'll have to catch me first."

"You want to hide out like James Monahan?" The captain shook his head. "You don't have to resign. I'll assign you to stay and watch after these folks 'til they're out of harm's way. Our main duty is to protect the settlers."

"What if Mrs. Monahan refuses to go anywhere?"

"You'll have to persuade her. The sooner the better."

Rusty dreaded facing Clemmie. When she folded her arms and stuck out her chin, a mountain would be easier to move. He forced himself up the steps and through the door. She was in conversation with her father and Geneva, but her eyes cut him like a knife.

"You're not welcome in this house. We don't need you here."

He took off his hat. "You need me more than you know. I suppose they've told you?"

"That Caleb Dawkins thinks he's goin' to get rid of us? It'll take some doin'."

"He can do it. The war hasn't left enough law around here to stop him. Some of you are liable to get hurt, maybe killed."

"Maybe it's Dawkins who'll get killed." She threw her thin shoulders back and pointed at the door. "Git out!"

Geneva nodded almost imperceptibly, her eyes telling him this was not the time to argue with Clemmie. Rusty backed to the door, turned and went out onto the porch.

The captain asked with his eyes. Rusty said, "She ain't in a mood for talkin'. Maybe she'll see different in the mornin'."

"We'll have to leave in the mornin'. Got to see if we can overtake those other men."

The chance was slim to none, but Rusty understood. "I don't reckon you could leave Tanner here with me?"

"There aren't but five of us now. Four with you stayin' behind. Can't do it, Shannon."

They made camp on the south side of the barn, where the walls would protect them from the chilly north wind. Tanner built a small fire and warmed his hands. Whitfield had assigned him the night's first guard tour. Though their horses were penned, they were vulnerable to theft by either Indians or reckless white men.

Vince Purdy came down from the house, carrying a small cloth sack. "Thought you men might like to make a little coffee before you turn in. Brought some. Can't brag on it any. It's mostly parched grain with just enough coffee in it to give a little flavor. There's a war, you know."

"We hadn't noticed," Tanner said. He accepted the sack, opening it and smelling of the contents. "I wouldn't trade one cup of good old-time coffee for a gallon jug of whiskey. One of these days when the war is over I'm goin' to buy me a whole barrel of coffee beans and boil enough to float a boat from here to the river."

Purdy tried squatting on his heels, but his arthritic knees would not allow it. He sat flat on the ground. Rusty suspected he would need help to get up.

He asked, "You reckon Miz Clemmie will be a little more inclined to listen once she's slept on the idea?"

Purdy shook his head. "I raised me a real stubborn daughter. I'm afraid the only way to get her off of this place would be to tie her up and drag her away. But she'd turn around and come back if she had to crawl on hands and knees. Too bad James wasn't a better shot."

"We'll all have to keep talkin' to her."

"Me and Geneva been talkin', but Clemmie ain't listenin'. Looks to me like we'd best do some talkin' to the Lord."

Rusty said, "Pray for Him to drop a hailstone on Dawkins, one the size of a washtub."

Rusty stood the last watch before dawn. He observed the dimming of the stars and the first sign of light in the east, grateful that the night had passed without incident. Dawkins had probably known the rangers would be at the Monahan farm. However fanatic he might be, Dawkins would not want to risk confrontation with five armed and determined men.

Tonight, however, there would be only one. Two, including Vince Purdy. Rusty had no idea how well the old man could shoot. He knew he had been in the revolution against Mexico, but that had been nearly thirty years ago. He had scrapped with Indians in more recent times, but for all Rusty knew he might never have hit one. In all the Indian fights he had ever heard of, far more shots were fired than people wounded or killed on either side.

He watched as Whitfield and the others saddled their horses. The captain said, "I wish there was more I can do. Maybe Dawkins'll change his thinkin' when the dust has settled better."

"He's got blinders on, like a mule. He can't see but one thing at a time."

Whitfield wished Rusty luck and led out. Tanner lingered a moment. "We're never goin' to find them other fellers. Maybe I can talk the captain into comin' back here once he sees that."

"Even if he did, he couldn't afford to stay. Dawkins'd just wait him out."

Glumly Rusty watched the riders angle away to the northwest to intersect the horse tracks. He hunkered at the rebuilt fire, sipping from a cup of lukewarm liquid that had to pass for coffee in these short-ration times. He arose as he saw Geneva coming down the steps and walking toward him. He tossed out the little that remained in the cup. It had gone cold anyway.

She said, "Why don't you come to the house? I'll fix you a decent breakfast."

"Your mother wouldn't want me there."

"*I* want you there." She touched his arm. "You can't just camp out here while you wait for her to change her mind. She may never change it. Come on." She caught his hand and tugged.

He made a weak show of resistance, then gave in. "All right, but if she comes at me with a chunk of firewood . . ."

"She won't. She'll try to freeze you with her eyes, but she won't draw blood. I think deep down she knows you did what you thought was right. She just thinks you were wrong."

"So do you, don't you?"

Geneva did not reply.

Unlike the night before, Clemmie did not order him out of the house. She simply glared at him, then left the kitchen to him and Geneva and one of the younger girls slow in finishing her breakfast.

Clemmie came to the door as Rusty finished a bit of salt pork, dragging it through gravy and following it with half a biscuit. She leaned against the jamb, studying him critically. "Me and Lon and Papa and the boys built this house with our own hands. If you think I'll let Dawkins scare me into leavin' it, you're mistaken."

"He doesn't strike me as a man who makes idle talk."

"It'll be a cold day in hell."

Rusty spent the day puttering around the farm with Vince Purdy, patching a broken place in a fence, putting several fresh shingles into the shed roof to repair hail damage. Every little while Rusty would look eastward toward the Dawkins farm, wondering where Dawkins was and what type of vengeance simmered in the man's twisted mind. It seemed inconceivable that he would risk injury or death to women and children. Yet Dawkins was fanatical about the war and hated the Monahan family. Passion could easily drive such a man across the boundary between reason and madness. Daddy Mike had encountered fighters in the Mexican war and Indian campaigns who lost all sense of caution or compassion in the fury of the moment. Isaac York had been such a one.

Purdy offered, "You can sleep in the room with me tonight if you don't mind an old man's snorin'."

Rusty demurred. "Clemmie wouldn't get much rest, knowin' I was under the same roof. I'll sleep in the shed like I did before."

He did not expect to sleep much. He intended to stay awake and on guard in case Dawkins came. But weariness overcame good intentions. He dozed off slumped on the edge of his cot.

He was awakened by a shout and a flash of light, the sound of horses moving. Fighting off a lingering drowsiness, he instinctively jumped to his feet, jamming his pistol into his waistband and grabbing the rifle he had loaded and left ready. He stumbled outside, nearly falling in his haste. Flames licked at the front of the house. Horsemen fired through the windows, shattering glass. In the flickering light of the blaze he saw someone emerge from the front door with a blanket and try to beat out the flames. Whether man or woman he could not tell. Horsemen raced down upon the figure and forced a retreat back into the burning house.

Against the flames he managed to outline a rider and bring the sights of the rifle to bear. The rifle roared, and a man shouted in shock, almost falling, leaning over the saddle horn as he lost himself in the darkness.

The flames swept upward, hungrily spreading across the front of the house. Rusty tried to reload the rifle as he ran. Two horsemen bore down upon him. He dodged, swinging the rifle like a club but missing. He raised the pistol and fired once.

Vince Purdy came around from the back of the house, firing a shotgun. A horse squealed and pitched and almost lost its rider.

Someone shouted, "We've done it! Let's go!"

Sprinting toward the house, Rusty saw Clemmie burst out upon the porch, carrying a rifle. She fired into the horsemen. With a squall of pain, a rider fell to the ground. He arose, hopping. A companion reached down and pulled him up behind the saddle. They raced past Rusty, almost running over him.

Another horseman spurred to the porch steps as Clemmie tried vainly to reload the rifle. He fired at her, and she fell. Rusty shot at the rider but knew the bullet went wild.

Flames were spreading across the porch toward Clemmie. Rusty dropped his rifle and hurried up the steps, arm raised to shield his face from the intense heat. Clemmie pushed up onto her elbows, her nightgown beginning to smoke. He lifted her and carried her into the yard, away from the blaze. He felt wetness soaking through his shirt. It was Clemmie's blood.

She pointed back toward the house. "The children! Get the children out of there."

For a fleeting moment Rusty considered trying to fight the fire, but he saw that it had grown too intense. "How bad are you hit, Clemmie?"

"Leave me. Go see that the children get out."

He set her on the ground as gently as he could, then ran back to the house, again shielding his face with his arms as he hurried onto and across the porch to the front door. The thick smoke choked him. The doorknob burned his hand. Inside, the flames lighted the house brighter than daytime. He saw Geneva and one of her younger sisters, carrying all the clothing they could hold in their arms.

"Get out of this house!" he ordered.

The smallest of the girls carried the family Bible. Geneva had probably thought of that.

Flames turned them away from the back door. Rusty saw that the front door had become completely engulfed. "This way, out a side window."

He raised the window and propped it with a stick. Geneva and the girls pitched out the clothing they had retrieved, then Rusty helped them through the opening. Geneva said, "There's more clothes in that chifforobe. Hand them through to me."

"This house is fixin' to fall down around us," he said, but he opened the doors to the upright chest and grabbed everything he could reach.

The fire was roaring, engulfing the house. It was unthinkable to go back inside. Geneva asked desperately, "Where's Mother?"

"Around front. You-all come on. She'll want to know that everybody got out."

The girls cried, and Geneva's voice broke as she called for her mother. The answer came in an urgent shout from Purdy. "She's out here."

Clemmie lay where Rusty had left her, her anxious face lighted by the dancing flames. The smaller girls ran to her, sobbing. Purdy grabbed them. "Your mama's hurt. You're liable to hurt her more if you touch her."

Geneva knelt at Clemmie's side and took her hand. "How bad is it?"

Clemmie tried to answer but had difficulty in speaking. Purdy said, "Bullet hit her in the side. Might've busted a rib or two, but I don't think it got any of the vitals." He looked up as the porch collapsed in a shower of fire. "That's the wound that'll hurt her the most, I think, losin' the house."

One of the girls said eagerly, "We saved a lot of the clothes."

"And the Bible," the smallest put in.

Clemmie managed to control her voice. "Is everybody all right? Nobody hurt?"

Geneva said, "We made it out just fine. Rusty helped us."

Now that he had time to think, Rusty began to suffer from a worrisome conscience. If he hadn't fallen asleep . . .

Clemmie murmured, "Everybody is here. Thank God for that."

Out past the barn, two stacks of hay went up in flames. The raiders had taken time to touch them off before they left. Clemmie lamented, "The house is gone, and now we've got no winter feed for the stock."

If the animals had to, they could survive on grass until the spring green-up, Rusty thought. But the prospect of the family spending the winter without a roof was much more troubling. "Clemmie, we'd better see after that wound."

He started to tear the gown where the bullet had ripped through, but she shoved his hand away. "Ain't proper. Geneva can see to it."

It struck him odd that at a moment like this she should let modesty take precedence. Only the direst of emergencies had caused her even to let him see her in her nightgown.

One of the girls asked fearfully, "You think they'll come back?"

Purdy stood hunched, staring at the blazing ruin that had been their home. "Ain't much to come back for, unless they take a notion to burn the barn and shed, too." The raiders had set fire to the old log cabin, but the flames had sputtered out after burning away much of the roof. The cabin would be unusable until that was repaired.

Rusty thought they probably would have had they not encountered more resistance than they expected.

"He ought to've killed us," Clemmie said bitterly.

"He?" Rusty asked.

"Caleb Dawkins. Who else? If he wanted to be shed of us, he ought to've killed us, because we ain't givin' up. We may have to go somewhere else for a while, but we'll be back."

Geneva asked, "Where could we go?"

"I don't know, but we ain't about to roll over and die. We'll build it all back big as it ever was."

"Dawkins would just burn it down again."

"Not if he's dead. He'd be dead now if I'd just been able to get him in my sights."

Rusty looked around sharply. "Did you see him here tonight?"

"No, because if I had, I'd've shot him. He must've managed to stay back out of the light."

Thunder rumbled, and lightning streaked the northern sky. Rusty could smell moisture in the air as the wind carried the smoke away from him. He said, "Everybody better get into the shed before it starts to rain." He supported Clemmie, helping her move under the roof. Geneva and the girls brought the clothing they had managed to salvage.

A downpour began. Even under the shed, Rusty could feel the cold mist as the wind drove it inside. "Pity it couldn't have done this an hour ago. They wouldn't have been able to light the fires."

Clemmie said grittily, *"What if* is a fool's game that nobody wins. We've got to deal with things they way they are. Come daylight we'll take stock of what's left and figure out what we can do, where we can go."

Rusty knelt in front of her. "I've already thought some about that. I've got a place down on the Colorado River. It's a pretty good ways from here, far enough that Dawkins isn't apt to follow. House isn't near as big as yours was, but it'll keep you warm and dry through the winter. Ought to be grass enough for at least some of your stock, too."

Clemmie seemed not inclined to accept. "James wouldn't know where to find us."

"Preacher Webb can tell James where it's at. Could even bring him. Nobody there would know James. He wouldn't have to sneak around in the dark."

"You were all set to turn him in once. Why wouldn't you do it again?"

"If I don't see him, I won't know he's around. And I won't be there. I'll be in camp at Belknap."

Geneva pressed, "Maybe by spring the war'll be over, and we won't have to worry anymore about men like Dawkins."

Glumly Clemmie said, "Sometimes I think this war never will be over with. I can't understand the men that started it. I don't understand what they were thinkin' of."

Rusty watched the rain pounding down, drowning the fire. It had come too late. Daylight would reveal nothing of the house but blackened timbers and sodden ashes.

He said, "They sure wasn't thinkin' of the women and children, and how much it was goin' to cost them."

Clemmie held her hand against the bound-up wound. Pain put a raspiness in her voice. "If women were in charge of all the governments, there wouldn't never be no more wars."

Rusty doubted that. He had read about queens running countries in Europe, yet Europe had wars. War seemed to be part of nature, whether man, bird, or animal. He had seen stallions in vicious combat and enraged bulls trying to kill one another. Once he had happened upon two male wildcats ripping each other with fang and claw, and had watched them battle to total exhaustion. One bled to death. The other slowly limped away the winner, yet barely alive.

It seemed to him that human beings ought to be smarter than the animals, but in some ways they weren't.

The sheriff grimly surveyed the damage, a silent anger in the stern set of his jaw. "Useless. Stupid."

Rusty limped along beside him, taking stock of what had been lost and what remained. "All because of the war, I guess."

"There are some people who use war as an excuse to do what they otherwise wouldn't have the nerve for. Recognize any of them?"

Rusty shook his head. "It was dark, and things were movin' too fast."

"I know for a certainty that you didn't see Caleb Dawkins."

"No, but he must've been here. Those had to've been his men."

The sheriff grunted. "Probably were. But he wasn't with them. He was in town all night."

"How do you know?"

"Saw him myself early in the evenin'. He was playin' cards. I asked around this mornin'. They said he stayed in the game 'til way after midnight, then went home with some folks I know who wouldn't lie."

Rusty did not know what to say. He would have bet all he owned that Dawkins had been here.

The sheriff said, "He ain't normally much of a card-playin' man. Ain't got the time or the patience. He did it to make sure plenty of people saw him and could vouch for his whereabouts."

"Just the same, he arranged for the raid. You know he did."

"I'd bet my best horse on it. But unless somebody tells off on him, no court will convict him. Not now, the times and politics bein' what they are. And nobody who really knows anything is goin' to talk. Dawkins will pay them off or scare them off. He can be a scary son of a bitch."

"Scares me, sure enough. A man who'd have a house burned down around women and kids, there's no limit to what he'd do."

"And not much way to stop him, short of murder. James Monahan tried that." The lawman walked to the shed where Clemmie sat with her children. "Mrs. Monahan, I think you folks ought to get away from here for a while."

Clemmie nodded woodenly. "We've talked about it. Ain't likely we can go to any neighbors. Been a couple come to see about us, then left real quick. They're afraid of Dawkins."

Rusty said, "I've offered them the use of my farm down on the Colorado."

The sheriff stared hard at Clemmie. "You goin'?"

"Don't look like we've got much choice. The cattle can take care of themselves if we leave them here. We'd need to take the horses along because there's some people'd steal them soon as they found out we're gone."

"I know a couple of boys who'll help you make the move."

Rusty asked the sheriff, "Would you get word to the captain at Belknap that I'm takin' leave of absence while I show the Monahans to my place?"

The minutemen organization was so loose and perpetually in need of help that even a private had considerable latitude in setting his own terms.

The sheriff said, "They won't pay you for the time you're gone."

"They haven't paid me half the time as it is. I didn't join for the money."

"I figured you joined to stay out of the Confederate army."

"Not at first. But it's a good reason to stay in."

The Monahans had two wagons, one strong and heavy, the other old and broken down so that it was used only for light work around the farm. Most of the household furnishings had been lost in the fire. The two wagons should be enough to haul whatever remained, provided the oldest did not collapse.

True to his word, the sheriff sent two schoolboys to help gather and drive the loose horses. Rusty guessed them to be fourteen or fifteen. They were too young to be conscripted into the army, though he had seen some of that age volunteer or lie about their birth dates to get in.

He felt that the boys should be warned of the possible consequences. "Caleb Dawkins may not like it, you-all helpin' the Monahan family. He might take it out on your fathers."

One boy said, "I don't see how he can. My pa is off in Tennessee someplace, fightin' the Yankees."

The other said, "My folks are dead. Worst thing he can do to them would be to knock over their tombstones. He's a little bit tetched, maybe, but not that crazy." An eagerness came into his voice. "You reckon we're liable to run into Indians? I'd sure like a chance at an Indian fight."

Bad memories stirred like a supper gone sour and rising back up. "Goin' south, it's not likely we'll see any." For the first time in a couple of days, Rusty felt a dull ache in his leg. "Fightin' Indians ain't as much fun as it sounds like."

He rode out with the two boys to round up as many of the Monahan horses as they could find. After two days of combing the country for miles around, they were still at least a dozen head short by Purdy's reckoning. "You never can be sure what-all has happened to horses," Purdy said. "Some stray, and now and then one will die on you. And then there's the wolves, them with four legs and them with two."

Rusty said, "Maybe the same wolves that got off with some of Colonel Dawkins's horses."

"Dawkins can afford the loss. We can't."

Since the war had shut off eastern markets, cattle had become dirt cheap, hardly worth a thief's efforts. Horses were far more valuable. From reports Rusty had heard, dry weather had set in down on the Colorado, so grazing was likely to be limited. His home place would probably do well just to accommodate the Monahan horses. The cattle would stay behind to shift for themselves.

"If anybody steals *them*," Purdy declared, "it'll be his own fault."

During the course of gathering the horses, Rusty was aware of riders watching from a comfortable distance. He suspected they were Dawkins's men, though they never came close enough to recognize. Dawkins would know the Monahans were leaving. Their destination would not likely be of great interest to him, so long as he knew they were on their way out. Rusty doubted he would pursue the vendetta to the Colorado River. He might if he thought James was there.

Despite the hard downpour the night of the fire, rainfall had been scarce in recent weeks, and grass showed the effects of deprivation. It would probably benefit the range to remove the horses for a while, regardless of the family's other problems.

Clemmie stood beside the wagon, her shadow stretching far across the yard in the winter morning's early sunlight. She stared at the ruins of her home. "It wasn't nothin' but a house," she said tightly. "Just a lot of wood and a little bit of glass. Wasn't no great effort to burn it down. But it won't stay down. We'll be back, and we'll build it just like it was only bigger and better. And Caleb Dawkins can burn in hell."

Rusty supported her as she climbed up onto the seat. Geneva was already there, holding the reins. Vince Purdy sat on the older wagon, ready to leave. The youngest girl sat with him. The other was on a horse alongside the two schoolboys.

"If we're goin'," Clemmie said, "let's be gettin' at it."

Rusty sensed that she would not need much persuasion to stay here and face Dawkins down with a shotgun. But the family was without menfolk now except for Purdy. In the short run she had to do what seemed best for her young ones. There would be time enough in the future to return and make a stand, to face the challenge of the land and Caleb Dawkins.

Clemmie shouted at the team, and Geneva flipped the reins to set the mules into motion. Rusty watched the two wagons set out on the dim trail southeastward. He rode back to where the boys waited. "We'll give them time, then fall in behind. No use in them havin' to breathe the dust these horses raise."

One of the boys pointed. "We've got company yonder."

He saw a man on horseback and a man in a buggy. They made no move to approach but watched from afar. Though at the distance he could not see the faces, every instinct told Rusty the man in the buggy was Caleb Dawkins.

"Come to watch the Monahans leave," he said. "He probably feels like he drew four aces. But these folks'll be back, and we'll see who laughs loudest then."

· 15 ·

Familiar landmarks set Rusty's pulse to racing. He came to a place where he and Mike Shannon had camped once while searching for unused grazing land during a dry year much like this one. He imagined he could hear his foster father's voice telling him about the Mexican war, well-remembered old stories Rusty had heard before and wished now he could hear again.

Vince Purdy pulled his wagon up close. "Kind of early to be campin'."

"Just studyin' about better times. We'll travel a little farther before sundown."

Thoughts of Daddy Mike led him to Isaac York and the terrible day Mike was shot. Stationed far from home, away from the familiar places that triggered old memories, Rusty had managed most of the time to relegate the past to a far-back corner of his mind. Now as he returned to the land he knew so well, the memories came in a rush, resurrecting an old bitterness he had not managed to overcome.

He hoped he would not encounter Isaac York. He would stay no longer than was necessary to get the Monahan family placed. He would avoid the settlement, where he was most likely to see York. On no account would he go near the York farm for fear of arousing an impulse he might not be able to control.

His heart quickened at sight of the Shannon cabin. From afar it looked just as he had left it. Then he noticed smoke curling from the chimney. That struck him odd. He allowed himself a moment of fantasy that he would find Mother Dora there, cooking supper. He knew better, but the image brought him an inner glow before cold reality dashed it.

Preacher Webb had promised to look in on the farm once in a while to be sure the roof had not fallen. Perhaps he was there now. Rusty motioned to Geneva, who drove the lead wagon, her mother sitting beside her. "That's the place. Just pull up to the dog run so we can unload."

He rode beside the wagon until Geneva stopped the team, then dismounted and reached to help Clemmie down from the high seat. Setting her feet on the ground, she fell against him, weary and barely able to stand. Days of slow travel had put deep lines in her face and dark circles under her eyes. The trip had aggravated the wound in her side. It was good that she would finally be able to get some rest.

He watched her survey the cabin and tried to read what was in her eyes. He realized this was not an adequate substitute for the home she had lost. She said, "The place is goin' to need a right smart of cleanin' up."

Trash had accumulated and weeds had grown around the cabin, something Mother Dora would not have tolerated. The woodpile out back was too small for winter. Maybe he could talk the two schoolboys into staying an extra few days to replenish it.

He apologized, "It won't be what you've been used to, but the roof doesn't leak. At least, it didn't when I left. Come on in. Let's see who's here."

He stopped in mid-stride as a man slouched out of the kitchen and onto the dog run.

Fowler Gaskin!

Surprise left Rusty momentarily speechless. Gaskin looked as if he might have stolen his clothes from a scarecrow in a field. His dirty underwear showed through holes in the elbows of his shirt. A piece of twine served in lieu of a belt to hold his ragged trousers in place. His face had not felt a razor in ages, and his beard was stained with tobacco.

Rusty got over his surprise enough to ask, "What the hell are you doin' here?"

"I been livin' here." Fowler's questioning gaze roamed over Clemmie and Geneva and the youngsters. Rusty saw apprehension in the rheumy eyes.

"I never gave you leave . . ." Rusty broke off, for Gaskin knew very well that he was trespassing. It was useless to tell him so.

Gaskin said, "You wasn't here, and I didn't know but what you might never come back. Fightin' Indians can get a man killed."

"But you've got your own place."

"We had a storm last spring. Taken off some of my roof. I had to have a place to live."

"You could fix the roof, you and your boys."

Eph and Luke were about as shiftless as their father, but at the least they ought to be able to repair a damaged roof and keep the rain off their heads, Rusty thought.

Gaskin said, "My boys are both gone off to the army. Fightin' for Texas and the Confederacy."

That did not sound like the Gaskin boys Rusty had known, but maybe the war had given them an unexpected sense of responsibility. More likely the conscription officers had come and taken them away whether they wanted to go or not.

Gaskin added, "My old woman died, and daughter Florey run off and got herself married. I been havin' to do everything for myself. It's hard, boy, awful hard."

For someone else, Rusty would have felt compassion. But Gaskin had never done much for himself and had done nothing for anybody else, so far as Rusty knew. "You'll have to gather up your stuff and move. These folks lost their home, and I've brought them here to live 'til they can do better."

Gaskin had the cowering look of a dog just given a whipping. "I don't know where I can go. My old house ain't fit to live in."

"You can find somebody to help you fix the roof. Doesn't

look like it's rained around here lately or is fixin' to any time soon."

Gaskin hunched, his voice trailing into a whine. "I'd hoped you'd turn out better, but you're just like your old daddy was. He never had no pity on the poor and helpless. I'll bet Saint Peter gave him a cussin' when he got to the gates."

Rusty had tried to summon tolerance, but it evaporated. "I said go, Fowler."

"I'll have to fetch my team. They're down by the creek."

"Then do it. I'll pile what's yours out here on the dog run."

The old man mumbled to himself as he hobbled off in the direction of the creek where two mules grazed. Rusty realized he had not seen any Shannon cattle on the way in. There should have been some. He would not be surprised to learn that Gaskin had driven them off somewhere and sold them for whatever little he could get.

Geneva helped her mother into the cabin. She turned back at the door. "We wouldn't want that old man put out in the cold on our account."

"You don't need to feel sorry for the likes of Fowler Gaskin. If he could be sold for his true worth, he wouldn't fetch six bits."

The kitchen was a mess. Rusty could well believe that Gaskin had lived here for months. It would have taken that long to accumulate so much grease and filfth. Mother Dora would be appalled if she could see what had become of her home. "I'm sorry," he said. "I had no idea the place would need so much cleanin' up."

He smelled something simmering on the stove. Squirrel stew. For a moment he felt hungry, but he quickly recovered, remembering how dirty Gaskin's hands had been. When Fowler Gaskin died, it would not be of food poisoning; he must be immune to that or he would already have gone to his reward. Rusty removed the stew from the stove and carried it out onto the dog run. "You don't want to eat that. It'd kill anybody but a Gaskin."

He crossed over the dog run and into the bedroom side. The blankets had a rank odor. Evidently they had not been

washed or sunned since Gaskin had been here. Rusty rolled
them and dumped them outside, along with a suit of Gaskin's
clothes he found draped across a chair. Wherever they had
been worn, he assumed it had not been to church.

He propped open the one window to let the chill wind
draw through. He returned to the kitchen and told the
women, "I'm afraid you may have to sleep outdoors another
night or two. It'll take a while to give this place a decent
airin'."

He walked to the barn as Gaskin drove the mules into a
pen. Gaskin brought out a set of harness. Rusty stopped him
as he started to put it on the first mule. "Wait a minute. That
looks like mine." He examined the harness and saw he was
right. He carried it back into the barn and found an old, badly
patched set he did not recognize. "That'd be yours."

Gaskin grumbled but made the change. Rusty did not want
to help him harness up, but he was so tired that as he watched
the old man fumble around, his patience quickly wore
through. He finished the job himself and hitched the mules
to Gaskin's old wagon to hasten his neighbor's departure. He
watched closely to see that Gaskin did not carry off more
than he had brought with him. He allowed the blankets to
go, though he recognized some as having belonged to Mike
and Dora. He would never want to use them. They would
forever carry Gaskin's scent, in Rusty's imagination if not in
reality.

Leaving, Gaskin hollered back over his shoulder. "I hope
you wind up in hell someday, because that's the only place
you'll find any friends."

Rusty grunted, "It'd be my luck to find him there ahead
of me. Then I'd know for sure that it *was* hell."

Geneva studied him critically. "You don't seem to have
much patience for a poor old man down on his luck."

"I've got all the patience in the world for folks who have
a run of bad luck that isn't their fault. Like you-all. But
Fowler Gaskin? He's too lazy to scratch when he itches."

After supper he started up the hill toward the oak grove
that shaded the small family cemetery. Geneva stepped from
the dog run. "A little late to start out huntin'."

"I'm not. I'm goin' up yonder to pay my respects to the folks."

"Mind if I walk along with you?"

Rusty was pleased at the prospect of her company. "You sure Clemmie's all right?"

"She's takin' her rest." Geneva walked out to join him, and they started up the long slope. He took her arm to give her support on the steepest part of the climb. He liked touching her.

She said, "I'm sorry I never got to meet your mother and father."

"So am I. You'd've liked them, and they'd've like you." It was on the edge of his tongue to add, *They'd've been tickled to have you join the family.* But that would be premature. He had not seriously toyed with the idea of asking her, and he probably would not until the uncertainties of the war were behind them. There was no way to know what calamities might be thrust upon them without any doing of their own. People had little control over their own destinies in such a time.

Rusty had already told Geneva something of Mike and Dora. She watched him pull weeds from around the markers. Someone had put a carved stone over Mike's grave, fairly well matching Dora's. Preacher Webb's doing, most likely, or perhaps Tom Blessing's. He would remember to thank them.

She said, "Your father died because of his beliefs, like mine."

"A lot of people are doin' that these days. Seems like there ought to be a better way—more talkin' and less fightin'."

"That's easy to say, but would you be content just to talk to whoever killed your father?"

Old anger arose in him. "No, I guess not. I still want to kill him. I suppose that makes me a hypocrite."

"It just shows you're human. I have the same feelin's toward Caleb Dawkins, but I know I'll never kill him. Somebody else may, but I won't. And if you try hard enough, you can get past the notion of killin' the man who shot your father."

"It'll take a lot of tryin'."

*   *   *

He did not want to delay his return to the ranger camp longer than necessary, but he disliked leaving the Monahans such a mess to clean up for themselves. He decided a couple more days should do no harm, considering how much time he had already lost in recuperation and in the trip here. Few Indian incursions had been discovered in recent weeks. He persuaded the two boys to stay, too. They could ride back together when they had the Shannon place in better shape, the woodpile replenished, and Rusty's cattle accounted for.

It was the latter task which brought him suddenly and unexpectedly face-to-face with Isaac York. He had hoped to avoid any such meeting. But after a wide sweep failed to turn up half as many cattle as he thought should be there, he decided to ride over to Tom Blessing's place and ask if Blessing knew anything about them. He had yearned to see at least a few old friends anyway, and Blessing was at the top of his list along with Preacher Webb.

Riding up to the Blessing cabin, he saw a face he knew well, the black man Shanty. Isaac York's slave sat on a bench beside the door, soaking up the winter sunshine. Rusty reined to a stop and considered turning back. But stubbornness demanded that he not retreat. He tied his reins to a post.

Shanty stood up, his face troubled. "Mr. Rusty. You back to stay?"

"Just another day or two. Came to see Tom Blessing."

Shanty jerked his head toward the door. "He's gone someplace. Mr. Isaac's inside, waitin' for him. You ain't come for trouble with Mr. Isaac, I hope."

"Didn't know he was here 'til I saw you. I wouldn't have come if I'd known."

"I've told you before, it wasn't Mr. Isaac killed your daddy."

The old man's honest eyes told Rusty that he believed what he was saying. But Shanty was a slave, and it was unlikely York would have told him anything that might later incriminate him. "I didn't come for trouble, and there won't be any unless he starts it."

"He won't start nothin'. Mr. Isaac's a sick man. He looks different than the last time you seen him."

The door opened, and Isaac York stepped outside. "Tom," he said, then stopped, dumbfounded at the sight of Rusty. "Heard talk and thought Tom had come back." He stood awkwardly, one foot on the step, one on the ground. He made no move to extend his hand, nor did Rusty.

Rusty felt paralyzed. It had not entered his mind that he might find York here.

Though Shanty had warned him, he was surprised by York's gaunt, pallid look. The man appeared to have shrunk. His eyes seemed sunk back into his head and surrounded by darkness.

Looks like the whiskey is finally about to get him, Rusty thought. But he sensed that the problem was deeper than simply drink. *Maybe his conscience is grinding him down.*

York appeared frozen in place. "I ain't armed."

Rusty's rifle was on his saddle. "I'm not either. This is Tom Blessing's farm. I've got no wish to bloody his ground."

York eased a bit. "I never did want a fight with you. What happened to your daddy, that wasn't none of my doin'."

Rusty did not believe him, but he was determined to let the matter rest for now. Someday when the time was right he would call for an accounting, if nature did not beat him to it. York's look indicated that he might not be long for this world.

"Tell Tom I came by. He'll understand why I didn't stay."

He swung into the saddle. He felt the rifle beneath his leg. It would be easy to draw it from the scabbard and shoot Isaac York where he stood. He had to struggle to keep himself from reaching down. But York was not armed. Killing him under these circumstances would be murder, as brutal as the murder of Mike Shannon.

Another time, then. Another place. He turned Alamo around and rode away. He would not allow himself to look behind him, though his back itched with anxiety. It would be easy for York to step into the cabin and fetch out one of Tom Blessing's rifles, to shoot Rusty from behind as Daddy

Mike had been shot. To turn and look would be to admit fear, and that he would not do, not for the miserable likes of Isaac York.

He felt a rising of confidence after he had ridden two hundred yards and strong faith after three. York was not going to shoot him. He wondered why.

A mile from Blessing's cabin he saw a wagon coming toward him, Tom Blessing's familiar figure perched on the seat. By this time Rusty's pulse had slowed back to normal. He raised his hand in greeting. Blessing sawed on the reins and stopped the wagon. A huge smile spread across his face.

"Rusty Shannon. Didn't know you were anywhere around."

Rusty shook with him. Blessing's big hands were strong enough to crush rock, and Rusty feared for a moment that his bones were going to break. "Just a few days. Brought some folks to stay on my place 'til the war foolishness slows down."

"You been to my house? Sorry I wasn't there. Been to the settlement to get some supplies to carry my wife 'til I get back from my trip."

"Trip? To where?"

"Up north of here, town of Jacksboro. I've been workin' for the Confederate army, buyin' horses. Supposed to meet some dealers up there the first of next week." He made a circular motion with his hand. "How about turnin' around and goin' back to the cabin with me? Wife'll fix dinner."

"I'd better not. I found Isaac York there."

Blessing's smile died a sudden death. "Rusty, I hope you didn't . . ."

"No, I didn't. Not that I didn't study on it some. Hard as it was, I left him be. For now."

"I'm glad. Lord willin', you've got a long life ahead of you. You wouldn't want to do somethin' foolish and ruin it."

"I don't see that it's foolish to want to even up the score for Daddy Mike."

"You think another killin' would make the pain go away? It'd just make you hurt different, and worse. I've killed men because I had to, and it hurts when I think about it. It'd hurt more if I knew I hadn't had to."

Rusty had talked all he wanted to about Isaac York, for even hearing or speaking the name made him sick to his stomach. He changed the subject. "I can't find near all the cattle I ought to have. You know anything about them?"

"Can't say I do, exactly, but I've got suspicions. I think Fowler Gaskin and his boys helped themselves 'til the conscript men drug the boys off to the army."

"I didn't figure they went of their own accord."

"You never heard grown men bawl and carry on like them boys did, or cuss like the old man. He kept hollerin' 'til they was plumb across the county line. Said he'd starve to death without them boys of his to take care of him."

"He wasn't goin' to starve as long as one beef critter was left on my place. Did you know he'd taken up livin' in my cabin? I had to run him off so the folks I brought would have a place to stay."

"I told him several times he had no call to be over there, but he kept tellin' me it was only temporary. I'm sorry I didn't run him off myself, but I've been away a lot, workin' for the government."

"It's done now. Come over the first chance you get and meet the Monahan family. They're good folks." Briefly he told what had happened to the Monahan men.

Blessing sympathized. "Been a many a wrong done in the name of the war. Someday folks'll have to learn to put the wrongs aside and get on with livin'."

Rusty took that as a reference to his problem with Isaac York. "It'll be hard. I don't know if I can."

"You'll have to. Either that or go to the brush with blood on your hands. I don't think you've got it in you to turn outlaw. Mike Shannon taught you better than that."

"Daddy Mike was a fighter."

"So are you. And the toughest fight you face may be against yourself."

*   *   *

He brooded all the way home, arriving at dusk. He turned Alamo loose and walked into the kitchen, where Geneva was almost done preparing the family's meager supper. She smiled in relief. "I was afraid you wouldn't get back in time to eat with everybody else."

"I could smell your good cookin' for the last two miles. I wasn't goin' to miss it."

He tried to smile, but he could not quite make it convincing.

She sensed his uneasiness. "What's wrong?"

"I'd figured on stayin' a few days, but I can't. First thing in the mornin' I'm startin' back."

She stared at him, holding a skillet until the handle's heat forced her to set it down quickly. "But why?"

"If I stay here I'm liable to kill a man."

"That fellow York?"

"I saw him today."

"But you didn't kill him."

"Not this time. But next time I might. It's best I don't take the chance."

She made a step toward him. "I was hopin' . . ." She broke off as her two younger sisters entered the kitchen. They left when they saw that supper was not quite ready. "What you need is time."

"I've been gone more than a year. Thought I'd put the worst of it behind me. But I saw him, and it all came back strong as ever."

"This is your home. You can't stay away forever."

"If I killed him, I'd have to. This way I'm just leavin' a few days quicker than I figured on. A few days don't make a lot of difference."

He saw a tear in her eye before she blinked it away. She said, "Everything is so uncertain in these times. A few days might be all we have."

She came into his arms. Old Vince Purdy walked in, stopped in surprise, then quietly withdrew.

Embarrassed, Geneva asked, "What do you suppose he's thinkin'?"

"The same as I am, I reckon. That it's high time I get myself back to Belknap."

He expected a stern lecture from Captain Whitfield about his having stayed away longer than planned, but the officer seemed glad to see him. He mentioned that he had lost a couple more men who decided to join the Confederate army, and only one replacement had as yet shown up.

"How we're expected to hold this line, I don't know," Whitfield said. "If the Comanches and Kiowas ever take it in their heads to come across in numbers like on the Linnville raid, there's no tellin' how far they might go. There have been rumors about Kansas Jayhawkers up in the territory, agitatin' for them to do just that."

Rusty had been hearing rumors about Jayhawkers and union activists ever since the war had started, and nothing of the kind had ever come to pass. The people who started such rumors were doing about as much to demoralize the frontier as the Comanches could.

He said, "The Indians don't need anybody from outside to agitate them. They've got reasons enough of their own." He thought especially of the Tonkawas, exiled in the midst of their enemies after long and helpful service to Texas.

Whitfield asked, "You hear any talk about horse thieves down where you went?"

"Didn't talk to many people, but Indians haven't penetrated that far in a good while."

"I'm not talkin' Indians. At least, I don't think so. Seems like there's been a mild epidemic around the settlements over east, horses turnin' up missin'. Most people blame Indians, but we haven't found that much Indian sign."

Rusty remembered that somebody had run off a number of the Monahan horses the night the Monahan house had been burned. And Caleb Dawkins had complained about missing horses after James Monahan's retaliatory raid, though Rusty was sure James had not taken them.

Whitfield said, "The army's buyin' all the horses it can

get and not askin' many questions. It's not likely it's buyin' any of them from Indians. As I see it, it's white men doin' the stealin'.' "

"Anybody in particular?"

"There are some people around Belknap I wouldn't trust with a blind mule. Or else it's some of the renegades in the brush, waitin' out the war. They're a mix of conscript dodgers and wanted men."

Rusty wondered if he was thinking of James. "Even if they snuck into the settlements and did the stealin', those men from the brush couldn't afford to be seen. Somebody would have to help them sell the horses to the army."

"That is the way I figure."

Rusty remembered what Tom Blessing had said when Rusty met him driving his wagon. "I've got a friend back home buyin' horses for the government. He told me he's fixin' to meet some horse dealers up thisaway."

Whitfield's interest quickened. "Did he say where?"

"Town of Jacksboro." Rusty's trips along the frontier line had never taken him quite as far as Jacksboro, but he knew in a general way where it was.

Whitfield's big moustache made several contortions while he thought over the situation. "Might be interestin' if we just happened to be passin' through when those horses come in."

Defensively Rusty said, "Tom Blessing is as honest as anybody you ever met."

"Blessing? I remember that name. Seems like I even rode with him a time or two."

"He used to be a friend of old Captain Burmeister. He wouldn't be a party to horse stealin'."

"Not intentionally, but if he lives way down on the Colorado River he probably doesn't know the people at Jacksboro, or around here either. He has to take them at their word."

"For that matter, *I* don't know anybody over there."

"But I do. They've had a right smart of Indian trouble since Jacksboro got started. Nobody's apt to get suspicious if we make a *pasear* over that way lookin' for fresh Indian sign."

Whitfield took Rusty, Tanner, and the Morris brothers. They set up camp west of Jacksboro, a small farming and stock-raising town of modest log and lumber houses, hard hit in the past by Indian raids and surviving hard times on the most tenuous basis. From afar, the rangers watched Tom Blessing arrive on the second day with his wagon, a saddle horse tied behind. He raised his tent beside a set of log corrals.

Rusty said, "I'd like to go and say howdy. I've known him as far back as I can remember."

Whitfield shook his head. "I don't doubt your friend's honesty, but he might say somethin' to flush our quail. Last thing we want to do is to attract undue attention. We're out here lookin' for Indians, remember?"

The following day Rusty saw a cloud of dust. Lack of rain had left the grass short, the surface dry. Anywhere an animal walked, it left a tiny dust trail slow to settle behind it. The size of this cloud indicated many animals. He limped to the captain's tent to let Whitfield know, but the officer had already seen. He held a spyglass to his eye and focused it.

"Looks like twenty horses, give or take a few." He folded the glass, a transient smile lifting his moustache. He was not given to smiling often. "We'll wait 'til they get them penned, then mosey down for a look."

The captain seemed cool and calm. Rusty was not. Whitfield moved slowly and deliberately, as if he had all day. Rusty felt his stomach tightening with tension. Whitfield admonished him, "Never get in a hurry when you don't have to. A man in too big a hurry makes mistakes he can't afford. Let the other man be the one who makes mistakes."

The volunteers had their mounts saddled and were sitting on them, waiting, when Whitfield finally got ready. He nodded. "Leave us go and look at some horses."

Their approach went unnoticed until they had almost reached the corral. Tom Blessing had his back turned. He was examining a gray horse's teeth and asking about the animal's age. When the man beside him answered, Tom said, "His teeth tell it different. He's a sight older than that."

Tanner's horse took a notion to neigh at those in the corral.

Blessing turned, eyes widening in surprise, then smiling as he recognized Rusty. "Rusty Shannon, you're about the last man I expected to see here so far from home."

The man beside him turned. Rusty recognized Pete Dawkins and somehow felt no surprise. Dawkins's face fell as his gaze swept over the rangers. Nearby, a rope in his hand, stood another man Rusty was sure had been with Pete the day they were trying to escape with the stolen Tonkawa horses.

Rusty said, "Howdy, Tom." He left it to Whitfield to advance the conversation.

Whitfield looked straight at Pete. "You are Colonel Dawkins's son, aren't you?"

Pete's only answer was an affirmative nod. He had the look of a coyote with his foot caught in a trap.

"I would assume these are some of the colonel's horses you've brought to sell?" A few bore the Dawkins brand.

Pete managed a weak "Yeah, part of them. Bought the rest from farmers around."

"I assume you have bills of sale."

Pete looked toward his horse. The man with the rope began walking toward the fence where his and Pete's mounts were tied outside. Pete said, "Got the papers in my saddlebag. I'll fetch them for you."

He climbed over the fence near his horse. Rusty heard him say something to his companion. Quickly they jerked their reins loose and swung into the saddle. They spurred the horses into a dust-raising hard run on the wagon road that ran through Jacksboro.

Tanner drew his rifle and aimed. Whitfield said, "Don't shoot. You might hit some innocent person in town."

Tanner lowered the rifle. "From what I've heard, there ain't no innocent people in this town."

"A few. Let's give them the benefit of the doubt."

"Them boys are gettin' away."

"I think we all know where they're goin'."

Tom Blessing stood gaping. "I'm just guessin', but I'd have to figure the government won't be gettin' these horses."

Whitfield said, "Not unless the government encourages

horse thieves. Johnny Morris, you stay here and take charge of these animals. The rest of you, follow me."

Rusty told Blessing, "Sorry to bust up your trade."

"You-all may need a witness. I'll saddle up and go with you."

Whitfield did not have to say where they were going. Rusty knew long before he saw the big house where Colonel Dawkins lived. Several of the Dawkins farmhands stood silently watching the rangers ride into the yard.

Rusty studied one face after another, uneasy. One order from Caleb Dawkins and none of the rangers might leave here alive.

Whitfield asked an elderly black man, "Is the colonel at home?"

"Yes sir, up at his house."

Whitfield stopped and studied the house before he dismounted. "Shannon, you come with me. Tanner, Morris, Mr. Blessing, you-all stand watch out here. You may have to cover our leavin' if things don't go well."

Rusty had a pistol on his hip, but he had always trusted the rifle more. He drew it and walked to the captain's side. They ascended the few steps up to the long veranda.

A man stood just inside the doorway that led into a hall. Caleb Dawkins, who had always looked seven feet tall, seemed smaller than Rusty remembered him. His broad shoulders sagged. His face appeared the gray of riverbank mud, his eyes dull and dispirited. His voice lacked the deep resonance Rusty remembered. "Come in, Captain. The men you seek are here."

Pete Dawkins and the other man who had fled Jacksboro sat in straight chairs in the parlor. They looked as if they had been whipped. A middle-aged woman stood beside Pete and wept.

The colonel said gruffly, "Amity, you'd best leave the room."

She cried, "You can't do this to our son."

"Our son has done it to himself. You'd best go and let me talk to the captain."

The woman left the room in tears.

Pete pleaded, "Papa, please . . ."

The colonel rubbed the knuckles of his left hand as if arthritis was biting him. Gravely he said, "Pete asked me to help him get away. He told me what he'd done, he and Scully here, and some of those renegades out in the brush. They stole from others, and they stole from me." He turned on his son with a flash of anger. "For this, I've kept you out of the army." The anger left him quickly, and a deep sadness came over him again. "I have had men hung for less than what he has done. He's my son. I can't have him hung. But I can turn him over to you and let the law take its course."

Whitfield gave the two culprits a long study. "I can't say what a court might do. Stealin' horses is a penitentiary offense."

Dawkins looked at the floor. "No Dawkins has ever gone to the pen. We've always gone the last mile to uphold the law. The thought of a son of mine in that place . . ." His voice trembled.

Rusty had never thought he could feel sorry for a man like Dawkins, and he resisted it now. But a touch of sympathy came unbidden. He had a hard time putting it down.

The captain said, "I might suggest one thing. I can take him into custody and turn him over to the conscript officers. He'd do his country more good in the army than in the pen."

Dawkins walked to the window and looked out into the yard, nervously flexing his big hands behind his back. When he turned, his mind was made up. "Son, you've shamed us. You've brought dishonor on the Dawkins family name. The army might give you a chance to redeem yourself."

Pete protested, "Papa, a man can get killed in the army."

"He can get himself hung for a horse thief on the outside. So you'll go and serve your country. You too, Scully. The army'll make men of you, or it'll kill you." He walked to the door through which his wife had gone. He turned. "They're yours, Captain. Take them."

He disappeared into the hallway. Rusty heard a door slam behind him.

Captain Whitfield motioned for Pete and Scully to stand

up. "You boys are under arrest. Try to run again and we'll shoot you."

Pete looked toward the door where his father had disappeared. He opened his mouth as if to shout something, then changed his mind and hung his head. "We won't run. Next time he'd hang us himself. He told us so."

Whitfield looked back toward the house as they rode across the yard. "Shannon, if you know some way to get word to James Monahan, tell him there's no use tryin' anymore to kill Caleb Dawkins. Pete has already done that."

"Colonel still looked alive the last we saw him."

"Walkin', breathin', sure. But this has hurt him worse than any bullet ever could. It'll eat on him like a cancer. It'll kill his soul."

In a peculiar way, Rusty felt that the Monahans had been avenged.

PART
IV.

· 16 ·

Buffalo Caller fidgeted in a vain attempt to find comfort. He had sat in the council circle so long that his arthritic joints had stiffened and were beginning to ache. A horse had stumbled and rolled over him during a buffalo hunt last fall, leaving him with chronic pains he had never felt before. If this interminable discussion ever ended, he would probably have to ask someone to help him to his feet. That was embarrassing to a man who in his prime had led ambitious raids far down into the Texas settlements and deep into Mexico. Once his war party had ridden so far that the horsemen from the open plains penetrated the edge of dark, humid forests and marveled at the excited chatter of funny-faced little people perched high up in the limbs.

Now the council was considering Buffalo Caller's proposal for an invasion on a scale not seen since the great raid that had carried him and so many others all the way to the big water, chasing terrified whites out into the surf. He was ready to do it again. It was high time that the land-hungry Texans felt once more the full fury of the People, that the blood cry of Comanche warriors rang in their ears at the moment of their deaths.

He had sensed from the first that the council did not share his enthusiasm for a massive strike. He could not understand the reluctance. He argued that the timing was perfect. Many reports from south of the Eckhoft Pahehona, the Red River, indicated that the white men had become so hopelessly embroiled in their war against one another that their defenses at home had almost fallen apart. They had sent most of their fighting men away to some distant country to kill their own kind in awesome numbers.

The white man's foolish ways would forever be a mystery. But it seemed equally foolish for the People not to take advantage of them.

Buffalo Caller voiced a strong opinion that the Texans were vulnerable enough now to be pushed back from all the lands the People claimed for their own. He was convinced that the spirits were moving to bring this about. How else could one account for the white men's destructive war against each other unless it had been willed by the spirits? How else could one explain the fact that the western line of Texan settlements was guarded only by a small and tattered group of men on horseback who had to range over long distances because they were so few and the land so large? Such a line should be easy to breach. With help of benevolent spirits, the destruction should be well under way and irreversible by the time Texan patrols discovered the signs of invasion.

Black Wing countered that several attempted penetrations of late had been discovered early and pushed back, some with painful loss of life. He felt that Buffalo Caller was much too optimistic. "You and I have both seen the Texans' settlements. Even with their war, the hair-faces have become thicker to the east of us than winter hair on the back of a horse."

Buffalo Caller argued, "There was a time we could have stopped them easily, but we waited. We thought the Mexicans would turn them back, or the land itself. But they continued to come. If we wait much longer, the white men's war will end and there will be twice as many of them. This is the time to be bold."

He used a pointed stick to draw a crude map in the sand. He indicated the course of the Colorado River, far south of the Red. "This is the Talking Water River. As a young man I hunted there. Many times since the Texans built their houses, I have gone and taken horses from them."

Black Wing knew. He had ridden along on a couple of the excursions and had acquitted himself with honor. He now owned many horses. But he cautioned, "Many more Texans live there now."

"And many more horses." Buffalo Caller hoped the appeal to greed would be persuasive if an appeal to patriotism was not. "The Texans to the south and east are not as ready as those to the north. They no longer expect us."

"But the searchers are out all the time. They will find our trail."

"Not if first we go far west, where they do not ride. Then we go far south before we turn and move into the Talking Water settlements."

"Are there not white men to the west?"

"Only a few. They are fugitives. Even if they see us, they cannot send warning. They hide from the white man's law."

Black Wing's frown told Buffalo Caller he was resistant to the whole notion. Black Wing was already rich enough in horses. And many of the People did not share Buffalo Caller's strong compulsion to drive the white man away. After all, most Comanches remained at large. Though they had lost homelands to the south, they still ranged in relative freedom across the high plains. Most had not allowed themselves to be gathered like cattle and confined to the reservation north of the Clay-Colored River, the way less resistant tribes had done, or the white men's pet dogs, the despised Tonkawas. The Comanches could still hunt buffalo unimpeded so long as they did not venture too far eastward into areas infested by the white men.

Buffalo Caller felt a sour letdown. Though the argument would go on and on, he already sensed that he would lose it. At least there was an alternative. Above all, a male Co-

manche was a free man, allowed to act on his own volition
if the way of the others did not please him. If the council
would not agree upon a huge raid, he could organize a
smaller one of his own. He had always found young men
ready to follow him. Seldom had they come home empty-
handed. Sadly, it was true that the last time he had led warriors into the land of the Texans, he had had the misfortune
of running unexpectedly into a ranging patrol. The warriors
had been obliged to give up some of the horses they had
taken and flee back across the river to sanctuary.

But that had not been his fault. One of the reckless young
men had chased an owl from its perch and made it angry.
Everyone knew that Mope the owl harbored dark spirits. The
same ill luck could have happened to anyone burdened with
unseasoned youngsters who did not respect the proprieties.

If he was obliged to make up his own raid, he would be
careful in choosing those who went with him. He had felt
compelled the last time to take some poorly seasoned men
who wanted the glory without regard to the requirements.

The conversation and the wrangling went on around him,
but mentally Buffalo Caller had already stood up and left.
He shut out the sound of others' voices and kept counsel
only with himself. Already he was visualizing the country he
would cover, the circuitous western route by which he would
make his way down to the Colorado River settlements with
the least chance of discovery. He knew the farms where he
had found horses and mules before and where he would
likely find them again. But this time he would do more than
simply take the white men's animals. He would make a con-
certed effort to take as many of their scalps as possible.
Those he did not kill, he would leave frightened for their
lives. The survivors would be glad to gather their families
and leave the land that had been Comanchería since the time
of his grandfathers' fathers.

He itched for the council to finish its deliberations, for he
had preparations of his own to make. He would need, among
other things, to repeat the vision quest ritual he had undertaken as a young man first seeking his guardian spirits. He
would ask those spirits for a renewal of the power he had

known in his youth, that he might bring down the People's full wrath upon the Texans. Granted that power, he and others would regain the land that was the Comanches' own by every right a warrior held sacred.

Unbidden, a loud war cry escaped him. He looked around quickly and saw that the rest of the council was as startled as he was. Everyone looked at him.

He was sure one of the warrior spirits had spoken through his voice. "The signs are good," he said. "Many enemies will fall."

Often in the past he had sought a vision, and usually one had come to him if he prepared himself properly to receive it. He entered the hide-covered sweat lodge naked and poured water on heated stones to force the impurities from his body, then cleansed himself in the river. His son Steals the Ponies rode beside him to the hill chosen for the vigil so he could take Buffalo Caller's horse back to the encampment.

Formerly known as Jackrabbit, his son had earned a new name after leading several young men in stealing army horses right out of the military corrals one moonlit night last fall. They had not so much as awakened a sentry. Any father would have cause for pride in such a bold stealer of the soldiers' mounts.

"Come for me in four days," Buffalo Caller said. "If the vision appears earlier, I can walk back."

He waited until his son had passed from sight, then unrolled the buffalo robe he had brought and spread it carefully on the ground. He built a small fire and lighted his pipe, blowing the smoke in each of the four principal directions, then down toward the earth and up toward the sky. He would not eat or drink until he saw a vision that would guide him. Often it came on the fourth day or night, for four was a number that held much power.

Four days was a long time, but Buffalo Caller could wait. Infinite patience was one attribute of a good warrior.

Several times recently a disturbing dream had visited him.

It was an old dream, actually. He had first experienced it after the great raid on the coast, when for a short time he had held the captive boy with red hair. In the dream he had seen his old friend Antelope, warning him that the red-hair was an ill omen, that the boy should be killed before he could bring evil upon the People. But Antelope had already been dead when the dreams had begun; the Texans had regained the red-haired boy. The dreams had eventually become less frequent, though he had never quite put them out of his mind. It seemed to him, when he allowed himself to dwell on it, that the spirits were saying Antelope had been right.

It was probably true enough that red hair was a bad omen, because Antelope, a fearsome warrior, had died trying to kill the boy who possessed it. To Buffalo Caller this meant that red hair had great power. The spirits were telling him to beware of anyone whose hair was red.

Fortunately there seemed to be few red-hairs among the Texans. The rest were fair game.

Fasting was little hardship for Buffalo Caller. He had done it many times on the war trail and in quest of a vision. The discomfort was small compared to the satisfaction of a victory or being visited by a dream of good portent. The first night he slept well. His dreams were an empty succession of meaningless images. He was not disappointed. He did not expect a real vision the first night or the second. Usually they did not come to him until the body had advanced beyond the distracting sensations of hunger and thirst and the mind was open to whatever message the spirits wished to deliver.

By the close of the third day his vision was blurring because of self-imposed deprivations. He considered this good. Unimportant details faded, and he could better see the intentions of the spirits, better hear their voices above the whisper of prairie wind through the dry grass.

He was not aware of dropping off to sleep. It was as if he drifted without effort from the conscious world to one in which dreams became reality. He saw around him a great mass of warriors and more horses than there were buffalo on the plains. He saw the white man's houses and felt the ground tremble as the invaders mounted a charge upon them. He saw the warriors' mouths open wide as they raised their voices in a grand cry for victory, yet there was no sound, only silence, only feeling.

It was a wondrous thing, but puzzling.

He saw himself on the ground and saw the Texan horsemen rushing down upon him, swarming like angry bees. But most passed on, disappearing into a haze. Only one remained. Buffalo Caller realized with a start that though this was a grown man, he had the face of the boy once captured, then lost. And his hair was red like blood.

Buffalo Caller awakened to a loud shout and realized the voice was his own. He was cold, yet sweating. He looked around him but saw little in the darkness except the sparkling of the stars above and a moon round and white and bright. He gathered the robe over his shoulders to stop his trembling. He wanted to grasp the dream and hold it in his hands for study to determine what it was meant to tell him. But dreams are elusive, and the details faded before his eyes. He could hold the essence of this one: the fall, the red-haired Texan, a sense of emptiness.

He poked at the remnant of his fire, adding a few dry sticks to coax the flames, then building the blaze with larger pieces of wood. He sat hunched in the robe, staring into the flames, trying to decide what the spirits had told him. They did not always speak clearly.

He had much to ponder.

Buffalo Caller wished he had not seen the horses. The discovery threatened a premature breakup of a carefully planned expedition.

He had led his group of twenty warriors, mostly young and eager for plunder, far to the west before dropping southeastward toward the Colorado River settlements. He counted on being able to make a deep penetration, as he had done several times in the past, before his band attracted attention.

Now, from the cover of timber along the river, he peered

out onto a rolling prairie where the horses were scattered, grazing. They were an inviting target. Too inviting.

Tall Eagle argued, "We have already come far. We are likely to be discovered soon, and we may be forced to turn back with hands empty. I say we should take these horses and be content."

Buffalo Caller struggled to control his temper. Only a poor leader had to shout and harangue his followers. "We agreed before we came. We would not strike a blow until we are deep in the Texan country. As we go out we will leave a trail of fire. Those who survive will run like rabbits and our land will be rid of them."

The warriors had departed the encampment days ago fired with enthusiasm, but now he was disappointed to see how easily the young men could become distracted from the larger goal by discovery of a lesser prize. He had seen wolves snarl and fight over the right to one buffalo calf when there were many more close by, easy to bring down.

"We know where these horses are," he said. "They will still be here when we return. Be patient, for there are many more horses farther on. We can have those and these as well."

He feared some of the young men would follow Tall Eagle and spoil the grander plan, for they were not bound to follow Buffalo Caller should they at any time disagree with his leadership.

Tall Eagle pointed through the trees. "There stands a white man's house. You seem more interested in blood than in horses. We can take them by surprise and kill them all, then capture the horses."

Buffalo Caller remembered this log house. He had picked up several horses and mules here once, adding them to a large band taken farther to the east. Now the chance of discovery had forced his warriors to stop riding in daylight, and they had taken cover along the edge of the river, waiting for darkness to hide them as they traveled. He had been studying the house a while, trying to determine how many might be living there and how strong their defense might be. So far he had seen only one man, and by the way he walked he was old. He had seen two women and two or three children. He thought it probable that the young men of the family were away to the big war.

"I say we go farther, because once we strike, there will be no more surprise. Everywhere else, they will gather and wait for us. The spirits have favored us so far, but if we are foolish they will turn away."

Tall Eagle acknowledged the logic but hated to pass by an easy prize for a larger yet chancier one. "You dream. The white men will never give up our lands. There are too many, and they keep coming. We can no more kill them all than the wolves can kill all the buffalo. But we can do like the wolves and feed from them. We can take their horses. We can even take their cattle and trade them to the Mexican Comancheros."

Buffalo Caller had never understood that defeatist sentiment. He had never doubted that the People could defeat the Texans if only they would steel their hearts and minds to accept the high cost of the fight. Nothing of value was gained without work and sacrifice.

Steals the Ponies said, "My father is right. Why be content with the hooves and tail when we can have the whole animal?"

Buffalo Caller turned, pride warming him. His son was not inclined to speak often, but when he spoke he showed he had inherited his father's wisdom.

Tall Eagle gave in reluctantly. "The next time we find many horses, we will take them and turn back."

The band remained in the timber, waiting for darkness to cover their movement. Shortly before dark, another white man arrived at the cabin. Several of the people inside came out to greet him. He and the old man led the new arrival's horse to the barn and turned him loose.

The young men were pleased, because this meant one more horse for the taking. Buffalo Caller was pleased because this was one more white man to die when the time came.

· 17 ·

Rusty Shannon was brushing Alamo's back when he saw a rider approaching the ranger camp in a lope, his horse lathered with sweat.

Private Tanner was leading his own horse back from the water. He jerked his thumb over his shoulder. "Feller comin' yonder must be carryin' a powerful message. He's fixin' to kill his horse."

Rusty put the brush into a wooden box and squinted. Something about the rider looked vaguely familiar. "I do believe that's James Monahan. He wouldn't come out of hidin' without there's a strong reason for it."

Tanner stopped abruptly. "Monahan? Ain't he the one who . . ."

"That's him."

Rusty tied Alamo to a tree and sprinted toward the camp headquarters. "Captain Whitfield. Somebody comin'."

Whitfield stepped out of the open-fronted tent as James slid his horse to a stop and hit the ground trying to run, stumbling in fatigue. James's anxious gaze fell immediately upon the captain. "You the man in charge?"

"I am, sir. What is your business?"

"Indians. A sizable bunch of them, a good ways west of here and on their way south."

"You saw them yourself?"

"Sure as hell did, me and a preacher. He found their trail, real fresh, and we both followed it a ways 'til we almost ran up on them from behind."

"How many?"

"Twenty or so. Enough to do a right smart of mischief."

The captain appeared convinced, yet suspicious. "You say they were a long way west of here. There's very few people to the west of this place. What were you doin' out there?"

For the first time James spotted Rusty. He made a tiny nod of acknowledgment. "Tryin' to stay out of sight."

Rusty realized that Whitfield had not seen James before and had no reason to recognize him. He wished now he had not said anything to Tanner. Though the lanky ranger was a talkative sort, he could hold his silence when necessary. Rusty intended to tell him it was necessary.

The captain said, "Why would Indians ride so far west if they are on the warpath? There are no people out there for them to raid except maybe a few camps of deserters and renegades." His narrowed eyes made the implication clear.

"Me and the preacher, we figured they were tryin' to travel without bein' seen. They'd go south, maybe down as far as the Colorado, then cut east and hit the lower settlements."

"And where is this preacher?"

"He figured to circle around and get ahead of them, then warn the folks livin' in their way. I come to fetch you and your company."

Whitfield gave the order for most of the company to be ready to ride in twenty minutes, leaving only a skeleton guard. He told James, "We'll furnish you a fresh horse. You intend to come with us, don't you?"

"Damn betcha. I got folks somewhere down yonder."

Rusty threw his saddle on Alamo. Whitfield pointed out a horse for James, and Rusty caught him. As he transferred his saddle, James said quietly, "You could've given me away. How come you didn't?"

"Looks to me like he's pretty well figured you out as it

is. He's got you pegged for a fugitive from the conscript, and maybe one of them renegade horse thieves in the brush to boot. The only thing he doesn't know is that you're the man who tried to kill Caleb Dawkins."

"You goin' to tell him?"

"I'll keep my mouth shut unless he asks me. But I won't lie to him." Rusty had not forgotten that James once contemplated killing him. "You took a big chance comin' here."

"Wasn't no choice. Preacher Webb knows how to find my family and warn them. I don't know where your farm is."

Rusty jerked his head, motioning for James to follow him to his tent. "We'll pick up some grub. It'll be a long, hard ride."

James explained, "Me and Preacher Webb been keepin' pretty close touch. He was on his way out to see me when he come upon that fresh Indian trail."

Rusty put some jerky, cold bread, and coffee beans into a cloth sack. "If it hadn't been for worryin' about your family, would you have come and told us about the Indians?"

"I don't know. I'd've had to think about it a while."

That at least was an honest answer.

Rusty counted ten rangers, including himself, plus James, mounted and ready to ride. On Whitfield's command they set out in a trot. The temptation was strong to run the horses, but the animals would tire out and break down long before they reached the Colorado. At best it would be a hard two days' ride. The captain's strategy was to travel straight south. If James's theory was correct, that the Indians would turn eastward at some point, the rangers should intersect their trail without wasting extra miles.

Rusty suggested, "Captain, I can point you to my farm down there. Not many people live to the west of it."

"Then do so, if you please."

Much later they stopped in a stream to water the horses. The captain pulled up beside James. "I don't believe I heard your name."

"I don't see where that matters."

"I've been rememberin' a description I heard. Do you know a man named Caleb Dawkins?"

James flashed Rusty a look of resignation. "I do."

"I believe you are the James Monahan who attempted to kill him. Would I be guessin' close?"

James shrugged. "Close enough."

"I can't say that I criticize your motive. I do criticize your marksmanship."

"I was a little excited. Next time I'll try to keep my head."

"It's my job to see that there is no next time. Consider yourself under arrest."

"You're not sendin' me back now, are you?"

"I can't spare the men. Do you give me your word that you'll stay with us?"

" 'Til we see about my folks and them Indians. After that, I ain't promisin' you nothin'."

"Fair enough. But understand this: afterward, if you try to run it'll be my job to stop you. Even if it takes a bullet in the back."

"Looks to me like we understand one another." James looked at Rusty. "Is that your feelin', too?"

Rusty had let him go once, though he had little choice. "Like I told you last time, I follow orders."

They rode in silence, trotting a while, picking up into an easy lope for short stretches, then trotting again. The pace put miles behind them quickly, but not quickly enough to ease the persistent burning sensation where Rusty's rump met the saddle. He could not put aside a fear that they might be too late.

They rode far into the night and made a dry camp, resuming the march at first light. The second night Rusty guessed that they were near the river, though he could not be certain of the distance. Whitfield ordered a halt.

Rusty argued, "If we keep goin' we ought to strike the Colorado pretty soon."

"We may do it afoot if we don't rest these horses."

James declared, "While we're restin' there's no tellin' what may be happenin' to folks downriver."

"We can't help them if we can't get there, and we'll never get there on dead horses." But Whitfield eased a bit. "We'll let them breathe an hour or so, then we'll see."

The horses may have rested, but Rusty did not, nor did James. They paced back and forth until in exasperation Tanner said, "I wisht you boys'd set yourselves down a while. You're makin' me tired just watchin' you."

James retorted, "You ain't got folks down there to be worryin' about." He glanced at Rusty. "For that matter, neither do you."

Rusty's mind had been dwelling on Geneva since they had begun the trip. "Maybe I do. Or will have someday."

Whitfield had been lying on his spread-out blanket. He arose and rolled it, tying it behind his saddle. He was irritatingly calm. "All right, boys, time to travel."

Rusty sighed in relief. James was already in the saddle while Rusty tightened the girth he had loosened so Alamo could breathe easier. Rusty took up his position to point the way, though it was not necessary. They had been moving as nearly due south as the terrain would allow.

In about an hour he came upon a wagon road, visible in the light of the full moon. It ran generally east and west. "I know this one. It follows the river."

Shortly he was on the riverbank. "There ought to be a farm on the other side, just a little ways up."

The cabin looked black against the moonlight, and Rusty feared it had been burned. Nearing it, however, he realized he had been fooled by the deep shadow. The cabin was intact. Motioning for the others to stay a safe distance behind, he put Alamo into a walk and carefully approached the house. He listened for sounds of life, but the place was silent as a tomb.

He wished he knew how he could shout quietly. The last thing he wanted to do was make a lot of noise. "Anybody home?" he called.

No one answered. He felt a chill, fearing the worst. Perhaps the Indians had already visited. If they had been here, they almost certainly had struck other farms to the east, including his own. He moved to the door, where he found a piece of paper held down by a bent nail. He could not read it in the shadow, so he tore it off and held it up to let the moon's light fall upon it.

It said, *Indian sign. Gone to Shannon place.*

He swung back into the saddle and carried the note to Whitfield, telling him what it said so the captain would not have to waste time trying to read it in the moonlight.

Whitfield grunted. "Then let's go to the Shannon place, too."

By the stars Rusty guessed it was midnight or a little later by the time they reached there. He agonized all the way, fearing that he would find the place in charred ruins, its occupants slaughtered. Somewhat to his surprise he found himself whispering a prayer. As he rode in, James close beside him, he saw that the cabin was dark but intact. A large number of horses were held in a corral.

The Indians had not struck here. Not yet, at least.

"Thank God," Rusty said in a husky voice.

James responded, "I thank Him, too. I sure as hell do."

A shot was fired from the far side of the corral. A sentry's warning, Rusty surmised.

"Hold on," he shouted. "We're comin' in."

He recognized the distant voice as Vince Purdy's. "Who's out there?"

"It's me, Rusty Shannon. With some rangers."

"Well, come on in, and welcome. We've been expectin' company, but not you."

Several men materialized from the shadows, carrying rifles. Rusty realized that several neighbors had come together for mutual protection. Purdy pumped Rusty's hand, then hugged his grandson. "Preacher Webb told us you'd rode for help. But it's liable to cost you, son."

Rusty said, "He came here under arrest. Where's the preacher?"

"He rode on to warn others. Said he was goin' to Tom Blessing's first so Tom could help him spread the word. He ain't been back, and we been worried about him. From the sign he showed us down on the river, there was a war party came by here a couple of nights ago. They could've taken us then. We wouldn't't've known they was around 'til they was on top of us."

"They were savin' you for their return trip."

"That's the way we see it. If it hadn't been for Preacher Webb, no tellin' what might've happened."

"It still could."

"But now they won't catch us by surprise. We're fixed to give them a dandy scrap."

James asked urgently, "Is everybody all right? Mama and them?"

"Your mama's made out of rawhide. That bullet slowed her down a little, but it was a long way from killin' her."

James turned back to the captain. "I'm goin' up to the house to see my folks. Any objections?"

Rusty said, "I'll go with him." He tried to make it sound as if he were volunteering out of a sense of duty.

"Go ahead. We'll set up camp at the corrals. There won't be any horses stolen out of here tonight."

Purdy went ahead to awaken the family. Clemmie and Geneva came out onto the dog run so quickly that Rusty doubted they had ever gone to bed. With the threat of a raid hanging over them, they probably could not sleep in any case. Clemmie clasped her son in her arms and wept.

"Preacher Webb said he'd fetch you down here when he could. We didn't figure on it bein' this way." She raised her gaze to Rusty. "You got him under arrest?"

"The captain has."

She said to James, "You could take your horse and lose yourself in the timber down by the river. You could be far gone by daylight."

"I'm ridin' a ranger horse, Mama, and he's plumb give out from the trip."

"There's plenty of fresh ones in the corral."

"And bunch of men there to see that I don't take any of them. No, I'm stayin' here 'til we know the Indian trouble is over with."

Geneva took Rusty's hand and eased him off the back side of the dog run, into the shadow. She leaned to him and kissed him. "I was hopin' you'd come. I've missed you."

"It hasn't been all that terrible long since I left here."

"I was already missin' you while I watched you ride away."

Tanner came along after a while. "Captain says he'd like to see you and James Monahan down at the corral. Says you belong with the rest of the company." He gave Geneva a moment's quiet study. "Sorry to pull him away."

She said, "We can sleep now, knowin' the rangers are here."

Tanner smiled. "I expect just one of them would've done, provided it was the right one."

As he started to leave, Rusty heard a groan of complaint coming from a dark shape lying beside the cabin. A querulous voice complained, "A body can't get no sleep around here, people talkin' loud all the time."

The voice was Fowler Gaskin's.

Purdy walked with James and Rusty and Tanner. He said, "Fowler was the first one to come here after word got out about the Indians. He was scared to stay by himself down yonder in his cabin."

Rusty warned, "He won't leave 'til you run him off with a club."

"You've got to feel sorry for him. Word came a few days ago that both of his boys been killed."

"Eph and Luke? I never thought the army could get them that close to the fightin'."

Purdy looked back to be sure no one else could hear. "They told the old man the boys died in battle, but Tom Blessing whispered in my ear that it wasn't that way atall. They got in a fight over two French women in a New Orleans fancy house. That was the nearest them boys ever come to a battlefield."

Daylight brought a sense of relief, for there had been no sign of Indians. Though it was generally believed they did not like to fight at night, that was their favorite time for stealing horses, protected by darkness. Rusty saddled Alamo and made a circle around the corrals and down to the river. He saw no fresh tracks that would indicate passage by the raiding party. Unless they had decided to give the farm a wide berth, they were still somewhere downriver.

Captain Whitfield gave the men time for a quick breakfast before announcing, "I'll leave a few men here to help guard this place. The rest of us will move east and see if we can intercept the hostiles." He sought out Rusty. "I'll take you with me, Shannon. And your prisoner, too." He nodded toward James. "I want to keep him in sight."

"*My* prisoner?"

"You lost him once. He's your responsibility."

James did not change expression. He spoke softly, so that only Rusty could hear him. "You goin' to shoot me if I take and run?"

"I guess I'll have to decide about that when the time comes."

"My sister wouldn't take it kindly."

Rusty suspected James was trying to determine the depth of his feelings for Geneva. If he took a notion to run, he would have to count on their being strong. In a sense James was using his sister. That irritated Rusty. "I wouldn't take too much for granted, was I you."

James said, "If we run into Indians, I won't be much help without a gun."

The captain overheard. "If that happens, I'll give you your gun back. But not before." He looked around. "Everybody ready?" He motioned with his hand and led the way, setting his favorite dun horse into an easy trot. The rangers' mounts had received only a short rest after two hard days of travel. Whitfield was being careful not to overtax them without cause.

Rusty counted eight riders paralleling the river. That seemed the most likely route for the Indians' return.

James said, "There's twice as many Indians as there is of us."

"Daddy Mike used to tell about the big fight on Plum Creek. He said the rangers were outnumbered four or five to one, but they whipped the Comanches anyway."

"Took them by surprise, I guess."

"No, the Indians knew they were there. They just thought their numbers made them safe. They didn't expect the volunteers to hit them so fast and hard. It threw them off balance, and they never got back on their feet."

They rode by the Gaskin place. The roof had been patched,

after a fashion, but it was the sort of slapdash job Rusty would have expected of Fowler. He managed to muster some sympathy for the old man in the loss of his sons despite years of grievances at Gaskin hands.

James knew little about the Gaskin family. He said, "It would be a mercy if the Indians burned that place down. Maybe the neighbors would get together and build a better one."

"They would for sure, if they could build it fifty miles away."

Farther downriver lay the Isaac York place. Rusty would rather have passed it by, for the thought of seeing York brought a bitter taste rising up from his stomach. He hoped York would not be there. Perhaps he had heeded Preacher Webb's warning and had gone to the settlement.

Captain Whitfield raised his hand in a signal for a halt. "Quiet!" he ordered. "Listen."

Rusty heard distant gunfire. The York place was under siege.

His first thought was that the Comanches would do for him what he had not been able to do for himself: administer justice to Isaac York. He took quick satisfaction in the thought, then lost it. He felt shame for letting himself harbor such an unworthy sentiment.

No comment was necessary, and Whitfield made none. He signaled for an advance and set his dun horse into a run. James spurred up beside him. "You promised me my gun, remember?"

Whitfield reached into his saddlebag and brought out the pistol he had taken when he placed James under arrest. "I'll want that back."

James made no promise.

Rusty pushed Alamo hard, trying to keep up. He suffered a confusing ebb and flow of conflicting emotions pulling him forward yet trying to hold him back. He was tempted to drop behind and leave the rescue of Isaac York to the others, but he could not bring himself to draw on the reins. Outnumbered, the rangers needed every man they had, and more. His feeling of duty to them was stronger than his hatred for York.

The cabin came into view on a slope easy water-carrying distance up from the river. The Comanches were circling it on horseback, loosing arrows at the windows and a broken door that sagged half open. A dead horse lay at the doorstep. Rusty guessed that a warrior had tried to smash the door by backing his horse into it. The rider evidently had escaped, but his mount had not.

White smoke arose from the two windows and around the door as defenders inside fired sporadically at the attackers.

The Indians spotted the incoming riders and broke their circle. They quickly formed into a group, then surged toward the rangers.

Oh, hell, Rusty thought. *They're fixing to meet us head-on.*

The sight of the oncoming Comanches, stripped down to little more than breechclouts and warpaint, shouting in defiance, set Rusty to shivering. His blood was like ice. But Whitfield did not temper his speed, nor did the other rangers. They plunged headlong toward the mass of warriors. Some of the men raised an exuberant yell to match that of the Indians.

Whitfield shouted, "Chastise them, boys! Hip and thigh!"

The Comanches split suddenly, avoiding an actual collision. They swept around the rangers, who struggled to circle about and give chase. Rusty heard the whisper of arrows and instinctively dropped down on the side of his horse. He saw a minuteman tumble from the saddle, an arrow in his shoulder. A horse fell, hit in the chest.

So far as he could see in the wild chaos of the moment, only two Comanches had rifles. One rifle fell to the ground as ranger pistols barked.

He glimpsed a large gathering of horses farther down the river, prizes of the Comanche raid.

The Indians regrouped and made a wide circle back toward the horses. They did not intend to give up their booty without a fight. The cabin door was forced open, and three men stepped out to fire at the Comanches as they passed. Rusty recognized Preacher Webb, Tom Blessing, and the slave Shanty.

He did not see York. Perhaps the Indians had done to him what Rusty had long yearned to do.

Whitfield shouted, "Keep poundin' them, boys. They can't fight us and drive their horses too."

Rusty was uncertain for a moment which the warriors would choose. Then he knew, for they formed a long, ragged line and came forward in a run, ready for more battle. The rangers spread out to meet them. Rusty found himself at one extreme end, racing toward a Comanche who seemed to have chosen him as his specific target.

The Indian swung a war club. The stone head looked as large as both of Rusty's fists. He knew it could crush his skull. He tried to line his pistol sights on the man's broad, painted chest, but the motion of his running horse kept the barrel bobbing up and down.

The opposing riders were no more than ten feet apart when Rusty squeezed the trigger. He saw the other horse scotch at the flash, just enough to prevent the war club from striking Rusty's head as it swung in a wide arc. It hit him across the shoulder so hard that it knocked him loose from the saddle. He felt himself falling. He landed on his back, jarring most of the breath from his lungs. His hat rolled away. He looked up as the Indian wheeled his horse around and came back, swinging the club again. Instinctively Rusty brought up the pistol and squeezed the trigger, but the hammer fell on an empty chamber.

Buffalo Caller had been in high spirits over the success of the raid. Though he had been thwarted in gathering scalps—most of the farms the warriors visited were either deserted or too well defended for a frontal assault—they had done well in gathering horses. It appeared they had somehow lost the element of surprise, but most of the Texans had been more interested in saving their lives than in saving their animals. The war party had rounded up horses in more abundance than he had dared hope.

He had not been surprised when their approach to the

small log cabin was greeted by gunfire. Most of the warriors had been willing to pass it by and settle for the four horses they saw in the corral, but Buffalo Caller fretted over not having taken Texan scalps. The cabin looked vulnerable, and he had led the assault.

Now they stood in danger of losing all the horses they had gathered and perhaps a few of the warriors themselves. He dreaded the blame the young men would fasten upon him. He had taken a rapid count of the horsemen approaching and had decided the whites were too outnumbered to attempt a fight. Surely they would back away. He would have to give up the attack on the cabin, but at least the raiders should be able to move on with their horses.

To his surprise, the Texans mounted a charge. There had been nothing for Buffalo Caller's warriors to do but meet it and try to break it up. He was confident the white horsemen would disperse when they saw the superior force riding down upon them. But they did not. They kept coming.

Buffalo Caller wondered what manner of madmen he was dealing with. The Texans' failure to be intimidated left him rattled, unsure what he should do.

The young warriors made the decision for him. They would try to save the horses. Surely the inferior band of Texans would realize they were too outnumbered to take the horses back. Surely they would pull aside and let the warriors pass.

But it quickly became evident that the teibos had no such intention. Buffalo Caller had no choice but to lead another charge. It was poorly organized and quickly began disintegrating as the opposing bodies neared one another. He looked around desperately for his son Steals the Ponies. He could not see him in the confusion of running horses and shouting men.

Buffalo Caller found himself facing a single rider. He had fired his rifle in the first charge and had not had a chance to reload. He did not trust his aim with an arrow from the back of a running horse against another moving horseman. He chose to use the war club.

He was almost blinded by the flash of the rider's pistol.

The bullet missed him, but the blazing powder set his face afire. He felt his club connect with the white man's shoulder so hard that it would have been jarred from his grasp but for the leather thong that bound it to his wrist. The rider fell from his horse and landed on his back.

Buffalo Caller quickly brought his horse around for another run, determined this time to crush the teibo's head. Blinking, trying to see through the lingering brightness of the flash, he raised the club, then stopped. He looked down in surprise and growing horror, for he saw what he had seen in his dream. The white man's hair was red.

Buffalo Caller burned all over. Instinct told him to smash this man quickly, for the red-hair was evil medicine. But his hand seemed paralyzed. He felt a struggle of opposing powers, his own against that of the red-haired Texan. He tried to bring down the club but could not move it.

He heard a shout and saw another white man bearing down upon him. As Buffalo Caller turned to meet the new threat, he felt a renewal of power. He swung the club back for momentum, then felt a terrible blow to his side even as he heard the shot fired. He once had been kicked by a mule, but that was nothing compared with the impact of the bullet. He almost fell from the horse. He managed to grasp a handful of mane, but he could not see to guide the animal. He could feel that it was still running, but he had no idea where it was going.

It did not seem to matter. A slow paralysis came over him. His hand loosed its grip on the mane. He knew the sensation of falling, of pain when he struck the ground. Then he was lying on his back, sunlight filtering through tree branches above and burning through the lids of his closed eyes. He felt himself drifting away as if floating in the river.

The last thing that came to him was a renewal of the vision. Once again he saw the man with the red hair. And once again the face was that of the boy he had taken for his own but had lost in the turmoil and fire of Plum Creek.

*   *   *

Rusty felt a terrible pain as a hand gripped the shoulder the club had struck. He cried out, and the hand jerked away. He recognized James Monahan's anxious voice before he was able to focus on the face.

"Are you shot?"

Rusty had trouble bringing out the words. "He hit me with his club. Feels like he might've busted my shoulder." He reached up to examine the source of pain. "He was fixin' to fetch me another lick when you rode up. Thanks. You saved my life."

"It ain't worth thankin' me for." James straightened up and looked around. "I'll go fetch your horse. Looks like our Indian got away, but he won't go far. I put a bullet in him."

While James rode out to catch Alamo, Tanner reined up and swung a long leg over the cantle of his saddle. He bent down to give Rusty a searching look. His anxiety faded, a smile creasing his face. "Fell off of your horse, did you?"

Rusty did not see the humor. "Got clubbed. If James Monahan hadn't come along, I'd have my brains scattered all over the grass."

"Wouldn't've been enough to make much of a mess. Come on, I'll help you up."

Rusty felt shaky on his feet, and Tanner held him until James brought the horse. Tanner boosted Rusty into the saddle. Rusty asked, "Where's everybody else? What went with the Indians?"

"Scattered to hell and gone," Tanner replied. "Looks like we busted up their party. You know how it is with Indians. They'll go off in six directions and meet up later, somewhere they don't figure we can reach them."

James observed, "They've left their horse herd behind."

Rusty was grateful for that. "But they'll be back. They'll try again. Maybe not today, but sooner or later."

Tanner said, "That means me and you can hang on to our high-payin' job." He pointed his chin toward the York cabin. "Looks like the boys are startin' to gather over there. Guess we'd best go join them."

James looked toward the river. It was only fifty yards

away. "Maybe they won't notice for a while that I'm not with you."

Rusty frowned. "You leavin'?"

"I promised to stay 'til the trouble was over. It is, so I'm gittin' while the gittin's good."

Tanner said, "They'll blame Rusty for you gettin' away."

"Tell them it happened while him and that Indian was havin' their set-to. Wasn't nothin' he could do about it. Ain't much either of you can do now except shoot me in the back."

Tanner drew his pistol and studied it. "I ain't had time to reload. Don't reckon Rusty has either."

James smiled. "Then adios, Rusty. Take good care of my sister. See you when the war is over."

Rusty grimaced. "The war back east has got to end one of these days, but I'm afraid the one out here may take a lot longer. Don't let some Comanche raise your hair."

He watched James disappear into the timber, then shifted his attention to the York cabin. "Guess we'd better see what's goin' on."

Captain Whitfield stood with his hands on his hips as Rusty dismounted, his shoulder stiff. "I don't see your prisoner."

Rusty grimaced. "Neither do I, sir. Things got kind of mixed up out there for a little bit."

"Caleb Dawkins will be upset if he finds out you had him, then lost him again."

"Somehow, what Caleb Dawkins thinks doesn't mean a damn thing to me right now." Rusty rubbed his aching shoulder. He decided it was not broken, but it would probably turn black as a bucket of coal. "Anyway, he's got other troubles on his mind. And deserves them every one."

"There's no reason he has to know, unless somebody has the poor judgment to tell him. I don't know anybody in this company that short of good sense."

"Truth is, Captain, if it hadn't been for James Monahan, I'd be layin' out yonder with my head stove in. It's a lucky thing he was there."

Preacher Webb stood at the door. "Just luck, you think?

Likely it was Providence that James was close by when you needed him."

Rusty shook the minister's hand. "I wouldn't be surprised."

"And it was the Lord brought you and the minutemen here in time. We were might near out of ammunition."

"I'm glad we got here, for your sake. As for Isaac York, I wouldn't care if the Indians plowed him under."

Webb stared critically at Rusty, then motioned him over to the side of the cabin away from the others. "It's time you know the truth. Tom and me, we tried for a long time to tell you we weren't sure Isaac shot your Daddy Mike. Now we know he didn't."

Rusty swallowed hard. "What do you mean, he didn't?"

"When word came about Fowler Gaskin's boys bein' killed, I went over to try and comfort the old man. He let the truth slip. Eph and Luke did it. They were afraid to sneak up close, so they mistook Mike for you. It was you they meant to kill."

"Me?"

"You'd just had a fight with them, and you whipped up on them pretty good."

Rusty leaned against the cabin wall. He felt that otherwise he might fall down. Remorse burned like a long drink of bad whiskey. "I came awful close once to killin' Isaac York."

"Hate is a heavy load to carry. Especially when it's for nothin'."

"Is Isaac inside the cabin?"

"He took an arrow. Shanty and Tom are doin' what they can for him."

Rusty dreaded going in. But it had to be done. He owed Isaac York for a wrong he was not sure he could ever set aright.

Blessing and Shanty leaned over York, stretched out on a cot, groaning. A bloody arrow lay on the dirt floor. Blessing was washing a chest wound with a whiskey-soaked cloth. Shanty was murmuring, "Don't you go and die on me, Mr. Isaac. You take a tight grip and hang on. You hear me, Mr.

Isaac? I don't want to belong to somebody else." Shanty's voice broke.

Blessing said, "It's bad, but it missed the heart. He'll make it. Guess it sort of makes up for him shootin' those Indians on the reserve that time. When his time comes to die, it'll be the whiskey that kills him."

In a voice so weak as to be almost inaudible, York murmured, "Preacher, pray me through this. I swear I'll give up drinkin'."

Webb said, "The Lord expects a man to live up to his promises. Were I you, I wouldn't go makin' any I couldn't keep."

Rusty said, "Mr. York, I'm sorry."

York became aware of Rusty's presence. He struggled to find voice. "Boy, whatever troubles you've got with me, they'll have to wait."

"I've got no trouble with you. I'm sorry I ever did. I just found out what really happened to Daddy Mike."

The man's puzzled expression made Rusty realize York did not know. "I found out it was the Gaskin boys shot him."

York was slow in absorbing the information. It seemed too much to digest at one time in his weakened condition. "I had some differences with your daddy, but not nothin' I'd kill him for."

"Maybe someday I'll learn to be slow about makin' judgments. Forgive me, Mr. York?"

York began muttering incoherently as shock took hold. Shanty leaned over him again, grasping his hand. "You just take a strong grip, Mr. Isaac. I'm right here."

Webb and Tom Blessing walked out with Rusty. Blessing said, "Takes a man to admit he's wrong. Looks to me like you've grown up, Rusty."

"I reckon it was high time."

Captain Whitfield was assembling the company. Rusty shook the two men's hands.

Webb said, "You've taken a load off of Isaac York. The Lord is smilin' on you."

"He must be, because all of a sudden there's a load gone off of me, too. Come up to Belknap when you can, Preacher.

There's folks up there who could sure stand some gospel-learnin'."

He mounted Alamo. Preacher Webb asked, "Anything you want me to tell the Monahans?"

Rusty shook his head. "Nope. I'll be goin' by and tellin' them myself." The rangers were riding away. Rusty spurred to catch up to them, thinking of what-all he wanted to say to Geneva and to the rest of the family.

His shoulder ached, but it was not enough to overcome the warm feeling that arose within.

He *had* a family now. He was no longer alone.

Buffalo Caller lay on damp ground. Looking up through a haze dense as smoke, he knew he was in the midst of timber along the bank of the river. He had fallen from his horse. His side burned like fire where the bullet had smashed his ribs. Carefully he pressed his hand against the wound. The blood flowed warm and much too freely. He realized his life was draining away. He did not want to die lying on his back. He wanted to push up, to meet death in a sitting position, but he lacked the strength.

He blinked, trying in vain to clear his blurred vision. He sensed that a horseman was moving toward him. One of the Texans, coming back to kill him, he thought. He felt no fear, for the teibo could do nothing more to him. He was dying anyway.

The voice that called softly was not that of a white man. "*Powva?* Father?"

Steals the Ponies had found him. The young warrior dropped to the ground and knelt by Buffalo Caller's side. He gave the wound a swift appraisal. "I am here to take care of you, Father."

Buffalo Caller struggled to find voice. "It is too late. Even if I could ride, my horse has run away and left me."

"We lost all the horses, Father, except the ones we rode. There will be other times and other horses."

"For you, my son. Not for me. Our grandfathers are waiting for me."

Steals the Ponies choked off a cry. It was not becoming for a grown son to weep in the presence of his father.

It was a hard thing to die, knowing his last mission had been a failure. But Buffalo Caller could feel the darkness coming over him, the long darkness from which there would be no waking. "You will keep fighting, *Ner-too-ahr*—son. Take my bow and my shield. Every time you fight the Texans, I will be with you."

"I *will* fight them, Father. I will fight until they are gone or *I* am."

Buffalo Caller found strength to raise his hand, to touch his son's arm. "But beware the red-haired ranger. His medicine is stronger than mine. Stronger, perhaps, than yours."

He sighed then, and the long sleep closed his eyes.

Steals the Ponies remained beside him long after the breath was gone and the strong heart had ceased to beat. He did not understand what his father had said about the ranger. Perhaps Buffalo Caller would come back in a vision sometime and explain.

As darkness came, Steals the Ponies took his father into his arms and lifted him up, laying him across his pony's back. He heard a whisper of wind through the trees and thought for a moment it was the voice of Buffalo Caller, trying to reach him.

"What did you mean about the red-haired ranger?"

There was no answer. Head bowed in disappointment, Steals the Ponies realized he had heard only the wind after all.

Time had come to begin the journey. Time had come to take his father home.

Forge

Award-winning authors
Compelling stories

. . . .

Please join us at the website
below for more information
about this author and other great
Forge selections, and to sign up for
our monthly newsletter!